AVENGING ANGEL

AVENGING ANGELS SERIES
BOOK 1

KRISTEN ASHLEY

ROCK CHICK
P R E S S

AVENGING ANGELS SERIES **BOOK ONE**

AVENGING ANGEL

A ROMANCE NOVEL BY

KRISTEN

NEW YORK TIMES BESTSELLING AUTHOR

ASHLEY

To all the Rock Chicks out there.

They're all for you,
but this one in particular
is my love letter to our history...
and our future.

ONE

NATURAL BADASSERY

"I'm gonna go in."

"Are you *insane*? You can't go in!"

"I'm just gonna have a look around."

"What if you're right? What if this guy is the actual guy?"

"Then I'll call the police."

"What if he sees you?"

I sighed. "Luna, this isn't my first rodeo."

"Exactly!" she cried in a Eureka! tone. "So, yeah, let's talk about that, Raye."

Sitting in my car, talking to my bestie on the phone and casing the house in question, I cut her off quickly before she could start in— *again*—about how she felt about what I'd been up to lately.

"I'm just going to wander across the front of his house and look in the windows. No biggie."

Truthfully, I was hoping to do more than that, but my best friend of all time, Luna, didn't need to know that.

We'd had chats about what she called my unhinged shenanigans, or my lunatic tomfooleries. Then there were also my deranged mischiefs (Luna read a lot and her vocabulary showed it).

But I did what I did because, well…

I had to.

Luna spoke into my thoughts. "Okay, so if *I* kidnapped a little girl from my church, and *I* was holding her for things I won't even contemplate why someone would do that, and some woman I'd never seen in my neighborhood casually strolled in front of my house and looked in my windows, what do you think *I* would do?"

"Sic Jacques on them, whereupon he'd lick them and dance around them and race away, only to race back, bringing his toys so they'd play?"

Jacques was Luna's French bulldog. He was gray, had a little white patch on his chest, and I considered myself for sainthood that I hadn't dognapped him yet. I was pretty sure I loved him more than Luna did, and the Tiffany's dog collar I'd splurged and bought him (which she refused to let him wear because she said it was too bougie, like that was a bad thing) proved my case on that.

"This isn't funny, Raye," Luna said softly.

That got to me, her talking softly.

She was yin to my yang, Ethel to my Lucy, Shirley to my Laverne, Louise to my Thelma. Dorothy to my Rose/Sophia/Blanche (and yes, I could be all three, dingy, sarcastic and slutty, sometimes all at the same time, I considered it my superpower).

You get the picture.

We were opposites, but she loved me.

And I loved her.

"I promise to be careful. It's gone okay so far, hasn't it?" I asked.

"Luck has a way of running out."

Hmm.

I struggled for a moment with the use of the word "luck," considering I thought I was pretty kickass, but I let it go.

There was a little girl missing. And I had a feeling I knew where she was.

"I need to do this, Luna."

It was her turn to sigh, long and loud.

She knew I did.

"Call me the instant you get back to your car," she ordered.

"Roger wilco," I replied.

"You don't even know what that means," she muttered.

"It means I heard you."

"Yes, it also means *you will comply with my orders*. That's what wilco is short for."

See?

She totally read a lot.

"Okay, so, samesies, yeah? I heard you, and I'll call."

Another sigh before she said, "You won't call because either, a, you'll be tied up in some villain's basement, and I'll then be forced to put up fliers and hold candlelight vigils and harass the police to follow leads. This will end with me being interviewed, weeping copiously, naturally, saying you lit up a room in a Netflix docuseries about solved cold case files once some hikers find what's left of your body at the bottom of a ravine in fifteen years. Or, b, you won't get anything from the guy, so you'll start devising some other way of figuring out if it's him or not. You'll then immediately begin scheming to implement plans to do that, at the same time you'll remember you forgot to buy tampons for your upcoming cycle, and you need to pop into CVS, after which you'll realize you're hungry and you'll stop by Lenny's for a cowboy burger and a malt."

She was hitting close to home with that first bit, and she knew it. Including when my period was coming, something she always reminded me to prepare for because I always forgot, and as such, was constantly bumming tampons from her. Though, her remembering this wasn't a feat, since we were together so often, including working together, we were moon sisters.

"I will totally call," I promised.

"If you don't, I'm uninviting you to my birthday party."

I gasped.

"You wouldn't," I whispered in horror.

Yes, you guessed it. Luna threw great parties, especially when she was celebrating herself.

"Try me."

"I'll call. I'll absolutely call. Long distance pinkie swear."

"Lord save me," she mumbled, then stated, "If you hit Lenny's, *definitely* call me. Since I brought Lenny's up, I now realize I need a malt."

After that, she hung up on me.

I leaned forward and put my phone in the back pocket of my pants, my eyes on the house that was just right of the T at the end of the street where I was parked.

There was a light on to the right side of the front door.

He was home.

He was home, and he might be the kind of guy who grabbed little girls to do things it wasn't mentally healthy to contemplate.

Maybe Luna was right. Maybe this was madness.

Though...

Her name was Elsie Fay. She was six years old. She had a cute-as-a-button face.

And she'd been missing for nine days.

What could happen, even if he saw me?

He wasn't going to storm out of his house and confront a stranger who was out for an evening stroll.

I was just getting the lay of the land.

I was correct in what I said to Luna.

No biggie.

That said, better safe than sorry.

I leaned across to the glove compartment, opened it and nabbed my stun gun. I then got out, locked the doors on my bright yellow, Nissan Juke (not exactly a covert car, I needed to consider that on upcoming operations) and shoved the stun gun in my free back pocket.

I'd dressed the part. Navy-blue chinos and a navy-blue polo shirt with a yellow badge insignia at my left breast.

Sure, under the yellow badge it said Puppy Patrol, and this was my uniform when I did moonlighting gigs for an online dog walking/pet sitting service. But if you didn't look too closely, it appeared official. If someone asked, I could say I worked for code enforcement or animal control or...something.

I'd seen in an episode of *Burn Notice* that the best way to do something you weren't supposed to be doing, somewhere you weren't supposed to be doing it, was to look like you were supposed to be there doing what you were doing.

And if a burned TV spy couldn't guide me in a possibly, but not probably, dangerous mission, who could?

Okay, so I was seeing some of Luna's concern.

Nevertheless, I walked up the sidewalk toward the house in question like I'd personally designed the neighborhood. I hooked a right at the T, walked down the street a ways, crossed, then walked back up on the possible perp's side of the street.

And then across the front of his house.

Good news, his window shades were open.

More good news: I was right, he was there. And as I'd already ascertained, and this cemented it, he was sitting, watching TV, and he looked the nondescript everyman version of your not-so-friendly local kidnapper. The image of a man whose neighbors would appear on TV and say, "He gave us a bad vibe, but he was quiet and didn't cause any trouble, so..."

I kept walking, thinking she could be in there.

In that house.

Right now.

Scared and alone and so much more that, for my mental health, I refused to contemplate.

Not many homes in Phoenix had basements, and his place was a one-story ranch. I couldn't imagine he'd be stupid enough to keep the shades open in a room he was keeping a kidnapped little girl in, but who knew? Maybe he was.

I couldn't call the cops and say, "Hey, listen, hear me out about this guy."

I had to have something meaty.

At the end of the street, I turned right, then hooked another right to walk down the alley. It was dark, impossible to see the words Puppy Patrol on my shirt. I was counting the houses in my head at the same time coming up with a plausible explanation of why I was wandering down the alley should someone stop and ask.

I hit his back gate without seeing anyone and tried the latch.

Of course, locked.

If I owned a home, I might lock my back gate to deter intruders. But it'd be a pain in the ass when I took out my garbage.

If I was holding a little girl I'd snatched, I'd definitely lock it.

Hmm.

The dumpsters and huge recycling bins were just outside his gate.

Perfect.

This meant I could get into his yard to look in the back windows, though I might not be able to get out.

I'd figure that out later.

I climbed on top of the dumpster (not easy and all kinds of gross), stood and looked over the top of his fence.

Clean landing on turf.

He should xeriscape. We were in a water crisis. No one should have lawns anymore in arid climates.

Right, I totally needed to learn better focus.

I looked at the house.

Light on in the kitchen with no one in it (did this man *not* hear about climate change?). No lights on in the other side of the house. I couldn't tell from that far away, but it seemed like no blinds were closed over the back windows, because I could see the light shining in from opened doorways to a hall.

Except the last room, but it might just be the door was closed.

This could mean he had nothing to hide.

It could also mean he was an idiot.

Well, I was currently harboring fifty thousand forms of bacteria on my hands and clothing from my climb onto the dumpster. In for a penny, in for a pound.

I put one foot to the top of his fence then leaped over. I landed on soft knees and it still jarred me like a bitch.

Ouch.

Right away, I set the pain aside and returned my attention to the house.

No movement in the windows. I didn't think I was making that much noise, but, if he could hear it, I hoped my climb onto the dumpster sounded like someone taking out their trash like people often did at seven at night.

Though it appeared I was good.

Sticking to the fence, I moved left, forward, then crouching, I went in.

Coming up from the crouch just enough to see over the windowsill, I noted it was a window to the dining room, through which was a galley kitchen, through which was the living room and him sitting in a recliner watching the Diamondbacks on TV.

Okay, good. He hadn't heard me and come to investigate.

Onward.

Crouch-walking under the window, I hit a back patio. The first window there, from the dim light shining in from the rest of the house, I saw was a bathroom.

The next room, door open from the hallway, more light shining in, appeared to be an office.

The next room, there were blinds, they were down and closed.

"Shit," I whispered.

I went around the side of the house, which was rife with mature trees, not a lot of room to move. I shimmied my way in, but the blinds on the window on that side were also closed.

Open windows everywhere else, except this room.

That was fishy.

Right?

Still not enough to call the cops.

I couldn't now say, "I have a feeling about this guy, and the blinds on one of his rooms are closed, though I can't tell you how I know that. So obviously, that's cause to break down the door and search the house ASAFP."

They weren't going to rush an urgent call to assemble the SWAT team on that intel.

Time for tampons, Lenny's and scheming some plan to find a way to get into that house and check that room.

I was thinking a trip to a T-shirt printer and some time on my computer creating a bogus notice from the city for a mandatory visit from pest control.

Gophers.

I'd heard gophers were a sitch in the Valley.

Though, not so much inside houses.

Again, I'd figure it out.

I was about to move out of the trees, hoping the lock on the gate was easy to navigate from the inside, when I noticed movement at the window.

I froze.

I'd brushed against the trees, but I didn't think I'd made much noise. Surely not enough he'd hear me three rooms away over the TV.

That was when she appeared.

Just her head.

Dark hair: messy.

Cute-as-a-button face: terrified.

Lips: moving with words anyone could read, even in the dark.

Help me.

Adrenaline surged throughout my body, making it tingle top to toe.

Tears flooded my eyes, making them sting.

My heart clutched and memories battered my brain, trying to force their way in.

I couldn't give them free reign or they'd paralyze me.

It took mad effort, but I held them back using the aforementioned adrenaline and the sight of her face in that window.

I was right.

She was there.

I had to call the cops.

Now.

I put my hand to the window, nodded to her, tried to smile reassuringly, my mind cluttered.

Should I call from where I was? Would he hear me? If he did, what would he do with her? He had access to her. I did not. He had access to his garage. I did not. And I was at least a five-minute run away from my car, and in my current situation, couldn't even easily get around to the front of the house to see which direction he'd have gone. Had a neighbor heard me, one who would maybe warn him someone was lurking on his property, or they'd called the cops and their sirens would do it? Would me being in his backyard, trespassing, mess up the investigation?

I had to get to the alley and make the call.

Pronto.

It's going to be okay, I mouthed back to her. *Someone will be here soon.*

Panic filled her little face. Even if I suspected she couldn't read my lips, my guess was she knew I had to leave. She shook her head.

I pressed my hand into the window, not that she could notice the added pressure, so I got closer and mouthed, *Promise. Hang tight.*

She kept shaking her head, but I was on the move.

I didn't stick to the fence. I ran right to the back gate.

The latch locked from the inside, but with an easy twist and lift, the door opened.

On instinct, I looked back to the house and froze yet again.

I saw a shadow moving through the hall across the door of the bathroom, headed toward the back bedroom.

"*Shit!*" I hissed.

I sprinted back to the dining room window and didn't bother crouching.

I looked right in.

I was correct about that shadow.

He wasn't in his recliner anymore.

He was headed to her.

"No, no, no, no, no," I chanted, panic creeping in, attempting to take a firm grip.

To force it out (because that would paralyze me too, and no way could I let that happen), acting fast, even though I was not able to think as fast, I had to go with it.

I went to the patio door and knocked, loud.

And I kept doing it until he showed at the door.

Okay, good.

Or, also, bad.

What the heck did I do now?

The door was made of glass.

Through it, he looked at me.

He looked at the patio beyond me.

He looked at me again.

And I looked at him.

On the wrong side of middle age, my guess, closer to sixty than forty. His shoulders were broad. His hair was thin. He had a little gut. He needed a shave. And he had to be four or five inches taller than me.

I had a stun gun and thirty years less than him.

But he could probably take me.

Expressions chased themselves across his face. Shady. Incredulous. And regrettably, he ended on angry.

He opened the door and demanded, "Who are you and what are you doing on my back patio?"

"Hi!" I exclaimed. "I'm so sorry." I pointed to the badge on my chest. "I work for Puppy Patrol?" I told him in a question, like he could confirm I did. I didn't wait for his confirmation, I babbled on.

"And I was walking one of your neighbor's dogs. He slipped the leash and ran off. I'm trying to find him. He's a little Chihuahua. I'm freaked! He'd be a snack for coyotes."

"We don't have coyotes in the city," he informed me.

"Yes, we do," I contradicted. And we did. I had a Puppy Patrol client (actually, it was a Kitty Krew client, same company, brown uniform, whole different ball of wax) who'd learned that the hard way. "They come down from the mountains and in from the desert, easy pickin's for people who let their cats go outside and stuff."

RIP Gaia.

"How did you get in my backyard?"

"Your gate was unlatched," I lied. "And I could swear I saw little Bruiser dash in here from the alley."

He leaned out to look toward his gate.

I leaned back, my hand moving toward my pocket and my stun gun.

When he looked back at me, I knew he saw through my story.

And it was on.

I didn't have time for the stun gun. Not now.

He lunged.

I tried to evade.

He caught me anyway and pulled me right inside.

Totally knew he could take me.

Damn it!

We grappled.

I went for the gonads with my knee and hit his inner thigh.

This caused him not to let me go, but instead grab my hair and pull, *hard*.

Jerk!

I went for the instep, slamming down on it with my foot, and that was better. He yelped, his hold loosened, I ripped myself away from him (pulling my own hair, because his grip hadn't loosened that much, *ouch!*), and I yanked out the stun gun.

He recovered too quickly, nabbed me, and even if I knew he

could take me, I was still surprised at his strength when he wrenched me around at the same time throwing me down to the floor with such force, I hit the tile and skidded several feet. My head then struck a corner of his kitchen cabinet.

Worse than the hair pulling. Seriously.

While I blinked the stars out of my eyes, he came after me, reached down to grab me again, and I remembered I had my stun gun in my hand.

I turned it on, heard it crackling, his attention went to it, and ill-advisedly in our current positioning, I touched it to him.

He went inert, then dropped, all two hundred some-odd pounds of him landing square on top of me.

"*Oof,*" I grunted.

Fuck! I thought.

I dropped the stun gun to try to shift him off, when my breath that had just come back stopped because he was suddenly flying through the air.

He landed on his back several feet away from me, his head cracking against the tile with a sickening sound.

But I didn't have any attention to give him.

I didn't because there were two men standing over me, and these two dudes could totally take me. I didn't know who they were. They might be associates of the bad guy. But they were so gorgeous, for a split second, all I could think was that I'd be okay with that (the them taking me part, that was).

One was tall, very tall, with black hair, green eyes and an age range of thirty-five to a very fit, healthy-living, great-genes forty-five. He also looked familiar, but I couldn't place it in my current predicament. And last, he'd had some goodness injected in him from, my guess, a Pacific Islander parent.

The other one was also tall, very tall, just not as tall as the other guy. I'd put him in the thirty to thirty-five age zone. He had dark-brown hair, full, short, but the top and sides were longish and slicked back in a stylish way. He had a thick brown beard that was trimmed gloriously and gray-blue eyes.

For a second, I thought he was Chris Evans.

Then he spoke.

Angrily.

"What the fuck are you doing?"

Wait.

What *was* I doing?

Oh yeah.

Suddenly confronting a Chris Evans doppelgänger, I'd forgotten about Elsie Fay (that sounded really bad, but trust me, with these guys, who wouldn't?).

I shot to my feet and dashed through the kitchen.

That was as far as I got before I was whipped around with a strong hand on my arm and Chris Evans was in my face.

"Again, what the fuck are you doing?" he asked.

"Who are you?" I asked back.

"I asked first," he returned.

"Do you know that guy?"

"What guy?"

"The one who owns this house."

"No."

Okay, I was going with he was a good guy. Maybe a cop. Maybe they were onto this guy like I was.

Yeah.

Anyway, if they were in cahoots with the bad guy, they wouldn't have cracked his head on the tile.

So I was going with that because there was no more time to waste.

"Elsie Fay," I said, tore my arm from his hold and raced through the house.

I made it to the door to the room at the end of the hall and was in such a rush, when I turned the knob, I slammed full-body into it because it was locked.

I then grabbed the knob and jostled it and the door violently, like that would magically open it.

I was pushed aside with an order of, "Stand back."

I did as told.

"Are you a good guy or a bad guy?" I belatedly asked in order to confirm.

"Even if I was a bad guy," he said while positioning in front of the door, his eyes aimed at it, "I'd tell you I was a good guy."

Excellent point.

He lifted a beefy (those thighs!), chocolate-brown-cargo-pants-clad leg and landed his boot solidly by the door handle.

The door popped open.

I slipped in front of him to enter the dark room.

I immediately tripped over something, but stopped, righted myself and called into the darkness, "Elsie Fay?"

No movement. No sound.

Chris Evans entered behind me, *close* behind me. So close, I could feel his heat and the natural badassery that wafted off him (this apparently happened with guys who knew how to bust open doors with their boot), and I felt him move.

On instinct again, I spun and whispered, "Don't turn on the light."

The other guy was standing in the doorway.

I turned back to the room, and gingerly, my eyes adjusting to the dark with weak light coming in from down the hall (trying to ignore the fact this room would be pitch black without the door open, and how that would affect the mind of a little girl), I called, "Elsie Fay? It's me. From outside? You know, the window? You're okay. We're gonna get you out and call the cops and your parents and—"

I didn't finish because a six-year-old hit me like a bullet. She slammed into my legs so hard, I nearly went down. And I would have if I didn't run into Chris Evans and his hands didn't span my hips to hold me steady (told you he was close).

I didn't have time to consider how those hands felt on my hips.

Elsie Fay was clawing up my chinos.

I bent and pulled her into my arms. She was heavy, as six-year-olds were wont to be, too big to be held, too young to realize it, though in this instance, she needed it, and I didn't have time to consider her weight as she clamped onto me with arms and legs. She, too, fisted her hand in my hair and she did it tighter than the bad guy. She also shoved her face in my neck.

"It's okay," I whispered to her. "You're okay. You're safe now. Okay?"

She said nothing.

I turned to Chris Evans and his hottie partner.

"Is he neutralized?" I asked.

"Yes," the hottie partner answered.

"Then let's get her out of here," I stated, and didn't wait for their response.

I pushed through them and got that little girl the hell out of there.

TWO

CITADEL OF DENIAL

I was in denial.

Of a lot of things.

The first part of that denial was what had happened an hour earlier, when Elsie Fay's parents showed at the police station, haggard, harried, both of them in tears of joy that their nightmare had ended, and that end didn't lead them to another nightmare. Also, they were tears of fatigue and residual terror because the nightmare they'd endured was hideous.

I knew all about that.

Triggering much?

Hell yes!

The thing was, Elsie Fay would not let go of me. She wouldn't even lift her face out of my neck.

This was part of the reason why I was at the police station.

The other part was that I didn't have much choice (say, *any*). The police needed my statement, and as iffy as that statement was going to be, considering the kidnapped child was clutching me in a death grip and she lost it anytime anyone tried to pull her from me, I had to go.

The thing was, her parents were frenzied, and she was freaked way the eff out. And, for obvious reasons, the moment they made it to us, they tried to tear her from my arms.

She just wouldn't let me go.

So, with several cops, Chris Evans and his hottie partner looking on, I took a step away from them, saying gently, "I'm sorry. So, so sorry. Hang tight a second." And then I dipped my lips to Elsie Fay's ear and whispered, "It's okay, honey. Stay right where you are. I got you. But do me a favor." With effort, juggling her in one arm (not that she'd go anywhere with the hold she had on me, I just wasn't taking any chances of letting her fall), I gently pulled her filthy, ratted hair away from her face and urged, "Just a peek. Look. It's your mom and dad. Take a quick peek. They're right here, and they can't wait to hold you."

She shoved her face deeper into my neck.

I heard her mother swallow a sob.

"Elsie Fay, honey, listen to me. I wouldn't lie to you," I promised. "You're safe and your parents are here to take you home."

It took a second, and it was both horrible and adorable, the timid way she peeked at her folks.

The next second, she let me go, twisted in my arms, planted her feet in my pelvis and launched herself toward her parents.

It was good she possibly ruined any future plans I had to carry children so I could concentrate on the pain in my girlie parts, such was the strength of her using me as a launching pad, and not lose my shit at watching her mother and father catch her, huddle around her, and their weeping turn into uncontrollable sobs.

I was then taken into a room with Chris Evans and Hottie Partner. There, I sat silent—partly due to the fact I was in shock at what those two were saying—mostly because they didn't let me say anything—as they explained to the cops (another term you could use was lied) they were private investigators hired by Elsie Fay's grandparents to look into the matter of her kidnapping.

The lie part was that I was on their team.

So, this was why they were at that house. They'd figured out the same thing I had.

They then shared I, being the least intimidating of the three (this was vexing, but true), made the approach. The bad guy made me, and promptly assaulted me, making the first move, so they had to move in. As we'd breached the house, and I'd already ascertained Elsie Fay was there, we carried on getting her out.

At least that last part was true.

By some miracle (which included some official looking older officer in a spiffy uniform coming in and asking the detectives to leave the room to "have a word"), this was good enough for the police.

Thus, with no ado whatsoever, they let us go.

The whole interview lasted, at most, fifteen minutes.

The thing was, I'd been escorted to the police station in the back of a cruiser, Chris Evans at my side, which meant my Juke was back at the bad guy's house. And I was uncertain about a call to Luna for a ride from the police station.

This uncertainty was embedded in the real fact I'd never hear the end of it.

I mean, even Dorothy might leave Rose if Rose went off and did something Dorothy expressly advised her not to do, and a few hours later, that ended with a call for a ride from the police station.

(Okay, no. No way Dorothy would leave Rose hanging (maybe Blanche), but Shirley might do that to Laverne.)

I could call Tito, but on his way, he might get sidetracked by a biker bar or tiki lounge or remember the whereabouts of a speakeasy that was on his way, and I'd be there all night.

It was going to have to be a Lyft, which was money I didn't have to spare, but whatevs.

However, I would find in short order I didn't need a ride.

Oh no.

I was "escorted" (this, a nice way to say I was somewhat compulsorily guided) to a black GMC Denali, stuffed in the back seat and whisked here.

Which was part two of my denial.

I wasn't sure what "here" was.

I knew it was an impressive set of offices in downtown Phoenix (and by the by, we drove by Lenny's on the way here, and I now totally needed a vanilla malt).

I also knew that either these dudes didn't put a lot of time into office organization, such was their desire to get the job done for their clients, or their business was new, what with all the boxes of unopened computers and flat screens and other shit I didn't know what it was stacked around. Not to mention furniture that had been delivered, but not had its protective wrapping taken off. Nor had it been positioned, including desks, chairs, couches and a line of office chairs, which stood at attention along a wall, waiting for badass asses to rest in them.

I would rather have had them take me to my car so I could go home, have a bubble bath and descend into my Citadel of Denial, a place I'd had nineteen years to design, and it was impenetrable. It had ramparts and trebuchets, and vats filled with boiling tar and everything.

It was the shit.

It kept me safe.

With these guys I didn't feel not safe, but I also didn't feel safe.

I was sitting in one of the few chairs that had been unwrapped, across a handsome executive desk (that had also been unwrapped, but the top of it was completely bare), staring down the Hottie Partner.

I did this while Chris Evans stood against the wall behind the desk, arms crossed on his wide chest (thus, pecs popping, *Lord*), knee bent, one boot against the wall, blue-gray eyes scowling at me.

By the by, he could scowl very well.

Therefore, no matter how much I whipped up my trusty steed (her name was Cinnamon) to get me across the drawbridge and into the bailey of my Citadel, I knew I was screwed.

Not to mention, the staring contest I had going on with Hottie

Partner, who seemed more like he was Hottie Head Honcho, was lasting a long time.

In the Denali, after I'd asked if they were taking me back to my Juke, and Chris Evans had replied with a curt, "No," I decided further discussion could happen once they'd reamed me for being an idiot who frequently involved myself in deranged mischiefs (though, they didn't know the "frequent" part of that).

The thing I had on my side was...I'd saved the girl.

And that was a big thing to have on my side. At least I thought so, even if they were right on my tail in that endeavor.

Finally, Hottie Honcho spoke.

"Let's start with how you knew it was Donald Walken."

"Sorry?" I asked.

"How did you know Walken had Elsie Fay?" Hottie Honcho rearranged his question.

Oh.

"I went to Elsie Fay's church," I answered.

Hottie Honcho didn't say anything.

I read this as he wanted more.

"So, you know, whoever took her had to have opportunity. Right?"

Hottie Honcho nodded. Once.

"And he had to have seen her, and from there, probably followed her, researched her, so he knew when he could take her."

Hottie Honcho said nothing and made no move.

I read that as agreement.

"So...school, neighbor, friend of family, employee of a grocery store they frequented, stuff like that. All of which the cops were going to sort through with a fine-tooth comb. But days passed, and she wasn't found. Then her parents asked the reverend at their church to be their spokesperson with the media, so I figured they were religious. If they went to church, Elsie Fay did. And maybe the bad guy did too. So I went to their church."

"And?" Hottie Honcho prompted.

"And, they *are* religious. The mom teaches Sunday school. The dad is a deacon. I went to church that first Sunday after she went missing. The reverend asked everyone to keep them and Elsie Fay in their prayers, and if they heard anything, or saw anything, to report it to the police immediately, no matter how small or seemingly insignificant. Elsie Fay's folks were there. Everyone was glancing at them. Or trying not to and looking sad or upset. Except, well..."—I shrugged—"*him.*"

Hottie Honcho looked over his shoulder at Chris.

Chris looked at Honcho and shook his head, also once.

Honcho turned back to me.

"Obviously, that was weird," I shared. "What was weirder was that he seemed to *diligently* avoid looking at them or having any reaction. Therefore, I followed him home from church. Then I went to my place and"—I lifted my hands, mimicked tapping on a keyboard, wished I hadn't because I undoubtedly looked like a dufus, dropped my hands and concluded—"did some Google magic, and found he was not to be found, at all, anywhere. He rented his house, that was as far as I got. No social media. No LinkedIn. No nada. Which was even weirder. Therefore, I had to take a closer look."

Honcho again said nothing. Chris didn't either, nor did he move, though he was back to glowering at me.

"So, how did you know?" I asked.

Honcho answered, "Donald Walken's name is really Paul Nicholson, and he's on the sex offender list. He's already done time for some sick shit. This is why he illegally started using a new identity. Also why no one in his neighborhood or at the church knew he's messed way the fuck up."

Ah.

There you go.

I kept my mind firmly off the "sick shit" and that he had time to do that with Elsie Fay and focused on something else that was pertinent.

"Can I go now?"

When he leaned into his elbows on his desk, fingers linked, resting his chin on them, and penetrated me with his perfect jade stare, I figured that was a no.

"Do you know where you are?" he asked.

"No," I answered.

"Do you know who we are?" he went on with a slight jerk of his head to Chris.

"Well, that'd be nice to know, considering we're spending so much time together," I told him.

"I'm Kai Mason."

Why was that name familiar?

"And that's Julien Jackson," he continued on another slight jerk to Chris...or Julien.

I felt a strange, but far from unpleasant, electrical pulse jolt through me at learning his name.

Well then.

I ignored the pulse and focused on the fact that I liked his name. It was unusual, at least his first name was. It didn't really look like him, but it also did, in an odd way.

"And considering you're the Avenging Angel, you probably should know who the players are on the street," Kai Mason carried on.

Uh-oh.

Seemed he knew more than just my name.

I sat back, clasped my hands in my lap and tried really hard not to suck my lips between my teeth in order to bite them, that being in order not to groan at my own stupidity.

Mental note: A girl can be sassy, but no one should be cocky.

"What are you talking about?" I asked.

Mason sat back too, in order to be more comfortable when he shared, "This is Nightingale Investigations and Security."

"Okay," I said slowly.

His lips quirked like he found me amusing.

The gall!

Even if I couldn't bust open a door, I was kickass, not amusing!

At this point, Jackson moved. He lifted his hands and pretended to type on the keyboard.

He did this saying, "Look it up when you get home."

First, I was glad I was going home. I mean, it didn't seem in question, considering the cops just let these two dudes go, didn't ask me a single question, not even my name. And thinking about it, something I didn't have time to do with a six-year-old attached to me, the police had treated them with respect from the minute they'd showed.

Like, all kinds of respect.

But still.

Second, it was every shade of annoying he was making fun of my pretend typing.

I shot him a glare.

My glare hit his badass forcefield and became imaginary butter-flies that flitted away, or at least that was what I imagined considering his stoic (but gorgeous) face registered nothing from being the target of my glare.

Ugh.

"We have three offices," Mason kept talking. "One in Denver, one in LA, and a new one." He pointed to his desk. "Here."

"Right," I said tersely.

So that explained the boxes and wrapped furniture.

"Are we hanging so I can help you unwrap the furniture and position it?" I inquired. "Because that might have to wait for tomorrow. I need a malt, then a bubble bath."

Though, I was probably out of luck with the malt. Lenny's closed at ten. I needed to get moving if I was going to make it.

Mason again looked over his shoulder at Jackson.

Mason still seemed amused.

Jackson did not.

Mason came back to me. "See, this is the thing."

I wasn't sure I wanted to know the thing.

He told me anyway. "We have experience with people like you. Namely, *women* like you."

Oh boy.

I might be getting mad.

"You don't know what kind of woman I am," I retorted.

"I know we had a friend who thought she could take to the streets and right all the world's wrongs. She got shot twice, chest and gut, for her troubles. She almost didn't make it. It's a flat-out miracle she did."

Yikes!

"You should have reported your concerns to the police," Mason kept at me.

Before I could say anything, Jackson cut in, "Barring that, when you cased his house, you shouldn't have sat in your ridiculous bright-yellow car and had a ten-minute phone conversation while obviously casing his house."

I knew my car was a problem.

I loved my car (I called her Tweety, for obvious reasons).

But she wasn't so good in a stakeout.

Now Jackson kept at me. "Or jumped the fence from a dumpster."

I still needed to wash my hands, and every other inch of me, not only due to the dumpster sitch, but also that Walken collapsed on me.

Serious *euw*.

Jackson wasn't done with me. "Or directly confronted him with nothing but a stun gun and a Puppy Patrol polo."

He was hot and all, but he was all kinds of infuriating.

"Okay, all's well that ends well—" I started.

"So you know this is gonna end well?" Mason asked.

"Tonight it did," I pointed out.

"Two weeks ago, when you roofied that football player who was the ringleader in the gang rape of a girl, dragged his ass to a warehouse, poured honey on him and let loose a bunch of ants, then told him to, 'Behave himself, the Avenging Angel is watching', that wasn't smart."

See?

Stupid cocky.

"Are you talking about that college guy?" I asked fake-innocently.

"You know I am," he answered, knowing I was playing fake.

"Well, he'd slut-shamed her into dropping the charges. He and his buds' bullshit on social media destroyed her after they'd already violated her. She's quit school. Girls have committed suicide over stuff like that. Gotten into drugs. Cutting. Their lives are forever ruined even if they pull through it and find help to carry on in a healthy way," I returned. "So, I don't know anything about this Avenging Angel person, but if they did that, I applaud them."

"I'm not defending him," Mason pointed out. "He's a piece of shit. Him roofied, naked, alone, and somewhere he doesn't know where he is or if worse is yet to come, covered in honey and crawling ants would not be the way I'd deal with him, but it works. The point I'm trying to make is, you're not a piece of shit. And you could get fucked up by doing that crap. He's too humiliated to press charges. But the next guy you run up against might not be the same."

"I'm not this Avenging Angel," I lied again. "I just..." Nope. Not gonna go there. "Got interested in Elsie Fay's case. I'm a true crime buff." Lame! (Though true.) "You're right. I should have called the police. There won't be a next time, but should that very unusual incident occur, I promise to call the cops. Now, will one of you take me back to my car? Lenny's closes soon."

Mason turned to Jackson and lifted his brows.

Jackson pushed away from the wall and grunted, "Come on."

He would not have been my choice, mostly because, in any other circumstance but this one, he totally would be my choice.

But whatevs.

I got out of my chair and said, "Nice to meet you, Kai."

"Mace," he corrected me. "Only my wife and mother call me Kai."

"Right," I mumbled, gave him a salute with one finger to my brow and out, ignored him appearing amused again, then followed Jackson out of the office.

"Can I make a pit stop?" I requested. "I have dumpster hands."

He said nothing, but reversed directions to take me to a bathroom in their office suite.

It was swish. Black walls. Recessed lighting. Backlit mirrors. White bowl sinks looking stark and stylish on a matte black counter. Contrasting blond wood floors and matching wood stalls. An attractive white planter in the back corner with a healthy green plant in it.

It did not say PI's office. It said five-star hotel.

I did my thing, then I did it again for good measure. I considered a third go but decided that was maybe a hint over the top. After that, I walked out to Jackson waiting.

He was silent through the reception area and into the hall. He was also silent down the elevator to the parking garage (their offices were on the fifth floor of the high-rise). He remained silent as he bleeped the locks on one of seven shiny black Denalis lined up right next to the elevator. And he was silent when we got in. He pulled out and we were on our way.

It was me who broke the silence when he pulled into Lenny's drive-thru.

Okay, maybe he wasn't *totally* infuriating.

"Thank the good Lord above," I said.

He had no response.

He didn't quite make the menu board when he stopped and turned to me.

"Just the malt?" he asked.

I shook my head. "Also a cowboy burger. No tomato. Stress that. I don't want even one slimy seed to ruin the perfection of the burger. Tots. And the malt needs to be vanilla. Oh! And a root beer. No, Orange Crush. No! Root beer."

Jackson didn't move, just kept staring at me.

"Root beer," I firmly decided.

He looked forward then the SUV inched forward.

I was realizing how this wasn't going to be a great thing (even if it was a great thing, Lenny's was always great, even though, if you went inside the one on Central, you might be eating your burger or pastrami next to a meth addict, a couple sex workers, some hipsters, some skaters, and a Scottsdale socialite slumming it to cheat on her Whole30 diet where no one could see her—in other words, the vibe could be mixed, though, in my opinion, that was part of the fun), because this wasn't McDonald's. The drive-thru at Lenny's took a while.

Part two of this predicament was that I'd left my wallet in my glove compartment in Tweety.

"Um, my wallet's in my car," I told him.

"My shout," he said.

"I'll pay you back," I promised.

"You bet your ass you will," he murmured so low I barely caught it, but couldn't ask after it since he was leaning forward to pull out his wallet due to the fact the cashier had opened her window.

After he dealt with paying, as we sat waiting, I queried, "What did you mean?"

"About what?" he asked, his head turned away from me, apparently fascinated with the goings-on inside at closing time at Lenny's.

I jogged his memory. "The part about me betting my ass I will. I'm good for it."

Again, it'd bite into my monthly fun-money budget, which wasn't an astronomical number to begin with, but since Donald Walken/Paul Nicholson was caught, and Elsie Fay was with her parents, I had free time. I'd just sign on for more dog walking and cat sitting and sort myself out.

"Though, I don't have any cash on me. I'll drop it at the office tomorrow," I told him.

"Right," he said.

"Really, I will," I confirmed.

"I believe you."

"You don't seem like you believe me."

"Well, I do."

"Okay," I mumbled.

We continued waiting.

He drummed the steering wheel with his fingers.

I watched as he did so.

His fingers were long. The ends squared. The back of his hand deliciously veined. And he had a tan, his skin a beautiful caramel color. But there looked to be some scars on his knuckles, like he'd been in a fight (or more than one).

I was thinking about those hands on my hips earlier. I was thinking about them in other ways too. I was one hundred percent drifting into my Blanche of the *Golden Girls* personality of the trio I embraced, so I decided for safety's sake to start a conversation.

"So, you're a PI."

"Yup."

He didn't seem old enough, but what did I know? He was the first private investigator I'd ever met (along with Mace, of course).

"How long have you been doing that?"

"Awhile."

Hmm.

Not chatty or forthcoming.

I tried a different tack. "So do you have a cool nickname like Mace? Do people call you Jack?"

"Cap."

"Cap?"

He finally turned to look at me. "Yeah. Cap."

"What's that short for?"

"I haven't decided about you yet," he said instead of answering my question.

"Sorry?"

"I haven't decided about you yet," he repeated.

"I heard you, I just didn't get you."

"Part of that is not knowing if I want you to get me."

I didn't say anything to that because I still didn't know what he was saying, though what I thought he was saying was annoying.

Therefore, I turned away and whispered to myself, "You're hot, you know it, but get over yourself."

I didn't know if he heard me, I also didn't care.

Fortunately, a few minutes later, my food was passed through.

He gave it to me and said, "You're welcome for dinner."

There it was.

He heard me.

"I'm paying you back," I reminded him.

"Right," he repeated his earlier, enigmatic sentiment.

Whatever.

I was paying him back. He'd see.

"Can I eat in your car?"

"Knock yourself out," he replied as he drove to the exit.

I left the burger for later, chased the tots with the root beer, and was glad traffic was light so he could get me to my car, and with any luck, I could get home before my malt totally melted.

When he pulled alongside my car, for some insane reason, I turned to him and spoke.

"I didn't know she was in there. I was just checking. Once I saw her in the window, I was going to go to the alley and call the police. But I saw him headed her way. I had to do something. I couldn't know you and your partner were on the case and at my back."

"She's safe. With kidnapping her, he's gonna get life. That waste of humanity will die in prison. You were right. All's well that ends well."

I felt weird because I was attracted to him, and as such, obviously, I didn't want him to think I was a dork.

On the other hand, I had a feeling he knew I was attracted to him, and he hadn't "decided" about me, and he was drop-dead gorgeous so he probably just had to crook a finger and any heterosexual woman would fall all over themselves to follow wherever he went, and he oh-so-totally knew that. So I thought he was likely a conceited jerk.

And outside of popping by his office, which he clearly didn't spend much time in, say, unwrapping furniture, this was possibly going to be it, and he hadn't asked for my number.

Of course, he was a PI. He could probably find my number, easy.

"Are you gonna get out or are you gonna sit there until that malt is milk?" he prompted.

Okay, still attracted to him, but he was a total jerk.

"I feel like I need to say something, like 'thank you for pulling that nasty asshole off me and telling the cops I was on your team so I didn't have uncomfortable 'splaining to do.'"

"You're welcome," he said shortly.

Right then. Decision made, at least on my part.

This was done.

"Have a good life," I bid and lifted my malt. "I'll mail the check to the office."

"On me," he replied.

"Nope." I shook my head, struggling, with all my drinks and food-stuffs, to open the door. "No way. I'm paying you back."

"Hey," he called when I jumped out.

I looked back to him.

"What's your name?"

"Kelly Garrett," I lied, slammed the door with my foot and turned to Tweety, putting Cap and Mace and Donald Walken/Paul Nicholson in the dark forest I never visited surrounding my Citadel of Denial.

Not looking back, I got in my car, and even though the Denali didn't move, I pulled out and drove away.

THREE

MARCONI UNION

While snarfing down my burger and sipping my malt, I googled Nightingale Investigations and Security.

And discovered how I knew Kai Mason.

He was Stella Gunn's husband. That being Stella Gun, lead singer and guitarist of the Blue Moon Gypsies, award-winning, multi-platinum, cool-as-all-hell rock band. I'd seen him in dozens of pictures by her side when she went to award ceremonies and such.

He was also a celebrity in his own right, being a top-notch snow-boarder who turned into an equally successful surfer.

This somehow segued into him being the owner of the most sought-after celebrity security firm in LA, providing security for such stars as Viola Remington, Dee-Amond and Imogen Swan.

However, recently, his business, MTS Security of LA, had merged with Nightingale Investigations of Denver, whereupon NI had become NI&S, and as Mace told me, they'd expanded to open an office in the Valley of the Sun.

He and Stella had some book written about them, so I bought the eBook but left it and clicked through all the stuff about Nightingale Investigations.

The guy who owned it, Liam Nightingale, also had a book written about him. But that was probably the least fascinating thing about him, his firm and his superhero-esque crew.

I mean, they made the Denver news more than the Hemsworth brothers made international. And an image search showed me Nightingale's crew made those Aussie boys look just plain.

I know, it sounded crazy, but it was all kinds of true.

I guessed they were going to go with the same hiring strategy down here in Phoenix, if Cap and Mace were anything to go by.

I sucked the last dregs of the malt down, even if I was lamenting my addition of the tots. My belly was so full (who was I kidding, the malt was enough, I shouldn't have ordered the burger either) and headed to my tiny bathroom to run a bath.

My Citadel was under attack. The parapets were shaking. I should have known, with what happened that night, even a vanilla malt wasn't going to be able to tame the onslaught.

I needed a bath bomb, bubbles, a face mask and some candles.

Moving through my apartment, which was also tiny (living room up front, bar beyond which was a U-shaped kitchen, hall with bath to one side, laundry closet to the other, lone bedroom at the back), I sorted that all out.

Cueing up Marconi Union's "Weightless" on my Bluetooth speaker, I got in the bath, spread the sheet mask on my face and sat back in the warm water, the foam moving in to cocoon me.

I should have known it wasn't going to work.

And it didn't.

Five minutes in, I was curled into a ball, face shoved against my knees, shoulders heaving, the name *Macy, Macy, Macy, Macy, Macy* echoing in my head.

I huddled in my Citadel as the arrows flew and the cannons boomed, and it took me a while to get there. To be able to do what my counselor taught me to do, one of many things I tried, the only thing that worked (sometimes).

I anchored myself where I was. I felt the warm water. Listened to the music. Smelled my tobacco cedarwood candles. Felt the cool mask still clinging to my face.

And I reminded myself I was Rachel "Raye" Armstrong, with emphasis on the "strong."

I'd navigated the trauma and made it here to this place.

And I was safe.

Now.

In my bath.

But also, in my life.

Alive. Breathing.

I had friends. I had a job I liked.

I had a life.

No, I'd *made* a life.

And I was living it.

I was healthy. I had cute clothes. I worked hard to give myself a little extra.

I was okay.

No again.

I was good.

I was happy.

"Okay," I whispered to my knees, laid back again, smoothed the mask on my face, gently pressing it into my skin, and closed my eyes.

I needed a gummie and rest. I had a shift tomorrow.

Tomorrow.

Today was done.

And I had tomorrow.

I peeled the mask off, massaged the serum into my skin, got out of the bath, pulled the stopper, dried off, lotioned up, put on my silky green robe with the big pink flowers that hit my knees and tied the belt tight.

Then I headed out of my bathroom toward the back of my tiny apartment and my bedroom.

I got one step into my bedroom and let out a little scream.

Julien "Cap" Jackson was standing there, right beside my bed.

Holy shit!

"Two questions," he said conversationally, like I'd invited him there and let him in, not like he'd broken in completely silent while I was in the bath (with my bathroom door open!) and now he was in my bedroom. "One, what the fuck is this shitty music? And two, what the fuck is this?"

He then flicked a finger at my wall.

"What are you doing here?" I demanded.

"I decided about you."

"So you broke in?" My voice was rising.

"What's this, Rachel?" he asked, now stabbing his finger to my wall.

Hmm.

He now knew my name.

Also, where I lived.

Seemed while I was doing research on Nightingale Investigations and Security, he was researching me.

"Did you see me in the bath on your way to helping yourself to my bedroom?" I demanded.

"I heard you so I didn't look when I walked by," he answered, and for some reason, I believed him.

What could I say? Outside fibbing to the police in order to get my fat out of the fryer, he didn't seem a guy prone to prevarication.

"You can't just break into my house," I informed him of something he should very well know.

I said it standing several feet away from him.

In the blink of an eye, I was pressed to the wall, and he was pressed to me.

My breath took a hike.

"That friend," he said in a soft, dangerous voice. "The one Mace told you about who got shot?"

I nodded, too freaked out to do anything else.

Sure, I should be pissed and worried some dude I just met broke into my house and now had me pressed to a wall.

But this close, I could smell him. He smelled like my candle, manly and woodsy and fresh and comforting and safe.

And if he was hot at a distance, this close, those gray-blue eyes searing into mine, his magnificent face *right there*, I was having an entirely different reaction.

"She saved my life," he continued. "She saved my brother's life. Outside of my brother, my mom, and Law's husband, she's the most important person in my life. And I've got a huge family of people I care about. When she got shot, when we didn't know if she was going to make it, my brother got shot too. It was the worst few hours of my life, waiting for the doctors to tell us they were okay. And I've seen things, I've done things, I've been places that were literal hell on fucking earth. But that was the worst, the thought of losing her, losing him. So tell me,"—he got closer—"what *the fuck* is on your wall?"

I opened my mouth but didn't get any words out.

My front door crashed open.

Another blink of an eye, I wasn't pinned to the wall. I was shoved behind the tall, lean-hipped, broad-shouldered frame of Julien "Cap" Jackson, and he had a hand to his back waistband, fingers curled around the butt of a gun where it had been shoved.

Whoa!

Times two: the gun, and him from behind.

Yowza!

Great hair. Great beard. Great eyes. Great shoulders. Great hands.

Superior ass.

I tore my gaze off his ass and peered beyond him.

The front door was a direct shot to the back of the apartment, and I saw a crazed Luna standing there, her usually perfectly executed messy bun askew, her vibe manic.

Oh snap.

I forgot to call her.

Her head turned toward my living room then she came back to us.

"*You went to Lenny's without me?*" she shrieked.

Seemed like I should have cleared the evidence off my coffee table before I had my bath.

"That's my friend Luna," I told Cap. "She's safe. You don't have to shoot her."

He relaxed, took his hand from his gun but didn't step out of the way.

This might be because Luna slammed the door then planted her hands on her hips.

"You didn't call me, but you *did* go to Lenny's, and picked up a hot guy to boot!" she accused.

"Listen, Luna—" I started.

That was as far as I got. She was marching down the hall, bitching me out.

"It's all over the news. Elsie Fay was found. The bad guy arrested. I'm at home, watching this, waiting for your call, knowing where you were not but hours ago, and—"

She halted abruptly and sniffed the air.

Then she shouted, "Oh my *God*! Did you take a bubble bath with a hot guy you picked up after you saved a little girl from a monster?"

Like Cap and I could both fit in my bath.

Though that might be impossible, it'd be fun to try.

I felt Cap's eyes on me, so I looked to him and said, "I don't pick up hot guys all the time."

With zero hesitation, Luna outed me.

"She totally does."

I made an *Eek!* face at Cap. Then I shrugged to indicate the veracity of that statement.

After that, I stood transfixed as a smile flirted on his lips.

Wait, with all the rest, I hadn't noticed his lips.

Dayum.

He had nice lips (or at least the lower one was *fine*, the upper one was hidden by the mustache part of his beard).

Okay, generally, the man was good-looking. Scowling, he was also good-looking. Stoic, same.

Smiling, be still my heart.

And it wasn't even a full smile.

I came to when Luna snapped her fingers in my face. "Earth to Raye, pissed-off best friend in the room."

"Sorry," I muttered.

"What? Are you a cop?" she asked Cap.

"No," he answered.

She swung her head to me, brows raised in a silent demand for an explanation.

"He's a PI. Elsie Fay's grandparents hired his firm. He was kinda in on the, um...rescue operation."

"Rescue operation?" she asked.

Here we go.

"Um..." I didn't quite answer.

"You told me you were just looking in his windows," she snapped.

"Well, in one, I saw Elsie Fay."

"Just hanging out, watching some *Wild Kratts* with her abductor?" she asked sarcastically.

"What's *Wild Kratts*?" I asked back.

"It's a kid show," she told me.

"How do you know kids' shows?"

"Hello?" she called. "I have a nephew and a niece since Dream is working on making baby daddies of as many dudes as she can divest of their sperm."

Oh yeah, right.

Luna's older sister, Dream, was an interesting one. I wasn't sure she resided on our same planet.

Then again, Luna's parents were a lot like Dream, though a little more down to earth.

Luna hadn't entirely fallen far from that tree, but she didn't live in a house in Tempe obscured by an overgrown garden, owning and fostering more cats and dogs than was probably legal, and using her spare time to march in every protest organized, or standing outside grocery stores asking for people to sign petitions.

Nor did she flit from dude to dude, casually getting knocked up, and having babies she treasured who she put in cloth diapers because the disposable ones didn't biodegrade (or whatever).

The diaper bucket at Dream's house featured prominently in a number of my nightmares. Just sayin'.

"Raye, I've been worried sick," Luna said, taking me out of my reverie about why, exactly, she didn't put Jacques in that Tiffany's dog collar.

"Okay, I looked in more than his front window," I admitted.

She threw her hands up, stared at the ceiling, then turned to Cap.

"And you fed into her crap?" she demanded.

"When he'd thrown her on the floor of his dining room, she'd stun-gunned him, and he collapsed on top of her, Mace and I interceded."

I was wrong earlier.

Now, here we go.

I felt my eyes get big and my mouth cried, "Oh my God, dude! Total snitch!"

Luna turned to me and yelled, "You confronted the guy?"

"He was headed in Elsie Fay's direction."

"Did you have your phone on you?" Luna asked.

"Luna, I—"

"Did you?" she pressed.

"Yes."

"And you know what hitting the digits nine one one will get you?"

I looked to Cap.

He had his arms crossed on his chest and an expression on his face that teetered between entertained and tacit agreement with Luna.

"So, no help from you, then," I groused.

He looked to Luna and "helped." "My bad about Lenny's. She'd left her wallet in her car, so I covered it for her."

"That isn't exactly help," I informed him.

His lips flirted with that smile again.

I liked it again.

Someone, shoot me.

I turned back to my friend. "I'm fine. He's fine. Mace is fine. Most importantly, Elsie Fay is back with her parents and she's fine."

Or she would be if they bypassed religion and took her to see a child psychologist. Jesus was good for a whole host of things, and he might be the son of God, but he was also a carpenter, not a counselor.

"Did you also take her by CVS and get her tampons?" Luna asked Cap.

Right.

I was done.

I went to my bed, and making sure my robe stayed closed in all the important places, I fell backward on it.

"No," Cap drawled. "We missed that errand."

"Okay then," Luna said to Cap. "She's fine. You're fine, in more ways than one, by the way. Whoever this Mace is, is fine. Elsie Fay is too. Someone needs to go to CVS, because it's two days and counting, but that's not gonna be me. I've had enough of Raye's harebrained deviltry for one night. I'm outta here."

Told you she had a good vocabulary.

I sensed her walking away and knew she was doing it when she bid, "See you at work tomorrow."

"See you," I mumbled.

She made no noise since she was wearing a pair of her beat-up Toms, but I heard the front door close.

Then I felt the bed depress as Cap sat, his hip by my hip.

He leaned into a hand on the other side of me so all I could see was him.

My brain took this unfortunate moment to remind me how much I liked his hands.

Also, his beard.

"So, you can tell me tomorrow when I take you out to dinner about that shit on your wall," he declared. "Now, tell me what this music is."

I didn't have it in me to fight anymore.

So I said, "Marconi Union."

"Why are you listening to it?"

"It's ambient. It's relaxing."

"Fleetwood Mac's *Rumors* is relaxing. Ray Lamontagne's anything is relaxing. Joni Mitchell, Jack Johnson, James Taylor are relaxing. Miles Davis and Billie Holiday are relaxing. If you gotta go there, Enya is relaxing. Nick Drake is the essence of relaxing."

Wow, I was impressed with his knowledge of music.

"This is just weird," he concluded.

"I like it," I pointed out the obvious.

At that, he did something very, *very* bad.

He smiled.

No flirting with it, it was full-out this time.

Oh man.

I was screwed.

"I like your friend," he said.

"Don't let her fool you, she's crazier than me. She just hides it better."

He kept smiling.

Shit.

"Listen, Cap—" I started.

"I'll be here tomorrow, six thirty, to pick you up. I don't mess around when it comes to food. So wear something nice."

My mind immediately split between my closet and my bank account, the one side telling me it contained nothing that would do for a date with Julien "Cap" Jackson, the other side telling me I didn't have enough to splurge on a new dress (and shoes...and handbag).

I corralled my mind's wayward ways and noted, "I didn't say yes to the date."

"No woman stares at a man's hand like you stared at mine when she doesn't want that hand doing something to her."

Oh my God!

"You weren't even looking at me."

"I'd adjusted the side mirror so I could see you."

Damned technology making side mirrors adjustable with interior buttons clever PI guys could use so they could watch you while you didn't know they were doing it.

"That's sneaky," I announced.

"It's part of my job."

Huh.

"You're very full of yourself," I stated.

"Yeah, you said that already. Six thirty."

"Cap—"

He bent to put his face in my face at the same time his free hand slid up my neck to cup my jaw.

I smelled him again, this time with that beautiful hand on me, and I stilled in silent, expectant anticipation.

I thought he might kiss me.

But he didn't, and idiotically, I was disappointed about that.

Instead, he said, "And no woman, who doesn't want a man in her bedroom, lets him break into her house and then doesn't do dick about him being in her bedroom."

Busted!

"Rachel. Six thirty. Dinner. And the story behind that shit on your wall." He said this like a warning.

"That's none of your business."

"I'm making it my business."

"I'm not letting you make it your business."

I shivered as he slid his fingers along my jaw, his touch light and titillating, doing this as he took it away.

Also doing it as he said, "We'll see."

The bed moved when he got up.

And then, as silently as he showed, he was gone.

FOUR

THE SURF CLUB

The next morning, I swung into the back employee entrance of
The Surf Club, only five minutes late for my shift.

A personal best.

To lift my mood after a wild, emotional night, I'd gone devil-may-
care with a Parisian circa-1960s flair with my outfit. Black capris
that had a cigarette pant feel with a side zipper and a high waist that
rose to my lower ribs. Black and white striped, boatneck, long-
sleeved top that was cropped to just under my breasts. Black ballet
flats.

All I was missing was the beret.

Instead, I'd wrapped the black, pink, red and white Alexander
McQueen scarf I'd scored on an online resell site, backwards kerchief
style around my hair, tied just above my forehead in a neat little knot.
My blonde hair was twisted and pinned at the back, the floof of its
curls sticking out of the top of the wrap.

I'd decided to channel my Lucy vibe that day. After the successful, yet madcap night I'd had, it seemed apropos.

I went straight to my employee locker, stowed my purse and
made my selection from the many different colored server aprons I

had hanging there (I picked hot pink to go with the pink in the scarf). I tied it around my waist.

I then walked through the tiny kitchen and called a hello to Lucia, our cook.

She was prepping for the lunch crowd, and she could be intense (think Carmy from *The Bear*, except female, and she didn't use tweezers to dress any of her dishes, though she did mumble to herself, "needs more acid" a lot). Therefore, she didn't even look up at me.

This was not unusual, so I didn't take offense.

Shortly after, (our kitchen wasn't very big, though it was meticulously clean and tidy, by the edict of Lucia), I hit the bar area of the main room.

The Surf Club was neither for surfers (no surprise, considering Phoenix was landlocked) or a club. It also didn't have surfer décor. In fact, I had no idea why Tito named it The Surf Club, except he was Tito, and if you knew Tito, you'd know this wasn't uncharacteristic.

The bulk of the main room was chaotic.

A long, turquoise padded bench ran the length of the back wall, two- and four-top tables in front of it, mismatched chairs in front of those.

A huge mural was painted on the wall, which had a softly abstract, Mona-Lisa-smiling woman in the top corner. Instead of hair, though, she had dots and squishes that resembled flowers in varying shades of pinks and yellows against a background of greens and blues that flowed across the wall. In the middle of that space, painted into the flowers was the word LIVE!

The rest of the floor space was taken randomly with tables or seating areas that had armchairs and couches and beanbags. There were standing floor lamps that looked like they came from vintage stores dotted here and there, and some tables had small lamps on top of them.

A pothos plant sat in another corner and it had to be prehistoric, because the trails of its foliage were so long, tracking up and out so far, they were tacked to the walls and even the ceiling. There were string of pearls plants sprinkled around the space, hanging with vines dangling five feet.

The Surf Club was a coffee and cocktail bar on Indian School Road, which also served food, that Tito had opened sometime in the aughts.

So there was a long, curved bar made of a highly polished ash at the front, which had stools with backs and seats covered in marine blue. The bar back was filled with bottles of liquor and a wide, double-filter, cream-colored espresso machine.

There was exceptional Wi-Fi, and outlets and USB jacks everywhere, some even embedded in the tables or the wood floors, so people could charge while they hung.

And hang they did.

It was only now, early morning, when the parking lot wasn't jammed with cars of people who came, drank copious amounts of the ridiculously good Guatemalan, Ethiopian or Columbian blends Tito sourced from mysterious suppliers, and tapped on their keyboards for hours, sucking up Tito's electricity. Or folks who drank Jessie's, our mixologist, riotously inventive cocktails with lunch or dinner from Lucia's ever-changing menu of fusion food.

And Lucia didn't discriminate with her fusions. It could be Asian-Italian. It could be traditional fish and chips with a chipotle tartar sauce. It could be French-Mexican. You never knew with Lucia. You just knew it'd be good.

Also, around the corner from the bar, just in from the front door, for those who wanted to drink and dash, there was a strictly coffee cubby that had our second espresso machine, shelves filled with bags of the coffee we brewed that you could buy and take home, and a display of muffins, cookies, brownies, Danish and macarons we got from Willow's Good Stuff. Willow being a talented baker who didn't have a storefront, she just supplied us and had pop-ups at farmer's markets around the Valley on weekends.

Our fare was amazing, but the place was weird and eclectic,

personified by who was in the back corner on the bench seat right then, and nearly all the time.

Tito.

His name wasn't actually Tito. No one knew his real name. Luna and I guessed he called himself Tito since he drank so much of that brand of vodka (including tipping it in his coffee in the mornings).

He had lots of white hair, a white beard, and a pudgy body that rose, at best, to five foot four. Thus, he looked like a demented Santa Claus who'd gone astray in his efforts to go incognito on vacation.

In other words, he was always in Hawaiian shirts, and even inside, he wore sunglasses.

But that, and the fact he silently sat in the back corner booth most of the time (no one but Tito sat there—ever—partly because his butt was usually in that seat, partly because his stuff was jammed all around, making it look like an open office, but mostly because everyone knew that was Tito's space).

If you came to SC, you'd see Tito ensconced in his nook, surrounded by books, tapping on his iPad, or writing in copious journals.

But that was the only thing (visually) with Tito you could count on.

He had flip-flop days. Then red Keds days. There were checkerboard Vans days. There were slides with tube socks days.

There were also Panama hat days. And bandana days. Not to mention fedora days. Also Life is Good baseball hat days. Though, always, his long, fluffy white hair poofed out at the sides of whatever he put on his head.

There were days when his sunglasses had bright red frames, then the next day he'd switch to white, or yellow, or Wayfarers, or aviators. Honest to God, I didn't know the color of the man's eyes, since I'd never seen them. I also couldn't count the number of sunglasses he owned, there were so many of them.

He was always in shorts, but these could be Madras (and those clashed with the Hawaiian shirts, big time), or cargo shorts, Bermudas, sometimes even boardshorts.

And his extreme tan that veritably screamed impending melanoma was a constant, even if I had no idea how he maintained it when he was inside most of the time.

Tips were decent at The Surf Club, but it didn't matter. Tito paid well above minimum wage, offered insurance, even to part-timers, and gave five percent to the 401(k)s he also offered. We all had regular schedules so we could live our lives not at the mercy of when The Man decided to put us to work. And every year, he gave epic Christmas bonuses, along with a bottle of Dom, doing this at the Christmas party he closed the Club down to throw.

The weird part about this was, he might look like Santa, and be just as generous, but he didn't show at the party he threw. Never.

However, I knew he'd bail me out of jail (eventually, once he meandered there) or knock himself out to find a specialist doctor to deal with a rare disease if I contracted it. And I knew this in a way that thought was iron tight and unshakeable.

But I'd been working here for four years, and I knew practically nothing about him, except he fostered long-term employees by hiring well and paying well and providing zero management.

You were hired, everyone there taught you the way of things until you knew what to do, so you just did it, and he let us alone to get on with it.

I had no idea how it worked, I just knew it did.

I also knew I loved it here.

Luna worked at SC for a year before she coaxed me from my job in retail to join her.

It had been the best decision I'd made in my life, and both Luna and I knew, as long as there was a Surf Club, we'd be working here.

Yep, you guessed it. This meant I had no ambitions outside maybe one day owning my own little house somewhere in the Valley and the separate bank account I had that I added to every payday without fail would get me there (maybe in another hundred years).

Any ambitions I might have started to foster had been irrevocably quashed one horrible day when I was eight, and they'd been thus in a way no kernel could ever take root and grow in the time since.

As for Luna, she had her own reasons to have a job that had zero stress, meant you had cash in your wallet at all times, and no one got up in your face if you were late to work.

Which that morning, she wasn't.

She was behind the bar polishing the high shine to a higher shine while I heard Otis, the man who ran the coffee cubby on weekdays, steaming milk for a patron around the corner.

"Yo, Tito!" I called when I hit the room.

Tito didn't look up from scribbling in a journal.

Again, I took no offense. This was an everyday occurrence, even if the journal might be a book or some YouTube video he was watching on his iPad.

I then approached Luna.

My girl Luna, by the way, had burnished dark-blonde hair I'd witnessed a variety of people get into full-fledged verbal fights as to whether it was blonde or red (I liked my descriptive version best). That hair was full of bouncy curls.

She also had upturned, almond-shaped, silvery light-blue eyes and beautiful, full, pouty lips that had creases in the corners when she smiled, even a little bit.

She was one inch taller than me, standing at five-eight. And, like me, she assiduously maintained her T&A with profuse consumption of Willow's baked goods and Lucia's fusion with intermittent injections of things like Lenny's.

Today, she was in a lacy, white swing dress with a deep ruffle on the very mini-miniskirt, a plunging vee neckline and super-flowy, three-quarter sleeves (straight up, guaranteed good tips in that dress from the hetero men who'd show, which was one, if not the only reason she wore it).

If that didn't shout boho loud enough at you, she'd topped this with a fawn-colored rancher hat.

"Am I uninvited to your birthday party?" I asked.

"I'm thinking on it," she returned. "My first inclination is, yes. However, my vision for the party hinges on your sangria, and I don't think I have time to alter the theme."

Good news for me, but unsurprising. My sangria was the shit.

"That's good, because if you shut me out, I would be forced to save your birthday present for next year, and the present I got you *rawks*."

This was a total lie. First, I hadn't got her present yet. Second, I was the worst gift-giver in history.

I didn't know what my deal was. I just got incapacitated by the stress of it all.

This might be why she shot me a disbelieving look.

"Okay, it's *gonna* rawk," I amended. "I swear, I'm gonna do better this year. I'm on a mission."

"The Nordstrom Rack gift card didn't suck last year," she said.

See?

Totally uninspired.

"Ugh. Don't remind me," I groaned.

She held up her right index finger toward me, on which was a slim, gold band fashioned with a teeny evil-eye, which had a little baby sapphire embedded in it, sitting midi on it.

"I got this midi-ring with that gift card," she reminded me. "And this midi-ring is da bomb. I love this midi-ring."

"I should have just bought you that ring."

"You did, in a way." She studied me a sec before she said, "You are so weird about gifts."

"You're my bestie!" I cried. "It has to be perfect."

"You dragged me to seven stores before you found that tie-dyed bandana for Tito last year. And he wears it once a week."

We both looked to Tito.

Tito was now staring out the massive, restaurant-wide side window that had an impressive view of Lucia's planter-boxed herb garden, beyond which was an unimpressive view of the parking lot (though, Tito had planted multiple palo verde trees in the lot for shade and aesthetic purposes, so it was a nicer parking lot than most). He was doing this in an absent way where I wondered if he might be asleep sitting up.

I wondered that a lot.

I looked back to Luna. "He's just being nice."

"Whatever," she replied. "Tell me about Captain America."

"Oh my God," I whispered as it hit me.

"What?" she asked.

"That must be why he's called Cap. He looks like Captain America."

"He's called Cap?"

"Yeah."

"Then...duh."

I was totally off my game last night if it took me this long to figure it out.

I shook off that thought and told her, "I'm glad you brought him up, because we have a lot to talk about with that guy."

"And I'll repeat...duh." She circled a be-ringed hand (that midi-ring wasn't the only ring on it, there had to be twelve other little rings adorning her fingers—regular, thumb, pinkie and midi). "Hit me," she invited.

"First, he's kind of a jerk," I began, and she tipped her head to the side.

"This isn't starting great," she pointed out.

"Though, he's hot," I said.

"I hate to admit this, but I could get over 'kind of a jerk' when a man is that hot. Because he's so hot, he's scary hot. He's ignore-red-flags hot. He's entertain-thoughts-of-baby-daddy-even-if-you're-not-ready-to-push-one-out hot. He's—"

I cut her off. "Yeah, yeah, I know. I spent hours in his company. It was far from sunshine and roses and intense conversation that hint at a lifetime of shared intimacy, and still, I thought he was going to kiss me when he left, and when he didn't, I was disappointed."

Her brows shot up in surprise. "You didn't have sex with him?"

"We were kinda busy saving Elsie Fay, and then I had some work to do defending my Citadel."

Her expression instantly grew soft with understanding and concern.

She knew all about my Citadel and why I'd built it, one of only three living beings who did (outside my dad). The other two were Jessie and Harlow, who both also worked at SC and were honored members of our posse.

I waved my hand between us and warned, "I'm not going there."

"Okay," she said gently.

I had to navigate us around her gently, pronto. Luna's gently always got to me.

So I did.

"Now, he says we're going out tonight, and I don't know if I should, harking back to that kind of a jerk part. But also, if I do, he said to dress nice, and I don't have anything to wear."

One of her eyes squinted in incredulity at that statement.

She explained this reaction by saying, "Raye, you have so many clothes, some of them are at my house."

"Luna, *he looks like Captain America.*"

"I get your point," she mumbled.

"And between now and tonight, I don't have time to walk ten dogs and feed seven cats to pump up my clothing budget, but I *need* to find the perfect outfit."

"So, you're going."

"Luna, *he looks like Captain America,*" I repeated.

"Gotcha," she replied. "Late lunch, we'll hit up Tuesday Morning."

"I'm not sorting through the wares of Tuesday Morning for this date. It has to be The Rack."

"Okay then, late lunch, we'll hit up Nordstrom Rack."

"What if they don't have anything?"

"Then wear that off-the-shoulder black thing."

"That's too dressy."

"Then wear that satin skirt with an oversize tee knotted at the waist."

"Too casual."

"Then wear your billowy white poplin skirt and a white racer-back tank with some sexy sandals. The nude ones with the thick straps and that big buckle at the side of the ankle."

I grabbed hold of her and shook her, crying, "Oh my God, that's it!"

"Are we still going to The Rack?"

"Totally."

She grinned.

I smiled.

"Is someone gonna serve me, or what?"

We both turned to see Byron standing on the other side of the bar.

Byron was a regular. He came in every day. He was a computer programmer. Or an app designer. Or an internationally hunted hacker who didn't actually look like the man in front of us, because he was wearing an expertly crafted plastic face in order to evade Interpol. I didn't know what he did. I just knew he did it on a laptop and had a mess of floppy sandy-brown hair that fell over bright eyes due to the fact that he was always ludicrously caffeinated. He also had a crush on Lucia, even though she had three kids and a husband who would cave in his face if he knew that fact.

"The usual?" I asked.

He nodded. "With a cinnamon apple muffin."

I nodded in return, then he loped off to his usual table, that being the one at the back in the opposite corner to Tito.

The morning crowd started gathering, which rolled into the lunch crowd.

Jessie came in for her shift, so did Harlow, and Hunter joined Otis.

The crowd had thinned, denoting it was time for me and Luna to take off to go shopping, and that was when he came in.

That "he" being Cap.

I knew he showed when Harlow, behind the bar with me, whispered reverently, "Holy...Mary...*Mother of God.*"

I looked where she was looking.

And...yeah.

Cap was enough, but with him this time was a tall Black dude with a sinfully handsome face and soulful brown eyes who looked to be around Cap's age.

Cap smiled at me as he came my way.

Watching him do it (both the moving and the smiling, mostly the smiling), parts of my body tingled, other parts rippled.

And Harlow whispered, "I hate you so much," before she grabbed her iced lattes and took off to a table.

"Hey," Cap greeted when he arrived opposite me.

I approached my side of the bar. "Hey."

My gaze went to his bud.

"This is Liam Tucker," Cap said. "He's one of our Phoenix crew."

"Hey, Liam," I greeted.

"Rachel," he replied on a wide smile.

Super cute.

But I had other thoughts on my mind.

Primarily, Cap knew my name, and I didn't tell him. He knew where I lived, and I didn't tell him that either. Now I knew he knew where I worked, and ditto me not telling him.

So...how much about me *did* he know?

I mean, even for your average, everyday person, it wouldn't be hard to learn certain things about me. Certain things it was nobody's business to know, but it was public record, not to mention, it'd been splashed all over the media nineteen years ago.

Therefore, someone like Cap could probably dig even deeper and know it all.

I didn't like this. That kind of thing was for me to share, or not, at my choice.

"You know where I work," I said to Cap.

"Yeah, it's kind of my business to find shit out about people," he replied.

"Can I hold on to hope that you only did prelims on that?" I requested.

He held my gaze steady and stated honestly, "Sorry, Rachel, not with what I saw on your wall last night."

Okay, so I had to give him the fact that what I'd meticulously crafted on my wall was something anyone, especially someone like him, would find interesting and even alarming.

But I didn't like this either.

At all.

I opened my mouth to share that with him, all the while struggling with that bloody wound I harbored deep down inside. A wound I could ignore normally, because I'd had nearly two decades of practice. Not to mention, I'd carefully curated some kickass, comfy décor in my Citadel so I could chillout in my denial without worrying if I had the right toss pillows.

But I couldn't ignore it right then.

However, to my utter shock, suddenly, Tito was there.

Cap didn't miss it, and Cap dwarfed him, so Cap had to bend his neck really far to look down at Tito.

The minute his eyes hit Tito's aqua-framed sunglasses, Tito said, "Thank you for your service."

After he said that, he shuffled away on his tube-sock, slide-covered feet.

Evidence as to why Tito hired so well, he could read people.

Like, he was a master at that shit.

Cap watched him go then turned back to me, entirely unaffected by an odd little man in a Panama hat, plaid shorts, a Hawaiian shirt, tube socks and slides approaching, speaking, not waiting for a response, then leaving.

"Were you in the military?" I asked, even though I suspected Tito was never wrong about this kind of thing.

"Yeah. Army," Cap replied.

"Right," I murmured, impressed at this news, at the same time a tad bit thrilled to learn more about him (okay, more than a tad, this guy got to me, *argh*!).

"I came by to say, face-to-face, we got shit that came up for tonight I can't get out of," he told me. "I have to postpone our date until tomorrow. That good for you?"

It totally was, and it totally was not.

I got into the totally was part.

"I feel at this juncture I should repeat my uncertainty about this date."

Though, I kinda wasn't exactly uncertain, because, you know, he was *him*, so, in reality, it was more like I *wanted* to be uncertain, but I was absolutely not.

"So I'll repeat at this juncture, I'm taking you out," he shot back.

I looked to Liam.

He'd taken a couple of steps away to give us privacy and was staring at his feet.

I still saw the smile playing at his lips.

Luna slid in beside me with a "Yo," aimed Cap's way.

"Hey, Luna," he greeted.

"In for coffee?" she asked.

"Wouldn't turn it down," he answered.

"What's your poison?" she inquired.

"Americano, double shot, room for cream." He turned his head. "Liam?"

"Latte, iced, full fat," Liam ordered. He finished with, "Thanks," and a bright, white smile.

"Coming up," Luna said, after she recovered from witnessing Liam's bright, white smile, though she turned to the espresso machine still a little hazy.

"Can we—?" I started to say to Cap.

I got no further, because Dream trundled in, a baby strapped to her front, a toddler bouncing on her back, a brightly colored hippie tote dripping heavily from her shoulder, her face makeup free, her hair a wild arrangement of Luna's bouncy curls, except longer and redder, her frame willowy-thin, due to the fact she was chasing after kids all day, or, like now, toting them around. She was wearing the stressed expression she adopted when she was about to unload on her sister, or if I was in the vicinity, me.

"Oh my *goddess*, thank the divine you two are here," she exclaimed, even though she knew our schedules, which were seven o'clock to four, Monday through Friday (in other words, not hard to memorize), so she knew we would be.

She walked right behind the bar while pulling her daughter out of the pouch at her front and shoving her in Luna's busy hands in a way Luna had to quickly drop the portafilter she was packing in order to catch her.

She then expertly swung her son out of the carrier at her back, and in mid-swing, landed him smack in my torso so I had no choice but to grab hold.

Yes, she did this, even though she held no discernible employment, and both her sister and I were at our place of work...*working*.

And yes, you can read from this, I wasn't a tremendous fan of Dream's. It wasn't that she was trippy or lived her life in a way I'd never live mine.

It was because she was often a mooch, could be a user, could also be a manipulator, and unless she was dealing with her children, almost always acted selfishly, with massive doses of thoughtless attached to that.

Luckily, how I felt about her sister caused no problems between Luna and me, because Luna felt the same way, and then some.

"Momster and Dadman are at work," Dream announced. "My normal babysitter is sick." Like she had a normal babysitter...*not*, unless you counted Luna, and sometimes me. "And I have a reading I *have* to get to. Ambrosia said I can't bring the kids anymore. She says they mess with her chi and block her third eye chakra, which skews the readings. Last time she told me I was in for a windfall, and the next day, I found out I'd forgotten to pay my APS bill."

Not-so-newsflash: Dream "forgot" to pay her bills a lot.

"Is Ambrosia ever right?" Luna asked while bouncing her niece, who was named Feather (by the by, the kid I was holding was called Dusk, and yes, Luna and I had already discussed, when the time was right, how to teach both of them how to deal with bullies when they hit school, and further by the by, our strategies had nothing to do with leaving it to karma or turning the other cheek).

"It isn't an exact science," Dream retorted. "Even science isn't exact science."

"That's because science is a never-ending quest for answers to all of life's questions," Luna shot back. "The dudes in the lab coats didn't discover penicillin then say, 'Right. We cracked that. Time for an eternal cocktail,' whereupon they hung up their white coats and left their lab to get covered in dust and cobwebs. They moved on to the next thing that might help us understand and better our world, our lives and the universe."

While Luna said this, Dusk struggled to get out of my arms, so I set him down, but only because Dream was not a stranger to The Surf Club, thus neither were Dusk and Feather, and I knew what he'd do.

He did it instantly, toddling precariously from behind the bar in a direct trajectory to Tito.

Once he got there, wordlessly, Tito picked him up, put him in his lap and handed him his iPad, whereupon Dusk started bashing it violently against the table.

Tito didn't stop this.

He looked out the window and...well, that was it.

"Jujubees!" Dream cried, taking my attention back to her only to see she was forming the sign of the cross with her fingers and directing this at Cap. "Toxic masculinity *in da howwwwse.*"

Cap simply smiled at her.

At the smile, my body parts started tingling and rippling again.

But my mind had other ideas.

Before I even knew what I was doing, I snapped, "Bitch, uncool."

Dream's upper body swayed back in affront as her eyes swerved to me. "My sister, did you just call me a bitch?"

"You said something bitchy, so I called you a bitch," I replied.

"Here, take her, I'm making coffee," Luna mumbled to me, depositing Feather in my arms.

I cuddled her closer because she was cute and cuddly and smelled like a baby, so it was a moral imperative to cuddle her closer, even if her mom was acting like a bitch.

"Oh no, he's not yours, is he?" Dream asked me.

"I'm hers," Cap stated (yep, more tingling and rippling).

"He's not mine, you can't own people," I said after he spoke. "He's just...we're just..." Gah! "Dating."

"This place feels really fucking familiar," Liam muttered to Cap, making Cap smile again.

"Yeah," he replied, sounding oddly content about whatever they were referring to.

"No offense," Dream said belatedly to Cap.

"None taken," Cap said back.

"Well, *I* take offense," I said into this exchange. "You formed the sign of the cross and insulted him right to his face. You have no idea if he's toxic. You don't even know his name."

Though, on the face of it, semi-kinda-kidnapping me instead of taking me to my car, then breaking into my house seemed to reside in the red-level zone of toxic.

But then he also bought me Lenny's.

Contradiction.

Though, Dream knew none of this.

Dream assumed a solemn expression and added a heartfelt hand to her chest to drive it home before she turned back to Cap. "She's right. I jumped to judgement. That was wrong of me." She put her other hand palm-to-palm with the one at her chest and did a little bow. "You have my sincere apologies."

"Do you listen to Marconi Union?" Cap asked.

"Of course," she answered. "They're wildly talented."

At that, Cap aimed a smirk at me, right before he winked.

The tingles and ripples hit overdrive.

So, obviously, I held Feather safe, well to my side, bent forward and thunked my head against Surf Club's highly-polished bar and left it there.

I felt a hand cup the back of my head, and that hand had only touched me twice, but I knew whose it was.

"We gotta go, babe," Cap said quietly.

Yep, that's whose hand it was.

I lifted up and saw he and Liam had their coffees.

I had no choice in the current circumstances but to say, "Great, thanks for coming by and sharing our change of plans face-to-face."

"See you tomorrow night," Cap replied.

"Yeah, yeah, see you."

Cap shot me another smile.

I steeled myself against hurdling the bar and throwing myself at him.

Thankfully, I succeeded in this as Liam said, "Nice to meet you, Rachel."

"You too," I replied.

Cap fished out a twenty, put it on the bar, and they sauntered away, all loose-hipped, hot guy.

I watched.

Luna watched.

Every woman and gay or bi man in the joint watched.

Even Dream watched.

"He'll make beautiful babies," Dream said rather dreamily.

There it was again.

I was totally screwed.

FIVE

DON'T CALL ME BOSLEY

W hat was that saying about repeating things that didn't work being the definition of insanity?

Well, that night, that was what I was doing, and Cleo lay behind me in Tweety while I was doing it.

I'd scored a dog-walking gig with Cleo, who was half Labrador, half chow, and I understood her struggle, because she was always at war with the two parts of what made her, never knowing if she should be overexcited and unconditionally loving (Lab) or a diva ice queen (chow).

I had more personalities than that, so we vibed.

I'd walked Cleo before, so her owners knew me, and they were all the way down with how I went about taking care of her when they were away, this time, for a long weekend.

The way I took care of her was, I just took her and she stayed with me. No reason for me to head to their house three times a day for a walk and not enough playtime, if her parents were groovy with that. She slept with me. She went to work with me. And she alternately ignored and loved obsessively on me and anyone in her vicinity.

Her parents were thrilled I'd signed on to take the gig last minute after they requested me, because they knew they got the added benefits for their girl when they got me, and only had to pay dog-walking (not sitting) fees.

I was thrilled because I dug Cleo.

Also because they always left me a twenty-five percent tip.

This would score me over two hundred bucks, which wouldn't cover the dress and shoes and Havaianas I didn't need that I bought at the Rack that day while lugging around Feather and Dusk with Luna, but it would help.

Now, with a free evening, I was doing what I often did during free evenings.

I was sitting in my car in the parking lot of The Slide, a strip joint on Van Buren on the east side of downtown, which was where the first woman worked who went missing.

I was waiting for him and watching him, because, since the first time I laid eyes on him, I had a bad feeling.

Or watching *for* him to come out of the club.

Cleo wasn't watching. Cleo was flat-out in my back seat, snoozing.

Along with watching, I was thinking.

I had no idea what to do about the feeling I had about this guy. That feeling being something that cautioned me not to get close, absolutely not get caught watching him, and one hundred percent not to do something stupid, like follow him.

However, to move this forward and maybe find out what the hell was going on, I had to do *something*.

That something could not be in Tweety. In fact, *I* shouldn't even be there in Tweety.

They had cameras outside the club, and I parked at the very edges, as far away from lights as I could manage, so maybe those cameras wouldn't catch me. Even so, Tweety gleamed bright and cheerful like a beacon. I also never went inside the club. But someone would eventually notice me hanging out there yet not patronizing the establishment, if they hadn't already.

And women were going missing.

They were strippers and sex workers, so, as per historical protocol, the powers that be didn't feel inclined to knock themselves out figuring out where they'd gone.

But I scoured the *Arizona Republic* on the daily, and these police bulletins garnered attention in the form of short articles about the women who'd disappeared.

Sure, the info shared was minimal, and the news was treated almost as an aside. And it didn't happen daily, weekly or even monthly.

But by my estimation, seven strippers or sex workers had vanished in a little over two years (those being the ones who were reported missing, considering the occupations, there might be others who were not), and that seemed like a lot to me.

I was about to give up, go home and pour myself a glass of wine while I considered for the millionth time dismantling the wall I'd painstakingly crafted, and thus at long last abandoning this mission, when he came out.

Not tall, not short. Not young, not old. Not handsome, not ugly.

But he was bad to the core. I felt it, even in a car a parking lot away, staring at him through my windshield.

He gave me the shivers.

He was talking to the bouncer just outside the front door, and I knew it was time to leave.

"Ready to roll?" I asked Cleo.

Her response was a snore.

I took that as a yes.

I started up and headed out and didn't look in the direction of the club as I rolled out of the parking lot onto Van Buren.

I headed toward the city.

I headed home.

I parked in the only spot my unit guaranteed me, which was

covered, thankfully, and noted, per usual, the three visitor spots were taken.

My apartment complex didn't offer a lot, but I loved it anyway.

Cleo and I got out and headed to the gate. I punched in the code, pulled open the gate and walked by the bank of mailboxes (to the left) and the bike rack (to the right) to the inner courtyard common space.

The pool for our complex was there, because this was Phoenix. If you didn't have a pool, you wanted one, and if you did, and you had to maintain it yourself, you wished you didn't have it.

Since I didn't have to maintain it myself, I loved our pool.

It wasn't big, but it was always cool, because that square set of apartments with its inner courtyard had been there since the seventies. So the trees around it had plenty of time to grow high and shade the space. It was a bitch for Mark, our pool cleaner, because of the leaves, but it was heaven on a summer day in the Valley.

It could be a hundred and ten outside that space, but it was ninety in the courtyard and it was eighty in the pool.

Perfect.

I couldn't say our landlord gave much of a shit about the place, but he wasn't a total loser. He kept it clean and safe.

No, it was the tenants who gave it its personality.

Inner walkways led to the doors of the units on two levels, and most of us had decided to use these walkways as our own personal patios. So they were all adorned with an eclectic mix of planters, lawn chairs, lights and outside décor.

The pool furniture was relatively nice, but it was Patsy, the resident green thumb, who kept the planters peppering the courtyard bursting with color and greenery. And it was Bill and Zach, one of our gay couples, who'd strung the lights that went from the railing of the upper balcony down to ornamental poles they'd planted in the grass that surrounded the pool deck.

All of this, with the trees and the aqua waters of the pool, now illuminated with a light that was timed to turn off at ten, gave that space a cheerful, tranquil feel that smacked a hearty *Welcome Home* every time I hit it.

There were renters that came and went, of course, but such was the awesomeness of Oasis Square, most were long-timers, like me, who'd been there five years. In fact, I knew the waiting list to get a unit was a mile long, and I knew this because Luna, Jessie and Harlow were all on it.

We held complex-wide parties in the courtyard, and we definitely had extended family, like Luna, Jessie, Harlow, Otis, Lucia and Hunter (I'd asked Tito, he'd come twice, spoke minimally, and even if it was a nighttime event, never took off his sunglasses), who would come to our get-togethers, as would friends and family of others.

My apartment might be small, but the rent didn't break my back, and I'd had plenty of time to establish my Urban Outfitters with shades of Anthropologie, large doses of Target and hints of Z Gallerie boho-girlie-glam-multiple-personality décor.

In other words, I loved my apartment too.

And as Cleo and I made our way up the switchback stairs to the upper level, I was looking forward to pouring a glass of wine, putting my feet up, and firing up my Kindle to maybe start reading that book about Kai Mason and Stella Gunn.

My steps slowed as I got close to my unit, however.

This was because light was coming through my shades, which, on the inside, were covered in pretty, rose-colored chiffon window panels.

I was relatively sure I didn't leave my light on when I left.

It wasn't late, just before eight, and considering it was September, I'd left when it was dark.

But still, not only did I care about climate change, I cared even more about my electrical bill, and I hadn't left the light on.

Was Cap done with his business that took him away from our date that night?

And if he was, would he break into my house again in order to spend time with me?

Last night was extreme, and because of it, I could forgive his intrusion...once.

Him just helping himself to my place...hell to the *no*.

I was juggling Cleo's lead with pulling off the strap to my purse in order to dig out my phone, wondering if I should hit up Bill and Zach to take my back when I went into my apartment (because it might not be Cap, and even if it was, a statement needed to be made). Or maybe head to Jacob, who worked crazy-long hours and endless days of construction sometimes, doing this so he could make enough money to take lots of time off in order to hang around and get high other times. But even if he was high, he could probably take care of business, because he might not be super tall, but he was solid and built.

These were my activities, and thoughts, when the door to my apartment opened.

A very pretty Black woman, who I guessed was a little older than me, had large bosoms, slim hips and long legs, and was wearing a white suit Olivia Pope would get in a bitch-slapping contest over, took one step out on her pencil slim, four-inch, patent-nude Louboutin heels, and asked, "Well, are you coming in?"

"Who are you?" I returned.

She walked my way.

I braced.

And unfortunately, Cleo took that opportunity to become one with her Labrador, so she was full body shakes due to her tail wagging and straining the leash to get a lick or two in as the woman approached.

She ignored Cleo but opened her white Birkin with black stitching, exposing the sumptuous red leather interior.

From it, she pulled a manila envelope.

She offered this envelope to me.

I didn't know why (out of habit? shock? whatever), but I took it.

"Don't call her Charlie. And don't call me Bosley. I'm Clarice."

And with that, she strutted away in the manner only a woman in

Louboutins could strut, in other words, there was no better strut in the world.

I watched her go.

Cleo watched her go.

When she was out of sight, I dashed to my apartment, Cleo having no choice but to dash with me.

I closed the door, locked it, took off Cleo's leash and hung it on the golden arch that was adorned with medallions shaped in the cycles of the moon with hooks under each moon.

I then went to my circular, glass-topped coffee table with the white cutaway panels underneath that supported a shelf, on which I displayed my Pucci coffee table book that had a hardback exterior of a Pucci print (and it *rawked*).

I dropped that envelope on the table like it could grow teeth and bite me.

Five minutes later, I had a glass of chilled white in my hand, and I was standing at the coffee table, staring at that envelope.

"Shit," I whispered, rounded the table, sat on my pale-blue velvet, tufted-back couch, sucked back some wine, set it aside and reached for the envelope.

Cleo sat on the floor beside me and watched, panting, as I opened it and upended what was inside onto the table.

Some papers came out, as did a car key fob and a business card.

I reached for the fob first. It had a tag attached to it.

On the tag were the words, The Parking Spot, a letter, number (in other words, location where the car was parked), an email that appeared bogus, some goobledygook letters, numbers and characters and the message, *Download the app, username, password, use that account to pay.*

"What the fuck is going on?" I breathed.

I set the fob aside and nabbed the business card.

The cardstock was thick and expensive.

It said, *Clarice Davis and Associates, Attorney-at-Law*, with phone number, email, address, and on the back, in pretty but professional handwriting, *Emergencies only*, and a telephone number.

I set that aside and grabbed the papers.

They were stuck together with a gold binder clip (all of this was freaking me out, but not enough not to note that gold clip was pure class), the front page blank.

I flipped it over.

And ice filled my veins.

I dropped the papers like they'd burst on fire, grabbed my purse, pulled out my phone and called Luna.

"Who's Kelly Garrett?" Luna asked casually, standing, sipping and flipping through the papers that were in her hand.

Papers I hadn't touched in the time it took me to call her and demand she get her ass to my place. I only sifted through them when she got to my place, gave Cleo a rubdown and poured herself a glass of wine.

Papers that were given to me, but after glancing at them once I had the moral support of my bestie at hand, I saw contained a brief letter at the front that was addressed to Kelly Garrett, and said, simply, *Things you might wish to know. x-A Friend.*

"Jaclyn Smith. One of the original Angels."

"Oh yeah, right," she muttered, flipping to the next page.

"When Cap asked my name, I gave him that one," I told her.

Her head shot up. "Kelly Garrett?"

I nodded.

"Holy cow. Do you think this is from him?"

"No. Yes. I don't know!" I cried. "He sure didn't seem thrilled I involved myself in Elsie Fay's situation. He also seems pretty honest and straightforward, not prone to subterfuge. I couldn't imagine him sending the righteous chick Olivia Pope wished she was with a weird

envelope filled with"—I circled my finger at the papers in her hand—
"whatever the hell that is."

"It looks like a list of all the dudes who raped that co-ed," she said.
"And I know that because at the top, it says, 'List of Co-Ed Sexual
Assaulters.'" She waved the papers. "It seems whoever she is thinks
your job is unfinished."

"I fucked up on that assignment."

She dropped the papers on the table and crossed her arms, being
careful not to spill her wine as she did so.

"Assignment?" she queried. "An assignment is something
someone *assigns*. It's kinda in the word. What you did to that asshole
was all you."

I couldn't dispute that, so I didn't.

Instead, I asked, "How does whoever this is know it was me?"

"Okay." Luna moved to my sky-blue velvet armchair and sat down.
"We got Cap, the guy who was with Cap today, and whoever that
Mace guy was you mentioned last night, who know about this, yeah?"

"I don't know if Liam knows, maybe Cap told him. But no way
it's Mace. He was totally against me doing the vigilante thing, and he
didn't hide it."

"So the guy today?"

"Liam?"

She nodded.

"I don't know. Does he seem like a guy who can afford an expensive attorney, who carries a Birkin bag, to act as his go-between and
someone who can provide me with a car so I won't get made doing my
thing in Tweety?"

She shook her head. "Not so much."

"So not him either."

"So someone else knows what you're up to."

I swung a hand to indicate my coffee table. "Uh...*yeah*."

"And they want you to keep going, and they're giving you the
resources to do it better and more thoroughly."

"Uh..." my pause was longer this time, and my stress on the next word was stressier, "*yeah.*"

"So what are you gonna do?"

"I know what I'm not gonna do. I'm definitely not going after those rapists. After I dealt with the ringleader, they're all gonna be on their guard. It wasn't easy rounding up a roofied tight end. I don't need to attempt to wrangle the offensive line."

"I think this is a good call," she mumbled.

Why was she acting like this was no big deal?

"Luna, babe, this Clarice lady was *in my house waiting for me.*"

She reached for the papers and flipped through them.

I downed the rest of my wine and got up to get more.

I brought the bottle and topped Luna up too.

"What's this?" she asked.

"What?" I asked back.

She handed me the papers that had been flipped deep to the back of the stack.

In fact, it was on the last page.

There was a decent-quality, color, photocopied picture of a white woman with a mass of blonde hair, a lot of eyeliner, and the plate denoting it was a mugshot under her chin.

Underneath the picture it said, *Missing women. Divinity. Roosevelt, between* 16*th and* 24*th Streets. Evenings. Take $200 cash. CD will reimburse.*

"Holy shit," I croaked.

"What's it mean?"

I tossed the papers on the table again. "Whoever this is knows I'm looking into those missing women."

Luna held her wineglass and tapped its side with her finger as she stared at me.

"Luna, are you there?" I demanded.

"Right, first, we go see this Clarice lady."

What?

And...

We?

"We also go get that car, or at least look at it," she went on.

"Are you *insane*?" I asked.

"Aren't you curious?" she returned.

I shifted in my seat. "Yeah. Sure. But—"

"Raye, calm down and think. Divinity is a lady of the evening. 'Take two hundred dollars,' means you're gonna have to pay her for info, and that means she probably *has* info. The stuff about Roosevelt is Divinity's patch, where we'll find her, on Roosevelt between Sixteenth and Twenty-fourth. CD is Clarice Davis, and she'll reimburse you for said info. Whoever this is, knows something about those missing women, and whoever it is can't do anything about it. Something's up. Maybe it's a cop whose hands are tied or something like that. But we can't talk to Divinity unless we get a feel for this Clarice woman. So we're gonna talk to Clarice first, then we're gonna go look at whatever car that is, because..."—she reached, grabbed the fob and brandished it at me—"this is to a Mercedes. So whoever this is, is *not* playing."

She was right.

They were not.

Because it wasn't just the Mercedes.

The bulk of that stack of papers, which I hadn't entirely gone through, were detailed dossiers of the men who assaulted the co-ed.

And when I said detailed, I'd only glanced at them, but still...they were *detailed*.

"Don't you think this is dangerous?" I asked.

"Yeah," she huffed out. "And I thought the tight end was dangerous. And Paul Nicholson. And that wife beater whose car you poured sugar into the gas tank. And—"

"All right, all right, you've made your point."

"So are you gonna stop now? Or is the last year of work you've got pinned to your bedroom wall, with pink yarn twirled around tacks, pointing to places on a map of the Phoenix metro area and Post-its with descriptions of possible players, gonna be just a weird piece of artwork of a slightly unbalanced mind?"

"I'm not unbalanced."

"It depends on the day," she said into her wineglass.

Honestly?

I couldn't argue that.

Her tone had changed when she said, "I didn't like that Paul Nicholson business because it cut too close to Macy."

I tried not to flinch.

I failed.

"Honey," she said carefully. "By some miracle, you tracked down Elsie Fay. And that's good. I'm glad. But, girl, that hit too close to the bone."

"I know," I whispered.

"But this,"—she tossed the fob to the coffee table—"I don't know. Something about it is intriguing. I also don't like you going out there alone. But if we go together..."

She let that hang.

"I'm not a fan of that," I informed her.

"Welcome to how I've been feeling the last year."

That hit me, and it did it hard.

So I said, "Maybe I should just quit."

"And maybe you should just go talk to this Clarice woman. It's just a chat. Call her. Set it up. If we don't like the feel we get, we're out. But...why not?"

I wondered how many people, before they met their grisly end, asked "Why not?" prior to engaging in the endeavor that led to their grisly end.

I had a feeling that percentage was high.

Even so, I was me.

And women were missing.

So I replied, "Yeah. Okay. Why not?"

It was later.

Luna was gone.

Cleo and I were lying on my bed.

I was in my nightie, on my back, upside down in bed, my heels resting on my scallop-topped, pale-yellow padded headboard.

Cleo had her butt aimed toward my face and her head on a pillow.

Ice queen mode during cuddle time, friendly puppy when a strange lady carrying a Hermès bag was walking out of my apartment toward us after breaking into it.

Figured.

I had my head turned to what I'd meticulously been building on my wall.

It had taken me a year after I'd cottoned on to what I thought was a pattern before I kicked it up to high gear.

But I was no detective.

I had a ton of info on that wall and zero idea what any of it meant.

"What the hell am I doing?" I muttered to myself.

My phone rang.

I reached for it on the pink, peach and yellow butterfly print comforter on my bed.

The screen told me it was an unknown number.

But I took the call because…

Why not?

"Hello?"

"Hey, babe."

My belly dipped.

It was Cap.

I rolled to the side, into Cleo, and came face to face with a dog butt.

I lifted up on a forearm and looked at my Alexa on the nightstand.

It was ten to ten.

I fell again to my back and asked, "Is your thing over?"

"Yeah."

"How'd it go?"

"We got the job done."

I figured that happened a lot.

"Go you," I replied.

"How was your night?"

"Weird."

"Just a stab in the dark, but my guess, that's not unusual."

I started laughing and turned away from Cleo to lie on my side.

Cleo's Labrador took control, and she shifted so she could rest her chin on my waist.

I reached for her head and started scratching.

"Why are you calling?" I asked, hoping he wasn't going to postpone our date again.

Yeah.

Okay.

It happened. I couldn't help it.

I gave up the fight.

Because I was into him.

"I'm calling because I was supposed to take you out tonight, I didn't get to do that, that sucked, so I wanted to hear your voice before I wind down and go to bed."

Great.

He could be sweet.

And great part two.

He was leaving me at the end of the night with thoughts of him going to bed.

"What do you want to hear my voice saying?" I asked. "I have the Pledge of Allegiance memorized, as any good American should. Or the lyrics to Fall Out Boys', 'Sugar, We're Goin' Down.'"

"Great song, but a fucked-up one."

"Word."

"Arguably, The Killers did it better with 'Mr. Brightside.'"

Hang on.

"Whoa, you think 'Sugar, We're Goin' Down' is about a woman cheating?" I asked.

"Absolutely."

I thought about it. "I see that."

"What'd you think it was about?"

"Voyeurism."

"Man was bumped for a new model," Cap said. "He just couldn't let go."

"Something you probably cannot relate to at all. You're undoubtedly always the bumper, not the bumpee."

He burst out laughing.

I found this surprising.

"You've been bumped?" I asked, not hiding the shock in my voice.

My phone binged with a text.

"Sent you a picture," he told me.

"Hang tight," I said, pulled the phone from my ear and opened the text, then the picture.

It was of a scrawny, short, acne-ridden kid standing next to a tall, handsome Black kid, who had his arm slung around the scrawny guy's shoulders.

I put the phone back to my ear. "Who's that?"

"Me and my brother."

Say what?

I looked at the picture again.

I didn't see it.

Okay, maybe around the eyes, and the hair.

But...wow.

I put the phone again to my ear. "Your nickname should be Swan."

"Why?"

"Ummm...." I drew that out, such was my surprise at the looks he'd grown into, having painted myself into a very unfun corner.

"Babe, I know I was the ugly duckling. I shouldn't have asked. I get it."

"Your nickname stems from Captain America, doesn't it?" I asked for confirmation.

"Not my choice. Some buds in the Army saw a picture of me when I was younger, they came up with it. It stuck."

"Well, it fits."

There was humor in his tone when he replied, "If you say so."

Time to change subjects.

"That's your brother?"

"Yeah. Roman. He's called Roam. We're both adopted. We were foster brothers first. Got adopted as teenagers."

At this news, my heart lurched for him, and I said softly, "Oh."

"The mom nature gave me was a piece of shit, babe. The mom I earned is the finest woman on the planet. We made out more than all right in the end."

I was still going soft when I said, "I love that for you."

He was now going soft when he said, "Yeah."

This was because he knew.

Heknewheknewheknew.

"Cap—" His name was husky.

"Rachel, baby, I know what happened. I just don't know what happened to you. Only you can give me that, and I'll only take it when you're ready to give it to me."

Tears hit my eyes at how profound and perfect and under-standing that was.

He got it.

He got it.

It didn't happen to me, but it happened to me all the same.

And that was mine to give him.

I didn't like that he knew, but I liked that.

"That's something else I didn't want to wait to tell you," he said. "You needed to hear it."

He was *so right*.

"Yeah," I agreed.

"There's something else I need to leave with you," he said.

"What?"

"It's tough. I wanted to get into it over dinner. I couldn't do that, but I don't think it should wait."

Oh shit.

"What?" I repeated.

"The police told Mace that Elsie Fay's parents told them she wants to see you."

Oh God.

"They don't know who you are or what happened," Cap assured. "I didn't tell Mace either, but I did say you got a history where that has to be up to you, and if you say no, everybody has to be okay with it."

Again with the sweet.

And also protecting me.

I liked that a whole lot.

However...

"I'll see her," I said.

"Baby," he replied gently.

"I'll see her, Cap. It's okay. It's good. If she needs me, I'm there."

"I was afraid you'd say that, but sleep on it. It's late. I'm not gonna say anything to anyone until tomorrow anyway. Give it time to think about what it'd do to you."

"She's home. It's fine."

"Rachel—"

"Okay, Cap. I'll sleep on it," I gave in.

"Good," he murmured.

"Can we talk about songs again?" I asked.

"Give me your favorite."

"What? By genre?"

"Of all time."

"Are you crazy?" I demanded. "I'd have to go into a deep medita-tive state. That is, after spending three straight days creating a playlist that might last three straight weeks that I'd have to fully listen to in that meditative state so I can decide. And I'd probably have to listen to that playlist twice. And take notes. Which will take me out of my meditative state. Which would mean I'd have to start from the beginning. To wit, that's impossible."

He'd started chuckling halfway through my diatribe.

"Okay, then, movie," he suggested.

"Favorite?"

"Yeah."

"By genre?"

He burst out laughing.

I smiled, listening to the deep timbre of it, which, frankly, was beautiful.

In fact, it might be the most beautiful thing I'd ever heard.

When he was done, he asked, "How about top fives?"

"By genre?"

He started laughing again.

I smiled again.

When he quit, I asked, "How about you?"

"'Baba O'Reilly,' The Who," he stated instantaneously. "And four-way tie between *Fargo*, *Shawshank*, *Memento* and *Babe*."

My heart thumped.

"*Babe*?"

"Don't dis. That movie's the shit."

"It totally is," I agreed.

Cleo, now in full Labrador mode, rounded me and curled into my front. I curved around her.

And Cap and I talked music, movies, TV, books, fave foods, and this segued into me learning he'd only lived in Phoenix for a little over six months, and since he was a foodie and liked to cook (a man who liked cooking! heaven!), I told him my top spots for good eats and made sure he knew about AJ's Fine Foods grocery store (he did).

I was drooping and trying not to when he said quietly, "Gonna let you go before you fall asleep."

I didn't want him to.

But I had to work the next day, and at a glance over my shoulder, I saw it was nearing midnight, so considering he probably had to be sharp for what he did, I had to let him go too.

"Okay."

"Call me tomorrow with a definitive about..."

He let that hang.

Being protective again.

Right, so he was a good guy.

He came on strong.

But he was a good guy.

"I will."

"Later, Rachel."

"You can call me Raye," I told him.

"Okay, baby," he whispered, then, "Later, Raye."

"Later, Cap."

"'Night."

"Goodnight."

He disconnected.

I threw my phone on the bed and wound my arm around Cleo.

Her tail wagged twice.

"I think he's a good guy," I told her.

Her tail wagged again, this time more than twice.

"Yeah. That was exactly what I was thinking," I said.

And after that, once I programmed Cap into my phone, Cleo and I righted ourselves in bed and went to sleep.

SIX

WHOA DOGGIES

I woke with Cleo shoved up against me and Cap on my mind.

This meant I woke with a smile.

I did my morning thing wondering if Cap silenced his notifications when he was sleeping so a text wouldn't bother him.

I decided he wasn't a centenarian who didn't know how to work his phone, so if he didn't want to be bothered, he'd see to that.

So before I left my apartment, I tapped in,

Good morning!

FYI, I've decided it's a definite yes for EF. If you could let me know how to sort that, it'd be great

I liked talking to you last night. I'm glad you called.

Have a fab day and see you tonight.

I tacked an emoji face with hearts around it at the end and hit go.

I then leashed up Cleo, grabbed my bag, shoved my black-rimmed, cat eye Prada sunglasses on my nose (another online reseller score) and headed down to my car.

On my way along the landing, I saw Patsy wearing her work blouse and skirt, though she had Crocs on her feet, because she was out watering the planters.

"Yo!" I called a greeting to her.

"Heya, Raye," she called back, hoofing it from the pool area to the entry (where she'd also placed a couple big vibrant planters—see? total welcome home).

Uncertain which personality she was going with for the morning, Cleo sniffed Patsy when she got to me.

"Did you see the notice on the notice board?" she asked.

I turned to the glass-fronted bulletin board Bill and Zach had mounted above the mailboxes. They also maintained it.

It had business cards for housekeepers and dry cleaners, and a rotating array of takeout menus of new restaurants and announcements of local concerts and events.

What it did not have was info on pet sitters, since I looked after everyone's pets in the complex if they went out of town, and I did it for free (though, everyone paid me with gift cards and such).

On it was a bright-pink sheet of paper that shared Dreamweaver Inc. had purchased the complex.

I got closer to the bulletin board, mumbling, "Oh snap."

"I know, right?" Patsy said. "It's a done deal. John Campos is out, and this corporation is in."

John Campos was our, apparently former, landlord.

I was listening to her, and also wondering if that was legal—selling a complex like ours without notifying the tenants— and being proficient at multi-tasking, also reading.

And further, not believing my eyes.

First, the notice assured us that rents would not change.

Then, the notice told us there would be upgrades to the complex happening beginning Monday, and we should be advised that there would be workers and delivery people on the property, and soon, we would have to assist in their endeavors by moving our cars.

Next, it listed all the things that were going to happen in the coming month or two.

Things that made it shocking...nay, downright impossible that rents weren't going to rise.

In other words, the pool deck was going to be lifted and a new cool deck installed. This winter, the pool was also going to be drained and new pebble finish applied, with a pool light upgrade. Topping that, the courtyard furniture was going to be replaced and the barbeque area updated.

Further, the exterior of the complex was going to be painted, solar panels added that would reduce our electrical bills, and a new sign erected.

Onward from that, new, updated security fences and gates would be installed, along with cameras trained on the parking lot.

If that wasn't enough, the blacktop of the lot was going to be replaced with a heat reflecting surface. JuiceBoxes to charge electric cars were going to be affixed in the carports, metered to the unit the space belonged to. A compost bin was going to be built in a corner of the parking lot. Window boxes were going to be fitted to the outer building windows and the greenery planted would be maintained by building management. And a new recycling service had been contracted, so the four narrow rooms (upstairs and down) at the two north corners of the complex that held the garbage chutes would have new recycle containers, compost collectors and a plastic bag bin.

"Did I wake up in an alternate universe?" I asked the bulletin board.

But it wasn't the bulletin board that answered.

It was Patsy.

"Linda's freaked," she said.

Linda being the longest-standing resident at Oasis Square. She'd moved in about five years after the complex was built. She was a retired schoolteacher who never married. She was in her seventies, and as such, on a fixed income.

"She's sure they'll raise our rents after all this work is done. And she barely survived Campos's last rent increase," Patsy went on.

Every year, bar none, John Campos had increased the rents.

This was annoying, but it wasn't out of hand. It happened every-where, and especially in our area, which was pretty safe (for city living) and popular, just north of McDowell on Seventh, not a five-minute drive from downtown.

Rent in Phoenix was astronomical, and although this rent was affordable to me, it was because I did some moonlighting work. I'd barely be scraping by if I didn't, and probably would have to move somewhere that was not nearly as nice.

It would totally blow if Linda had to move after living there for forty years.

"Has anybody emailed that address?" I asked, pointing toward the contact info at the bottom of the notice.

"Bill and Zach are on it," she told me. "They'll hit the email chain with anything they learn."

It was Linda who started the complex-wide email chain. She made it her mission to hit up any new tenants to get their comms info, partly so we could invite them to our pool parties and partly so we could collectively bargain when Campos was falling down on maintaining things.

Bill and Zach looking into this change was good. If anyone could get the complete lowdown, Bill and Zach could.

"Right," I said to Patsy. "Never a dull moment, I guess."

"I like animals, but I don't want to have to walk dogs on top of dealing with doctors all day in order to live here."

Patsy worked reception at a primary care physicians' office.

"Word," I replied.

We bid adieu, and Cleo and I had barely hit Seventh on our way to Indian School when my car told me my phone was ringing.

The display on the dash said it was Cap.

I was weirded out about my new landlord, but seeing his name made me smile.

I took the call with a, "Yo."

"Mornin', baby," he said, sounding sleepy.

Those tingles and ripples he caused went positively volcanic when I experienced his deep voice sounding sleepy.

Not to mention, he obviously woke, saw my text and called right away.

Nice.

"You sleep well?" I asked.

"Yeah. What you up to?"

"Cleo and me are on our way to work."

"Who's Cleo?"

"I pick up pet sitting gigs for extra bank. She's my gig for the weekend. Say hello to Cap, Cleo."

Cleo didn't adhere to my request. She sniffed the wind coming in from the window I'd opened for her.

"Sorry, she's busy sniffing the wind," I told Cap.

He chuckled.

Then he asked, "You sure?"

I knew what he was asking.

"I'm sure."

"Okay, I'll set it up and let you know."

"Thanks."

"I gotta hit it, so I'll let you go."

"Groovy," I lied.

His voice wasn't as sleepy anymore. But I liked listening to it.

"Have a good day, babe."

"You too, Cap. See you later."

"Later."

He disconnected.

Cleo and I continued on our way to work.

We made it through the morning and lunch crushes without Dream dumping her kids on us for her Reiki or cupping, or whatever appointment (fortunately), or Hunter, who was bi, so his array of targets was larger than most, hitting on one of the customers (unfortunately—Hunter was a master at flirting and it was always extraordinary to watch).

Though, I'd received a text from Cap asking if he could pick me up at 5:30, rather than 6:30, for our date, so we could swing by Elsie Fay's house for a visit on our way to the restaurant.

I knew his tactic.

We had something to do and somewhere to be, and if it was a nice somewhere, he'd have reservations we wouldn't want to miss, so the visit would have to be short.

That was sweet. Unnecessary, but sweet.

And although this would cut into my primping time (since my shift ended at four, it was cutting it close), I'd confirmed that was a go.

Cleo was snoozing on her back with all four of her paws up in the air on the bench seat next to Tito. I was at a table dropping some of Lucia's carne asada crepes. Jessie and Luna were behind the bar—Luna making someone a coffee, Jessie whipping up a couple of her signature Jessita Mojitas—when Scott and Louise came in.

My gaze shot to Luna at the exact same time her gaze shot to me.

Scott and Louise were her parents.

Scott and Louise both had jobs, working together—Scott as Managing Director, Louise as Development Director—at a nonprofit that dealt with affordable housing initiatives and helping with the homeless.

So neither Scott nor Louise showed at SC on a workday at two thirty in the afternoon.

In other words...

This couldn't be good.

"Eat hearty," I muttered to my customers as I hightailed it behind the bar.

Jessie had already cottoned on and, still mixing drinks, smoothly transitioned to take a position closer to Luna, who had left the espresso machine to stand opposite the bar from her parents.

This had to do with moral support.

It also had to do with being closer and hearing better.

What could we say?

The whole place was filled with busybodies (except Otis, he was the kind of *If you want me to know, you'll tell me* guy).

"Hey, guys," I greeted when I got there.

Scott shot a grim smile at me.

Louise gave me a weak wave and said, "Hi there, honey."

Oh boy.

I approached Luna. "I'm on the coffees. What we got?"

"Another dirty for Byron. An iced skinny vanilla, sugar free, for the chick in the basket chair."

"Got it," I said and moved to the espresso maker to finish up Byron's dirty chai and the skinny vanilla latte with sugar free syrup she'd started.

And I tried not to brazenly listen in, but that was difficult with the machine gurgling loudly. At least I wasn't steaming milk. That would make it impossible.

"Sorry to disturb you at work, sweetie," Louise was saying. "But we need a family meeting."

"We need an intervention," Scott corrected.

"It's not that bad," Louise snapped.

"She owes us over seven thousand dollars. It's that bad," Scott snapped back.

Oh Lord.

"Is this about Dream?" Luna asked after the obvious.

"She's pregnant again," Scott announced.

"Whoa doggies," Jessie muttered as she put back the bottle of rum next to me, then loitered there for better eavesdropping positioning.

"Feather isn't even six months old," Luna noted irritably.

"A woman is fertile within weeks of delivery, snook'ums," Louise noted.

Louise, by the by, was proficient in endearments. Her daughter had a vocabulary of maybe twenty thousand more words than the average person. Louise had the same in sweet nothings she'd call you.

"This is unbelievable," Luna groused.

"My sentiments exactly," Scott agreed.

"Babies are wonderful," Louise said.

"The girl doesn't have a job," Scott returned. "If it wasn't for the ACA, she wouldn't have insurance to birth those babies."

"Scott," Louise said soothingly.

"She's into me for over fifteen hundred," Luna told them, and I whirled around, because this was news to me.

"Say what?" I demanded.

Luna turned to me and pressed down both her hands in front of her. "Cool it, sister. I didn't tell you because I knew it'd piss you off."

"Damn straight," I replied. "I take it this isn't money she owes you for babysitting her kids all the time."

Luna shook her head slowly.

I harrumphed.

"Raye, they're my niece and nephew," she explained. "What would you do?"

I got her.

But tarot readings, Reiki and cupping, not to mention acupuncture, IV therapy, the occasional séance and entry to taco festivals cost cake, so Luna wasn't just helping to keep those cute kids in cloth diapers.

Sadly, she knew that better than me.

"You're part of the family, Raye. You need to be in on this intervention," Scott declared.

I loved he thought that, and he was not wrong.

I'd moved to Phoenix when I was nineteen and met Luna at my first job working at J. Crew, which meant I'd only known them for eight years. But Luna and I had been thick as thieves from the moment we bonded while folding T-shirts on a board my first day.

And Scott and Louise adopted everybody, and I was no exception.

I spent holidays with them, just sayin'.

Louise pressed her lips together.

I had so many things to say to Dream, I didn't hesitate to accept his invitation.

"Tell me when and where, and I'm there."

Scott nodded his satisfaction with my response because Scott was Luna in dude form, so he and I were tight.

"She's in a delicate way right now," Louise said, hinting at why Dream was like Dream was.

Louise was a pushover, and Dream was pushy.

"Women drop kids while working in rice paddies or dragging buckets of water three miles home from the closest well," Luna stated. "Dream can be knocked up and sit in the living room she grew up in and hear some home truths."

"Word on that, sister," I chimed in, just as my phone vibrated in my (today, mint green, it clashed righteously with the black, knee-length tank dress with the side slit I was wearing) server apron.

Even if I hoped it was Cap, saying something like, *thinking of you, can't wait for tonight,* I ignored it due to the sitch at hand.

"She needs a job, she needs to learn responsibility, and she needs to get those deadbeats to pay for the babies they made," Scott proclaimed.

"Right on, brother," I cheered.

Louise looked uncomfortable, or *more* uncomfortable, and I knew why.

None of those guys had signed on to be baby daddies.

Sure, they got the good stuff, and everyone on the planet above a certain age knew how babies were made, so if you didn't want one, you took precautions.

But we all knew Dream was Dream, and honest to God, I wouldn't put it past her to tell them she had things covered when she didn't in times she was ready to pop out another kid.

They still needed to be involved, monetarily and otherwise. She had two kids from two different guys, so at least whoever this joker was who'd put that bun in her oven was either a moron or he thought solely with his dick (which was another term for moron, but there was a nuance of difference).

Scott knew what Louise was thinking, which was why he said, "You do the crime, you pay the fine."

Louise stretched out her lips.

I couldn't hold on these drinks any longer, neither could Jessie delay on her Jessita specials. Late delivery cut into your tips.

So I repeated, "When and where and I'm there," before heading out with the drinks.

I glanced at Tito on my way, and it didn't surprise me he wasn't scribbling, reading or staring out the window.

His sunglasses were trained on Luna, Scott and Louise.

It was weird, but he missed nothing.

And honestly, if he had superpower hearing, and he could hear what was happening at the bar, it wouldn't surprise me if Luna had a fifteen-hundred-dollar bonus in her next pay packet.

'Cause that was how Tito rolled.

Case in point, the new tires I needed for Tweety last March that would have cut into my saving-for-a-house fund were reimbursed just like that.

You didn't say thanks. You didn't make a big deal of it. You didn't demur. Not that Tito would get pissed or insist. He'd just wander away from you while you were talking, so it'd be a wasted effort.

I'd dropped the drinks, and my phone had vibrated again to remind me of the text, so I pulled it out on my way back to the bar to get the water pitchers and do a loop on refills.

And I stopped dead in the middle of the space.

The text was not from Cap or anyone else I might expect.

It was from the person I would least expect.

The person I spoke to briefly on my birthday, his birthday, Thanksgiving, Christmas...

And Father's Day.

It was from my dad.

Feeling a feeling I knew but never liked, my hands shaking, I opened the text and read, *Hey there, darlin'. Coming out for a visit next week. Staying at the Hermosa Inn. I know it's short notice but would love it if you could carve out some time for your old man.*

I jumped and nearly dropped my phone when I heard a growled, "What is it?"

Scott was standing close.

I forced a smile toward his hard-with-disquiet face (was I that easy to read? yikes!), shoved my phone in my apron and said, "Nothing, just my dad."

Louise had also gotten close and they exchanged concerned glances.

"He's coming for a visit next week," I said faux-blithely.

Scott's lips thinned.

Louise's eyes got big.

Yep.

Totally adopted.

They might not know (or they might, Luna might have told them, but she didn't tell me if she did, and I was glad she didn't share that intel with me) what had happened to my family, but they knew my dad was not a big part of my life.

And Scott, especially, did not like it.

Luna was now in our huddle.

"What's going on?" she asked.

"Her dad is coming for a visit," Scott told her.

Luna's mouth dropped open.

I waved a hand—yes, you guessed it—fake-airily. "It's not a big deal."

"He's never been here," Luna pointed out.

"I know," I replied.

"In eight years," she went on.

"I know," I repeated.

"You've never been home," she continued.

"I know," I said yet again.

"What's up with *that*?" she asked.

"I don't know," I replied. "I'll call him later. Tomorrow."

Or the next day.

Or when I dropped off Cleo on Sunday, climbed into Tweety, and drove to Reno, whereupon I'd text him and say I was sorry to miss him, but I was on vacation, lady luck was smiling at me, I was up at the craps table, so I couldn't possibly come home to share some father/daughter time.

I didn't play craps or gamble at all (I couldn't buy second-hand Prada sunglasses if I did), but obviously, Dad didn't know that.

Luna opened her mouth.

"Leave it," Scott ordered firmly.

He might be a progressive liberal, animal-loving, craft-beer-drinking, TEVA-wearing, affordable-housing advocate.

But when he wanted his word to be law, it was just that.

Thus, Luna shut her mouth.

"I gotta do a water loop," I said before handing out good-bye hugs and making a beeline for the water pitchers.

I'd done the loop and taken and put in an order for some of Lucia's pulled barbecue chicken and cheddar nachos, Scott and Louise were gone, and Luna was all up in my space.

"You okay?" she asked.

"Sure," I answered.

"Don't pull that bull," she warned.

I sighed.

Then I said, "I'll call him. Later. Tomorrow. When I have time to emotionally handle it."

"I'll come over," she stated immediately.

God, I loved this bitch.

"That would be cool."

She socked my arm.

I looked to Jessie.

She winked reassuringly at me.

Luna had blabbed.

I smiled at her.

Then I got to work.

SEVEN

IT CAME NATURAL

A t 5:28, there was a knock on my door.

Not a buzz up from the gate.

A knock on my door.

This guy held wild magic.

But at least he didn't just let himself in this time.

I rubbed my lip-glossed lips together nervously, because I played the field, I flirted, I dated, I enjoyed the sexual side of myself, and liked all that.

But I was twenty-seven.

I thought maybe I might want kids one day (that was a big maybe).

What I knew was that I wanted a partner, even a husband (though my wedding would not be traditional, just a ceremony somewhere cool and a big party afterward, then, of course, a fuck-a-thon honeymoon).

I wanted someone to spend time with, to share my life with, to make memories with, to create history with. Someone who got me. Someone who would help lighten the load of day-to-day responsibilities.

Someone who loved me.

I wasn't immune to understanding that the carefree part of being my age was winding down, and I might need to start getting serious about finding that person.

And straight up, Cap had the hallmarks of all I would want in that person.

A brief, and far from exhaustive list: He was hot. He had a great laugh. Beautiful hands. Steady job. A protective streak. Didn't play games about the fact he was into me. He liked Luna. And he had great taste in music and movies.

I mean, one word: *Babe.*

The guy had been in foster care and could pick up a two-hundred-pound man and toss him through the air, and he'd picked a sweet story about an orphaned pig who wanted to be a sheepdog as one of his favorite movies.

So, yeah.

I was nervous.

I was also nervous about the fact that, all day, I'd successfully ignored Clarice Davis's visit, but Luna had texted fifteen minutes ago to share she'd taken a photo of her business card and she had set an appointment for us at ten in the a.m. on Monday.

I was leaning toward dropping that stuff altogether. It was getting way too weird.

But now Luna, who hadn't been a fan, was all over it.

And I wasn't sure that was a good thing.

Although I'd bought a new dress and shoes, since we were still in summer and I was still rocking the honey tan I allowed myself to have when I hung out on my off days at the pool (the trees did offer some sun, you just had to chase it around with copious lounger changes), I decided on the white outfit Luna suggested as a kind of end-of-summer farewell.

Not to mention, it was girlie at the same time as it was sexy as all hell.

So it was perfect, but it gave me something else to be nervous about, because right on schedule, I'd started my period.

Every woman's lot, the constant worry about leakage, when there couldn't be anything more natural than a cycle (something I used when I peptalked myself into wearing all white).

I'd done a little shimmery-dewy-fresh makeup look that took half an hour but appeared effortless (I had a dab hand with a makeup brush), tucking some subtle iridescent pink in the inside corners of my eyes that made the cornflower blue of my irises pop. I curled chunky curls in my blonde hair, leaving it long to tumble over my shoulders and down my back, which meant a flowing hank of it often fell over my left eye. I'd added some mixed metal bangles to my left wrist, slipped my large, Ippolita mother-of-pearl ring on my right finger, but decided to let the sexy shoes and my tits in the tight tank do the heavy lifting.

So I was ready.

I headed to the door.

I opened it to Cap, in dark-wash jeans, a hickory-colored blazer, which contrasted beautifully with the flawlessly white button down stretched across his chest. He wore oxblood oxfords on his feet. And his hair was slicked back with a little lift on the full side of his part that was so delicious, my clitoris, especially, reacted positively toward it.

"What, do you jump the gate?" I asked in a tease.

It took me a sec to note Cap wasn't in a teasing mood.

Cap was in a mood to make my nipples defy the light padding of the racerback bra that covered them, something I was sure they did as his gray-blue eyes roamed...

No.

Devoured me from head to toe.

Then I had his hands to my hips, I was pushed in, the door was slammed, I was turned, backed into it, and Cap was kissing me.

I didn't hesitate.

Not for a moment.

I opened my lips, his tongue swept inside, he tasted like mint and man, so I wound my arms around his neck and pressed into him.

His arms around my waist pulled me closer as he took the kiss deeper.

Okay...

Okay...

Good *God*, this man could *kiss*.

Around about the time my clitoris signaled her maximum approval of his kissing abilities, he eventually pulled his mouth from mine, but didn't go too far away, so our heavy breaths mingled as he growled, "I like what you're wearing."

"I got that," I forced out.

"If I told you how I bypassed the gate code, I'd have to marry you."

"At this exact moment, I'm not seeing an issue with that."

He smiled.

I mentally swooned.

And straight up, my lip gloss glossing his lower lip and mustache did a seriously hot number on me.

The light in his eyes changed, as did his tone and the way he was holding me. Don't ask me, he didn't move, but I felt it go from sexy to supportive.

This happened before he asked, "Ready?"

I knew what he was asking.

Elsie Fay.

I nodded.

He stepped away, then yanked me sharply to his side as he had to shift to avoid Cleo and do this not falling down or letting me do so. A Cleo who was up in his space, sniffing his jeans at his calf.

"Is this Cleo?" he asked.

At her name, she jumped up on him, tail wagging her body.

She might be uncertain which way to swing at any given moment, but she was a girl, so she knew how to swing with Cap.

He let me go to bend to her and give her head a good rub.

Right.

Brilliant.

He liked dogs.

Totally might be willing to pay the price to learn how to bypass a gate code.

"How you doin', girl?" he murmured, then jerked his head back while smiling when she tried to do what I fancied doing...lick his beard.

"Cleo, Cap. Cap, Cleo," I introduced like she was human, and I carried on in that vein. "Now, Cleo, back off and be good. Cap and I are going to be out for a while."

Cap gave her a gentle shove, she backed off and woofed.

"That's right," I said. "We'll be gone for a few hours. So no time for ragers. I don't want to come home to an apartment littered with pizza boxes and Solo cups and you getting it on with that cute Rottweiler who lives down the street."

She wagged her tail at me then panted toward Cap.

I got that too.

I went to my chair to nab my big, Banana Republic Stella straw clutch. The second I was in reach of Cap, he reached, wrapping his hand around mine and leading me out the door.

Even though Cap made sure I was on the inside of the open walkway like any true gentleman would, I still saw Jacob smoking a joint by the pool with his latest squeeze (I hadn't met her yet).

Alexis was also there. She lived directly across from me on the lower level (and she also had a massive crush on Jacob, but she was shy, which was probably why she was out there, to be close to him at the same time torture herself while he was hanging with one of his babes). She was preparing the barbeque, with a platter sitting on the table close to it covered in tin foil.

"Yo, dudes!" I called.

Alexis turned.

Jacob dipped his sunglasses down his nose and called back, "Yo, dudette. Nice score."

His chick just stared.

So did Alexis.

And they weren't staring at me.

"Tell me about it," I yelled.

Cap chuckled.

I was blown away after we exited that gate, not only that he'd landed the phantom open visitor spot, but that he didn't lead me to some big truck or something like a Charger, both of which I liked in a guy.

Nope.

He led me to a sleek, granite-colored Porsche Panamera.

Holy cripes!

He helped me in my side, closed the door, rounded the car and angled into his side.

While he did all that, I put on my sunglasses and pulled out my compact to fix my lip gloss.

He was turning the thingie to start her up when I remarked, "I take it being a private investigator earns some bank."

"Don't know," he replied, wrapping his arm around my seat to look behind us to reverse out. "But you don't do too badly as a member of the Nightingale Investigations crew."

I had a feeling his definition of not doing too badly and mine were madly skewed.

For instance, I didn't think I did too badly, and I owned a car that they'd stopped making years ago, and I thought it was cute and was glad I had it.

His car purred to the exit of the complex with an arrogant demonstration of expensive, cutting-edge technology and power.

My clitoris didn't like that as much as his hair, or his kiss, but it was close (to the hair, nothing came close to that kiss).

He pulled onto Seventh asking, "How was your day?"

Delectable damage fixed, I dropped my gloss and compact in my purse and answered, "Found out first thing our landlord sold to some corporation, and starting Monday"—yes, Bill and Zach got the scoop, and I got an email, the painting was to begin at seven a.m. sharp on Monday, along with the replacement of the fencing and gates, and installation of the solar panels, apparently Dreamweaver Inc. wasn't messing around—"they're doing major upgrades from pool to parking lot to security gates to painting to a compost bin, without raising rents."

"No shit?"

"Absolutely none."

"Interesting," he murmured.

"You can say that again. Then, Scott and Louise, Luna's parents, who have unofficially adopted me, stopped in at SC to invite us to an intervention. Because apparently Dream, you met her yesterday, she's kids-in-tow-sign-of-the-cross woman and Luna's sister, is pregnant again. That's three kids in less than four years by three different guys who are not in those kids' lives, including not paying support. And Dream has no job. Which was a mystery, how they got on, partially solved today when Scott shared how much she owed them, and Luna admitted she'd loaned her sis not a small amount of cash. So with baby three on the way, shit's got to give."

"Not good," he said.

"You can say that again too. And in the midst of this, my dad texted, springing on me he's coming for a visit next week, and I haven't seen him in eight years."

After I said that, the interior of the car was completely silent in a way I'd never felt. In a way I didn't know silence could feel. In fact, I didn't know silence could *have* a feel, but the oppressive, sweltering feel of the silence from Cap was overwhelming me.

I looked at him just in time to see a muscle jump under his beard.

"Cap?" I called cautiously.

"Not cool," he grunted.

Wonderful.

We were here.

Already.

"How much do you know about me?"

"I pulled back," he shared. "I know what you think I'd know, but when I found that out, I stopped. The rest is yours to give me. But I also know a father who hasn't seen his daughter in eight years showing in town without much warning is whacked."

This was true.

However...

"We don't have a bad relationship," I said quietly. "We just don't have...well, much of *any* relationship."

"Let's talk about it over dinner," he bit out.

"Are you angry?" I asked, even though the answer was obvious.

"I know more than enough about shitty parents who take that job and then fall down on it in every imaginable way. With the one-two punch of this Dream chick getting knocked up when she doesn't have the resources to care for her children, and your father showing, when he let loose the bonds he should do everything in his power to keep strong...yeah, Raye. It pisses me off."

He was in foster care and then adopted.

I probably should have had a mind to that.

Damn.

"Sorry, I should have been more sensitive," I said softly.

"I'm not pissed about me," he returned. "I'm pissed for you." A pause then, "And just generally, because this shit is fucked up."

"You're right."

"I know."

I fell silent.

He offered, "You want me to look into your new landlord?"

I turned to him again. "Seriously?"

"Are you worried about it?"

"I'm worried they're going to raise rent. They said no. But there are a couple of tenants we might lose who couldn't afford another increase so soon after the last one."

"Can you afford it if it happens?"

"Depends, especially considering how much work they're putting in. Though, my electrical is gonna go down, since they're putting in solar panels, and that might help. Even so, any rise is gonna suck."

"Yeah," he muttered.

"Thanks for the offer, but let's see how it goes. We're a tight-knit bunch at Oasis Square. Bill and Zach are kind of our community organizers, and they're on the case with this landlord. They found out a lot of the work is starting on Monday, and now they're gonna ask for some sort of official assurance that rent is gonna remain steady. I mean, it could just be they take better care of their investments than Campos did. The place needs a paint job, and I think the pool is in its original form from when it was built during our nation's bicentennial."

"All right, baby. I'll leave it. For now."

Why did I like him calling me baby?

First, it was too soon.

Second, dudes had called me that before, and I'd always found it a little skeevy.

With him, it not only came natural, it made me feel all warm and squishy and...

Safe.

"And just to say, I'm okay about this visit with Elsie Fay," I assured him.

"Raye—"

I reached, wrapped my fingers around his biceps and squeezed, temporarily thrown by the steel I encountered that had zero give, even if he wasn't flexing, but not thrown enough not to interrupt him.

"Stop worrying about me," I urged. "It's sweet, you being protective. But something to know about me, for the most part, I let it all hang out. But you know what I went through, and I've had a lot of time to deal and process, find tools and seek counseling, all of which I've done, in order to maintain a healthy mental state. I can't say it doesn't get to me sometimes, honey. But this...I've got a lock on this. Okay?"

He lifted up his hand, and I knew he wanted me to give him mine. So I did.

He held it to his (also steely, *nice*) thigh and only then replied, "Okay."

We drove to Elsie Fay's house and I took it out of the heavy by asking where we were going for dinner.

It got much lighter when he shared we were going to Vincent's then hitting Platform 18 for after-dinner cocktails.

Learning this, I girlie squealed with zero shame.

I did this because Vincent's was a James Beard award-winning restaurant that was very expensive, so I'd never been there, but had always (but always!) wanted to go.

And Platform 18 was at Century Grand. It was a faux, swanky rail car with windows that were screens that made it look like you were winding through a winter wonderland of mountains (or whatever). They served artisan cocktails that were supposed to be almost as good as Jessie's. You had to make a booking, including dropping a wad just to get that booking, to go there. You then had an hour and a half to down as many cocktails as you could before you were ousted for the next set of drinkers to come in.

I'd never been there either, and Luna, Jess, Harlow and I had talked about going for ages. We'd just never found the time to get our shit together and go.

"For someone who hasn't lived in Phoenix for very long, you sourced the perfect date, my friend," I told him.

He didn't reply.

But he did squeeze my hand.

Not long later, he pulled to a stop in front of a house, and I couldn't say I'd lied to him about being cool with this visit, but now that it was here, I had to admit I was a little rattled.

Cap either sensed my mood shift or just got it, because he didn't let my hand go and turned to me rather than switching off the ignition.

"I'm right here," he said shaking my hand. "To make our reservation, we have to leave in no more than twenty minutes. But you give me the sign, Rachel, I'll get us out of there in five if that's what you need."

Yep.

This so totally could be the guy.

I nodded.

He stared in my eyes, going so deep, I sensed him probing the heart of me.

He must have felt okay with what he saw there, because he said, "Let's go."

Only then did he release my hand and turn off the car.

He took it again as we walked up the drive.

The door was open before we hit the walkway to it, and Elsie Fay's dad was standing there.

I knew his name was Ben. His wife's name was Emily.

Cap pulled me a little back and took the lead when we made it to him, offering his hand.

"Ben," he said as Ben took it.

"Julien, right?"

"Yeah," Cap said then turned to me. "This is Rachel."

I shoved my sunglasses up and offered my hand. "Hi, Ben."

His jaw jutted out at the sides as he clenched his teeth and fought emotion, seeing as the last time he saw me I was holding his daughter who had been taken from him, then he took my hand and said, "Rachel. Delighted to meet you."

I smiled an understanding smile, and he stepped aside to invite us in.

We walked in to a tidy house that was decorated with a moderate hand. There was personality, and lots of comfort, but no one was going for any awards. They just wanted it to feel like family. And it did.

Emily stood in their living room holding Elsie Fay's hand, and in the background stood their reverend, with a woman who looked around his same age who was probably his wife.

I nodded to Emily and her company but let Cap go and approached Elsie Fay.

I crouched in front of her, my billowy, ankle-length skirt settling around me in a circle, and gave her a bright smile. "Heya, Elsie Fay."

"Are you an angel?" she breathed.

It was the white outfit.

"They do walk the Earth on occasion," I heard the reverend say.

I ignored this and opened my arms. "Can I have a hug?"

No hesitation, she walked right into them.

To hold her closer, I dropped to my knees and tucked my face into the top of her hair.

That night, she'd been dirty, her hair greasy, she didn't smell great, which I thought was a hint of good in all the bad, since it was clear he didn't bathe her.

Now she smelled like strawberries and felt like heaven.

And I was wrong.

I couldn't do this.

My battlements didn't just shake. The parapets didn't just rumble. The soldiers I had manning the trebuchets and boiling tar went on an ill-timed break, my Citadel was under attack, and the whole thing was in danger of crumbling to the ground.

Fuck.

I felt her getting uncomfortable so I instantly loosened my hold.

She stepped away, didn't go far, but studied my face, then patted my cheek like she was comforting me.

My throat completely closed.

She turned to her dad and lifted her arms. He picked her up immediately.

I stood, looked at Emily and pushed out, "I'm sorry. Just a second."

Then I raced out of there.

I stopped once I got to the side of the house, leaned into a hand on it, put the other hand to my waist, bent my head and deep breathed.

Seconds later, Cap was at my side, not close, not far, but he had his hand on my back and he was stroking my spine up and down, his touch light and not intrusive, just warm and *there*.

After some time, I heard Cap ask, "Can you give us a minute?"

I straightened and turned to see the reverend had joined us.

"Of course," he murmured, making a move to leave.

"No. I'm okay," I assured. "I just needed a minute. But I'm okay."

He nodded solemnly. "It's a lot. I know."

"She looks good, she looks good," I repeated myself. "Is she good?"

"Our church is blessed with many parishioners, including some social workers and psychologists. We're working to find a fit for Elsie Fay, Emily and Ben."

This time, I nodded.

Thank God.

Literally.

He took a cautious step forward, lowered his voice, and said, "I believe you need to know, the police have resources the family have already availed themselves of. Elsie Fay has shared. It seems he was attempting to..." He struggled. "Groom her..." More struggling. "Or break her." He took a deep breath. "Bottom line, Rachel, he didn't touch her. Not that way."

I let out a sharp, hitching breath that bucked my entire body then found myself plastered down Cap's side.

"Thank you for telling us that," Cap said.

"If you need to leave, I'll explain that to them," the man offered.

"I'd like to say good-bye to her," I told him.

He lifted his chin.

We went back in, and in a haze where I barely recalled what I was doing or saying, though I did not miss that Cap didn't leave my side, I spoke with Emily and Ben, a little more with Elsie Fay, met the reverend's wife, and then Cap whisked me out of there and into his Porsche.

He did not drive me to Vincent's.

He drove me home.

He did not hold my hand.

Because I was wringing mine together.

He did ask for my key to let us into my apartment rather than breaking in, though.

When we got in, I walked in farther, tossed my clutch on the chair and turned to him.

He was just a couple of steps inside, the door closed behind him.

"Do you want me to call Luna?" he asked.

Who was this man?

And how did I find him?

I shook my head.

Then I walked direct to Cap, shoved my face in his chest, he wrapped his arms around me, and I dissolved into tears.

EIGHT

THE BEST I'D EVER HAD

The next morning, Cleo jumped off the bed.

After that happened, Cap left it but pulled the covers back over me, tucked them in, and I opened my eyes.

He leaned over me.

"Go back to sleep, I got her," he said softly.

Then he kissed my temple and disappeared.

I did not go back to sleep.

I listened to him get dressed, the low whistle he let out to call Cleo, and not long after, the front door opening and closing.

I turned to my back with my arm over my eyes.

And lying there, I replayed last night.

Honestly?

I had no idea how we got to my bed. I'd lost it. I was consumed by emotion.

Though, I understood his choice, since my couch looked great, and for lounging, one person fit well.

Two, no way.

Not to mention, I'd had a death grip on him.

Eventually, I calmed down, but I did so on my own time with no hassle or encouragement from Cap. Lying pressed into him, front to front, he let me cry, and he held me and stroked me and said not a word, letting me get it out.

When it was out, he reached to my nightstand and came back with a bunch of tissue he shoved into my hand, and it was only then I realized Cleo was tucked tight to my back.

Lab or chow, a dog was a dog, and when shit got real, they stuck.

Then, I had no earthly clue why it happened, but it happened.

I wiped my face, blew my nose, pressed my cheek to Cap's chest, and said, "She was taken from a playground."

He lifted my arm and rested it on his waist then gathered me closer in both of his.

Yes.

That was better.

"She was with a friend," I went on. "The playground was just down from our house, across the street from her best friend's house. Her friend's mom could see them from her living room window. Kids played there all the time. *I* played there all the time. And our parents watched from their windows. The guy literally walked right up to her, and within seconds, picked her up, and she was gone."

I swallowed.

Then I whispered, "That was the last time anyone saw her."

"Yeah," Cap whispered back, running his hand up my spine and curling his fingers reassuringly around the back of my neck.

Weirdest of the weird?

Having his hand there, even telling him this story, I felt reassured.

"Her name was Macy," I told him. "I was two years older than her. We got along great. We were close. Normally, I'd be at that playground with them. But I was at a friend's birthday party, and she wasn't invited." I shook my head, but it didn't go very far, seeing as it was pressed into his shirt. "I will never, not ever, forget the look on my dad's face when he came to pick me up. All the kids were gone by then. It was hours later than he was supposed to come get me. My friend's parents were acting funny and giving each other looks I didn't get then, but I do now. Seriously, you could *taste* the fear."

I stopped talking.

"You don't have to do this now," Cap said quietly.

"Is it too much for you?" I asked.

"If you wanna give it, I can take it. I just want you to know you don't have to give it."

"I wanna give it."

"Okay, honey, whatever you need," he murmured.

I pulled in a deep breath and let it go.

"There are milestones," I shared. "The time of having hope. The time that hope dies. The time you want the news they found her, but she's gone, so you don't have to worry what's happening to her, or if it was bad, you know it's over. There are also good things. We forget how it really is. How it is every day. We get caught up in the news. The divisiveness. The messages telling us that person in the grocery-store line, wearing a baseball cap you don't like, is your enemy because they voted for someone you didn't vote for. When that's fucked. Every day, in a hundred different ways, we live together in kindness. In thoughtfulness. With care. Or at the very least, just courtesy. And when something like that happens, Cap, people are so good. So, so *good*. Loving and supportive. Listening and trying to understand. Angry when you are. Sad when that turns. Not understanding why something like that can happen, and not afraid to show it so you don't feel alone in that. It's a beautiful thing. We live that beauty every day with the way we get along. And people miss it."

"You're right."

I knew I was.

I knew I was, because that was all I had to cling to for nineteen years after someone who didn't live in that world took my little sister.

"They never found her. Never even had any leads. He was a ghost. Just some guy who drove in a neighborhood that wasn't his, snatched a six-year-old girl, then vanished into thin air. To this day I don't know if she's dead or alive. And I hope equally she's dead at the same time I hope she's alive."

"That has to be hard," he said. "And confusing."

"I don't know," I mumbled. "It doesn't really feel like anything. It's just always been my life for as long as I remember. Because the time before she was gone, when we were a family, it feels like a dream. Because it was so very *gone* after she was taken from us."

"Fuck," he groaned, turning into me so I held some of his weight.

God, it felt good.

And I needed it.

For this part especially, I needed it.

Because losing Macy was the worst thing that could happen.

And it wasn't just losing her that made it so.

"Dad got lost in his rage. He was angry all the time. Angry at the police. Angry at Macy's friend's mom. Angry at Macy's friend, who was six too, and she gave a description, and shared what happened, but she was only six. Not much she knew to say could help. Angry at my friend's parents because Macy wasn't invited to the party, when no one but people in our class were. Dad was just was angry at the world."

"Hate to admit it, but I don't blame him," Cap said.

"Yeah," I agreed, drew in another breath and let it go before I shared, "Mom disappeared inside herself. Became a ghost. I don't know how either of us missed it, what was coming. When she killed herself five years later on the anniversary of Macy going missing, we should have known. We should have seen the signs."

Cap's arms closed tighter around me.

"You were too young," he stated.

"Maybe," I replied.

He gave me a tight squeeze. "Definitely."

"Okay," I wheezed.

He loosened his arms.

"After that, Dad became a shell. Filled with shame and guilt. I don't know how he brushed his teeth and went to work. He was there and he was not. He woke up breathing, so by habit, he just went through the motions."

"So you were alone."

"I was, until I met Luna, then she gave me her family. Got a job at sixteen, saved every penny, and when I thought I had enough money, I got in my car and drove as far away as I could get from all that. Hit Phoenix, got a shitty studio apartment, a job at the mall, and here I am."

His hand at my neck gave me a squeeze. "Here you are."

"Yeah."

"My mom beat the shit out of me."

My head snapped back.

"Cap, you don't—"

He looked down at me. "I gave myself the name Julien Jackson, Raye. No one knows the name I was born with, except Roam, and no one ever will. This could be something, you and me. We could go the distance. And you will never know that name because it's meaningless. It's ash. It's gone."

I nodded to indicate I got him.

The significance of his statement cut through me like a razor.

But I got him.

He carried on.

"Julien for Jules, that friend I told you about, a social worker who worked at the runaway shelter where me and Roam, and our buddy, Park, used to hang. Jules. Juliet Lawler, now Crowe. She loved us, *fuck*, Raye." His hand still at my neck, tightened. "She loved us. It was the first time I'd ever felt love like that from a female. The first time someone took care of me, looked after me, wanted with everything that was her that I would thrive, and she knocked herself out to make that so. Until Shirleen, my adoptive mom. Her last name is Jackson."

So that was why his name didn't fit him, but it still did.

"That is so incredibly cool you got to claim the good things you were given that way," I said.

"Absolutely," he replied.

"I hate that your mom—"

He shook his head on my pillow and gave me another squeeze to quiet me. "It wasn't the beatings. They sucked and she was a bitch, and at the time, I hated her. There was nothing good about her. My dad left before I was old enough to put two thoughts together, and I don't know what her deal was. If she was bitter or if she took her anger out on me that she had to look after me when she didn't want to be saddled with raising a kid. I don't know. I don't care. She hated me too, and she didn't hide it. There was nothing between us. No connection. Definitely no love. So it wasn't about that. It was that she brought men home and most of them weren't okay, they were just assholes. But one of them woke me up in the middle of the night, touching me."

Oh no!

I pressed tight and whispered, "Cap."

"I pushed him off, ran out of my room, to her—"

"Honey."

"And the bitch said, 'What's your problem? Suck it up. I do.'"

"Oh my fucking God," I breathed.

"Yeah. That night, grabbed some of my shit and got out and never went back, and then I met Park and—"

"Oh my fucking God," I repeated.

But the way I did, Cleo popped onto her feet and woofed.

"Raye."

I tore from his hold to sit up so I could screech, "*Oh my fucking God! Seriously?*"

Cleo woofed louder.

Cap sat up too and put both hands to my neck. "Baby, it was a long time ago. I barely even remember what she looks like. Honestly."

"Holy shit, that's fucking *lunacy*."

"Calm down, Raye, look at me. I'm okay. I'm good. I got a good life. A big family."

"Okay, but *still*," I snapped.

"My sister wasn't snatched, and my mom didn't commit suicide, and my dad didn't bury himself in his own shit and forget to take care of me—"

I shook my head and slapped a hand on his chest, then fisted his shirt in my fingers.

"Oh no. We're not playing that game of who had it worse, Cap. We both had it bad, and I like you. You're hot and have a beautiful laugh and like dogs, and I am one hundred percent *not okay* with your birth mom being such a goddamned *cunt*."

For a second, he stilled.

Okay, maybe I took that a shade (or a hundred of them) too far.

Then he started laughing.

My head fixed to explode.

"You think this is funny?" I shouted.

"I haven't seen the woman in nearly two decades. She does not factor in my life."

"Do you know where she lives?"

"No. Why?"

"Because I wanna go there and cut a bitch."

He started laughing again.

Cleo snuffled us.

"Stop laughing!" I yelled at Cap.

Cleo scooted away as I landed on my back with Cap's chest pressed to mine.

His face in my face, he said, "She's not worth the effort."

"I hate her," I declared.

"She's not worth that emotion."

"I still hate her."

His lips were twitching as he replied, "Right. Go for it. The hating her bit. But I don't know where she lives, and I don't give enough fucks to find out. Even for you."

Ugh.

Moving on.

"Is my makeup ruined?"

"Yes."

"Are you mad we missed Vincent's?"

"No."

"Are you mad you're gonna lose your booking deposit for Platform 18?"

"No, again."

"Are you hungry?"

"Yes."

"Well, I can cook, and I like to cook, but I'm unprepared to craft the first meal I'll ever serve you, which has to be an occasion. It has to have a wow factor. No way I'm blowing that. But I'm hell on wheels with DoorDash. So what do you want?"

I did not pay for the DoorDash, Cap did.

He took off his blazer and shoes, I took off my shoes, we ate in my bed while we talked, and Cleo stared at us with pleading eyes and failed in not slobbering (I felt for her, we'd ordered Raising Cane's, and that fried chicken smell was probably torture for the poor pooch). In the end, I asked him to spend the night, and he said yes.

So I did my nighttime prep and showed in the room in my nightie to find Cap in my bed, covers up to his waist, shoulders to my padded headboard, his glorious chest on display (it was tan too, and glorious didn't quite cut it as a descriptive word, I'd have to ask Luna how to describe it, maybe sublime or divine or awe-inspiring or transcendent, but you get the picture).

I crawled in beside him. We cuddled, kept talking, and I fell asleep while doing that.

It was the shittiest first date on record.

Yet it was the best I'd ever had.

I threw the covers off me, went to the bathroom, did my business, brushed my teeth, hit the kitchen, started coffee, grabbed my phone and went back to bed.

There, I called Luna.

"Yo, how was the date?" she answered.

"I lost it after seeing Elsie Fay. Cap brought me home. I cried in his arms for maybe twenty minutes, but probably more like an entire hour. I then bared all about Macy. And Dad. And Mom. He told me some shitty stuff about his life. We ordered DoorDash. He spent the night platonically, and that isn't just about the fact I'm on my period. And now he's out walking Cleo for me. Though, he liked the outfit you picked out so much he kissed me about two seconds after he saw me in it, and the man knows how to use his tongue. I didn't have an orgasm, and still, my clit was completely satisfied."

"Holy crap."

"*I know.*"

"You told him about Macy?"

"Yep."

Her voice was rising. "On the first date?"

"He already knew the basics. He'd researched me. But, outside sharing about my Citadel, I gave him it all. He held me and listened to me then gave as good as he got. Completely open. Seemingly adjusted. Not daunted by my drama. Not fucked up about his. Not even a little bit, on either, Loon."

"I...don't know what to say."

"Well figure it out, because he's out walking a dog so he won't be gone forever, and I need to sort this out."

"You didn't even get to the restaurant?"

"I barely remember the car ride home from Elsie Fay's, I was so messed up. But just to say, the restaurant was gonna be Vincent's, with Platform 18 after that, and he gave no shits we missed either booking."

"My Lord," she breathed reverently. "Vincent's is an ace-in-the-hole, guaranteed blowjob date on its own. But he also booked Platform 18?"

"Yep."

"For a first date?"

"I know. Those are totally Valentine's Day or birthday or fiftieth wedding anniversary locations."

"He's in as deep as you," she proclaimed.

My heart stuttered to a halt.

"You think?" I asked.

"What man gets up before eight on a Saturday to walk a woman's dog, that's not even her dog, after she blubbers in his arms, lays some heavy shit on him and makes him lose his Platform 18 deposit? It's a sheer miracle he didn't sneak out in the middle of the night to go home and then immediately block your number on his phone."

She spoke truth.

Holy wow.

He was in as deep as me.

"And, you know, Raye," she went on. "Not many men take time out of their day to hit up a woman's place of business to share face to face he has to change their date plans. I was impressed then. I mean, one-two punch, he was so interested, he wanted to see where you worked, at the same time see you. He's in, and that in is *deep*."

"We've known each other a couple of days and had one very bad, totally awesome date."

"All I gotta say to that is, life is shit, and it's totally awesome, so if you can sort through your shit and think being with him through it is awesome, you best be pulling out the trifle bowl."

This referred to making my famous chocolate pudding.

For Cap.

My trifle bowl saw a lot of action. Every Easter, Thanksgiving and Christmas at Luna's folks' house. Every Oasis Square get-together. And nearly every girls' night in at my place.

I once showed at our Oasis Square Independence Day Extravaganza without it, and I was shunned. Until I dashed out to Fry's and did my best with the time I had (I liked my pud to cure overnight, it was still good, because what made it couldn't be bad, but it wasn't my best effort).

"This is what I know," Luna broke into my pudding reverie. "You have never told a single date or boyfriend the story of your sister. Not because you're ashamed of it, but because you didn't deem them worthy. You deemed this guy worthy. And you are one together bitch.

It isn't about hormones or hotness. This guy has got something that reaches you. Which means I'm making dinner for him Sunday night after our Dream Intervention."

This was big.

Huge.

Luna had never invited one of my guys to her house for dinner.

It took Luna a year to invite Hunter to one of her soirees.

She was an ace hostess, but the woman was picky.

"That's Sunday?" I asked after the Intervention.

"Actually, you should invite Cap to it," she said...*insanely.* "He needs to know what he's getting into with our family."

Our family.

Oh snap.

I might cry again.

"Don't make me emotional. I glanced at my face in the mirror as I brushed my teeth and my eyes are scary puffy. In fact, I need to get off the phone and get my eye mask out of the freezer so I can get a minute or two with it on before he gets back."

"Your phone goes with you, bitch."

True.

I got out of bed and headed to the freezer, saying, "Still, I shouldn't be on the phone gabbing with my bestie when he gets home. He'll know we've been talking about him."

"He doesn't strike me as a dunderhead."

Dunderhead?

Where does she get this stuff?

She kept going.

"If he doesn't figure you did it while he was walking Cleo, he'll know it's gonna happen eventually."

I grabbed the mask and headed back to bed. "I'm not going to ask him to the Dream Intervention."

It was like I didn't speak.

"I'm gonna clear it with Mom and Dad. They'll say yes. Dad especially. He'll wanna look this guy over."

Oh my Lord.

"Luna—"

"Gotta make a call. Byeeeee."

She disconnected.

I sighed, turned around to make myself coffee, went back to bed and strapped the mask over my eyes before I aimed my coffee mug to my mouth.

I should have done that in another order.

Still, I got some joe down my gullet.

Blindly, I set the mug on the nightstand and laid back.

It would take a while before I realized just that.

It had been a while.

A *long* while since Cap and Cleo left.

What? Did he set about ghosting me while stealing my client's dog?

On this thought, I heard the front door open.

I shoved the mask to my forehead, threw my legs over the side of the bed and hit the door in time to see Cleo, in full Lab mode, charging toward me with a new rawhide clamped in her teeth, the label still dangling from it, trailing her leash. I moved my eyes to watching Cap walk toward the kitchen carrying four Fry's bags in one hand, a tray with two Starbuck's coffee cups in the other.

"You went grocery shopping?" I asked while alternately avoiding an overexcited Cleo and wandering down the hall.

"I wasn't sure you'd have all the ingredients for my chocolate chip pikelets with caramelized pear and chocolate sauce."

At his words, I stopped dead in the opening to my kitchen and stared at him as he unpacked groceries.

"I can confirm I don't have pears," I said as he unearthed one.

"There you go," he muttered.

"What are pikelets?"

"Mini pancakes. It's an Aussie/New Zealand term."

Okay, maybe I should invite him to the Dream Intervention.

Because I was hanging on to this dude for a good long time.

I wasn't ready to go there yet.

But still.

Maybe that good long time would be *forever*.

My kitchen wasn't that big, two people in it was close to two too many, and anyway, he seemed to be on a mission, so I rounded the column that delineated kitchen from living room and hiked my ass up on one of my stools (baby-pink, tufted-button back, quilted front, silver nail-edged seat, chrome bottom, adjustable with footrest bar, pure glam on a pole—and they were comfy).

"Got you a latte," he said. "Your name is on the side."

I hadn't finished my coffee.

I still reached for the cup with *Ray* scribbled on it.

I forgave the Starbuck's barista for missing the "e" on my name after I sipped.

I then asked, "You put Cleo in your Porsche?"

"Sure," he replied.

I was getting closer to that *forever*.

"I called Luna," I announced.

He stopped investigating my kitchen at the same time pulling out things he needed from where he found them and looked at me. His eyes swung up to the gel eye mask on my forehead, his lips tipped up, then those delightful blue-grays came to mine.

"Yeah?" he asked.

"She wants you to come over for dinner tomorrow."

He didn't wince or go stiff, or visibly freak out in any way at this alarmingly quick escalation in our relationship after our first very bad/incredibly awesome date.

Nope.

He started opening and closing cupboards again, asking, "What time?"

"Um...after we hit Dream's Intervention."

That got his attention.

He looked at me again. "Sorry?"

"You're invited."

"To the intervention of a woman I barely met...once?"

"Okay, Mr. Jackson, it's time I came clean."

He moved to the counter opposite me and settled his weight into his hands on the edge, leveling his gaze on me.

Man, he looked good in my kitchen.

"About what?" he asked.

"You see, I'm a little nuts."

"That's not news."

"And Luna is a little nuts."

"That isn't really news either."

"And seeing as Scott and Louise made her, they're a little nuts."

"Right."

"And I told you they unofficially adopted me."

"Yup."

"And I've never told any guy I've ever dated about Macy. Or Mom."

He nodded his head.

Once.

"Got it. So what time is this intervention?"

I blinked. "You're going?"

"You're into me."

"Yes," I confirmed.

"I'm into you."

"I hope so."

"I'm into you, Rachel."

I made big eyes, and my chin went into my neck as my lips spread tight and tipped up with my happy smile.

His lips tipped up too, but he didn't look like a five-year-old who just opened a present to unearth the doll she'd always wanted.

Not even close.

He also shook his head in an, *isn't she cute?* rather than an, *isn't she scary as fuck?* way, which I took as good.

"We're gonna spend the day together," he stated.

"We are?"

"Yes."

"Okay," I whispered.

"And the night."

"Okay," I whispered again.

"No pressure. I want you. You know that. But that's on your terms. I'm still spending the night."

I wanted him too, obvs, and usually, I had no hang ups with that.

But with Cap, I wanted it to be special (and that special couldn't be when I was on my period—my first day was always a heavy flow, and I was over that, so it didn't last long...still).

Thus, we'd see.

"Okay," I repeated.

"That means we'll be spending tomorrow together too. So it doesn't matter when this gig is. We'll just hit it when it happens."

"Right."

"You wanna help me or do you want me to cook for you?"

I guessed that was that.

And I was okay with that.

"Do you want me to help?" I asked.

"I wanna cook for you."

"*Mi cocina es tu cocina, mi amigo.*"

He did that, *isn't she cute?* head shake again.

Then he got to work on pikelets and caramelized pears.

Spoiler alert...

When I finally shoved that stuff in my mouth, I fell in love.

With his cooking.

But I was sensing that was just the beginning.

NINE

SWINGING LOW

After breakfast, Cap left to go home and shower and pack some stuff to spend the night.

I took this time to hop in the shower too, and being the multitasking wunderkind I was, while in the shower, I carefully crafted the perfect reply text to my dad. One that would be both welcoming at the same time establish boundaries.

Therefore, when I got out of the shower, I texted him I was excited for his visit, asked him to email me the particulars, then shared I hadn't had enough warning to get time off from work, but we'd meet up for dinner.

I then shot off a text to Luna, letting her know I was spending the weekend with Cap, what I'd said to Dad, and Cap was in on the intervention as well as for dinner at her place the next night (it was a long text).

I was doing my makeup when I got back from Dad, *That works, honey. We're renting a car so we can entertain ourselves until we see you. Email sent!*

I had to take a break from blending to stare at his text.

Because...

We?

I didn't ask. I'd had a rollercoaster week. I couldn't take anymore. So I let it lie.

I was back to blending when Luna returned, *Good. Mom and Dad are in with the addition of Cap. Three at theirs. Have fun with your hot guy. Later, bitch.*

I finished my makeup and was confronted with the impossible task of sorting a Spend the Day with Cap outfit.

The dress I wanted to wear was at Luna's, and I lost some time wondering why I'd benched that dress over at Luna's when it was super cute.

I notched a trip to Luna's to cycle out my wardrobe on my mental to-do list, marking it high priority.

The runner-up I decided on didn't suck, though.

I pulled out my babydoll dress that had a mixed floral and band pattern of blues, pinks, reds and peaches, with full three-quarter sleeves gathered at the ends and a vee neck. I buckled on some tan, flat sandals with thick straps that had scalloped edges, spritzed with perfume, added some gold hoops and rings, and switched out my bag to a cute, little tan crossbody, just in time for Cap's arrival.

I'd given him the gate code so he didn't have to deplete his magic by bypassing it anymore, thus he knocked on the door.

I opened it to see him wearing beige Bermuda shorts, an ashy-dark taupe, untucked button-down with the long sleeves rolled up high to over his elbows, and some white Chucks. He had a worn, but still awesome, leather backpack slung over his shoulder.

Before Cleo, who was crowding me to get to Cap, could do it, I threw myself at him.

He caught me, and giving me little kisses in between sweet smiles, he shuffled me in.

His little kisses weren't near as good as having his tongue, but I wasn't complaining.

He dropped his pack to the floor.

Still pressed up against him with my arms around his neck, I asked, "What do you wanna do today?"

"You've been in this city a lot longer than I have, what's there to do?"

"Can I take you to my favorite place in all of Phoenix?"

"Perfect."

We took Cleo out for another stroll to tide her over while we were away because only service dogs were allowed where we were going, and we had to leave her behind. Then we loaded up into Cap's Porsche.

As such, I guided him to the Desert Botanical Gardens.

I'd been there bunches of times before. In fact, Luna and her family and I went there every Christmas season to do the luminaria extravaganza.

But as much as I loved them (and the luminarias), no visit I'd taken there was as fabulous as strolling the paths hand-in-hand with Cap.

Indeed, doing that made the place flat-out *magical*.

We took our first selfie together under the big shady tree just up the way from the patron mosaic (and it was hard to stop looking at that snap, because, straight up, we were perfect together—so perfect, it was going to take all my willpower not to print it out within twenty-four hours, find the ideal frame and put it pride of place in my pad).

Eventually, we had a late lunch sitting outside on the patio at Gertrude's.

We ended the visit by stopping by the gift shop, where I bought two succulents. One for my house and one to adorn Tito's table at SC.

Late afternoon, we let ourselves into the gate of the Oasis, holding hands and each of us carrying a pot in our free one.

Just to say, on the whole, Cap was a hand-holder, not just when things were emotional.

I loved it.

No, wait.

Strike that.

I loved it.

Once inside, we spied Martha and Linda hanging out in the seating area by the barbeque.

"Yo!" I called.

"Get over here," Martha called back.

I stifled a smile, because Martha was a hoot. But she was also a lot.

We wandered over while I warned under my breath, "That's Martha, brown hair, and Linda, gray. Linda's lovely, but try to ignore everything Martha says." I paused then finished, "Or does."

"Gotcha," Cap said under his breath.

"Hey, guys," I greeted when we got to them and stopped.

"Heya, Raye," Linda replied.

"Who are you?" Martha asked Cap.

I motioned to him with my plant. "This is Julien Jackson."

"Everybody calls me Cap," he put in, let me go, made his approach and offered Martha his hand. "Nice to meet you."

She stared at his hand like it was covered in slime.

Not missing a beat, he moved it toward Linda.

She took it.

"Hi, Cap. I'm Linda, and this is Martha," Linda said.

"Hey," he replied and moved back to my side.

Linda looked at me. "Did you get the email?"

"What email?" I asked.

It was then I belatedly noticed they were drinking champagne.

It was also then, calling from her opened door, Patsy shouted, "Are we starting? I'm not done with the salad yet!"

"Is it five, girl?" Martha shouted back. "No, we're not starting. Learn to read a clock!"

Patsy, used to Martha, returned. "Okay! Hi, Raye! Dig the plants!"

"Hey, Patsy!" I called.

Her door closed.

"We're having an impromptu party," Linda explained. "Bill and Zach got written confirmation. They're not raising rents."

"For two years," Martha added, before sucking back some champagne from a plastic champagne glass.

A funny vibe came from Cap.

"Wow. That's great," I said, because it so totally was.

"And get this," Martha put in. "They capped Linda's rent."

That funny vibe from Cap got funnier.

"I got my own email," Linda added. "They told me, due to my long-term residency, and as such, investment in the property, my rent will never be increased. Ever. They're sending me a lease that, even if they sell, the new owners will have to abide by."

"That's short for, she's old and doesn't have a lot of dough, so they don't wanna be the heartless, greedy, pissant ogres who put her ass out," Martha translated.

Martha wasn't young, but she didn't have the same number of years on the planet as Linda, by about a decade and a half. And as such, she still was gainfully employed. Not to mention, she'd been able to bank the entire price of the house she'd sold prior to her arrival at the Oasis because it was paid off when she sold it.

At this juncture, Alexis bounced onto the scene.

"Hey, all!" she cried.

She was all lithe grace, considering she was a ballerina with Arizona Ballet.

"Isn't it fantastic news?" she asked.

Before anyone could answer Alexis, Cap turned in their direction before I knew they were there, so I heard rather than saw Bill state, "Awesome. Raye's here. Did you make your pudding?"

I turned too.

Bill was looking at me.

Zach was checking Cap out.

"No. I just heard the news," I told him. "We were at the Botanical Gardens."

Bill's eyes narrowed. "Is there time?"

See?

If it wasn't so damned good, I'd lament ever inventing that recipe. My pudding was better loved than me.

"She can't snap and make a trifle bowl full of pudding appear, William," Martha bit out. "It's quarter to five, for goodness sake. This shindig begins at five." She turned her steel-gray eyes to me. "Though, you probably have time to throw together some of that Asian slaw."

I didn't have the ingredients for my Asian slaw.

"We have to go up and take Cleo out," I told her, because I didn't know if Cap was up for an Oasis get-together, so we needed a confab.

"You know the rules, you can't come empty handed," Martha warned.

"Man, hat's off to you. Shit," Jacob strolled up saying.

His squeeze was at his side.

He was carrying a platter stacked high with raw hamburger meat formed into patties covered in plastic wrap.

"Longest date in history," Jacob finished.

Alexis's pretty cheeks went pink in Jacob's presence, or because she was upset he still had his chick with him, or both.

"Now that's how it's done," Martha confusingly stated, pointing at Jacob and his woman. "Watch and learn, Raye." She swung her finger and jabbed it at Cap. "He's too pretty. And you're too pretty. Everyone knows, if you're pretty, you swing low and get someone who isn't as pretty as you. Gives you the upper hand in the relationship. Jacob's a good-lookin' man. He knows to swing low."

This was met with complete and horrified silence.

Linda broke it by snapping, "Martha!"

"Am I wrong?" Martha asked Linda. She didn't wait for an answer. She looked to me and her mouth kept moving. "My Jeremy, not much to look at, but in the bedroom department, shooie! He had to work harder to make up for other things he lacked. And work he did. *Lawd.* Your pretty boy probably thinks his looks will do the work for him." Her gaze swung to Cap. "You'd be *wrong.*"

"I'll apologize for her," Linda said to Jacob's squeeze, moving her gaze to Cap to include him in the apology that wasn't hers to give (still, it was nice she gave it).

"Don't worry. Jacob warned me about her," The Squeeze responded.

I took a moment to wonder if I should petition our new landlord to put a sign out on the gates that said Beware of Martha.

Then, even if I was still swimming through my horror that Martha said Jacob's woman wasn't as hot as him right in front of her, I realized this was a point to ponder.

Because Alexis was all petite, slender, ballerina loveliness, with gorgeous peaches and cream skin, amazing cheekbones and big eyes, and I'd always thought she was the perfect foil to Jacob's rough and ready, muscle-packed, black-hair-and-bearded good looks. And he was maybe only three inches taller than me, but he was six inches taller than her.

Perhaps he knew the until-just-now-unknown rule of "swinging low."

Before Martha could say anything else that might make Cap pack my belongings and move me somewhere else in fear of my mental health, I grabbed Cap's hand, saying, "We need to go see to Cleo. Later!" and then I dragged him to my apartment.

Once inside, I put down my plant, divested him of his, pulled off my crossbody, slung it on the chair, turned to him and ran it down.

"Right, Linda. Retired schoolteacher. Really sweet. Everyone loves her. Never married, but since she is who she is, she's kind of the mom of the complex. Jacob, in construction, and when he's not on a job, he spends his time getting stoned and or laid. Nice guy, though. Bill and Zach, partners, not married yet, they have one of the two-bedrooms. They're our community organizers. Really nice guys. Patsy, who called from the door, works at a doctor's office and takes care of the plants and flowers around the complex. Alexis is a balle-rina, and completely in love with Jacob. So much, it's hard to watch. I keep hoping he's biding his time, but now I think he might be swinging low."

I took a deep breath.

Then I launched into Martha.

"Martha has three boys and a dead husband. Jeremy contracted some rare form of cancer a few years after their youngest was born. This means she spent her life dealing with his treatments and him being in and out of remission, at the same time raising three rambunctious sons on her own, being the primary breadwinner most of the time. All of this, only for him to pass a few years after their youngest went to college. This also means she's had her hands full all her life and instead of being cowed by it, she became a take-no-shit warrior. After they all graduated from college, she sold the house because she was done with AC repairs, cleaning a pool and dealing with tree limbs falling on her roof during monsoons. She lived at the Oasis in her swinging-single twenties, what she calls, 'The Glory Days,' and came right back the minute a unit opened. She has two grandkids who are in the pool a lot during the weekends. She also has no filter, as you've seen, but she'd put herself in front of a bullet for you."

"Do you know everyone in the complex?" Cap asked.

I thought about it.

Then I said, "Yes."

He studied me, an expression I couldn't read on his face, but it veered toward good, while saying slowly, "Right."

"We don't have to go to the shindig. We can do what we want."

"Do you want to go?"

Of course I did. Oasis shindigs were the best.

Outside Luna's parties, that was.

Cap must have read that on my face, because his beard twitched in the area around his mouth, and he said, "Let's make a deal. I'll check out what you got in the kitchen that we can throw together and take to the party, you take Cleo out, because she's been a good girl, but she's gotta go."

I jumped to him happily, gave him a quick kiss, then headed to my hooks to get Cleo's lead.

"Raye?" he called as I was clipping it on her.

Still bent over, I looked up at him. "Yeah?"

"I wanna look into this new landlord."

Hmm.

"Why?"

"Investing hundreds of thousands of dollars into upgrades without rent increases, and capping a tenant's rent..." He shook his head. "Sometimes, a good thing is a good thing. Sometimes, a good thing masks something bad."

I finished with her lead, and Cleo danced around me as I asked, "What could be bad?"

"Don't know. That's why I wanna look into them."

"Go for it," I said.

He jerked up his chin on a small smile and urged, "Get her to some grass. She's dying."

I smiled back, then Cleo and I took off.

Cap and I were lying in my bed.

Update: Cap fit in with the crew. He was laidback and friendly and super good at small talk.

As for me, when the sun went down, Bill and Zach's lights came on, the pool illuminated— making the Oasis an oasis—and drinking, eating, hanging and communing with people I cared about, with a comfortable and outgoing Cap at my side, felt like a slice of heaven.

Update times two: Tonight wasn't the night for us to *go there* with intimacy, mostly because I was seriously buzzed. Cap whipped up an insanely good pasta salad for the party (one could just say Lucia would approve of his ability to balance with acid), and I made a batch of my sangria.

Yes, I wasn't much of a sex-on-your-period person (though, I could make exceptions, but not normally for the first time).

Mostly, I wanted a clear head and to be totally into the moment when that happened with Cap.

Anyway, I was getting off solely on this getting-to-know-you time. It felt like the more we had, the deeper the meaning would be when we went there.

So I was waiting for my instincts to tell me when that time came.

We'd made out a little, and it was awesome, but Cap, as promised, added no pressure.

So we were cuddling and chatting when Cap announced, "He's biding his time."

"What?"

"Jacob."

I got up on a forearm and looked down at him, even if it was dark. My blinds were open and I could see him through the streetlights and moonlight.

"Really?" I asked excitedly.

"Absolutely. He's got some notches he wants to score into his belt. He's not ready to settle and commit, which is where he's gonna take it with her."

My excitement died a fiery death.

"That's messed up," I stated heatedly. "She can't pine for him forever. What if she finds someone in the meantime? Also, him parading his women in front of her is uncool. Also to the also, him dallying with other women when he's into Alexis is totally uncool."

"I didn't say what he was doing was cool. I said he was into her, he's just not ready to take it there, because he cares about her, and he's not gonna involve her in his life while he's sorting out whatever he's gotta sort out in his head before he gets serious."

I flopped back to the bed on an, "Argh."

Cap curled his arm around me and pulled me closer. "She ever bring a guy to one of your things?"

I shook my head. "No. Honestly, she's all about Jacob."

He nodded. "Yeah. And just to say, if she finds someone, that shit he's gotta sort out is gonna get sorted real fuckin' quick. He's the kind of man who would put up with what he's making her put up with for about a second. He'll move in the minute she shows in the courtyard for one of your parties with a guy at her side."

"He does strike me as a bit of a caveman," I noted. "A part-time stoner caveman, but a caveman all the same."

There was humor in Cap's, "You'd be right."

He then gave me a slight shake before he launched into some education.

"I think women look at men like him and see what he wants you to see, not what he's hiding. It isn't that Martha has no filter. Martha's a fucking genius. Because, my guess, Jacob thinks Alexis is too good for him. That's what he's gotta sort out in his head. It isn't right, but he doesn't even know this man-whore shit he has going on is serving double duty to prove to himself he's got a big enough dick to swing around, but also prove it to Alexis. And what Martha did was pump him up at the same time she was telling him he'd be the low swing for Alexis, when he isn't. Martha knows that. But she also knows he thinks he is. In other words, they'd match, fit. They'd work. He could do his thing for Alexis in a different way and keep her up on the pedestal he's put her on. And he'll do that the minute he figures out what Martha gave me shit about and insulted Jacob's woman in order to tell him. He's what Alexis needs. They're gonna work."

I saw this.

So I breathed, "Oh my God. That *is* genius."

"Yeah."

"But...why do men play games like that?"

He laughed softly then said, "Baby, the same powers that be that make women think they gotta put on makeup and be the ones to take the calls from school and leave work and deal while their man does his thing, are the powers that tell men we gotta provide and protect and have big dicks to swing around. It's insidious. It's ingrained in you before you even know someone is implanting it. Until we get to the point where women who want to wear makeup wear it, and women who don't, don't, and men realize they're just as responsible for dealing with what's happening at school as their woman is, and if they leave work, it's no hit to their manhood, we gotta navigate these games."

He was so right.

Again.

I pressed closer, asking, "How did you get so smart?"

"Wait until you meet Shirleen," he murmured. "And Jules. Indy. Jet. Ally. Ava. Roxie. Sadie. Daisy. And Stella."

I had no idea who most of those people were, he'd never mentioned them.

But if they had a hand in making Cap, I couldn't wait to meet them.

IT WAS the next morning and we were sitting outside Elsie Fay's church watching the congregants drift away.

We'd hit up Bosa on the way there, and sat eating the donuts we bought as we waited for the services to end.

My stomach was tied up in knots, and I was rethinking my decision to do this, my decision to talk Cap into taking me to do this (he thought it was unnecessary and worried it would be too much for me, which wasn't surprising, considering the last time we faced this, I cried in his arms for an hour), and the added decision to stuff my face with fried dough before doing this, when Cap asked a pertinent question.

"Are you sure about this?"

The reverend had already clocked us (two people munching donuts in a Porsche was hard to miss).

But that wasn't it.

I searched my feelings, and yes. This was about pride and some shame. I felt badly about how I'd reacted in front of Ben and Emily.

They had no way of knowing I was triggered. But they were dealing with so much, and I walked into their house and threw a drama. So I wanted them to know why I did.

But most of me was beginning to realize that maybe me being highly selective about who I deemed worthy to know about Macy wasn't healthy.

I'd told counselors how I'd dealt, and I'd had one who'd cautioned I should be more open. I'd had another who said I should go with my gut, not force myself to deal in ways that didn't feel comfortable.

I'd been doing the last.

Maybe I needed to talk about it.

Maybe I needed to cry about it.

Maybe I needed to allow myself to *feel* it.

It hurt, but it was a hurt that would never go away. Hiding in my Citadel and shutting it out was a coping mechanism.

But maybe it was time to ride Cinnamon over the drawbridge and into the unknown, carrying memories of Macy with me, including the fact we lost her.

It was more, though.

There were going to be dark times Ben and Emily would have to navigate. They snuck up on you even when you thought you had it covered. Friday night was proof of that.

And even though my story wasn't theirs, and not only because they got Elsie Fay back, I wanted them to know that it was a horrible, twisted kind of luck, but they were lucky all the same, with how their story ended.

I turned to Cap. "I wanna do this."

He tipped his head to the steps of the church. "Then let's do this."

I turned back to the church and saw the congregants were gone, but the reverend was waiting for me at the top of the steps, his wife beside him.

We got out, and Cap didn't take my hand when he hit my side.

He slung his arm around my shoulders.

I slid mine along his waist.

As he seemed wont to do, this made me feel better.

Attached, we climbed the steps.

"Rachel, Julien, what a pleasure to see you again," the reverend said as we let each other go, and he shook both our hands.

"Reverend," Cap murmured.

I smiled at him and his wife, then I requested of him, "Can I take a little of your time to speak to you? And ask a favor?"

"Of course." He motioned to the doors. "Would you like to come in?"

I shook my head. "You have a busy day and this won't take long."

He settled in.

His wife (I was so hazy when I met her, I forgot her name, though I was sure someone told me), wrapped her fingers around her husband's arm, totally feeling my vibe.

Welp.

I was here, no going back.

So I launched in.

"I want you to know that, yes, what happened to Elsie Fay was a lot. But the reason I reacted the way I did was because my sister Macy was taken when she was six."

"My dear," he whispered, his body jolting at hearing this news.

His wife's fingers visibly started clutching his arm, and it occurred to me then how his job had a lot to do with helping people navigate the shitty parts of life.

In other words, he had to bear some of that weight, and considering how much of it he probably had to take on, that weight must feel like he was carrying around a mountain.

It sucked I had to add to it, but at the end, they'd see the light.

Though, I had to give him more weight first.

"She was never recovered," I went on.

The reverend moved, like he was going to grab hold of me, probably to give me a hug, but he stopped himself.

Yeah, he knew how to do this.

I kept going.

"The favor I need to ask, and I know this isn't about me, and it's definitely not the time...I also know that if anyone will understand when the time is, you will. So I wanted to ask you to explain that to them. I didn't handle our visit well, and I'm embarrassed I had my episode when they're dealing with so much. So it's that. But also, I hope they'll learn healthy ways to deal with it, but we both know they'll never get beyond what happened. I just want them to understand they can hold on to the joy that they got her back."

"That *you* got her back," the reverend said.

"Well..." I demurred.

"The way you reacted, Rachel, said you cared," he told me. "That's it. They thought nothing of it. When something like that happens, we need to remember how very many people are out there who care. I think you've learned that. Am I right?"

Oh, I'd learned that.

I nodded.

"So don't worry yourself about it. But yes, I'll do you that favor. I'll find the time. And I'll share your story so they'll remember to hold onto that joy."

"Thank you."

"My pleasure. Thank you for trusting me with your history and giving me the honor of sharing it with Ben and Emily."

What a nice guy.

We said our farewells, and with his arm around me again, Cap took me back to the Porsche.

We got in and he turned to me. "You good?"

I nodded. "I'm good, honey."

"Can we get some real food now?"

He could eat after two donuts?

Whatever.

If we went somewhere to eat, I could sling back some mimosas. I just did what I'd just done, and in four hours, we had our showdown with Dream. I needed to begin preparations for the next onslaught, pronto.

"Sure," I said.

"Hash Kitchen?"

"We'd have to wait an hour for a table," I warned.

He started up the Porsche.

"I got AC in this ride. We'll be good," he replied.

Yeah, one thing that was certain and getting more so the more time I spent with him.

We'd be good.

TEN

PINWHEELS

I was seeing the error of Luna's and my ways as the Porsche oozed to a stop in front of Scott and Louise's house, which was all but hidden behind a jungle of overgrown plants.

We hadn't gotten there yet, me and Cap. Partly because we were new. Partly because, let's face it, I didn't want to.

I'd given my big speech to Cap on Friday night, but when it came to getting along generally in society versus finding someone to spend time with and your philosophies on life melding, well...those were two very different kettles of fish.

But I liked him.

A lot.

And the more time I spent with him, the more I felt that.

And women like me and the boho-glam-living-paycheck-to-paycheck (mostly), low responsibility, devil-may-care lifestyle I'd curated, and men like Porsche-driving, gun-in-his-waistband, comfortable-in-a-police-station Cap, didn't seem to mesh.

Anyway, everyone worried about people they cared about meeting someone they were growing to really care about, and all those factions getting along.

I'd never done this before, introducing someone like Cap to people like Scott and Louise. Therefore, it hadn't hit me how important this was.

And in that capacity, I was sensing impending disaster.

So I had to give him the lay of the land so he knew what he was walking into.

In other words, it was time to go there.

Damn.

I turned directly to him after he switched off the ignition and announced, "Right, you're in Tempe, which is a whole different ball of wax than the mixed sitch of Phoenix, and the entirety of A Z."

"Sorry?" Cap asked, looking confused, and I didn't blame him.

"This is a college town couched in a big city. And Scott and Louise are very *college town* people."

I hoped my choice of words to stress shared my meaning.

Thankfully, Cap was sharp as a whip.

He got my meaning.

I knew this when he turned fully to me, paused a moment to ascertain he had my full attention (he very much did, now and pretty much always), then he spoke.

"I carry a gun for work. I have no issue with people owning them if they hunt or shoot at a range. I also have no issue with people owning them if they feel they need them for their protection, but only if they keep them secured, get training in how to handle them and handle them regularly, so they know what the fuck they're doing. And I own a personal weapon for that purpose. That said, bottom line, a gun is a weapon. Period. It's just a weapon. So I think we need stricter gun safety laws so they don't get in the hands of people who should not be anywhere near a weapon. And in the Army, I used an assault rifle. Because I was in the Army. No citizen in a civilized society needs an assault rifle. Ever."

This was good.

So I nodded.

Cap kept going.

"It's my opinion that it's fucked I even have to state that a woman should have total control over the decisions that are made about her body. If the need is there to consult a healthcare professional, that's her choice too. No one else should have a say in that. And any person should be free to fuck or love or marry anyone they want. Who you do that with bears no reflection on who you are. And I don't give a fuck who or what anyone identifies as. It's not my business. Don't tell me how to live, I won't tell you how to do it. You harm no one, I wish you no harm. And I know a lot of good cops, really good ones, Raye. They do shit and face dangers on the daily most people can't comprehend. I also know there are shitty cops who should not have a badge. And I agree, shitty cops who shouldn't have a badge are a huge fuckin' problem. I don't have the answers for fixing that, but I feel someone should work at finding the answers so everyone can feel safe with law enforcement. But I respect and work closely with law enforcement. It's part of my job. It's also just who I am."

I nodded again.

Cap went on.

"I don't give a shit who anybody voted for. I give a shit how you treat people. I give a shit how you operate in your community. You're an asshole, I'm not gonna like you. You're a good person, I'm gonna like you. You judge me for who I vote for or that I own a gun or that I work with LEAs, you can fuck off."

"Okay," I whispered.

"You judge me for any of that?"

"No. I agree with all of that."

And I did, and I could not express how glad I was that I did.

"They gonna judge me?" he asked, jutting his chin toward Scott and Louise's house.

"I...I don't—"

I didn't finish stammering because his gaze cut beyond me.

I looked over my shoulder to see Scott was wending his way through the vegetation toward the Porsche.

"I guess we'll find out," Cap said, and I heard his door open.

I guessed we would.

Shit.

He got out.

I got out.

Cleo trundled out behind me.

Scott called, "You guys okay?"

"We're good," I called back.

He stopped a few feet from us, and his torso swung back. "Shit, son. That's quite a ride."

I stared at him, because Cap's Porsche was not electric, and both he and Louise had had electric cars since the Prius was born.

Not to mention, he'd given me a gentle lecture when I'd bought my Juke, which was also not electric. I'd had to promise him my next car would be electric, and now that I was getting a JuiceBox, that could happen.

Though, I wasn't letting go of Tweety anytime soon. I loved her, and she needed me.

"How fast does that puppy go?" he asked.

"Speedometer says one-ninety," Cap told him.

Scott whistled.

"Are they okay?" Louise's voice sounded from somewhere amidst the jungle.

"Yeah, woman!" Scott called back. Then he shared, "Raye's man has himself a Porsche!"

"What?" Louise shouted.

Scott twisted at the waist to holler toward the house, "Raye's man owns a Porsche!"

"Some borsht?" she yelled back.

"*Porsche!*" Scott bellowed. "The car!"

Louise emerged from the foliage. "Oh my goodness!" She clapped her hands, eyes to Cap's car. "Isn't that pretty?" She looked to Cap and saw the whole extent of the pretty, I knew, because she stopped dead and her face went slack as she stared at him.

"I'd be jealous if I thought she had a chance in hell," Scott shared with Cap, taking his hand and thwacking him on the shoulder, all man-to-man greeting. "Scott Nelson. That's my wife, Louise."

"Heya!" she called, shaking herself out of the Cap Stupor.

"Cap Jackson," Cap introduced himself.

"Fucking hell," Luna said, showing at our party. "That car is *dope*."

"Come in, come in, I've got hummus," Louise said, circling her arm to invite us inside at the same time turning and disappearing in the bush.

Cap claimed me with his arm around my shoulders again, and we followed them as I said low, "She always has hummus."

"Are they vegan?" Cap asked.

"Vegetarian."

"Got it."

"Yo, dude," Luna greeted him when we got to her.

"Hey, Luna," Cap replied.

"Yo, Cleo," Luna greeted Cleo.

Cleo turned her nose up at Luna and followed the scent of hummus.

We navigated the jungle only to enter a different kind of jungle.

Louise wasn't a hoarder, *exactly*.

But she did decorate with a heavy, unbalanced hand that veered wildly between Native American, African, Southwestern, Cape Cod, Japanese, rustic, Wild West, mid-century modern, art deco, and protest sign.

Cap didn't even look around in wonder (or horror). He strolled right in.

"Have a seat." Louise gestured to their new vegan leather couch, ignoring her dogs, the dogs she was fostering, and Cleo sniffing each other then pouncing and rolling around in a massive, playful, canine wrestling match.

I didn't know how many pups there were, there was too much fur flying and too many tails wagging to count, but at a guess, I'd say seven.

Their cats, unsurprisingly with this going on, were nowhere in sight.

Their couch sat against the wall with a coffee table in front of it laden with bowls of hummus and pita chips. And not only that, there was also salsa, corn chips, a platter of cheese slices intermixed artfully with crackers, olives, nuts and grapes, another platter of carefully placed finger veggies, a bowl of tzatziki, a display of what looked like two different kinds of tortilla-wrapped pinwheels, and finishing this spread were puff pastry shells filled with some cheese mixture inside.

I suddenly didn't know if we were at Dream's intervention or Cap's and my impromptu engagement party.

I braced for fifty people to jump out of their hiding places and shout, "Surprise!"

"What do you drink?" Louise asked Cap. "Scott has ten thousand different types of beer. I've got a bottle of white opened. We also have some sparkling water and strawberry iced tea."

"Iced tea would be great, Louise. Thanks," Cap said.

She shot off like a dart.

"Mom's nervous Cap isn't gonna like them," Luna leaned in and whispered to me.

Cap heard, I knew, because he turned and smiled at me.

I smiled back, realizing belatedly the common denominator to all these people was me.

So I should never have worried.

"So!" Scott boomed, clapped his hands, then clamped them together, pumping his palms while he did. "How 'bout them Diamondbacks!"

"Dad's nervous too," Luna added.

I heard Cap's swallowed laugh.

I liked he was amused.

But this felt.

It felt...

Really fucking beautiful.

I'd never told a guy about Macy, and, as mentioned, I'd never brought one "home" to Scott and Louise.

That they got what was happening, and it meant something to them, meant everything to me.

We settled in, and Louise, knowing me so well, brought me a glass of white, Cap's iced tea, and the men talked baseball while Louise fidgeted, and we waited for Dream to show.

Normal people would give the interventionee a later time so they could get their ducks in a row before they arrived, but I figured they told Dream three o'clock because she was going to show a half an hour late (at least) no matter what time they said.

The thing was, we weren't getting our ducks in a row.

"Um...she's your daughter," I butted into the baseball discussion. "And your sister," I said to Luna. "So maybe it's not my place to say. But shouldn't we get our ducks in a row? Or did Cap and I miss that part?"

"This is how it's gonna go," Scott declared. "I'm gonna tell her the Bank of Nelson is closed, the Tempe branch *and*"—he jerked his head at Luna—"the Phoenix branch. She needs to get a job. She needs to find decent daycare. And she needs to cease dumping my grandchildren on us, her sister and you while she flits around getting needles poked in her and shit. She also needs to contact those clowns who helped her get into this situation and tell them they're in for five hundred bucks a month, and if they've got a problem with that, she'll see them in court. And if she doesn't like any of that, tough shit."

"I think maybe we should go a little more cautiously," Louise said, then elevated her ass out of the armchair she was in to lean forward and lift the plate of pinwheels Cap's way and ask, "Cap, doll. Care for a pinwheel?"

Out of courtesy, I could tell (he'd had a big plateful at Hash Kitchen), he took one.

He and I were on the couch together, me sandwiched between him and Luna. I nabbed him a napkin because they were out of his reach.

And I did this trying not to giggle at Louise calling Cap "doll."

"Going cautious got us in this predicament," Scott pointed out.

Louise put the plate down with a clatter and sat her ass back in a huff.

Oh boy.

"Scott, you and I disagree that we should leave our pregnant daughter and the mother of our two grandbabies high and dry," Louise said sharply.

"Louise, you and I have been disagreeing on what we should be doing with Dream for a solid thirty years," Scott bit back.

Uh-oh.

Luna was a year older than me.

And Dream was thirty.

Suddenly, this got contentious and historical, and that was a volatile mix.

"I know I'm not lending her another dime," Luna chimed in, reaching forward and grabbing a cheese puff.

A Yorkie escaped the fray, leapt through the air and landed in Cap's lap.

He did nothing but start to pet her.

She lay down across his lap and panted.

Cleo noticed this, got jealous and loped over to stake her claim on Cap.

Cap slid the Yorkie so she was half on his thigh, half off, wedged between us, and he used both hands to pet them.

Cleo's black tongue oscillated in and out on a happy rhythm.

Okay...

Holy shit!

I'd known him mere days, and I was totally falling for the guy.

And with that thought, another one hit me.

The sad truth of it was, it was a high probability my sister would never fall in love.

Because she was more than likely dead.

But I was here, with these fine people, and I'd found this man.

As these thoughts assailed me, Louise and Scott, across from us in armchairs, forgot they were starting to argue. They looked at Cap, then at each other, and Scott sat back in his chair and contentedly rested his linked hands on his belly.

Tacit approval of Cap.

Louise asked Cap, "Anything else you need, sweetheart? I know Luna's feeding you after this, but if you're peckish, I made some white chocolate chip, macadamia nut cookies yesterday."

Explicit approval of Cap.

"I'm good, Louise. Thanks," Cap replied.

"Did Luna tell you about Macy?" I blurted.

Cap went still at my side.

Scott and Louise's gazes raced to me.

"Raye—" Luna started quietly.

"Did she?" I asked Scott and Louise.

"Sugar bun, she did," Louise admitted, talking like her daughter.

"I'm glad you know," I told her. "Because I'm realizing that I didn't have the strength to do it. But if you know me, you need to know that. Because it's part of me."

Cap stopped petting the Yorkie and wrapped his fingers around my thigh.

"Okay, sweetheart," Scott said.

"You're good people. You're good, *good*, kind people," I told them. "And maybe you're struggling with the fact that Dream's a bit messed up, and you might have had a hand in that."

Cap's hand at my thigh squeezed a warning that I was taking this too far.

But I kept going.

"But she's alive and healthy and you have her. She's also an adult and making very adult decisions. So it's time she acts like an adult. Maybe it's not the right call to cut her off cold turkey. But enabling her for any longer isn't the right call either. You would never, ever let anything harm her or Feather or Dusk. But it's not gonna come to that. She *will* get her shit together because she won't have a choice. I'm not looking after her kids unless she pays me. I'm certainly not doing it at the same time I'm at work. Not anymore. And I'll share that with her when she gets here. Luna isn't gonna give her more money. And Scott, you have to quit caving, Louise, you have to quit pushing him to cave and let Dream be all she needs to be for those kids. She loves them with all her heart. She'll get her head out of her ass. What's gonna go down whenever she gets here isn't gonna be fun. But it'll happen and then it'll be over. And she'll eventually get her head out of her ass to look after her kids."

"Well, I guess I know what Mom asking me over is about."

All our heads swung to where Dream was standing, laden down with children and her hippie tote just inside the door.

Whoops!

I wondered how much she heard.

She told me by asking, "Who's Macy?"

Apparently, Luna's sharing didn't include her sister.

"My little sister who was abducted from a playground when she was six and we never got her back," I announced.

All the color raced from Dream's face and her hand went up reflexively to curl around Feather's head.

"After that, my dad lost himself in his anger and my mom couldn't deal so she killed herself when I was thirteen."

"Oh, Raye," Dream whispered.

"I haven't seen my dad in eight years," I went on and pointed at Scott. "Yours is right there." I pointed at Louise. "Your mom is right there. And they've been *right there* for you too much, for a long time. You have absolutely no idea what you have in them. Get your head out of your ass, Dream."

Dream stood immobile.

"What she said," Luna put in.

"Papa! Papa! Papa!" Dusk shouted from Dream's back.

Scott got up and grabbed his grandson.

"Oggie! Oggie! Oggie!" Dusk yelled, pointing at the dogs who had abandoned their wrestling match and were now crowding Scott to get to Dusk.

Scott put him down and Dusk disappeared under a pile of fur, which the Yorkie dashed across Luna's and my laps to get in on (Cleo couldn't be bothered), but we could hear his squeals of delight.

"You guys are cutting me off, hunh?" Dream asked her parents.

"You're a thirty-year-old woman with two children and one on the way, petal," Louise said carefully. "Your father and I didn't decide to have those children. It was your decision. You must understand the burden you're putting on us by thinking you can live like a teenager when you're a mother. There will be times some years down the line when your kids have their own pursuits where you can spoil yourself. But now, you need to concentrate on providing for your family."

Dream came farther in and plunked her tote down by the side table next to Luna.

But she said nothing.

She also didn't take Feather out of her swaddle and drop her on Luna, so that was something.

Her gaze strayed to Cap, and she asked, "Why's he here?"

"Because he means something to Raye, and Raye's a part of this family," Scott answered. "That's why."

"How the hell am I gonna find a job when I'm knocked up?" she asked the room at large.

It was Scott again who answered. "Love you, kiddo, but you should have thought of that before you got knocked up."

"This blows," she said on a sigh.

"You should have thought of that too," Luna told her.

She looked down at her sister, her manner changed, and she sniped, "Perfect Luna, Daddy's favorite."

I got tense, mostly because that pissed me off.

Though, I thought it was telling that Dream, surprisingly easily, seemed to be coming to terms with what was going on, but the minute Luna got in her sights, she turned ugly.

I just didn't know what that told.

Cap's hand still on my thigh squeezed.

He felt me getting pissed off.

"Dreamy Dream, Mommy's favorite," Luna shot back. "Don't pretend you had it tough. We were both loved. I just never took advantage of that."

Dream flinched.

Louise took her feet.

"I cannot believe you stood in this very room and listened to Raye tell her story and you're trading barbs with your sister," she snapped at Dream. "Raye doesn't know what became of her sister, and yours is right there. My goodness, I didn't think I could be this ashamed of one of my own children."

"Momster—" Dream started in a whiny voice.

Louise gave her The Hand, shaking her head.

"No. No. Your father's been right all these years. I'm too much of a soft touch. But not anymore, Dream. Not anymore."

With that, she swept from the room.

Well, it seemed the intervention worked, just on a different person.

"Enjoying this?" Dream asked Cap snidely.

"More than you, I reckon," he murmured.

I bit back a laugh.

"I don't need this shit," Dream hissed. "Dusk, come to Momma."

Dusk didn't come to Momma. He was too busy trying to shove the ear of a golden retriever in his mouth.

So she went and picked him up, grabbed her tote and swanned from the house without another word.

We all looked at each other.

Then we all jumped (well, Luna and I did) as Dream swanned back in, miraculously having deposited Dusk in the carrier on her back in the two point five seconds she was gone.

She went direct to the coffee table, reached into her tote, pulled out an empty gallon-size Stasher, snatched up the tray of cheese puffs, upended it in the Stasher, sealed it, shoved it in her tote and huffed out again, all of this without making eye contact with a single one of us.

One thing you could say about that.

Dream came prepared.

"That went about as I expected. Sorry, kids, gotta look in on Louise," Scott said before he walked out.

Luna leaned forward to catch Cap's eye.

"Welcome to the family, bud."

Cap smiled at her.

Then he leaned forward too, and casually grabbed another pinwheel.

Honestly.

This guy wasn't for real.

And I was glad.

"So Tex comes running out, and I told you, the man's beard is down to here." Cap indicated his navel with his hand. "It's parted in half, flying out at the sides of his neck. I'm stunned he got out. Even more stunned the big man could run that fast. Then I had to take cover, because the warehouse he escaped exploded behind him."

Luna and I burst out laughing.

We'd been doing that a lot while Cap told us stories about his family in Denver.

It was no wonder he didn't blink at my nuttiness...or Luna's, Tito's, Scott and Louise's, etc.

We had a ways to go to compete with that crew.

We were at Luna's.

It was after a dinner of her famous cacio e pepe with Caesar salad tossed with her homemade dressing, and garlic bread.

Jacques in her lap (after the intervention, before we hit up Luna's for dinner, Cap and I took Cleo home to her mom and dad, and we could just say parting from Cap was bittersweet sorrow for Cleo, I could see her parents were weirded out how much she whined when Cap walked away), Luna asked, still laughing, "The warehouse blew up?"

"Tex had jerry-rigged a bomb."

"Oh my God, that's insane and hilarious at the same time," I said, also still laughing.

And by the by, those two adjectives seemed to pretty much define his friend Tex.

Luna took a sip of her wine before she noted, "Your posse up in Denver seems like the total shit."

Cap took a slug from his bottle of beer and replied, "They are."

"Not to be intrusive, you don't have to answer," Luna began. "But if that's the case, why are you here?"

Cap didn't hesitate responding. "Roam and I are tight, I mean, closer than blood brothers. But I was the runt."

"That's hard to believe," Luna mumbled.

She hadn't seen the pictures.

But I suddenly wasn't finding anything funny with the way Cap described himself.

Cap kept talking.

"Then I wasn't the runt anymore. He always took care of me, him and Park. But I no longer needed him to take care of me, and the dynamic shift could have come between us. I needed to find my own path, see who I was out of the shadow of Roam. One of the reasons I went into the Army. And Roam needed time to get out of the habit of looking out for me."

"Who's Park?" Luna queried.

"Our other brother. He died. Got hold of bad dope. Someone had cut it with something, he injected it, Roam, Jules and me found him dead in an alley."

My body went solid.

Luna looked at me.

Curled into him on Luna's loveseat, I pulled myself out of my shock in order to put a soothing hand on his chest.

He turned to me.

"It's okay," he murmured.

"It's not," I replied.

His smile was small. "You're right. It's not. But there's no changing it. Roam and I have talked about it a lot since then, and we both figure it would have happened one way or another. He was a daredevil. Fearless. He needed constant challenge. If he'd had a different life, maybe being in organized sports or something that would claim his focus would have helped. But I don't even think that would work. No joke, if he'd lived, he would have become a racecar driver or a paratrooper. He was an adrenaline junkie."

"Okay," I said, watching him closely.

"His death led Jules to Vance," Cap explained. Vance being Jules's husband, a member of the Nightingale Investigations crew up in Denver, and, from Cap's accounts, a man who became kind of a big brother mixed with mentor to Cap and Roam. "Vance led to us being a part of the RCHB and Roam and I having Shirleen. So it's like"—he tilted his head in an odd manner, as if he was trying to stretch some tension out of one side, so I cuddled closer and pressed my hand harder into his chest—"even in death, Park was looking after us."

The RCHB was the Rock Chick/Hot Bunch, how the Denver gang referred to themselves.

And FYI, "Rock Chick" was part of the title of the book about Kai Mason and Stella Gunn.

"Let's stop talking about this," I said.

"Yeah, let's," Luna agreed.

"I had him, baby," Cap said quietly. "I loved him, I lost him. You know something about that."

It struck me that I did. It was the worst, but we had that in common.

And as much as I hated what happened to Macy, and the aftereffects of that, if it hadn't happened, I might not ever have moved to

Phoenix, met Luna, earned her family, started working at Tito's, found my place at the Oasis.

So I understood him.

"Time for dessert!" Luna thankfully cried.

She got up, taking Jacques with her, then dumping her pup in my lap before she headed toward the kitchen.

"Dessert?" Cap muttered. "Jesus Christ, I'm gonna need to run for an extra hour to work off all this food."

"You run?" I asked.

"This body doesn't maintain itself," he answered.

"Allow me to congratulate you on the caliber of work you put into it," I replied.

He started laughing.

Jacques heard his momma doing something in the kitchen, so, naturally, he leapt off my lap and headed that way.

"Just to say, babe, Roam's considering joining the crew down here," Cap told me.

Interesting.

"How do you feel about that?"

"Shirleen and Moses are also considering it. They're tired of snow and cold, and she's uncertain anyone we can find down here can set up the office to her standards. Mace's office manager in LA is an older version of Wonder Woman, so Mace has been trying to get her to move to Phoenix, but he hasn't been successful, and that's a role they haven't filled yet. As for Shirleen, most importantly, I'm down here. If Roam comes, that'll seal the deal."

Shirleen managed the office at the Denver branch of NI&S.

It was an incestuous group. They all were in cahoots one way or another.

It sounded awesome.

He still hadn't answered my question.

But first things first.

"Who's Moses?"

"Shirleen's husband. They've been married, I think it's twelve years now. Like him a lot. Solid guy. Treats her like a queen."

Excellent.

"Okay," I said. Then pushed, "So is that a good thing? All of them moving here?"

He ran a finger along my jaw. "Not a good thing, it'd be a great one, having them here. And she'll like you."

Okay then.

It worked for him.

So it worked for me.

But I really hoped he was right, and she liked me.

WE WERE MAKING out in my bed.

It was hot and heavy.

I was leaning toward this being it. Cap having aced his weekend trial by fire, the fact he was pretty but still knew very well how to "do the work" between the sheets if my rock-hard nipples and wet-ass pussy were anything to go by...

It was time to take us there.

I arched into him.

And Cap stopped kissing me.

He uncurled his fingers from my breast, touched his lips to my nose, my forehead, then down to my chest before he put his lips to mine, and said, "Not tonight, baby."

"Why?" I whispered, still pressing into him.

"Because this weekend has been a lot for you."

"I know. So?"

"So, when it happens, I want you to be past that extreme and all about us."

Shit.

He made sense.

"I hate it that that makes sense."

He chuckled, touched his mouth to mine briefly, and said, "I hate it too, honey. But I'm right."

He was.

Us connecting in that way was important. It was a huge step in what we were building.

It had to be all about us.

Ugh.

He slid off me, rolled me so my back was to his front, then he lifted his knees, taking mine with his, and tucked me tight to his body with his arm around me.

God, he could work a spoon too.

This man.

Yum.

"I'm glad you were there through it," I said into the dark.

"I am too."

"I miss Cleo," I went on.

"Me too."

I knew what I wanted to say next, I just didn't know whether or not it would freak him.

Then I thought, if Martha hadn't, and Dream hadn't, and well, *I* hadn't, then this wouldn't.

"Did you pack enough clothes in that backpack to get you through sleepovers for the next week?" I asked.

He started laughing and through it said, "No." He then shifted so he could kiss my neck, and in my ear, he said, "But I'll take care of that tomorrow."

I relaxed into him.

"Go to sleep," he ordered.

"Okay," I mumbled, the entirety of the last few days rushing in all at once, making me suddenly sleepy when I was anything but two minutes ago.

Cap pulled me closer.

I sprinted toward dreamland.

I was catapulted out of it when he said into the back of my hair,

"The extreme of the last few days saved you from our talk about what's on your wall, baby. But just so you know, we're gonna get to that soon."

Well...

Great.

Just...

Great.

ELEVEN

ONE OF A KIND

M y alarm sounded (meditation music, Cap was probably going to hate that).

But I woke to an empty bed, so he didn't hear it.

I turned and saw a note on his pillow.

I picked it up and read, *Out for a run, baby.*

I didn't like waking up without him, but at least he didn't hear my wake-up music.

I told Alexa to quit it with the music, got out of bed making a mental note to program a musical change for tomorrow, did the prelims of my morning thing, including having a shower, and I was sitting in my robe and some panties at my bar with my laptop and a mug o' joe when Cap came in the front door.

He was wearing some drawstring running shorts, running shoes, nothing else and was slicked with sweat.

Lord.

Well, that explained the tan.

"I think I slept off my extreme," I informed him. "Can our first time be me jumping you on my living room rug?"

He grinned, walked to me, and I took it as a promising sign when he gently fisted my hair, pulled my head back and laid a lot-of-tongue wet one on me.

Alas, he pulled away and answered, "No."

"Bluh," I replied.

He grinned again, let me go and looked at my laptop. "What are you up to?"

"My morning scan of the *Republic* and checking emails. Are you allergic to cats?"

"No."

"Do you like cats?"

"Yes."

"Do you have an issue if I say yes to Jenn's cat coming for a visit? She has to head home because her mom is having hip replacement surgery. I can pop over for feedings and stuff, but Patches likes company."

He'd met Jenn at the shindig. She was a tenant, upper level, across from me, but down a few doors.

"Sure," he replied, then his head tilted to the side. "Is this a paying gig?"

"Jenn leans toward Anthropologie gift cards."

He shook his head giving me that, *isn't she cute,* look I liked so much, then he hit the shower.

I soldiered through his shower and me knowing he was naked in it by making a bowl of oatmeal and eating it.

I was on my second mug o' joe when he came out dressed in army-green cargos and a short-sleeved linen-colored Henley that stretched across his pecs, was tight on his biceps and showed off the veins in his arms (and his tan).

I was running low on reserves, but I managed to soldier through that too.

He made himself some coffee.

I watched.

When he was done, I remarked, "My dad arrives Wednesday. He's made a reservation at Lon's that night. Wanna come?"

He leaned against the back counter, leveled his eyes on me, and answered, "Yes," then took a sip of his coffee.

That gave me a good deal of relief.

And that thought made me wonder if I should be concerned about the level of relief it gave me, and the fact that Cap's and my first date had so far lasted sixty-one hours.

"Are you weirded out our first date has lasted sixty-one hours?" I asked.

"No. Though I am mildly disturbed you counted the hours," he teased.

I shot him a grin.

"Are you?" he asked.

I shook my head. "No. So, you showing tonight with more clothes, what do I stock to prepare? Protein powder? IV hydration packets? Raw meat? Ninja stars?"

He burst out laughing.

I kept smiling as he did.

"I'll cover myself," he said and lifted the coffee in his hand. "You got a travel mug, baby? I gotta hit it."

That meant our first date was over.

Which sucked.

I frowned.

But he'd be back that night.

I grinned.

"Jesus," he whispered.

I focused on him to see him very focused on me.

My nipples tingled.

"What?" I asked.

"Waited fifteen years to find you."

My breath left me with a *whoosh*.

So it was a wheeze when I repeated, "What?"

"One of a kind," he replied.

But he said no more, and for some reason (self-preservation? me not doing the seemingly impossible and running him off by launching myself over the bar and ripping his clothes off?), I decided to let it go.

"Travel mugs are hidden behind the coffee mugs," I told him.

He saw to that, came around and did the hair-pulling, loads-of-tongue kiss thing.

He lifted away to say, "The schedule of my day is never guaranteed, but I'll keep communicating. I'd like to cook for you tonight, don't know if I can do that. But you'll know in time to make your own plans."

"Okay."

"That set of keys on the hooks by the door your extras?"

"Yes."

He lifted his brows.

"Take them, honey."

He smiled on the outside.

I smiled on the inside.

He kissed me again.

And he was gone.

ON OUR WAY to Clarice Davis's offices, I was troubled by two things.

One, the amount of effort Luna had put into making this meeting, which included telling Tito we needed to take a few hours off and her talking the weekend shift into coming in to cover us.

Two, that Cap and I had a sixty-one-hour first date, a lot had happened, a lot had been shared, and I hadn't told him about Clarice Davis's visit.

Honestly, it hadn't really crossed my mind with all that was going on.

Still.

I'd have to rectify that, even if I sensed Cap wouldn't be a big fan of whatever this was. But it was clear we were both riding the same wavelength of what was going on between us, and I couldn't inject subterfuge into that, not ever, really, but definitely not at our beginning.

Clarice's offices were in a high rise two blocks down from NI&S's Phoenix branch. Parking required validation, so Luna was sure to bring the ticket with her, and when we hit her offices on the tenth floor, even after seeing her Louboutins and Birkin bag, I was taken aback by how swish they were.

The credenza behind the reception desk was all but covered in a massive bouquet of fresh flowers, which had to have cost at least three hundred bucks, just sayin'.

Once we announced ourselves, we were immediately led back to a corner office. I was filled with trepidation, but Luna was strutting through it like she paid the lease.

"Aren't you nervous?" I whispered to her.

"Why?" she asked. "It's just a chat."

Right, right.

That was all it was.

Just a chat.

We hit her office, and it was all modern glass and chrome, and lots of pristine white (including the fluffy rug that looked like fur under her desk), with Clarice sitting behind the desk, this time wearing a figure-skimming, fire-engine red dress with a notch at the collar and cap sleeves.

On her feet were patent black pumps, no red sole, but I still knew they were designer.

Seriously, the woman was top-to-toe class, but I was thrown by the fact she'd scored a primo corner office like this one. She had to be a really good lawyer or come from money to have this setup, and she didn't look much older than us.

"Glad you came," she said, standing but not approaching us. "Coffee? Sparkling water? Soda?" she offered.

"I'm good," Luna told her.

"Me too," I said.

She nodded to the receptionist, who took off without a word, then she gestured to the white leather chairs in front of her desk.

We sat.

She sat.

Then, with no further ado, she launched right in.

"What we can offer is resources. For instance, if you need extra stun guns, Tasers, or surveillance equipment, like telephoto lens cameras, you'll text a number I give you, and within an hour, that will be sourced for you. You need a pickup, you text, and depending where you are, within ten to thirty minutes, that will be provided to you. You need research, data, intel, you share what you need, within twenty-four hours you'll have it, unless the dive has to be deep, but you'll have something to work with as fast as we can get it to you. You need additional transport, like a van, that will be provided for you. You need cash for bribes or to loosen tongues, you submit a request, and if it's approved, we'll get that to you too. The deal is, first, no guns. Second, you don't get your asses in a sling. If you're in the field, you're on your own. So my recommendation is you do not go out alone, and my further recommendation is you recruit some new Angels."

I sat, stunned silent, as she nodded to me.

"Your code name is Kelly Garrett, even if you're a blonde." She tipped her head to Luna. "You're Jill Munroe. For short, you're Garrett and Munroe."

I turned my head toward Luna to see she was doing the same to me.

She looked excited.

I wondered what my wild vigilante hair got us into.

Clarice kept speaking.

"There will be times you have to come to this office. If you do, make sure you don't have a tail. If this becomes more, and it's necessary, we'll create a headquarters for you."

A headquarters?

Damn.

I raised my hand like I was in class.

Clarice looked at me.

"Um…we're just servers," I told her.

"Everybody is something until they're a badass," she returned. "You lugged a two-hundred and twenty-pound tight end to an empty warehouse, gained access and taught his nasty ass a lesson. As far as we can tell, you've got a finely honed sense of justice, you've got intuition, you've got skills in planning an operation, you fly under radar, because you're 'just a server,'"—her tone did the quotation marks for her—"but you get the job done."

After saying that, she slid a manila envelope our way.

Luna didn't hesitate to reach out and snatch it.

"I took a picture of your wall," Clarice said. "We might have some names to go with those descriptions of players you've been watching that you wrote on your Post-its. You see if we got it right. We've added some intel. Now, it's up to you."

Luna had opened the envelope and had her head bent to it, fingers sifting through its contents without pulling them out.

I looked back to Clarice when she kept speaking.

"You get enough, you get it to me. I'll feed it into the proper channels. This isn't about takedowns. It's about getting things to people who need them and can do something with them."

"Getting them what?" I asked.

"Evidence. A solid lead. We aren't supporting you in meting out vigilante justice. This is about real justice, the kind that happens in a court of law." She slid another manila envelope toward us, this one much smaller, but it had some bulk. "Another car. You don't need to be cruising the seedy sides of Phoenix in a Mercedes. Though, you meet with a real player, you take the Merc. They need to know you have resources. And you don't take any ID with you, ever. In the field, only refer to yourselves as Garrett and Munroe." Another envelope came over the desk, slightly bigger, much bulkier. "The phones you use for ops. They're burners. Untraceable. Leave your own at home. The cars have tracking, as do the phones. We'll keep an eye on you that way."

"Who's we?" Luna asked while again reaching for the envelopes.

"As far as you know, 'we' is me," Clarice answered.

That was all she said.

At least about that.

"Learn vigilance," she went on. "How to spot a tail. Learn to trust your gut. If you feel like someone is watching you, they are. If you feel in danger, you are, so you get the fuck out of wherever *you* are, shake the tail if you got one and get safe."

"Why are you doing this?" I inquired.

Clarice's gaze locked to mine. "Because that tight end should be facing ten years, his buddies with him. What they did to her after was just as bad as what they did *to* her. And Paul Nicholson had rented a house in Montana. Two more days and Elsie Fay would have been gone."

Holy Moses.

I didn't know that.

Goosebumps popped out all over my skin.

"And women are going missing," she finished.

They totally were.

Something started stealing up my spine.

"You're not just a server, Garrett," she said quietly to me. "You've got natural instinct and history that drives you to right wrongs. Use both."

So, she knew about me.

Not a surprise.

"You do know this is completely crazy," I remarked.

She sat back in her white leather executive chair. "I laid out the deal. It's up to you to take it, or otherwise."

"We're not detectives, and I know you know that," I reminded her. "But I've gathered a bunch of info already, and I have no idea what to do with it."

"That's where the reporting-to-me part comes in," she replied.

"It's not up to you to do something with it." She looked between the two of us. "I laid it out. The choice is yours. I'll know you're in if you take those cars or we get a text for something you require. This isn't about pressure. This is about getting the job done. If it isn't your thing"—she shrugged—"then have a good life."

That was her, *I'm done, you can go now.*

Luna read it too, which was why she popped out of her chair, clutching the envelopes.

"Thanks for the chat," she said.

"My pleasure," Clarice replied.

"If we get headquarters," Luna went on, "are we gonna get to sit in a line of plush chairs in front of a desk you're behind and talk to 'we' on a speaker?"

Clarice cracked her first smile. "We'll see."

Luna grabbed hold of my hand.

"But—" I started, though said no more because my crazy bestie tugged me out of the chair and toward the door.

"Later," she called to Clarice, and we were out.

I waited until after Luna got her parking ticket validated by the receptionist, and we were in the elevator before I turned to her and inquired, "Have you lost your mind?"

"We're gonna go look at those cars. Then we're gonna go talk to Divinity. Tonight," was her reply.

"You have. You've lost your mind."

"What will it hurt?"

Honestly?

I didn't have a response to that.

And I couldn't stop thinking about those women who were missing, and I hadn't been able to since I discovered how many there were.

"I'll get the two hundred from my bank. No, three. Just in case," she said.

"Luna—" I started as the doors to the elevator opened.

We walked out and she said, "Either the cops don't have leads, or they don't have enough motivation to dive into finding those women. It's not like we're putting ourselves in danger. We're gonna go talk to a sex worker. There's no danger in that."

"Maybe," I replied as she beeped the locks to her dark-blue Prius (hand-me-down from Louise, Dream drove the hand-me-down from Scott, Louise and Scott drove newer models of the same thing—there were different electric cars to choose from, but they were a Prius family, for the girls that meant buying used cars cheap from their folks (if Dream paid for hers, but I knew Luna did)).

We got in and she turned to me. "Do you wanna know what's going on and maybe find those women? Or at least find out what happened to them..." she hesitated, and I knew why when she finished, "so their families know?"

"Yes," I said quietly.

She turned to the wheel and said, "Then we're doing this."

I'd started it a year ago. Why I would stop now, when she was right, there was no danger following this lead, especially now that we had some primo resources to help, I didn't know.

"Wait," I said. "Cap's offices are two blocks from here. He hasn't texted me yet about our plans tonight. And anyway, if he can visit me at my place of work, I can do the same. And I wanna see if they've unwrapped the furniture. Since we're this close, and we have validated parking, might as well hoof it up there. Maybe you can meet Mace."

She turned back to me. "You wanna run this by him."

"Actually, I'm gonna wait until I have him liquored up to do that. But Liam might also be there, and Cap told me that Jacob is as into Alexis as Alexis is into Jacob. And he's a man, so he'd know. He also told me Jacob would stop messing around the second he saw Alexis with another guy. So I wanna see if Liam might be into some pretend-boyfriend action to light a fire under Jacob."

Luna knew all about Alexis's crush on Jacob, and she was right there with me, hoping those two would get together.

"You are oh-so-totally made for this shit," she said.

I kinda was.

I grinned.

She grinned back.

We got out of the car and hoofed it the two blocks to Cap's building.

It being September, the heat was still on the Valley. It didn't really let loose its hold until October (if we were lucky). Though, it got milder as the days got shorter, and we'd had a nice, mild weekend.

The heat was back that day, so Luna and I hadn't jogged or anything, but we were still more than a little dewy by the time we hit the door to Cap's offices.

I was considering finding a hall bathroom to get to some paper towels to dab my forehead.

But Luna was pushing in the door so I had no choice but to follow her.

We entered to a hub of activity.

Four men in gray chinos and matching shirts were moving furniture around. There was a massive pile of plastic and thin Styrofoam wrap creating a mini-mountain in the corner. There was a stack of paintings leaning against a wall. And on a plinth in the corner, there was a gorgeous bronze statue of a rising phoenix.

More importantly, there was an extortionately good-looking Native American man sorting through boxes of a bunch of stuff that had lots of wires. Another extortionately good-looking, tall, dark-haired man was going through another box of what looked like surveillance cameras.

And a further extortionately good-looking, tall, dark-haired man was arguing with a very pretty, middle-aged-and-working it Black woman with a kickass, massive Afro. She was wearing Christian Louboutin pumps that were black at the front and bled into red at the back, and a red, wraparound, long-sleeved dress, which was so chic, she made Clarice look like she was playing dress up.

The last two were clearly facing off dead center of the space.

"Having the holding cell offsite is ridiculous," she was saying.

"It's done. Mace and I agreed this building is too populated for that. We don't need to be bringing that element in here. It's not safe," the dark-haired man returned.

"What's done can be undone," she retorted.

"If I wanted it to be, yeah, which I don't, so it won't," the man shot back.

"You need help?" the man with the cameras asked Luna and me.

Everyone turned their eyes to us.

Having their direct attention, it had never done it before, so I didn't know how I knew, but I still knew my heart had started palpitating.

I'd put all the men in the same age range as Mace, which, from what I could tell from the history Cap had shared, was around forty-five, or hedging toward too old for Luna and me.

I instantly changed my mind on the age range I'd accept for a dude.

But at a sweeping glance, only one of the guys didn't have a wedding ring (the one sorting through the cameras).

And the other two didn't just have wedding rings. They had wide, gleaming gold bands that screamed *I'm taken!* to all the women who had uteruses that instinctively urged them to throw themselves at these guys' feet and beg them to make mini-future-hot-guy babies.

Even me, and I had my own super-hot dude.

Luna elbowed me.

I snapped out of the miasma created by breathing in so much drifting testosterone and witnessing such an extremity of good looks.

"We're looking for Cap Jackson."

The Black woman turned to face me fully.

A door to the back offices opened and Mace strode out, increasing the hot-guy quotient significantly.

Totally what was happening to my heart was palpitations.

"Hey, Rachel," he greeted.

"Raye," I corrected. "Hey back, Mace."

I felt something pummeling me coming from the Black lady, it wasn't good, or bad, or indifferent. I didn't know what it was, and I also couldn't give it my attention since I had Mace's.

"Cap's not here. You good?" he asked.

"Yeah, just in the neighborhood and—"

The Black woman was all of a sudden right next to Mace.

"You're Rachel?" she asked.

"Yeah, hi," I answered.

"I'm Shirleen."

As this info hit me, unexpectedly confronted with Cap's adored mom, I reeled a little bit, afraid I would faint.

"What on...?" Luna mumbled, grabbing onto my arm so I wouldn't go down.

I'd done a couple meet-the-moms in my life. I'd fared well.

But this was *Shirleen.*

"This is...Cap's mom," I croaked.

"Holy..." She didn't finish that either, her head snapping Shirleen's way.

We both stared, mute, at Shirleen.

Oh God.

I had to get it together.

ASAFP.

But...

I'd just met Cap's beloved mom!

I kept croaking to introduce, "Luna...Mace, Cap's mom, hot guys. Hot guys, Cap's mom, Mace, this is my best friend, Luna."

"Nice to meet you, Luna," Mace said.

The other men approached, and it was too much. I had to fight the urge to wave at them to stay back. They got better the closer they made it to us, so by the time they stopped and huddled around, I experienced my very first hot flash.

"I think I've died and gone to heaven," Luna breathed.

"These are my partners, Lee Nightingale and Vance Crowe." Mace ignored Luna and indicated the man who was arguing with

Shirleen and the Native American man. "And one of our crew, Eric Turner."

I didn't hear the last part because...

The revered Jules's husband and Cap's big brother/mentor was standing right there.

Right in front of me.

I reeled again.

Luna clamped onto me.

Vance grinned a shit-eating grin.

"Of course he's married," Luna grumbled.

His grin got bigger.

"*Lord*," she breathed, now reeling with me.

The door behind us opened, we whirled and watched Cap and Liam walk in.

That was when Luna lost it.

"Oh my God! I don't know how much more I can take!" she exclaimed. "And I've already seen these two!"

A big smile hit Cap's face as he greeted me. "Hey, baby. What are you doing here?"

I vaguely noted he ignored Luna as well, so I suspected this reaction happened a lot.

But I couldn't think on that.

My hand, arm straight, finger pointed, indicated Shirleen. "I just met your mom."

"Cool," he said, watching me closely.

I adjusted my hand to Vance. "And Vance."

"I see that," he said slowly.

I dropped my arm, tardily remembering pointing was rude.

"I'm also fighting hyperventilating because I'm dewy and I don't have a meet-the-mom-and-big-brother-slash-mentor outfit on," I shared.

His beard around his lips twitched, he approached, took over holding me up from Luna by sliding his arm around my waist, then he bent and touched his mouth to mine.

Okay, I felt a wee bit better now.

But just a wee bit.

When he lifted away, he reminded me, "I attended Dream's intervention yesterday, Raye."

"Yeah. I know. But that ended up being more like a party, with dogs wrestling in the background and an ugly confrontation mixed in. This is *terrifying*."

"I had something on. I didn't have time to text to tell you they were in town. I found out this morning they'd flown in last night. Shirleen wanted to surprise me."

I nodded and couldn't stop doing it.

"I got it, you can stop nodding now," he said, beard again twitching.

I stopped nodding.

"She's not usually like this," Luna informed the assemblage. "She's just seriously into Cap."

I looked to Shirleen. "It really is a pleasure to meet you," I assured her. "I was just caught unprepared."

"I see that," she said to me, then to Cap, "Should we tell her Jules is in town too?"

Oh my God!

The idolized-first-female-to-show-him-love Jules?

Cap felt my reaction, so he answered, "Probably not, but too late now."

"We need to do a dinner," I hurried to announce. "My place isn't big enough, or I'd cook. But someplace nice." My mind blanked, so I called, "Luna?"

"Rustler's Rooste?" she suggested.

I shook my head. "Too touristy."

"The Tee Pee?"

"I'm not sure they have a big enough table to fit us all."

Though, maybe they could pull some tables together on their patio.

"Steak 44?"

"That might be too loud, unless they seat us at a back table."

"Oregano's?"

Oregano's famous pizza cookie came instantly to mind, I snapped my fingers and cried, "That's it!" I took them all in and asked, "When can you all do dinner?"

"We have a team meeting tonight, Raye," Lee said.

"Right, so, I have some time to, you know, plan," I replied.

Would the outfit I bought but didn't wear for our first date be too dressy for Oregano's?

Yes.

I needed to shop.

"Aren't you supposed to be at work?" Cap took me out of my thoughts of shopping.

"Luna and I had an appointment downtown," I told him, and seeing as he wasn't liquored up, and his family was surrounding us, I wasn't getting into Clarice Davis at the mo'. "Since we were close, we decided to pop by."

Luna came to my rescue. "We should probably get back now, though."

I turned to Shirleen. "I honestly am not like this normally. I was caught off guard. Next time I see you, I'll have it together."

"Child, I've been around these boys for a while. I know the wallop they pack," she replied. "And if you didn't give a crap, or pretended you didn't, that wouldn't be good. But you give a crap. That says all sorts of good things to Shirleen."

Whoa.

She could pull off referring to herself in third person.

I knew no one who could do that.

So it wasn't just her Afro and mom skills that were awesome.

I smiled at her.

She smiled back.

Okay, it seemed I hadn't put her off.

Shoo!

"I'll walk you guys down," Cap said, turning me toward the door.

"Wait!" I cried and looked to Liam. "Are you seeing anybody?"

"No," he said slowly.

"Would you be into pretending to be someone's boyfriend so the guy she likes will get his head out of his ass and make a move on her?" I asked.

"Raye," Cap warned low, trying to pull me to the door.

I was fighting it so I could get this done before we left, but Cap was strong, so I was not winning.

"She's a ballerina with the Arizona Ballet and super sweet," I cajoled as Cap all but dragged me to the door.

"Fucking hell, it's happening again," Lee muttered.

"I told you," Mace said.

"Cap know the players?" Liam asked me.

I nodded.

"I'll talk to Cap about it," Liam said just as Cap got me out the door.

"Thanks, Liam! 'Bye, Hot Bunch! 'Bye, Shirleen! So nice to meet you!" I shouted, as the door closed behind us.

"Yeah, 'bye Hot Bunch and Shirleen," Luna added on her own shout.

"Totally get that Hot Bunch thing now," I said to Luna.

"*Totally*," she said back.

"You're not involving Liam in Jacob and Alexis's shit," Cap said as we made our way to the elevators.

"Why not?" I asked.

He didn't answer, he inquired shrewdly, "Is that why you showed at the offices?"

"It was secondary to saying hey to you."

He hit the button on the elevator.

"I think it's an awesome idea," Luna chimed in.

"You would," Cap muttered.

I turned to Luna. "I don't know about Oregano's. Maybe I can throw a shindig in the courtyard."

"You can make your pudding," she replied.

Perfect!

That'd win them all over.

It won *everybody* over.

The elevator doors opened and we entered with Cap saying, "How about we deal with your dad first, and you can deal with my family after?"

"Your dad?" Luna asked.

"I forgot to tell you," I said. "He hits town Wednesday. We're having dinner Wednesday night at Lon's. Cap is coming." After I said this, I thought about it and hoped she wouldn't feel slighted since she was my ride or die. I didn't want her to feel left out, like I was replacing her with Cap. So I said, "You wanna come too?"

"You bet your bippy," she replied.

One hundred percent my ride or die.

"Do you two ever kick back and read a book?" Cap asked.

"Yeah, loads," Luna answered. "There are twenty-four hours in a day, you know. Plenty of time to shove it all in."

"I try to read," I told him. "But I usually get side—oh snap!'" I exclaimed when I remembered Patches. "I forgot to go over to Jenn's and get Patches." I looked to Luna again. "We need to make another pitstop."

"You got it, sister."

"Jesus," Cap said under his breath.

"I like your mom's Afro," I told him.

He stared down at me and he did this a long time.

When the elevator doors opened, he murmured, "Christ, you're something."

"Is that good?"

"Absolutely."

I smiled.

Cap walked us to Luna's car.

TWELVE

SIDE EYE

"Okay, this is all kinds of skeevy. How do men do this?" Luna asked, a shudder in her voice I felt in my crawling flesh at what we were currently occupied in doing.

"Because there are a ton of men who are skeevy," I answered.

We were in a nondescript, silver Honda Accord. It had a few years on it, but not many miles. The interior was neat as a pin. And we'd found a note in the glove box that said there were stun guns and Tasers under the two front seats.

We'd checked this out, and it was true, and the stun gun was a much better model than mine.

By the by, the Mercedes was *pimp*.

A black, fully loaded S-Class with tan leather interior.

The. Total. *Shit*.

I was coming to realize the "we" Clarice had noted meant there was an actual "we" behind all Clarice was offering.

She was an attorney, but this was seriously bankrolled. No rinky-dink, bargain-basement stun guns, no A-Class Mercedes. Even our flip-style burner phones had color screens. I knew nothing about burner phones, but I suspected that was a cut above.

Cap had eventually texted me and told me he was taking Shirleen out to dinner that night after their team meeting, so we had time to look for Divinity.

Therefore, that was what we were doing.

I wasn't sure if I wasn't invited to this dinner because Shirleen wanted to have a few words with her son in private after she met the lunatic he was dating, or if he was protecting me from further emotionally extreme hits coming at me so soon after the weekend we shared, and before I was going to see my father.

I'd ask him when he got to my place that night.

Luna and I had spent some time at a table in the back of SC after our shift ended going through the envelope Clarice had given us.

In it was an info sheet, which included the number Clarice had mentioned to text if we needed anything, the numbers to our two burners, plus a secure email address we were to use to send anything we discovered.

Also, a bunch of 8x10 pictures of men clipped to reports that included their names, ages, addresses, places of business, and no other way to put it, rap sheets.

Because they all had them.

Bar none.

Just by memory, I could match some of them to the descriptions I'd jotted down of guys I'd been watching that I put on my wall. I'd never taken pictures because I was too much of a scaredy-cat. I didn't want to get caught doing it. Before we got their dossiers, one thing I knew for certain about all of them, none of them were men who wanted a strange woman in a bright-yellow Juke snapping photos of them.

And *he* was among them.

The one that gave me the super-bad feeling was named Cyrus Gibbons.

He'd done two stints in prison, one for pimping the women (not of their volition) that worked at his strip club in Nebraska. One for extorting money and sex from some women who worked at the same kind of establishment in Denver, though he didn't own that club.

This wasn't good, and it made me suspect him all the more of being involved somehow, because the dude obviously had some screw loose and thus carried zero respect for the fairer sex. He used them however he wanted in order to get whatever he wanted from them. The end.

But the Denver angle gave me an even worse feeling.

The US of A was a pretty vast space with lots of cities in it.

This guy having been caught committing a heinous crime in Cap's hometown was a coincidence I didn't like.

Luna and I discussed this, and since the US of A *was* indeed a vast space with hundreds of millions of people living in it, it was highly likely it actually was a coincidence. Not to mention, Gibbons had gone down for that Denver stuff thirteen years ago, when Cap was seventeen. So he probably didn't know anything about it. Further, we weren't going out to try to find Cyrus Gibbons.

Therefore, we decided to go forth with our plan to talk to Divinity, and then maybe, when I told Cap about all this, I'd mention it to him.

And that was what we were doing.

Cruising Roosevelt, looking for Divinity.

And it felt skeevy.

We'd stopped a couple of times to talk to a few ladies of the evening, but we learned really quickly not to show her mugshot to them. They were friendly enough on approach, but they got hinky when you showed a mugshot.

The last one we asked (*sans* mugshot) said she didn't know her.

I didn't believe her, but we didn't push.

I was driving, Luna on the lookout for Divinity and a tail, and by this time, we'd done a back and forth on Roosevelt at least five times.

No Divinity.

She was pretty, maybe she was popular, which made her busy.

"There's another one," Luna said. "I think we should stop and see if she knows our girl."

"Maybe we should give up and try again some other time."

"Just pull in here," she ordered.

Man, Luna was into this shit.

On a sigh, I pulled into a 7-Eleven and parked.

"Let's walk back to her," she said, and didn't wait for my response.

She got out.

Considering the 'hood we were in, with my new-and-improved stun gun in my crossbody, I got out too.

We hoofed it to where the woman Luna had seen was standing, leaning against a dark building that looked like whatever it used to be, it had stopped being that about half a century ago. Not only was the interior completely dark, the cages over the windows seemed rusted, and there was a thick crust of litter that had been blown up against the building on the sidewalk that sun, wind and monsoons had transformed into a permanent addition.

It would take a sledgehammer to get that stuff loose.

As we approached, I had the same thought I'd had about the others we'd chatted to: that I hoped this was her choice of occupation, and no man or drug was forcing her into this.

When we got closer, we saw she was Latina, petite (or would be, if she wasn't in sky-high platform sandals), very pretty and carried some extra weight, which her skin-tight cami and mini-skirt showed off to full advantage.

"Hey," Luna greeted.

She looked us over. "What you two *gringas* doin' out here?"

"We're looking for Divinity," I said. "Have you seen her?"

My heart sped up when she replied, "She got herself a client. She's at the hotel," and she jerked her chin to indicate a seedy motel across the street.

"She been with him long?" Luna asked.

"What's it to you?" she shot back.

"We wanna talk to her, and I'd like to know how long we'll be waiting," Luna returned.

"Guy didn't strike me as an all-nighter type," she said. "Probably hand job only, so she'll be out soon."

"I'm Kelly," I told her, feeling kinda like a dick I didn't give her my real name.

This might be the only gig we did.

On the other hand, this might be the start of something. And she seemed friendly enough.

But when people did stuff like this, they needed to establish relationships, people in the know, people who saw things.

People who would talk.

"Good for you," she replied.

Okay, maybe not that friendly.

"And this is Jill," I kept at her since this was the first lady we'd talked to who was semi-kinda-talking back.

"Yo," Luna said.

The woman made no reply.

"Women are going missing," I stated.

Her gaze had shifted to look between us to check out the cars passing, but at what I said, her head snapped my way.

Electricity sizzled over my skin at her response.

Here we go.

"You missin' someone in your family?" she asked.

"No," I told her honestly. "I just noticed a lot of ladies of the evening are being reported gone, and it keeps happening, so it's obvious no one is doing much about it."

She pushed to standing from her lean on the wall, a white smile bursting through the dark. "Ladies of the evening. I like that. Gonna put that on my business cards."

Tentatively, I smiled back.

"Do you know any of the women who are missing?" Luna asked.

"No. But there's buzz, *gringa*. We're all a little jumpy."

"What buzz?" Luna asked.

"Wait," I said and then inquired, "What's your name? I mean, if you wanna give it to us."

"Jinx."

Well then, she didn't give her real name either.

"Hi, Jinx." I stuck out my hand. "Nice to meet you."

She looked at my hand, me, Luna, me again, then that flash of white came back to her mouth, and she took my hand.

"You're crazy," she said.

"I know," I replied. After squeezing it, I let her hand go. "Have other family members been out looking?"

"Yeah. There's a woman named Betsy who's been around. Her daughter was one of them. But she's been gone for a while, so Betsy has too. Don't know if she gave up. Do know her girl didn't show up."

"What's her daughter's name?"

"Don't know her name, but the name she used on the street was Bambi. And she was a real Bambi. All big eyes and stupid."

"So you knew Bambi?" I pressed.

She shrugged. "Met her once. Knew she wasn't gonna last long."

"How?" I kept at her.

"Like I said. She was stupid."

"How was she stupid?"

"You bitches are blockin' the view of my clients."

We both stepped to the side.

She watched us do this, and how fast we did it, and she remarked, "Shee-it, you really after this, hunh?"

"We care," I replied. "So, yeah. We're really after it."

"A'right," she mumbled. "So she was young and dumb. Wandered onto patches that weren't hers to work. Got in cars instead of meeting at a hotel. Shit like that."

"And the buzz?" Luna went back to our earlier subject.

"The dumb ones are goin' missin'," she answered.

"Like, the ones who would get into cars?" I queried.

"Like those, yeah."

"Only those?" Luna pressed.

"Bitch, I don't know. Other dumb shit you can do is talkin' to two white women who got a lot of questions."

I took that as the sign she was done answering them.

Luna did too. So, from her crossbody, she fished out one of the pieces of paper she'd put our burner phone numbers on before we headed out (see? totally into this shit). Once she had that, she fished out one of the hundred dollar bills she got from the bank that afternoon.

It wasn't the white of her teeth that we saw when she offered those to Jinx. It was the white of her eyes.

"Thanks, Jinx," Luna said as Jinx took what was offered. "Appreciate you talking to us."

Luna jutted up her chin and the bill and paper disappeared—poof!—like she knew sleight of hand.

I had a feeling, in her way, she did.

I didn't explore that feeling.

We began to move off.

"Bitches," she called.

We stopped and turned back to her.

"Watch your asses. Whatever this shit is, it can be nothin' but bad. Hear me?"

We nodded and I called back, "Hear you. Stay safe out here." Then, as an afterthought that was probably plain loco, I said, "You need anything, call one of those numbers."

"What would I need from you?" she asked, not ugly, curious.

"I don't know," I replied. "But we all have the same equipment, so we're in this together."

"You're totally crazy," she declared.

"We hear that a lot," Luna told her.

"I bet."

"Again, be safe," I bid and pulled Luna toward the car.

We got in and I drove back onto Roosevelt. Since I was too chicken to try left turns across busy dual carriageways with suicide lanes (it was all in the name, just sayin'), I turned right.

It took a second before Luna noted, "They make it easy for them. Get right in their cars."

"Yep," I replied.

"You think the strippers do that too?"

"No idea."

I flipped a uey as soon as I could, and we swung into the parking lot of the hotel Jinx indicated.

I backed into a spot, turned off the car, and we waited.

"Women go to strip clubs all the time now," Luna said as we waited. "Maybe we should hit The Slide and have a look around."

At SC, while we were going through our envelope, I'd given her the entire lowdown.

And I was thinking the same thing.

However...

"Kinda too close to Cyrus Gibbons for my liking," I told her. "And from what I can tell, he's there a lot."

"He doesn't own the joint, though. 'Occupation unknown' is what it said on his info sheet."

"He didn't own the joint where he was doing shitty business in Denver either."

"True."

We got silent and watched.

Luna broke the silence again.

"Just to make it official, I approve of Cap. He's da bomb. It was cool how open he was with stories about his family, not to mention he seems bulletproof from our posse's crazy, which isn't surprising considering the crazy he comes from. And obviously, I dig how he doesn't hide how into you he is."

"Yeah," I murmured.

We exchanged a happy glance.

Then I asked, "Did you notice how yesterday, Dream turned when you piped up?"

"Totes."

"I know you guys don't always get along, but wasn't that weird?"

"Totes," she repeated.

"You wanna talk about it?" I offered.

She shook her head. "It's not my damage. It's hers. She's got enough to worry about in the now. When it's time, I'll call you in to have my back."

I nodded my head. "Deal."

I ended this one word on a small scream as I jumped when someone knocked hard on my window.

My heart racing, I looked to see a man leaning down and peering in. He was white, unattractive, and not surprisingly, skeevy.

"Can I help you?" I yelled through the window, my hand going to the ignition switch.

"You women gonna rent a room?" he yelled back.

"We're waiting on somebody." I was still yelling even if he was right there, just a window between us.

"Wait somewhere else. Parking is for customers only. Get the fuck out of here. Now."

"Go," Luna murmured.

I hit the ignition and called, "Thanks for your courtesy."

He scowled and that made him downright ugly.

He also rapped on my window hard again, entirely unnecessarily.

"Get out of here before I flip this asshole off," Luna warned.

I pulled out because I didn't need Luna escalating anything. She tended to be pretty mellow, though she didn't take a lot of shit. Still, even as long as I'd known her, you could always learn new things, and I was right then learning she didn't have a lot of patience for impolite, skeevy guys.

"What an asshole," she pointed out the obvious as I pulled out of the parking lot under his heaver glower. "He could have said please."

"His momma didn't raise him right, that's for sure."

We were on Roosevelt when Luna gave out a little scream this time, doing it as one of the burners dinged with a text.

"Holy shit," she whispered.

"What is it?"

"I don't know. I'm scared of it."

"Read it!" I demanded.

She grabbed the phone off the console, flipped it open and read it.

Then she started laughing.

"What?" I asked.

"It's from Jinx. It says, 'Stupid bitches also park in the fucking lot.' And then there's about twelve rolling on the floor laughing emojis, the same of rolling eye emojis, but about twenty side eye emojis."

That was when I started laughing.

"I think I like her," Luna decreed.

"Me too," I said. "Gotta dig a woman who can pull off a good side eye, even in emoji form."

"Totes," she replied. "We done for tonight?"

It was nearing nine. Cap said he'd probably be in around ten, but we had to drop off the car, get ours back, and then get home.

"I am."

"You got a hot guy staying over, so I'll email this intel to Clarice."

"Gotcha." And thinking on it, I advised, "Ask her if she can look into this Betsy and Bambi. If Betsy's been asking around, maybe she knows something, and we should talk to her."

"Roger that."

We drove in silence for a while.

Luna broke it.

"We'd be safer at The Slide and look more like a girl party if we took Jessie and Harlow with us," she noted.

We would.

"Let's sleep on it," I suggested.

"Word," she agreed.

More driving in silence.

Luna broke it again.

This time, she was talking quietly.

"I get why you do this now. It's kind of the shit."

"There's normally more action," I pointed out.

"That'd be more the shit."

She wasn't wrong.

We drove on.

I woke when Patches' twelve pounds turned into fifty with that wicked cat magic they called up when they jumped off you.

Which meant I woke with a start and a grunt to see Cap, one hand on the sofa back, one hand in the seat beside me, leaning over me.

"Hey," I greeted sleepily.

"Hey," he replied.

God, he was gorgeous.

Abruptly I was up in his arms, he sat down, I was in his lap, then I was flat on my back on the couch with him on top of me.

Smooth.

And...

Nice.

And good to know my couch *did* fit us both. Or at least it did when one of us was on top of the other.

I filed that away for future use.

"How was your dinner?" I asked.

"Good."

"Does your mom think I'm a lunatic?"

His lips tipped up. "I'm not sure you were listening close enough when I told you some of the stories about the Rock Chicks."

"They weren't dating her son," I pointed out.

"She thought it was cute you were nervous. She thought it was sweet you wanted to plan a dinner. And she's down to hold off with getting to know you better until after we meet up with your dad."

I rubbed my lips together before I asked, "Did you tell her about... all of that?"

"I told her you had a rough history and were estranged from your father because of it. I told her he didn't give you a lot of warning before coming into town, so you're on your back foot with that. And she knows your part in the Elsie Fay thing because Mace noted it in the file when he wrote the final report."

"And she thinks about that...?" I prompted.

He grinned. "Babe, you really need to read the Rock Chick books. And my mom is a Rock Chick."

"There's more than one book?"

"They all have them."

Whoa.

I should have probably done that when I got home rather than claiming Patches for cuddle time then passing out.

As if he read my mind, Cap remarked, "Take it that's Patches."

Patches was white with black and brown splotches on his back, his full tail was the two latter colors, and he had one black ear with that color framing his eye, one brown ear, an otherwise white face, pink nose and tawny eyes about the color of Cap's mom's.

"That's Patches," I confirmed.

"He's cute," he muttered, his gaze aimed to the floor.

I twisted my neck to see Patches sitting close to the couch, tail sweeping my rug, staring at us with curious eyes, maybe because he hadn't met Cap yet and he was trying to get a bead, maybe because cats were just curious.

I stopped looking at Patches.

He was cute and all, but Cap was cuter.

"So Shirleen didn't want a just-you-and-her dinner to warn you you'd be disowned if you kept dating me?"

His attention cut back to me, and when I got it, I saw he appeared amused.

His tone held the same when he asked, "Why the fuck would she do that?"

"I nearly passed out in your offices today due to hot guy overload mixed with unexpectedly meeting people who are important to you."

"I told you she thought it was cute." He touched his lips to mine then said, "Stop worrying. She likes you. It was me who wanted dinner alone with my mom. I didn't want more pressure on you, but also, I haven't seen her in six months, and we're close."

"Oh," I mumbled.

"Yeah." He smiled. "And don't worry about doing a big dinner. Stella says everyone can come over to her and Mace's house. She rocks in the kitchen almost as much as she rocks a stage."

Did he say what I thought he said?

"Stella Gunn?" I asked to confirm.

"Yeah, Mace's wife."

"Stella Gunn, the award-winning, multi-platinum, kickass rock star?"

I felt Cap's body move on mine with his laughter. "Yeah. That Stella Gunn."

"I might pass out again," I told him.

His tone changed yet again when he murmured, "Wonder what I can do to keep you conscious."

I had some ideas.

I shivered as his hand slid up my side.

Yep, those were my ideas.

He angled his head and kissed me.

There was lots of tongue. There was groping. There was more tongue and more groping.

Then his lips, tongue, and the welcome new addition of his teeth, renewed their relationship with my neck, and the skin of my neck graciously accepted their offerings, though it was my nipples that experienced the bounty.

I'd wrapped my leg around his. He'd pressed his hard thigh tight to my girl bits, and they were more than happy to make its acquaintance.

I'd gotten my hands up his Henley to re-explore the hot, silky skin over steely muscle of his back...

And I was headed down to finally make my move into his cargos and introduce myself to his ass.

That was when he ended the kiss.

"Stop doing that," I snapped, narrowing my eyes at him.

He smiled, but noted, "You were dead to the world when I walked in."

"I'm wide awake now."

"You were up and showered by the time I got back from my run at six."

"I go to work at seven and I like to do things in the morning, not rush my getting ready, so I'm an early riser."

He brushed his lips against mine. "If you want me now, baby, you got me."

I considered this offer, and I realized something annoying.

He was correct.

The time wasn't right.

I didn't want him to do me on the couch.

I didn't know what I wanted.

I just knew now was not the time to get it.

"Guh," I grumbled in order to communicate my decision to him.

He brushed his lips against mine again.

Then he said, "Let's go to bed."

He knifed off me and pulled me from the couch.

We got down to the preparations of doing that, then we did it.

I was sauntering off to dreamland, Cap spooning me at the back, Patches having draped himself over our feet, and I was on that trip, eventually reaching my destination, not realizing I didn't mention anything to him about Clarice or Divinity or Jinx or Luna and my nightly activities.

Not a word.

THIRTEEN

HE TOOK HIS BAG

I 'd forgotten to change the music on my alarm, but that wasn't what woke me the next morning.

My hip was shaken, not rough, not gentle, but it got my attention and pulled me from sleep.

Added to that was Cap demanding, "Raye, get up."

I opened my eyes and turned to my back, beginning to smile.

My smile died on my face when he lifted his hand, his fore- and middle fingers holding a business card.

"What the fuck? You know Clarice?"

His voice was vibrating deeply and his handsome face was hard with anger. I'd never seen that look on him, heard that tone, and both scared me.

Not yet quite awake and facing an alarming unknown first thing, I asked, "What?"

"Clarice Davis. You know her?"

I looked to the business card, pushing up to a hand in bed. "Where'd you find that?"

I thought I'd tucked all that away in my TV/stationery/odds-and-ends cabinet.

Was he snooping?

"Who gives a fuck?" he clipped, then ordered harshly, "Answer me."

My attention shifted back to him, some of the sleep left me (though, it was important to note, not all), and as I was wont to do when I thought someone was being unreasonable, I got unreasonable back.

Or, another way to put it, *ticked.*

"Can I get up and brush my teeth before you interrogate me?" I snapped.

His answer was to scowl at me then turn and prowl from the room.

"What on earth?" I mumbled irritably and threw the covers aside.

I hit the bathroom and did my business.

I did this trying to get my head together.

It sounded like he knew Clarice.

He'd been in town six months, but he was a PI. Maybe he'd had run-ins with her, considering her occupation, and his.

Though, it seemed he didn't like her much.

I also was realizing I should have found the time to share with him about her.

Even so, him shaking me awake before my alarm even went off to get in my shit about it wasn't cool.

Finished in the bathroom, I hit the kitchen and ignored Cap standing in it with his hands on his cargo-clad hips (today, black, with a navy blue short-sleeved thermal) and went direct to the coffeepot where, fortunately, there was already coffee brewed.

Because I was confused, anxious, and annoyed—a volatile combination with anyone, definitely with me—I performed my version of getting up in his shit by making him wait even longer.

I opened the fridge, grabbed the creamer and made myself a mug before I turned to him and took a sip.

Only then did I repeat, "Where did you find that?"

"Again, who gives a fuck?" The card was still in his fingers, and he lifted it before he went on, "Tell me why you've got this."

I did *not* like his bossy tone.

Therefore, unwisely, I shot back, "Tell me why it's your business."

He flicked the business card so it slid across my bar.

He then proceeded to rock my world when he said, "Clarice was a kid who hung at the same shelter I did when I was a runaway."

Uh...

What?

Holy *shit*.

Now *that* couldn't be just a coincidence.

I stared.

"She's now a viciously successful defense attorney," he went on. "So again, what the fuck?"

"I—" I began.

"Raye..."—he learned forward and barked...actually *barked...at me!*—"*talk!*"

Oh no he did not.

"Do not speak to me like that," I fired back.

"Then use your mouth and explain that shit to me."

"Tell me where you got that card first," I demanded.

"It was sticking out of the cushion of your armchair."

Oh.

Well then.

Guess I wasn't very thorough in tucking all of that away.

"Raye," he said warningly.

"I don't actually *know* her," I told him. "She was in my apartment last week when I got home one night."

"In it, like, you didn't let her in?"

"In it like *you* were in it. Somehow, she broke in."

"When?"

"What?"

"When did this happen? Before Elsie Fay or after?"

I shook my head in confusion as to why that was relevant but answered, "After."

His hard face, if it was possible, got harder. "So you knew me by then, and you spent the entire weekend with me, and someone broke into your house, and you didn't tell me?"

Uh-oh.

I realized then why it was relevant.

"I didn't get around to it," I said, and even I thought that sounded lame.

Cap agreed it was lame.

I knew that when he replied sarcastically, "You didn't get around to telling me someone you didn't know accessed your apartment."

I wasn't fond of his sarcasm.

"A lot was going on, Cap," I reminded him.

"That's kinda fucking important, Rachel," he returned.

"I meant to tell you."

"When?"

"I don't know. Today?" I asked like he could confirm.

"Today is about however-many-days since she was here too goddamned many before you shared that shit with me," he bit out.

"I'm seeing that now," I retorted sharply.

"You should have told me the minute it happened."

A lot had been going on and at that moment I was freaked and angry, I couldn't put it together where he and I were at that time, but if memory served, we weren't a thing yet.

"We weren't a thing," I said.

"We weren't a thing," he whispered so sinisterly, it felt like the words slithered over my skin, and it didn't feel great.

I powered through that and affirmed, "We weren't a thing."

"We were a thing the minute you looked up at me from Paul Nicholson's floor."

This was kinda true.

Kinda not.

I was going with not at that moment.

"I didn't even know if you were a bad guy then," I sniped.

"Jesus Christ," he bit off.

"You need to calm down, Cap," I warned.

He didn't calm down.

He ordered, "Why was she here?"

"I'm not sure you're in the mood to listen to that at this juncture."

"I'm not sure you have a choice in that."

Was he serious?

"I'm not sure you get to tell me what my choices are," I replied heatedly.

"You get what I do for a living?"

"Yes," I snapped.

"And you get you're a server in a funky coffee bar?"

Oh my God!

Now I was whispering. "Tell me you didn't just say that."

"I'm angry because I'm worried about you."

That would be nice, if I wasn't so pissed.

"And I'm an adult, and I'd like my boyfriend to treat me like that, not a child."

"So I'm your boyfriend?"

Oh snap.

"I—"

"I am, Rachel," he confirmed, and I didn't get to praise hallelujah at that, not only due to my mood but because he kept talking. "Which makes you my woman. You were flat-out wrong in what you said to Dream. People can belong to each other. That's what relationships are. Making that commitment to look after something you hold that means something to you. And I can't look after you unless you *communicate with me.*"

I was close to yelling when I returned, "I'm a big girl. I don't need you to look after me, Cap! I know because I've been doing it for a really long time. I also don't belong to you or anybody, and I never *fucking will.*"

His demeanor changed in a way that made my stomach twist and that sinister whisper was back when he said, "Right."

And then, before I could get another word in, he shouldered past me, walked into the living room, grabbed the strap of a big leather bag that was in my armchair, and he shouldered that too.

Without another word, or even a glance in my direction, he was out the door.

"What just happened?" I stared at the door, my stomach still in a knot and now my lungs felt like they were on fire.

Patches ambled in and said, "Meow."

That wasn't an answer to my question.

That was "I want breakfast."

Meditation music floated down the hall from my bedroom.

"Shit," I whispered.

Then I got Jenn's cat his breakfast.

I POWERED through the employee entrance of The Surf Club and went right to my locker to store my bag.

I was in a rush because I saw Luna's Prius in the parking lot and I needed a Best Friend Confab like nobody's business.

I still wasn't breathing right.

This was not helped when I opened my locker and saw it stuffed full with a bunch of same-sized but different-colored paperbacks.

The one on top, which was a pretty blue color with a film strip across the front and a familiar title, had a Post-it, on which was Tito's handwriting.

And it said, *Read this one first.*

I didn't have time for that right then.

I pushed the books aside, grabbed the closest server apron at hand (it was powder blue, which only semi-worked with the muted berry tee dress I was wearing, but I was in no headspace to be matchy-matchy).

I tied it on as I hightailed it through the kitchen, my head too cluttered even to call my usual greeting to Lucia.

I hit the main area and spied Luna behind the bar taking a sip from a foam-topped mug.

She took one look at me, put it down, and we both ran to each other.

I thought she'd read my mood.

I was wrong.

She grabbed both my hands, lifted them up and girlie bounced twice before she announced, "I got a unit at the Oasis."

I blinked at her. "What?"

"I was sending that email last night, and I saw I got one from your new landlord, and it was notification that a unit was opening October one, and *I'm in!*" she squealed her last and bounced again.

Although, after her being on the waiting list for over a year, I was thrilled she'd scored a unit and that she'd be so close I could walk down a walkway or across the courtyard to hang with her, the timing was suspect.

But I couldn't handle another freaky coincidence in that moment.

"I think Cap and I broke up this morning," I announced.

She stopped bouncing and stared at me. "What? Why? How? Again...*why?*"

"He found Clarice's business card and went ballistic."

She let my hands go but didn't move away, and she appeared as confused as I was that morning.

"Why?" she asked.

"Apparently, Clarice was a runaway in Denver too, back in the day. And she used to hang at the same shelter Cap did."

"Whoa," she said, her eyes rounding in shock.

"Yeah," I replied. "I can't tell whether he likes her or he doesn't. I got the sense he was as uneasy about the coincidence as I was, but his uneasy came out as being bossy and a dick, which segued to me sharing she'd broken into my pad, and things, already careening, went downhill from there."

"Break it down, sister," she ordered.

"Well, he was pissed I didn't tell him immediately someone broke in, when we weren't even a thing then."

"Wait, I thought he'd asked you out by then."

Shit!

"Okay, we weren't *officially* a thing."

Her face got funny.

"What?" I demanded.

"Okay, I can see how he flummoxed you with his openness and sharing and sensitivity about the Elsie Fay-Macy issue."

I took her by the arms and gave her a shake. "Loon, he took the big bag I'd invited him to pack and walked out on me this morning. *Make sense.*"

Her brows rose. "You asked him to bring over a bag?"

I let her go and begged, "Luna, please, focus."

She nodded. "Right. I thought you knew what you'd signed on for when you signed on with him. Now, I'm not sure you did. So, okay, there are guys who are, you know, great guys who listen and share and treat you like an equal partner and are, well, the kids these days call it, *enlightened.*"

Oh boy.

I got where she was going with this.

And it gave me a very bad feeling.

She kept doing that.

"Then there are guys like Cap who can listen and share and treat you like an equal partner who are kinda still throwbacks to another time."

"He told me he was worried about me and wanted to take care of me. I told him I didn't need him to take care of me."

She stretched out her lips in an *Eek!* face.

Fuck!

I gave it all to her. "I also told him I didn't belong to him and never would."

"Yikes," she whispered.

"He was being a dick," I defended myself.

"I'm reading from this you didn't get a chance to liquor him up and tell him about Clarice and the whole thing."

I sighed.

After I did that, I pointed out the obvious. "No, Luna, I didn't get the chance to liquor him up and tell him about Clarice and the whole thing."

"You probably should have done that."

I turned to the corner of the bar where we were standing at the entry to the bar back, dropped my head to it and started pounding.

She pulled me away from the bar.

When I looked at her, she suggested, "Maybe he just walked away to cool off."

"And took his bag with him?"

Her face got sad.

I turned to pound my head on the bar again.

Luna pulled me away again. "Give him time to do that. Cool off, I mean. And then call him and work it out."

I was breathing, but even so, my lungs still weren't getting enough oxygen, and my stomach was knotted up so tight, I thought I might hurl.

"He took his bag with him," I whispered.

She got close. "This is the thing, Raye. It started hot and heavy and you guys spent a ton of time together. But you haven't known him very long. This is your first fight. It's gonna take time for you two to feel each other out and get the lay of the land. He likes you a whole lot, honey. He might call you, but even if he doesn't, you need to give it a little time and call him. Talk, listen, keep your cool, have a mind to the kind of man he is, while standing your ground about the kind of woman you are, and work this out. I believe in you guys. This is just a blip. Okay?"

I wanted to believe that, so I said, "Okay."

"Right, you good?" she asked.

I nodded.

Or at least I was good for now.

She changed the subject.

"So, the other thing I had to tell you was that Clarice, or someone, emailed back. I have an address for Betsy. I say we go tonight, sometime after five, so she'll be home from work."

I needed something else to think about, so I nodded.

"You done with your most recent drama?" Byron asked from across the bar.

Luna whirled. "Dirty chai, coming right up!"

I looked to Tito's table.

He wasn't there.

But the succulent I brought him yesterday was pride of place, smack in the middle of the table.

I saw movement out the window and turned my attention there.

I located Tito outside, spraying Lucia's herb garden from a hose. It was a Hawaiian shirt and board shorts day, but he'd mixed up the crazy with a flak cap and some puka shells at his neck. I couldn't see what was on his feet. But he'd made an attempt to it tone down by donning a pair of tortoiseshell wayfarers.

This attempt failed, of course, but points for trying.

I snuck back to my locker and grabbed the book Tito put on top.

Rock Chick Renegade.

I turned it to the back and read the blurb.

It was Vance and Jules's story.

Cap's story.

Right.

I planned my day.

Work first. Visit with Betsy next. Go home and start the book after that. And as soon as I knew he'd be home, maybe around nine, I'd call Cap, and we'd figure it out, that would be last.

Or, at least I hoped we'd figure it out.

But for my mental health and the well-being of my heart I was gonna go with that.

For now.

FOURTEEN

LET'S ROLL

L una and I used the time between our shift ending and going to see Betsy to sit out in front of Eat Up Drive In, snarfing down an early dinner of sandwiches (Luna, Main Chick, me, braised BBQ short rib) and discussing what Clarice and Cap knowing each other back in the day in Denver might mean.

Unsurprisingly, we came up with no answers, so we decided I should confront her with that.

As such, we called to make another appointment with her.

Her assistant told us, considering it was the end of the business day (which it was, it was two to five, *oops*!), she'd need time to consult Clarice's diary, and she'd get back to us on that.

We moved on to debating if we should recruit Harlow and Jessie into our thing, and we decided that we were too new to it, we shouldn't involve them just yet.

So it was going to be Luna and me hitting The Slide strip club as soon as we could. And that would be after I had dinner with Dad and knew what my plans were for his visit to Phoenix (he was leaving on Sunday), and after I smoothed things out with Cap (or, God, I hoped I did).

But we figured it might need to be a late-night thing, after I spent some time with Dad, and we preliminarily set that for Thursday.

We then shifted to the intel we were given about Betsy.

Her name was Betsy Markovic. She was fifty-two and single mom to Christina, who was now twenty-one.

Apparently, Christina was a handful growing up, and this went into overdrive when she was a teen.

The sitch got out of hand, and the two parted ways when Christina was twenty.

Once she left home, Christina didn't bother asking for an application from J. Crew. She hit the streets right away. She disappeared from those streets not long after, about a year ago.

The police didn't look too deeply into Christina's "disappearance" (the quotes were how the officials looked at it). Betsy and Christina had been going at each other for a while, getting so loud at one point when Christina was eighteen, the cops were called to calm things down.

The police didn't put a lot behind it because, first, they weren't entirely sure she was missing, but instead, they thought it highly likely she'd just taken off. She had a boyfriend and he was nowhere to be found either, so they thought the two of them drove off into the sunset, and since she didn't get along with her mom, she didn't let her know. And second, they didn't have a ton of resources to waste on a twenty-year-old woman who might have just left town with her guy.

This was a point to ponder, and Luna and I pondered it.

Because it could be that the police weren't falling down on the job.

People moved. Circumstances changed. Mothers had hip replacement therapy, and you had to go home and take care of them. And if you worked on the street, you didn't put formal notice in to your manager to share what was going down.

Luna and I didn't have a lot of experience, and maybe the girls were a lot closer than what we'd observed last night. But it might be these gals, especially if they were new, hadn't made connections in order to share they were taking off with their man or to look after their mom or whatever.

We made note to ask for info on Christina's boyfriend, because if we could track him down, we might find Christina, or get something else to go on. Whichever way it swung, he was definitely a lead we could follow.

We also took some time to marvel at how much information was provided in such a short period of time, again realizing just how much "We" was not messing around.

We then took Luna's Prius to go switch out cars, debating along the way if we should do Mercedes or Accord.

Since Betsy lived in a not-great neighborhood on the west side of the city, we decided on the Accord.

Luna driving this time, we headed her way.

We parked out front of her house, which was tidy, but Betsy should consider a xeriscape, since, taking in the massive dead patches intermingled with green ones, it was clear some of her sprinkler heads had given up the ghost.

I had Christina's picture on my wall at home. I got it from the *Republic*. She had dark hair, blue eyes and a snarky look on her face.

When we knocked on the door and the woman opened it, I saw immediately that Christina took after her dad.

Perhaps, since he was absentee, this was one of the issues these two had. Not fun to confront the man who left you alone to raise your daughter every time you looked at said daughter.

Betsy was a flaming redhead with light-brown eyes, an upturned nose, and a pear-shaped, petite frame.

She also had a kind, but haggard and sad face. A face that didn't scream *I fight with my daughter all the time!* So, to me, it was also a surprising face.

"Can I help you?" Betsy asked.

"Hi, Miz Markovic. I'm Jill, this is Kelly, and we're looking into the women who have gone missing," Luna greeted.

Her eyes got round, and without pausing to ask for ID or a badge, such was her desire to find her daughter, she instantly pushed open the somewhat rickety screen door for us. "Come in."

This said a lot to me.

We went in.

We then both had no choice but to rear back when we were confronted with a living room of Barbie pink walls, a shrine to Christina making up the gallery wall of pictures over a puce-green couch situated dead ahead of us. In front of that was a round of glass on top of a ceramic elephant sitting atop a rug that was a hodgepodge of every bright color known to humankind. Two loud armchairs sat opposite the couch. And there was a big mirror on one wall that reflected all this so it seemed like it went on forever.

I was feeling the need to Tito this sitch by putting on my sunglasses when Betsy tardily asked, "Are you girls with the police?"

"No, ma'am," Luna answered. "We're with a kind of...underground organization that looks into women's issues that we feel aren't getting the proper attention."

She planted her hands on her ample hips and snapped, "Well, I'll say. They don't even think my Christina is missing." She tipped her head to the side. "You're here to talk about my Christina, right?"

"Yes, we are," I told her.

"Please, sit down," she bid.

Luna took a bright-orange armchair. I sat in the dandelion-yellow one. Betsy sat on the couch.

I started it.

"We were told by an informant last night that Christina wasn't engaged in her, erm, occupation for very long."

"You mean, she wasn't a hooker for very long," Betsy stated bluntly.

"I believe they prefer the term 'sex worker' now," Luna corrected.

Betsy flapped out a hand. "Whatever. She just did that to irk me. Christina was good at finding ways to irk me. She was running out of ideas. So she became a hooker. And that *Jazz* she was seeing thought it was great. Now tell me, what man thinks his woman getting paid to have sex with other men is great? Hmm?"

I briefly entertained the idea of Cap in this same scenario.

My mind rumbled with an impending catastrophic earthquake, so I stopped entertaining that idea and again wondered how I'd blown it with our convo that morning so badly.

Luna was right. He was that guy.

He might not try to cave in someone's face for having a crush on me because of my pudding, like Lucia's husband would if he knew Byron had a crush on her (Lucia's husband, Mario, was very sweet, but that was because he liked me and I didn't have a crush on his wife, otherwise, he was a total caveman).

But I sensed Cap didn't reside in a zone too far from that.

In my defense, this happened when I'd just woken up.

And I was going to stick to that defense when I spoke to him about it.

"Jazz, her boyfriend. Do you know his real name?" Luna asked, taking me out of where my mind had gone six thousand, nine hundred and seventy-two times that day.

To Cap.

"No clue. He was a waste of space. I told her to scrape him off, but did she?" Betsy leaned toward us and answered her own question. "*No.*"

I got my head in the game, and in doing so stopped myself from noting it might not have been a good idea to tell a twenty-year-old girl you often had conflict with to scrape off her boyfriend.

I mean, I wasn't a mom, so even though that didn't seem like a smart idea, what did I know?

Especially considering I knew one thing about this Jazz dude, that he was okay with his woman being a sex worker, and as such, he sounded like an asshole any mother worth her salt would tell her daughter to scrape off.

"We'll look into him, but when was the last time you spoke with her?" I asked.

"She called me every day, my girl did. You see, people don't get it. So she could work my last nerve. I worked my mother's last nerve too. Girls do that. Amiright?"

I would have no idea, so I looked to Luna.

Clearly thinking of Dream, she replied, "Yes, you're right."

"It doesn't mean we aren't close," Betsy continued. "So, sure, we could end our phone calls yelling at each other. But who cares? I'm still her mother, and she loves me. And she's still my daughter, and I love her."

I hoped her use of the present tense was apropos.

"We were also told by our informant that you asked around about her," I remarked.

She nodded. "Yup. Sure did. I knew the first day when I didn't hear from her something was up. I called her again and again, no answer. Went by her place, she wasn't there. Called the hospitals, the police stations. Nothing. That's when I went in and talked to the cops. They didn't believe me. More days went by, no call, she was not at her place. Nada. I talked to the cops again. They told me that a lot of times *girls like her*," she snarled that last bit, and I didn't blame her, "turn up after a while. I should just be patient. Then, she didn't show to do her laundry that first Sunday, and I knew something was up. My Christina *always* comes by on Sunday to do her laundry. I went back to the cops. They said they'd look into it. As far as I could tell, they didn't look too far. So I was on the streets, up and down, looking for her my damned self and talking to anybody I could find to see if they might have seen her."

"Did anyone have any information for you?" Luna queried.

She shook her head. "Nothing. Like my Christina went up"—she clapped her hands—"*poof!* in a puff of smoke. No one goes up in a puff of smoke. *Somebody* knows *something*."

Somebody knew something.

We just had to get a lock onto that somebody.

"Do you know how to get hold of this Jazz?" Luna asked.

Betsy popped off the couch and walked to a chest that was painted parakeet blue saying, "Sure do."

Luna and I looked at each other.

It was Luna who asked, "He's in town?"

"I don't know, just got his number," she mumbled. She'd taken a pad of paper out of the bureau and was copying down a number from her phone. She ripped off the top sheet, came my way and handed it to me. "Last time I talked to him, he told me to eff off and called me an old bat. The manners on that man. *Awful.* I was asking after *my daughter.*"

"And he wouldn't answer," I noted.

"He told me if Christina wanted me to find her, I'd find her." She lifted a hand and wagged a finger at us before tapping her temple with it. "But I think he knows something. I think he's *hiding* something. I told the cops that. They said they couldn't find him to ask him. And that was that. How hard is it to find a lazy cuss? He probably hasn't moved from his couch since my Christina disappeared."

"No address on him?" I pushed.

She shook her head. "No address. Last time—"

She cut herself off and looked out the front window.

We gave her time.

She drew in a breath and turned back to us. "Last time I talked to my girl, we fought about him."

Yup.

I was right.

That wasn't something you said to a twenty-year-old woman.

Betsy continued, "She told me I was lonely and should find myself a man so I wouldn't be jealous of hers. No one believes this either, but I know..."—she leaned again toward us—"*I know...*"—she leaned back—"that all this time, Christina has been kicking herself those were the last words we exchanged. *I know.* She loves me, and I love her. She won't want to have left it at that. She'll come back, and she'll be sorry it was left like that, and we'll get along for a while, and then we'll start fighting again. That's our way. And I'll tell you one thing you can bet the house on. I cannot *wait* to fight with my daughter again."

The look on her face, the tears brightening her eyes she refused to shed, I'd take that bet.

"I'm certain you can assure us you already talked with all her friends and acquaintances, and went to places she liked to hang out," I said quietly.

She sniffed then replied, "Time and again. And the cops did too. At least they tried that."

Luna stood, already having one of her phone number slips of paper out, and she moved to Betsy to offer it to her.

"Sorry, we're out of business cards. But those are our numbers. If you can think of anything we might need to know while we search for her, please tell us."

She took the paper, asking, "Do you think you'll find her?"

"We don't know, but we can promise you we'll try," Luna answered.

Her shoulders drooped and my heart went out to her.

"Guess that's something," she muttered. "At least someone cares."

I stood too. "We definitely care, Miz Markovic."

"Call me Betsy."

We said our farewells and got in the Accord.

Luna pointed us on our way back to the Prius and issued orders.

"You go home and figure out what to say to Cap. I'll email this in and see if 'We' can get us anything on this Jazz character."

"I'm not gonna call Cap until around nine. He works odd hours. I want him to be home and in a place he'll listen to me."

"Good call. I'll still do the emailing."

"Right," I agreed. Then asked, "Is it only me that thinks it's weird a boyfriend would blow off the mother of his missing girlfriend?"

"It isn't just you, but maybe she *is* with him. Maybe it's a thing with those two, and Betsy telling Christina to scrape him off was the last straw."

My thoughts exactly.

However...

"She has a shrine to her daughter, Luna. I don't think she just put that up in the last year either. You don't put pictures up of people you don't love. You also don't call someone every day if you're not tight with them, even if that tight has no small amount of dysfunction. And even if you're really into a guy, you figure it out with the mom you love, and it doesn't take a year for you to figure it out."

"Yeah," Luna replied.

I laid it out. "So we have Jazz as a lead, and we still have to find Divinity, and we're gonna check out The Slide."

"Your dad has shitty timing," Luna remarked. "He's slowing our roll."

Man.

She could say that again.

I SAT ON MY COUCH, staring at my phone sitting on the coffee table.

Patches lounged on the back of said couch, flicking his tail.

It was just past eight, and I was trying to convince myself I could wait another hour to call Cap.

I'd lugged the new additions to my library up and attempted to get into the book about Jules and Vance.

After reading some of the first chapter, and being surprised at what a supreme badass Jules seemed to be, when it got to the part about how they all lost Cap's friend Park, I got overwhelmed by his loss, more overwhelmed at how I'd bungled things that morning, and I couldn't concentrate.

So I changed the sheets on my bed, threw in a load of laundry, ran the vacuum, started the dishwasher and wiped down all the counters.

Now I was thinking, maybe he was home.

Maybe he'd been at home, sitting on his couch, staring at his phone for the last two hours, waiting for me to call or psyching himself up to call me.

Though, he was Cap. He didn't have to psych himself up for anything. He was the single most confident person I'd ever met (barring Mace, Vance, Lee, Eric and Liam, also Shirleen and Clarice).

Okay, so he was the single most confident person I'd met who was my age (barring Liam and Clarice).

If he could call, he'd call.

Which meant he wasn't home.

Or he was still mad and didn't want to call.

Or he was so mad, he didn't want me to call ever again.

I was thinking on this so hard, I nearly fell off my couch when a loud knock sounded on my door before I heard a key in the lock.

Of course, he wouldn't call.

He'd just come over.

Because it didn't occur to me until just then, he may have taken his bag, but he didn't leave my key.

Hope bloomed in my chest as I took my feet.

The door opened, and Luna, hand still on the knob, swung only her torso in.

"Come on, bitch. Jinx called. She needs us."

This was such a surprise, all I could do was ask, "What?"

"Chop chop. Let's go. Jinx is in a fix, and it sounds serious."

I'd worn my black Vans with the multi-colored daisies on the stackform sole that day (and they totally clashed with my dress—I was *so* off my game).

I shoved them on. I snatched up my crossbody.

And we motored.

On the way to the Accord (which was out of the way of where Jinx was, that being in a room in the very motel we'd been kicked out of last night, so we really needed a more central location for ease with switch out), after Luna told me where we were going, I asked, "Could this be a setup?"

"A setup of what?"

"A setup of someone who isn't happy we're nosing around the missing women."

"Well, she could be the kind of woman who warns us to be careful one night, and then the next, swings our asses out there. But I didn't read that on her."

"Tasers locked and loaded anyway."

"I hear that."

We did the car switch out. Luna drove like a bat out of hell to the Sun Valley Motor Lodge. We parked. We both refrained from flipping the bird at the night attendant, the same guy from yesterday who was now sitting behind the counter in reception and scowling at us through the plate glass windows. And we took the steps two at a time to the upper level to hit room number twenty-three.

It was an old key lock door, no update to keycards for this joint, and Luna and I had seen enough TV and movies to know what to do.

I just hoped it wasn't locked. But the door was flimsy, so maybe I could do the Van in the door trick, like Cap did with his boot to get to Elsie Fay.

I didn't hold high hopes for that, but we'd figure that out if it became an issue.

Luna flattened herself on one side of the door, Taser up and ready, I flattened myself on the other.

But it was me who shouted, "Jinx! You in there?"

"Bitches, come get me loose!" she shouted back.

Luna turned the knob and pushed open the door, but it was me who curled in on a squat, Taser out, scanning the place.

All that was there was a naked Jinx with both wrists handcuffed to the bed, her phone on the pillow beside her.

I straightened.

"Motherfucker cuffed me to the bed, did me, took my night's earnings and jetted outta here. I think I sprained my back getting my phone from my toes to my hand 'cause that's the only thing he left me, but he threw it at my feet. *Motherfucker!*" she screamed.

Luna came in behind me and closed the door.

I went right to Jinx, and even if it gave me the heebie-jeebies to touch it, I pulled the comforter over her.

"I've had a good night, but it's been a slow month. How'm I gonna pay my electric bill now?" she asked. Before we could say anything, she pushed, "Hunh? Hunh?" Then she let loose a stream of enraged Spanish.

"Oh man," Luna mumbled.

"What? You don't got a key?" Jinx asked. "I always got a key, but the fucker took that too. How you two on the streets without a universal key? *Motherfucker!*" and more Spanish.

But that wasn't what Luna was referring to.

She was referring to me.

I was feeling what I hadn't felt since I doused an asshole rapist with honey and loosed an entire ant farm on him.

And she knew me.

I whipped out my burner, pulled up the only contact in it and tapped in, *Jacob Brewer's number, right now!* then hit send.

"We'll figure this out, Ra…Kelly. Calm down," Luna urged.

I didn't calm down.

I ordered, "Help her get dressed as well as you can." I looked to Jinx. "What was he driving?"

"Who gives a fuck?" Jinx answered.

"You want your money back?"

"Kelly," Luna warned.

"You can do that?" Jinx asked.

"Damn straight. What was he driving?"

"Blue Lexus."

I stormed out.

I raced down the stairs to the night clerk, waltzed into the grimy reception area and rapped hard on counter.

"I wanna see the parking lot camera footage from about an hour and a half ago, and I wanna see it right now," I demanded.

And no. I hadn't missed the cameras. They had four of them trained to the lot.

"And I wanna fuck Jennifer Lawrence," he retorted. "Looks like we're both in for a disappointing night."

I whipped my Taser around and pointed it at him. "Show it to me, asshole, or I'll send so many volts into you, you'll piss your pants and slobber."

He put his hands up. "Fucking shit, woman. Cool it."

"One of your patrons was robbed. Footage. *Now!*"

His eyes darted beyond me, and I turned to see Luna entering.

"Just fuckin' chill. I'll call it up," the guy said.

He called it up.

Luna and I stood behind the counter and watched one of the four monitors behind the desk.

No keycards in this place, but they had tight security, and it was on show. Probably so they wouldn't get robbed like Jinx had been.

It wasn't hard to spot the Lexus.

Or its plate.

"Pause there," I ordered, and he complied. "Text it in," I said to Luna as my phone binged with my own text.

I looked at it.

Jacob's number.

I walked out and into the parking lot where no one could hear me and phoned him.

"Fuck off and die," he answered, probably thinking I was a too-late-in-the-evening marketing call.

"Jacob, it's Raye."

"Raye? You okay? What's with this number?"

"Do you have a key to handcuffs?"

He chuckled. "You and Cap into some kinky shit and it got outta hand?"

"Jacob, a friend of mine picked up a guy, was handcuffed to a bed, she was robbed, and the asshole left her cuffed to the bed."

"Fucking hell," Jacob whispered.

"Now, do you have a universal key?" I asked.

"Where are you, sweetheart? I'll be right there."

Knew he'd be a good source for that.

But we were requisitioning a couple of those keys *and* the hand-cuffs that went with them for the Accord and Merc.

"Sun Valley Motor Lodge on Roosevelt."

"I'm on it."

He hung up.

Luna was right beside me.

"You text it in?" I asked.

"Yeah, Raye, honey. But you need to chill."

"Fuck that," I said and marched up to Jinx. When I got there, I told her, "Key's on the way. Maybe ten, fifteen minutes."

"*Gracias a Dios.*"

"What'd he look like?" I asked.

"Clean cut. Blond. Short. Skinny. Small dick," she answered.

I nodded, though I didn't need the dick info. I didn't tell her that.

Luna's phone binged.

She flipped it open, looked at it then showed it to me.

An address in Arcadia.

That particular area of Phoenix was money.

Lexus and Arcadia.

Loser had bank and was stealing from sex workers.

"Keep it in control," Luna warned.

"I'm good," I bit off.

"She kinda scary," Jinx said.

"She really doesn't like sisters getting fucked over,' Luna told her.

"I can see this," Jinx replied.

I moved out to the walkway to wait for Jacob.

He didn't mess around and was there in less than ten minutes. He saw me and jogged up the steps.

He handed me the key, asking, "She okay?"

I looked him dead in the eye. "Dude, ask Alexis out. She's so into you, she practically *is* you. You keep fucking that shit up, she's going to move on, and you're gonna kick yourself for the rest of your life."

His chin jerked into his neck.

"She's right," Luna said.

I turned. She was standing in the door behind me.

"And you'd be super cute together," Luna added.

I tossed the key to Luna.

She caught it and disappeared behind the door.

"She's a ballerina," Jacob reminded me.

"So? She's a tiny little thing that men can throw across a stage. She needs you. You're perfect for her. She'll feel safe with you. And she's head over heels for you. Stop the woman parade and jump on that."

He surveyed me, asking, "What's got into you?"

"I'm just sick of man shit today."

His black eyes went to the door behind me, then back to me. "I feel that."

"You gonna ask her out?"

"If I crash and burn, you gotta make me your pudding."

"Deal."

I HIT the doorbell at the house in Arcadia and I didn't take my finger off it until Luna pulled my wrist away.

"I think they heard it," she said.

They did.

Or at least he did.

A short, blond, not-very-attractive, but openly-arrogant man opened the door, looked between us, looked us up and down, and then asked, "Can I help?"

"You can give me the money you stole from the prostitute you cuffed to a bed." I gave him an all-around assessment before I added, "And your Rolex."

I heard Luna gasp.

He turned instantly shady.

"I don't know—" he began.

"Honey?" A woman called from inside. "Who is it at this hour?"

"You got two fuckin' seconds to hand over your watch and go get that money or your wife knows what a colossal piece of shit you are," I told him.

He started to close the door.

I put a hand and all my weight into it to stop him.

"If you don't think I can't bust down a door, you're a moron," I lied. "And you can call the cops, but you'd still be explaining to your woman why Sun Valley Motor Lodge has footage of your Lexus going in and out of the lot, and you following a sex worker into room number twenty-three, not to mention dealing with her complaint of you stealing from her."

"Honey?" the woman's voice was getting closer.

His face paled.

Then he griped, "This is fucking crazy," while taking off his watch.

"You're right. It is." I took the watch when he handed it to me and shoved it in my crossbody. "Money too."

"Hi, oh...hi," a pretty brunette came up behind him. "Is everything okay?"

At this point, I was really glad I was still in my tee dress and daisy Vans. I looked normal, even sweet.

And there was Clarice's note of flying under the radar.

"So sorry for the late visit. We had a huge list today. Shoo!" Luna said to her, also looking sweet in a muted floral dress with ruffles on the sleeves, short skirt and a smocked waist. "But you're our last and we thank you *so much* for the donation to Sun Valley Homeless Shelter."

The woman's smile faltered in confusion as she looked to her husband. "Bobby?"

"I forgot to tell you, I pledged," he said to her. "I'll just go get that."

"Thank you *so much*," Luna oozed.

After shooting Luna a killing look his wife couldn't see, Bobby took off, but his spouse remained at the door.

It felt shit, not sharing her husband was a scumbag, but our hands were tied.

Apparently, righteous extortion had its drawbacks.

"Long day for you gals," she said.

"Yes, but we collected at least twenty-five thousand in pledges today. Isn't that amazing?" Luna asked.

I fought a smile.

Twenty-five thousand was maybe what that Rolex was worth, possibly more. Though, pawned, probably less, but still, it'd keep Jinx covered for a good while.

"Oh my God, that's great," the woman enthused.

"People are so generous," I said.

Bobby came back and shoved a wad of cash in my hands.

The brunette's brows snapped together, her gaze on the cash.

"Thank you for your kindness, we'll leave you be. Good night!" I cried.

Luna and I turned away only to hear the brunette ask, "Where did you get so much cash, Bobby? Did you go to the bank today?"

The door snicked shut.

"Loser," I muttered as we headed to the car at the curb.

"Asshole," Luna muttered.

"Dickhead," I kept it up.

"Piece of shit," she put in.

"Creep."

"Perv."

"Skeeve."

"Prick."

"Jackass."

"Douchebag."

I was so angry, I was insulted out.

We got in the Accord and headed back to Roosevelt.

LUNA ROLLED up in front of Jinx's patch by the litter-strewn, rusted-cage-windowed building, and she put the flashers on.

She stayed in the car.

I got out.

I shoved the cash in Jinx's hands then dug into my crossbody to get the Rolex.

I handed that to her as well.

Jinx stared down at it with her mouth hanging open.

"Probably keep your electricity rolling for a while," I remarked.

She looked at me. "*Madre de Dios.*"

"No more handcuffing," I advised.

"They pay big for that kink," she told me.

"Your call."

"I thought you two were a joke."

"We are. But when shit gets real, we kick into gear. Now, I don't want a call from you for a while, unless you wanna meet for margaritas."

"You wanna sit down for a drink with a whore?"

Interesting.

Maybe they didn't refer to themselves as sex workers.

"I don't care what you do. Just as long as it's a good margarita." I turned away, bidding, "Later."

She said nothing as I folded into the car.

"Let's roll," I said to Luna.

Luna turned off the hazards, and we rolled.

FIFTEEN

FIFTEEN YEARS

L una idled in my apartment parking lot, staring at Cap's Porsche in the visitor spot.

I sat next to her, staring at it too and trying to remember how to breathe.

"How does he get that spot? They're never open when I come over," Luna said.

I was physically unable to reply.

I felt her attention come to me.

"Go get 'im, baby," she encouraged.

I looked to her, smiled a terrified smile and got out of the car.

I got through the gate, ran to the stairs, slowed on the stairs as anxiety overtook me, ran halfway down the walkway and slowed as the anxiety took hold again.

I put the key in the lock, opened the door, and nearly burst out crying when I saw Cap's big leather bag on the armchair and Cap stretched out on my couch with Patches on his chest, kneading his thermal and purring so loud, I could hear him from where I stood. Cap's long fingers were massaging Patches' ruff.

With Cap's gray-blue eyes tracking me, I walked in, pulled the crossbody over my head and tossed it without looking toward the armchair.

I stopped moving.

Cap cradled Patches and rose from the couch before dropping him on it and locking eyes with me.

"Baby, I was such a fuckin' dick. I'm so—"

He stopped talking when I dashed toward him and ran into the coffee table, slamming into it with my shin.

"Ouch! Damn!" I cried, hopping on one foot, lifting the other and bending to wrap my fingers around my shin.

He had a hand to my back and was leaned to me, saying, "Are you o—?"

He didn't finish that either.

Because all my life I'd been glad my monthly cycle only lasted a couple of days.

But in that moment, this fun fact made me *ecstatic*.

As such, I lifted up...

And pounced.

I was kissing him, my hands all over him.

Then he was kissing me, his hands all over me.

I grabbed his thermal and yanked it up. He lifted his arms, pulled it off and chucked it away.

I thought we'd start kissing again, but he bent and put a shoulder in my belly, and then I was up in a fireman's hold.

Oh *my*.

My clit pulsed and my pussy contracted.

He stalked down the hallway, turned on a bedside light, bumped his shoulder, and I went flying, landing on my back in the bed.

My clit pulsed again, but this time my pussy convulsed.

Cap fell on me.

We went at each other with hungry ferocity, groping and rolling and kissing and licking and scratching. I toed off my Vans and footies. Cap yanked off my dress.

I got him to his back, straddling him in my undies. I bent to his chest, sucking at his perfect nipple.

Lord.

He tasted *amazing*.

He growled, angling up, dislodging my mouth. And with a clit-tingling expert flick, my bra was undone, then he yanked it off.

He lifted one breast to his mouth, drawing hard on the nipple.

I gasped and bucked in his lap.

He moved to the other breast and did the same thing.

I whimpered.

He let it go and his head dropped back to look up at me.

I looked down at him.

Dayum.

He was so goddamned gorgeous.

I went after his mouth again, but he tossed me to my back on the bed, ripped my panties down my legs, threw one over his shoulder, the other one, and then he was going down on me.

"*God*," I breathed, threading my fingers into his thick hair.

With what he could do with his tongue in my mouth, I should have known he would be good at this, but he was so good at it, it was mind-boggling, masterclass worthy.

I was close, God, so close, writhing and fisting my hand in his hair and rubbing myself against him.

Then his mouth was gone and he was up on his knees between my legs pulling out his wallet.

"I...U...D," was all I was able to force out.

His heated, dark eyes came to mine. "Sure?"

I didn't want anything between us.

Ever.

I nodded.

He tossed his wallet aside, undid his pants and pulled them over his ass, his hard cock springing out.

It was thick and long and beautiful.

Wow.

He lowered himself to me, locking his eyes with mine, his hand between us guiding the way. I felt him catch, then in a slow, smooth stroke, he was planted inside me.

I drew in a sharp breath as I accommodated his size.

He pulled my knees up at his sides and slid in deeper.

Oh yeah.

Nice.

I mewed.

He laid still and held my gaze.

"Honey?" I whispered.

"Perfect fit," he said.

He was *so right*.

Tears stung my eyes.

He kissed me and moved inside me. He was there. I was definitely there. So he didn't go slow and soft, he went fast and hard, slamming into me.

I curled my nails into his ass, dug them in and dragged them up his back.

He groaned into my mouth, stopped kissing me, but didn't move away.

Our lips were touching, our breaths battling, our eyes glued to the other's. He slid a hand over my belly, down and in. He hit the exact right spot. I automatically swung my calves in, digging my heels into the small of his back, and at his touch, my world exploded into beautiful, bright stars. They shot out, zoomed back in, then glittered as the most magnificent orgasm I'd ever had coursed through me.

He kept thrusting, my body jolting, before he shoved his face in my neck and groaned, "*Raye.*"

At my name on his lips, and him emptying himself into me, my sex rippled around his still-driving cock.

Eventually, he buried himself inside me, slid his finger from my clit and wrapped that arm around me. His face still in my neck, some of his weight in his other forearm, we lay connected and quiet as we came down.

Now, *that* was what I'd been waiting for.

"Fifteen years," he murmured into my skin.

"Sorry, honey?" I asked, smoothing his hair back, then his shoulders, his lats, my legs now wrapped around his ass.

He lifted his head and gazed down at me.

"All the guys at the shelter loved Jules. She's gorgeous. Christ. Unbelievable. She could be a model or a movie star."

My hands stilled, then, as I sensed what he was doing, I curled my arms around him and held on.

Cap kept talking.

"But it was more. She was fierce. We all knew she'd go to the mat for us, every one of us. Anything she could do to make our lives better, to take away pain, to prompt healing. Getting us to work with the tutors. Sitting and rapping with us. And in the end, taking to the streets to keep the dealers away from the runaways, so what happened to Park wouldn't happen to another kid."

Oh yeah.

Jules was a badass.

I moved my hands to smooth his face and whispered, "Honey."

"A lot of us had never had that. Nothing like it. It was like being in a golf cart then suddenly finding yourself on a rocket. A lot of us also had our trust broken so bad, it felt like we'd never get that back. But she was always there, seeing everything, caring about it all. She was like a shooting star, bright and brilliant and streaking through our lives, lighting up the darkness we lived in, but she did it in a way where that beauty just never died."

In our activities, some of his hair had fallen on his forehead, but it didn't make him look boyish.

He'd had the boy chased out of him early.

I felt that in my soul as I tried to smooth it back, but it just fell forward again.

So I left it and kept listening.

"Park had a huge crush on her. I did. Think even Roam did, but he'd never admit it. Everyone did."

"I can imagine," I murmured when he stopped speaking. "She sounds incredible."

"She is. But then Sadie came along, and I thought, for me, it was going to be someone like her. I needed that vulnerability I could protect, that fracture I could work to heal, and if I couldn't heal it, bust my ass to hold her together so she didn't fly apart. It was the man I was going to become. The man Jules started forming, the man Shirleen cast in iron. It was me."

Oh yeah.

I knew what he was saying.

The tears threatened to come back as I ran my thumbs over his cheekbones.

"Jules was a force of nature. She was about fierce love. But Shirleen wasn't about tough love. She was just about love. And not the making-up-for-lost-time kind. She didn't try to smother us or buy us or any of that shit. She was just steady. Solid. *A parent*. We got our homework done or she got on our asses. We got good grades or she didn't hide her disappointment. She didn't like us to waste our time with too much TV or videogames, so she made us read or go out and do shit. She let us fuck up, and sometimes that meant a lecture. Sometimes, she let us learn on our own. And every day, the house was filled with groceries. So much food, all the time. When you're on the street, you don't know when you're gonna eat next. Shirleen's kitchen was always filled with food."

God, all he'd been through.

I tightened my legs around him.

"Sometimes she'd touch us, just to straighten a collar or pull our backpacks up on our shoulder. Love has a feel, Raye. You know that when you've never had it. So you know it when you get it. And she touched with love. Not fawning all over us and covering us with kisses and hugs. She gave us space. But when there was touch, it was all about love. She'd never had a kid, but she was so fuckin' plugged into what we needed, it was fuckin' unreal."

It was really, *really* hard not to let the tears flow.

But if I did, I might miss something.

So I didn't let them flow.

Instead, I whispered, "I love that."

"She got Hank to talk to us about becoming-a-man shit. She didn't go there. But from zero to thirteen, my life was straight up hell. From thirteen to fifteen, it was uncertain, finding my way on the streets, keeping clear of the dealers and other elements that would use kids for things that would alter them permanently. Park and Roam found me, Jules came with them. And then from fifteen to now I've had nothing but steady. Solid. Stable. But I watched the men. I knew what I wanted when it was time for me to have it."

"Okay," I said softly when he paused again.

"And then you raced to the door Elsie Fay was behind and shook it like you could tear it off its hinges, and then tore into that room when I opened the door. *Fearless.*"

The last word was so guttural, I felt it drive into me, like a stake to the heart, the piercing of which, my heart couldn't function ever again without it embedded there.

He kept going.

"She slammed into you and you picked her up and held her like she weighed nothing. You held that weight and held it and didn't let it go until it was safe to give her up. She felt the touch of love from you, Rachel, don't doubt it for a minute."

Oh shit.

"Cap."

"I knew it then, and I was fucking terrified of all I was feeling for you."

His name broke this time when I repeated, "Cap."

"I fought it, but that didn't last long. Dropped you at your car. Drove back to the office. Did a prelim search of you. I read what happened to Macy. What happened to your mom. And it was like my insides turned out. I couldn't get them right until I was back with you. I started to tear out of there, Mace came out of his office, put a hand to my chest, and I stopped. He said, 'She's the one, isn't she?' I don't know what I replied, but it was some form of yes. He smiled, dropped his hand, I got my ass in my car and drove back to you."

"Please stop talking," I whispered.

He didn't stop talking.

"Jules and Shirleen knew Roam and me needed men in our lives. Good men. Men we could learn the right things from. We started hanging at Nightingale Investigations when we were fifteen. They taught us everything we needed to know. I'm one of them, Raye. I know because, when Lee was ready for Indy, he'd moved in with her within a couple of weeks. Eddie moved Jet in with him in that same amount of time. Hank and Roxie. Jules and Vance. Ava and Luke. All of them." Some of the intensity drifted away from him and his lips tipped up. "But it was you who told me to pack a bag."

I was feeling too much, I tried to duck my face in his throat.

"Baby, no, look at me," he murmured.

I dropped my head back.

"I hope that doesn't freak you, because I'm down to slow things up. I'm down with anything you need." He dipped closer. "But I gotta ask that you let me look after you. It's what I've been waiting for for fifteen years. A woman I can call mine who's beautiful and fierce and strong and vulnerable and has a fracture, she turns to me to help her hold it together. I need to know she gets that from me. I need to know I give that to her. I need to know she can count on it. It's what I need."

"I'd just woken up and I was freaked out you knew Clarice, and I have to cop to having a bit of a temper, and I forgot who I was dealing with because the last time I had a man look after me was when I was eight. But he was taken away right along with Macy."

"Raye," he groaned and shoved his face in my neck.

After all he'd shared, I let him do that and ran my hands all over his back.

"You're going to have to give me some time to get used to having that back, honey," I warned.

In response to that, he kissed my neck.

"We didn't handle this morning well," I stated the obvious. "We might do better next time. We might not. But I've been worried all day I messed things up with you—"

He lifted his head. "I should have called or come by."

"I should have too," I replied. "We didn't. We might learn from that. We might not. But, Cap, it's only been a day and we're here now. Maybe it's good. Maybe we needed some space. But *we're here now*." I grinned. "And you give amazing head *and* apologies and your bag is back on my armchair, so it's all good."

He returned my grin and took his arm from around me so he could curl his fingers at the side of my neck and stroke my jaw with his thumb. "Mind the coffee table next time you attack me."

"Word," I agreed. "And just to say, the fireman's hold was the absolute shit."

He let out a soft chuckle, and it felt ridiculously good moving against me.

"I learned that from Luke. He carried Ava out of Vance and Jules's wedding reception after she told him she loved him for the first time, took her home and gave her the business. They came back and she had sex hair."

I started laughing, at the same time thinking I was really going to like these people.

"You need to clean up?" he asked.

I nodded.

He touched his lips to my mouth, my nose, my forehead, then he rolled off me.

I scooted off the bed, went to the bathroom, took care of business, then grabbed my nightie from the hook on the back of the door and pulled it over my head.

When I got back to the bedroom, Cap had his pants up, was bootless, still shirtless (his shirt was in the living room), walking toward the door and asking me, "Got a pen and paper?"

"What?"

He stopped, cupped my jaw and repeated, "Pen and paper?"

I was confused about this question, but I answered, "TV cabinet, top middle drawer."

He nodded and took off.

I located my panties and tugged them on.

He came back, sat on the side of the bed and ordered, "Lap."

I felt my mouth quirk at his bossy, but I didn't hesitate to climb in his lap.

He pulled my legs to the side, swinging them over his thigh so I was stable and all kinds of comfy. He wrapped an arm around me and still managed to hold the notepad so he could write on it.

I had no idea what he was doing, but whatever it was, he had my full attention.

"You got no pens that aren't pink and don't have little crowns on top of them," he remarked.

I pulled my shoulders forward and gave him big eyes.

"What can I say? I'm a girl."

He shook his head then turned his attention to the paper.

He wrote:

Who? – victim

When? – opportunity?

Where? – opportunity?

How? – opportunity?

Why? – motive

He formed a bracket on all that and swooped an arrow down to the last thing he wrote.

Who? – suspect/perpetrator

Then he pointed the little crown at the top of the pen toward my wall, then down, tapping it on the pad, and he said, "That's the basic outline of an investigation."

Oh.

My.

God.

"Cap," I breathed, not able to process what he was doing and saying, how enormous it was and how much it meant to me.

"You start with the victim. Who they are. What they do. Where they live and work. Who they know. Do they owe someone money? Do they have something someone wants? Have they pissed someone off? And that doesn't mean they're the asshole. Someone can get pissed off and it isn't the victim's fault. All your leads are not gonna stem from them. So don't lean too hard into that. They could have done nothing. It could be a crime of opportunity. Which is when you start digging into the when, where and how, which might also lead to answers to other questions. But always start with the first 'who' on your road to get to the second one."

I put a hand to his cheek.

He looked into my eyes.

"How did I score an awesome dude like you?" I asked him.

"That's what I've been asking myself for the last week, though, without the word 'dude' in the question."

God, he *rocked*.

I kissed him.

He dropped the pad and pen to the floor and twisted us so my back was to the bed, and he was on me.

It was getting hot and heavy, I was happily riding that, when an angry knock sounded on my door.

Cap lifted his head and stilled.

I turned mine to look at my Alexa.

It was nearly midnight.

I turned back to Cap. "Who could that be?"

"Stay here," he growled and knifed off me.

My bargain-basement stun gun was in my closet, so I got off my bed and dashed there.

I stopped moving when I heard Martha demand, "Where is she?"

I then heard Cap's low murmur, but couldn't make out any words.

I walked to the door to the hall and saw her standing in my living room with Cap (he'd put on his shirt, alas), a robe wrapped tightly around her body and flip flops on her feet.

She spied me and immediately jabbed a finger my way.

"There you are! I have a bone to pick with you!"

"Martha, it's nearly midnight," I informed her as I walked down my hall.

She ignored that and shared, "Five minutes ago, I knocked on Alexis's door to tell that girl to keep down the racket. And who answered?"

Cap rounded me as I made it to the living room and stopped, so he stopped close behind me.

Okay, yeah.

Now that I knew I had to open that door, I had a feeling it wasn't going to be hard to let him inside so he could have my back, because he felt perfect standing *right there*.

Martha also stopped speaking, and it was clear she wanted me to answer.

"Alexis?" I guessed.

"No!" she shouted, "Jacob!"

My mouth dropped open very wide in a happy "O."

One could say Jacob didn't let a single blade of grass grow under *that*.

Cap's hand came to rest on the small of my back.

"Don't look so cheery," she snapped. "Those two have been having *very loud* and *uninterrupted* sex for the last *two hours!*"

Yay!

"Right on!" I cried exuberantly.

Martha's eyebrows hit her hairline. "Right on? I live right next door."

"I know. I'm sorry, but—"

"And when Jacob opened the door, he told me you were to blame for this. So you talked him into *finally* extricating his head from his ass, go down there and tell them to move the festivities to his place. He lives next to William and Zachary. I know for a fact they sleep with a wave machine on, because they told me. Maybe that machine will drown out this incessant *copulation*."

"We've all been wanting them to get together for a long time," I reminded her.

"Of course we have!" she exclaimed. "But when he did her, I thought he'd take her to his place. She's dainty. With the noise I'm hearing, I'm afraid he's gonna fuck her in half."

I heard Cap start laughing behind me, and I couldn't stop the snort that came out as I held back my own.

"This isn't funny!" she yelled.

"Just be happy for them, and I'll find time to call Alexis tomorrow," I promised.

"Good God," she grumbled, shaking her head and moving to the door. "The things I do for you people."

I followed her, saying, "I swear. I'll handle this tomorrow."

She turned in the open door and warned, "You better."

I did the motions with my finger as I replied, "Cross my heart."

Her eyes went beyond me and up to Cap, who'd followed me to the door.

"You. Stud muffin. Keep it down. You have neighbors. These walls are solid, but they aren't magical."

She then put up her nose and huffed down the walkway.

Gliding an arm around my stomach, Cap pulled me from the door, closed it and locked it.

He then turned me to face him, shifted me around and shuffled me backward.

"You got Jacob to go for it?" he asked.

"I've had an interesting night," I admitted.

"Do I wanna know?"

"Probably not."

"Tell me anyway."

"Well, it involves a sex worker who got robbed by her john after he handcuffed her to a bed. I figured Jacob had a handcuff key, and I was right. He rode to the rescue. I gave him what for about Alexis after he handed it over. Obviously, he took it to heart. I then went to Arcadia to extort a Rolex from said john, since his wife was on her way to the door to see why someone was knocking after nine at night. I did this as well as demand the stolen earnings. I succeeded in these endeavors and returned the money and gave the watch to Jinx, who has a very foul mouth in English, and, I suspect, Spanish. She can probably now pay her electric bill for the next four years. And, uh... that's it. If you don't count earlier, when Luna and I went to interview one of the moms of one of the missing women on my wall."

We were stopped beside my bed.

Cap said nothing.

"Please don't be mad I didn't call you to get the handcuff key, you and I weren't in the right place," I requested.

"Mm," was his only reply, but fortunately, I didn't get a ticked feeling from him.

Therefore, I asked, "I was wondering if you could teach me the boot in the door trick?"

"I was right," he said.

"About what?" I queried.

"I didn't want to know."

I looked to his shoulder. "Gotcha."

"Baby," he called.

I looked to his eyes.

"I might not want to know, but I'm glad you told me."

I smiled.

He tilted his head to the side. "Wanna see if I can fuck you in half?"

I grinned and just caught myself from clapping my hands together and bouncing on my toes. "Yes, please."

He fell forward.

I fell back.

We hit bed.

And he didn't fuck me in half.

But he had mad power in his hips.

So it was close.

And it was *glorious*.

SIXTEEN

CHICHARRONES

M editation music drifted in the room, waking me up.
I was naked and sprawled on top of Cap.

I knew it woke him too when he grumbled sleepily, "Jesus Christ. What the fuck is that?"

I lifted my head and called, "Alexa, stop."

The music stopped.

Cap said, "Alexa cancel alarm."

She told us the alarm was cancelled.

Cap instantly went on, "Alexa, set alarm for five a.m. with any kind of music but that shit you just played."

Alexa shared her confusion about what Cap was asking.

I started laughing.

Cap gripped my hips and rolled me.

It was then, I focused on his face.

Oh my.

He didn't hesitate. He kissed my throat, then he went down.

We'd had maybe three hours of sleep, and I'd personally had more orgasms than I could count (or maybe I could count them, they were just so world-rocking, my mind was muddled and I couldn't distinguish one from the other).

Still, he was so good at this, it didn't take long for me to arrive at the destination he was leading me to.

I came down to Cap nuzzling my neck.

God, he wasn't just hot, he was all kinds of sweet.

I put my foot to the bed and heaved him to his back.

Then I went down.

"Baby," he murmured, sifting his fingers in my hair as I took him into my mouth.

I worked him, lips, tongue, suction and hand, doing this all the while Cap had his fingers curled around the back of my head.

He knew from the first time I went down on him last night I wasn't into swallowing, so he warned a thick, "Raye."

I slurped him out of my mouth and went at him with just my hand, but he had other ideas.

He reached and grabbed me under my arms, pulling me on top of him.

I settled astride his hips, grabbed hold and took him inside.

He gripped my hips and controlled the rhythm, alternately watching our connection, my body and my face with a dark, hungry expression on his that was mingled with contentment and something else. Something beautiful. Something I knew was building between us, but it was so big, I wasn't ready to go there.

Not yet.

I'd just come, and our activities (though mostly the look on his handsome face) were taking me there again.

Eventually, he ordered, "Fuck me faster, baby," as he slid his thumb to my clit.

I didn't know how he held off before he took me there again, but his thumb was almost as magical as his tongue, and he had a very big, very pretty dick, so I suppose it wasn't a surprise that I shot off again before he did.

My back arched and I bounced frantically into it, so while I was having mine, I heard the delicious growly groan and felt the pads of his fingers dig into my flesh when he had his.

"C'mere," he murmured when I'd slowed down to a lazy glide.

He added a slight tug on my hips that didn't disconnect us, but I knew what he wanted.

I rested on his chest, tucking my face in his neck.

He turned his head and kissed my forehead.

"'Mornin', babe," he whispered.

I smiled.

CONSIDERING our first-thing activities ate into my morning time, I forewent my scan of the *Republic* and pulled my makeup out to the kitchen bar to put it on while Cap cooked me breakfast.

I was nearing the finishing line and about to stroke on my mascara when Cap slid a stack of thick sliced brioche French toast, perfectly browned, toward me. It was covered and sitting in a pool of maple syrup and topped with an oozing pat of butter and fresh raspberries, blackberries and blueberries.

Yesterday (or the day before, or the day before that, you get the picture) I had no brioche (or fresh berries) in my house, so I looked at him quizzically.

"I hit the grocery store before I hit your pad last night," he explained.

"Sure of yourself?" I teased, pushing aside my makeup to reach for the plate.

He shrugged. "You're you, and I'm me."

We were *so* that.

I shot him a smile and forked in.

He leaned into his forearms on the bar across from me.

I took in his position and the focus he had on my face.

"Oh boy," I said around my first bite of his ludicrously delicious French toast.

"A couple of things our fuckfest didn't allow us to get into last night," he began.

I was me and he was him, and what we had together was a definite thing we were both in deep on, so instead of bracing for the worst, I circled my fork as an invitation for him to go on.

"A while ago, Luke taught me something important."

I speared a berry.

"What's that?" I asked before I put it in my mouth.

"When you get pissed and you're talking with someone you care about, and you don't wanna say anything you can't take back, or she's gonna say something she can't walk back, or she's said something that triggers you, you get the fuck outta there and take the time you need to cool down and clear your head."

"Ah," I murmured, thinking this Luke was wise, delighted he'd taught this lesson to Cap and thrilled to have an explanation of why he'd walked away the day before like he had, mostly so I'd know in the future what was going down if he did it again.

Not to mention, making note that Luna had been correct. She'd surmised this in our conversation about Cap leaving yesterday morning.

"Taking my bag was a mistake," Cap went on. "It was an asshole thing to do. I was pissed that you knew I was already pissed, and you made me wait until you got yourself a cup of coffee. It was a strike back, immature and fucked up. I shouldn't have done it. It made you worry where my head was at. And I was pissed, but I was nowhere near pissed enough to end us."

God, I loved it that he laid it out like that.

"Me making coffee wasn't real mature either, Cap. I was being a bitch."

"Let's try not to do that again," he suggested.

"Deal," I replied.

He gave me a smile.

I said, "Look at our growth. I think we should celebrate our newfound maturity by having a quickie on the kitchen floor. After I finish my French toast, that is."

His smile got bigger but he shook his head. "That's not all I need to talk about."

Bummer.

I took a huge bite then circled my fork again.

"I paid Clarice a visit yesterday."

I choked on French toast.

I downed it and asked, "You did?"

"Yeah."

Interesting.

"What'd she say?"

"She said her deal with you was for you to share with me. She knew we were together, but when she made her approach to you, although she'd heard I was in town, she didn't have any idea we'd connected. Her and me and you, it was a coincidence."

"Do you believe her?" I asked, dubious myself.

"Clarice doesn't talk shit. She never has."

Well, I believed that.

I went back to my toast. "What's her story?"

"While she was at the shelter, she got tight with Daisy, another of our crew. Daisy took her under her wing. Clarice got her high school diploma and went to the University of Colorado. She graduated top of her class and scored a place at Harvard Law. She graduated top honors there too. Daisy and her husband, Marcus, paid for her education. Clarice didn't want to come back to Denver, she didn't have a lot of good memories there, so Marcus set her up in a practice here."

I wasn't sure how I got tangled in this Rock Chick/Hot Bunch web.

Though, I was not complaining.

"The DAs are terrified of her," Cap continued. "When she came on the scene, she was young, fresh out of law school. They thought she was green. But she's a law savant, coupled with the fact she brings the rules of the street to a court battle. In other words, she's seriously fuckin' shrewd, never caught unaware and entirely unafraid to fight dirty. This means she kicked their asses. They thought at first, they were just underestimating her. They've learned that wasn't it."

I believed that too.

Cap kept going.

"She's also ambitious, quickly but carefully cultivating a firm of whip-smart attorneys that cover clients from criminal to family, corporate and tax law. She's a year older than me, been practicing for nine years, and has one of the premier law offices in Phoenix with over twenty attorneys working for her."

"Impressive," I whispered.

He nodded his agreement. "After I talked to Clarice, I got on the phone with Marcus to make sure they weren't involved with any of this, whatever it is, and he said they weren't. He also told me she paid him back four years ago for setting up her firm. She tried to pay them back for her education, but Daisy threw a shit fit, so she backed down from that."

Totes was gonna love this Daisy chick too.

He stopped talking and held my gaze.

Shit.

It was my turn.

While alternately finishing my French toast and my makeup, I gave him the lowdown about Clarice and "We."

When I was done, I watched in silent fascination as he stayed immobile, still leaning into the counter, waging an internal battle against his inner *Raye My Woman!* caveman idiot.

This took a while.

I knew my Cap emerged victorious when he cocked his head to the side and said, "Promise me one thing?"

I nodded.

"You get in a situation you don't like, you call me. No questions asked, I'll be at your back."

He...totally...

Rawked.

"I can promise that."

His inner caveman idiot took over as he lifted his hand and crooked a finger at me.

It was hot, so I tested the stability of my stool by pushing up on the foot bar to get close enough to give him a kiss.

There was tongue.

He tasted of Cap and coffee. I probably tasted of berries and maple syrup.

It was an awesome combo.

He broke the kiss and said, "Gotta hit it, babe."

I reached for my setting spray and reminded him, "Dinner with Dad is at six thirty."

"You doing okay with that?"

"You and Luna will be there, it'll be fine," I hoped I didn't lie.

He studied me a second, apparently approved of what he saw, rounded the bar, came in for another kiss (with more tongue), then he said against my lips, "See you tonight."

"Absolutely."

He took off.

I sprayed my face with setting spray.

When I went out to the car, I saw men disassembling the short security fence and wide gate by the mailboxes.

I called "Yo" to the workers as I strolled by.

They'd already stopped working and were checking out my legs in my short, rose dress with tiered skirt featuring micro-ruffles and ties at the shoulders.

Seriously.

How did men rule the world when they got distracted so easily?

I was almost to Tweety when I heard Alexis cry, "Raye!"

I stopped, turned and watched Alexis add to the workers' show by dashing gracefully in a part-prance, part-run, part leap, wearing a little swing skirt, a cropped cami bra and one of those wraparound long-sleeved cardigans dancers wore.

When she got to me, without a word of explanation (not that I needed one), she threw her arms around me and gave me a big hug.

I hugged her back.

The workers' show ended abruptly when Jacob sauntered onto the scene and shot them a murderous look. They abruptly became very interested in getting our old gate out of there.

Alexis prance-ran-leapt back to Jacob, and as if they'd been together for ages and practiced this a thousand times, with talent and elegance most people had to pay to watch, she executed a final leap so she ended seated on the side of his hip with her legs around him and arms around his shoulders.

He caught her effortlessly, one-armed with a hand firm on her ass.

I totally *knew* they'd be adorable together.

"Yo, Raye," he called.

We got the workers' attention again when I called back, "Move the fuckfest to your place, dude. Martha hammered on my door last night pissed as shit."

Alexis giggled gleefully.

"Will do," Jacob grunted, then carried her to his Jeep.

I got in Tweety and gave myself a second to idle at the exit as I looked down the length of the complex.

I'd vaguely noticed on Monday, workers had been out power-washing the building.

Again vaguely, yesterday, I saw it was primer day.

Today they were already at it, and it appeared the building was going to go from an outdated, faded seventies aqua, to a rich, ocean blue with subtly contrasting azure trim.

I approved.

And the old, dilapidated Oasis Square sign at the corner was already gone.

A new one that was a kickass mix of modern and retro tiki with a boarder of green palm fronds and bright-pink hibiscus flowers on an ocean-blue background with white lettering was in its place.

This reminded me of something I forgot to mention to Cap, so I cued him up and called him on the car speaker.

"All good?" he answered.

"I forgot to tell you," I said, pulling out on Seventh. "Luna got notified a unit opened at the Oasis. She's moving in October one."

"Great," he replied.

"It is. The thing is, she's been on the waiting list for over a year."

"Okay."

He didn't get it.

"And now suddenly she gets a unit? Don't you think that's weird?"

"You know everybody there. Is someone moving out?"

I thought on this.

I didn't know for certain, but I answered, "Robyn, who lives down from me, isn't a joiner, and she's never said, but I think the courtyard shindigs annoy her. I think this mostly because she rarely comes to them. And Mick, across the way, got pissed at something Martha said to him, and he never got over it. He's not a dick, though that's debatable since Martha said it to him, and he takes it out on everyone, so he can be surly. I could see him going. Then there's Ryan, down from him but on the first floor. He's a slick guy and the Oasis is totally a stepping stone for him. He got his real estate license about a year ago, and he's always working, so he's not around much. Maybe he's doing well and trading up. I mean, I do know he went from a Hyundai to a BMW a few months ago, so that would make sense."

"So it's likely someone is moving out. She's been on the waiting list a long time and people drop off lists like that, babe. They find somewhere else and settle in. Moving is a pain in the ass. Even if you're offered a crib in a kickass complex like the Oasis."

He was right.

And I loved he thought the Oasis was kickass.

"You're right."

His voice changed, and I knew why with what he said next, "There isn't bad lurking around every corner, honey."

There was.

And there wasn't.

But you couldn't live life like there was.

"Right again," I replied.

"I gotta go home to grab a blazer and fresh shirt for tonight, so I'm just gonna shower there and I'll be at your place at six."

"Sounds good."

"See you."

"Later, Cap."

We disconnected.

And as I drove to SC, I navigated seven people pulling out right in front of me, saw one person drive down the wrong side of the street until they were free to get into their lane, and crawled by a police and fire barricaded camper (circa the Partridge Family) that had an intact rear, but the entire front appeared to have exploded because it was a burnt-out shell.

None of this fazed me.

I'd learned a long time ago you couldn't take the Wild out of the West, so you just kept alert, got on with it and hoped you weren't next to a camper when it exploded.

I got to work before Luna, and I'd strapped my boring beige (but it worked with the dress) server apron around my waist and was sipping the dirty chai I made myself (after three hours of sleep, I needed caffeine fortification), when Luna strolled in.

She took one look at me, I took one look at her, I put the chai down, and we raced to each other, caught up our hands and girlie bounced.

When we stopped bouncing, I filled her in.

"We made up, we *did it*, multiple times, he gives *amazing head*, has an insanely pretty dick, said some unbelievably beautiful things to me, and it's all good."

She let me go, threw her hands up in the air and cried, "Yee ha!"

"After we were done, Martha came pounding on the door complaining about the noise Alexis and Jacob were making and how she feared Jacob was gonna fuck Alexis in half," I continued.

She threw her hands up in the air again and shouted, "Yee ha!"

"Are you gonna be able to get out of your lease?" I asked.

Her lease wasn't up until January.

"I have to pay a month's extra rent or lose my deposit, but I can cover that, so the Oasis is a go and I told them to send the lease agreement."

I threw up my hands and yelled, "Yee ha!" Then I told her, "Cap's gonna shower at his place and be at mine at six to go to Lon's. Want us to swing around and pick you up?"

"That'd be cool."

We both stared at each other, then simultaneously threw up our hands and exclaimed, "Yee ha!"

"Yeesh, are you two done?" Byron asked.

I turned to him. "Sit your ass down. I'll bring your drink to you."

"What's got into you?" he asked.

"I'm falling in love."

He smiled. "Congrats."

Then he went to his table.

It was after the lunch crush when they walked in.

Specifically, *he* walked in.

I knew it was him immediately. If the long-ass beard didn't give it away, then the messy gray-blond hair, the flannel shirt buttoned up to his neck (I couldn't see due to the beard, but the way it sat on his shoulders told me this), even though it was ninety-seven degrees outside, and the sheer enormity of his frame would have.

He was with a pretty blonde lady who was maybe ten, fifteen years his junior.

Oh my *God*.

I was dropping some of Lucia's chili-chorizo fettucine on a table.

Luna was close, doing a water run.

I knew she saw him too when she said, "Oh my *God*."

He looked around the space, caught sight of me and boomed loudly, "You Raye?"

In a flash—and if you'd asked me a second before, I would have told you no way he could move that fast—Tito was standing beside me.

Then again, there were mild hints of serial killer in the big, bearded man's affect.

"Are you Tex?" I asked.

He put his long, beefy arms out to his sides. "Who else would I be?"

Taking in all that was him, this was a pertinent question.

"You know him?" Tito asked.

I looked down at Tito. "No. But he's a friend of Cap's."

Tito nodded, turned to Tex and gave him a long look, then flip-flopped back to his table.

Luna and I went to Tex.

I jerked a thumb at Luna. "This is my friend, Luna."

He put his arm around the blonde, and even though we were standing right in front of him, he still was booming, "This is my wife, Nancy."

"Hi, Nancy," I greeted.

"Raye." She smiled a dazzling, kilowatt smile at me. She turned it to Luna. "Luna."

Tex was looking around, and still booming, he decreed, "This place is the shit. Though, your espresso machine is a bust. Two filters? Amateur. You need four."

"Okay," I said slowly.

"He's the barista at Indy's bookstore," Nancy explained. "He knows espresso machines."

"Incidental," Tex grunted. Then he asked me, "What do you need? Tasers? Stun guns?"

Apparently, he'd been briefed about me.

I shook my head. "Got those."

"Grenades? Smoke bombs? Tear gas?" he went on.

Luna and I were struck dumb by this offer.

"TSA would get up in my face if I packed 'em. Don't need the hassle of another prison sentence. Nance and the kitties need me around," he said. "Anyway, we needed wheels when we got here to look over the place, so Nance and I drove down."

Another prison sentence?

And...

The kitties?

Luna found her voice first. "You have grenades?"

"Sure," he replied (still kinda booming).

"Um..." I didn't quite respond. Then I steered it to a subject I could wrap my head around, "You have kitties?"

"Cats," Nancy put in. "Tex and I have a cat sitting business. Though we have our own cats too." She looked up at him. "How many do we have? I lost count."

"Nine," he said. "No, ten. Didn't like the feel of that asshole who brought us Oreo, didn't give him his cat back."

Uh.

What?

"You stole someone's cat?" I asked.

He leveled his blue gaze on me, and I fought quailing.

"I don't like the feel of you, you don't get your cat back."

"Okay," I agreed quickly, wondering how their cat sitting business continued to be a business when he occasionally stole client's cats.

"Raye sits people's pets," Luna told them.

"Yeah," I said. "I have Patches now. He's a calico. But his momma is super sweet," I assured. "She had to go home and look after her mom who had hip replacement therapy."

Tex nodded his approval of this excuse to abandon your cat with a sitter.

"Want a coffee?" Luna offered.

"What kinda grub you got here?" Tex asked. "We haven't had lunch."

I smiled up at him. "The best kind. Sit your asses down, and we'll get you sorted."

We got them to a table. We got them menus. And we dropped waters on them.

While they perused their choices, and in between taking care of other customers, I texted Cap, *Tex is here.*

I wasn't surprised when, about five seconds later, my phone rang, telling me Cap was calling.

I took the call.

"Yo," I answered.

"What the fuck?" he asked.

"It's all cool," I told him. "He seems nice. But he talks really loud."

I heard him swear under his breath and then, back to me, he said, "I should have warned you. My crew has big mouths. And they're nosy as fuck."

"Honestly. Like I said, it's all cool."

"It's not cool my crew just drops in on you while you're working, Raye."

"How fresh are the chicharrones?" Tex hollered all the way across the space from his seat at a back wall.

Everyone turned to look.

"Super fresh!" I hollered back.

"Could munch on some a' those while Nance is deciding!" He was still hollering.

"On it!" I was still hollering too.

"Christ," Cap said in my ear.

"Gotta go. See you later," I said to him.

"Raye—"

I disconnected and hit the register to punch in the chicharrones order.

I noted Tito's pumpkin-orange-framed sunglasses trained on Tex.

Tex noted it too.

"Yo!" he greeted.

Tito tipped his panama hat to Tex then to Nancy and went back to his book.

When I took their chicharrones to them, I told them, "The guy in the corner is Tito. He's my boss, and he owns the place."

"Right on, man!" Tex boomed at him then flicked a finger out to indicate the space.

Tito looked at him again and dipped his chin.

"He doesn't say much, but he's a super sweet guy," I informed him.

I knew Tex took this in, but then his gaze went beyond me and his back straightened.

I turned to see Cap stalking to the table, Eric following him.

Eric was looking around.

Cap was homed in on Tex.

Oh man.

I made an approach and tried to waylay him but there was no waylaying going to happen, so, with the arm he put around my waist when I made it to him, he essentially dragged me to Tex and Nancy's table.

"Yo, Cap," Tex said casually when we got there.

"You think to warn me you're gonna show in town and hit up my girlfriend at her place of business?" Cap asked.

"Can't get a proper bead on her if you warn her I'm comin'," Tex returned. "She'll try to be all nice and shit. Don't got time for that garbage."

He then crunched into a chicharron.

I thought I might have to draw on my health and safety training when his eyes bugged out of his head after he swallowed.

"*Fuck!*" he bellowed.

Again, everyone in the place turned to look.

"What? Are they okay?" I asked.

"What's this shit sprinkled on them?" he asked.

"I don't know. Lucia doesn't divulge her cooking secrets. Don't you like them?"

"They're the absolute shit." He shoved the entire chicharron in his mouth and munched loudly.

"This isn't Fortnum's, Tex," Cap said between his teeth. "You can't shout and curse and act like you have no manners because people are used to your shit."

After Cap said that, his head turned sharply and so did mine.

Again, Tito was right there.

He put a hand on Cap's arm, took it off right away, and said quietly, "We welcome everyone here, son."

He then looked around.

Cap looked around.

I looked around.

After the initial curse bellowed through the place grabbed their attention, now, no one was staring or paying us any mind.

Granted, we didn't have huge men with wild-ass beards and hair who shouted all the time frequenting our establishment (until now).

But Luna, Harlow, Jessie and I worked there.

Not to mention, like I said, you couldn't take the Wild out of the West.

Just sayin'.

Tito gave Cap a slight bow, one to Tex, then he shuffled back to his table.

"Like that guy," Tex declared and chomped into a chicharron sideways in his mouth.

"Fucking hell," Cap muttered.

Luna sidled up. "You guys have lunch?"

She asked this to Eric.

"Yeah, but I wouldn't say no to a to-go coffee," he replied.

Harlow shoved her aside, batted her eyelashes and said, "What can I get you?"

Jessie shoved Harlow aside and said, "I make a wicked dragon fruit refresher. Better than Starbucks."

We all jumped when Tex boomed, "Fuck Starbucks!"

"Word, my man," Jessie replied.

Tex crunched into another chicharron.

My three friends herded Eric to the bar, and I led Cap to a safe space, that being through the kitchen, the employee locker and break area, out the employee entrance and amidst the herb garden.

I then put both hands on his chest, leaned into him and said, "Okay, totally down with you looking after me. *Totally*," I stressed.

He knew what was coming, put his hands on my hips and started, "Babe—"

"But you don't have to protect me from your own people," I finished.

"Tex is a lot," he told me something I'd figured out on my own.

"Tex is down here because your people know you and I are a thing, and he wants to look me over. I love he cares enough about you to do that. It's amazing. It's beautiful, really. I mean, it isn't like he drove down from Flagstaff or something."

Cap looked into the windows.

I put my hand to his cheek and brought him back to me.

"I'm fine."

"You're seeing your dad tonight, and you don't need to put up with any shit on the run up to that."

Ah.

There it was.

I leaned deeper into him. "Honey, I promise. *I'm fine*."

His eyes moved over my face.

Then his hands moved to my ass, he bent his head and kissed me.

It got hot, it got heavy, and I'd wrapped my arms around his neck, and we were going for it when we heard Jessie shout through an opened pane in the window, "Get a room!"

"No! Don't! This is hot!" Harlow shouted out of another one.

Cap broke the kiss.

I twisted my neck to look over my shoulder to Tito's table.

His sunglasses, as ever, were covering his eyes.

But on his lips, there was a smile.

SEVENTEEN

INNER CAVEMAN

A t around 5:57 that evening, I was standing in my bedroom staring at myself in my full-length mirror, realizing how fortuitous it was that Tex showed at SC and provided a distraction.

I wore the off-the-shoulder, figure skimming, mid-shin-hitting, black jersey dress that Luna had suggested for my first date with Cap.

Inspired by Betsy's walls, I'd paired this with my bubblegum-pink, patent-leather, killer spiked pumps. I'd smoothed my hair back into an artful bun at the nape of my neck. I'd augmented this with a hammered silver collar and wrist cuff, along with a big silver statement ring. And I'd refreshed and augmented my makeup and perfume.

I looked like a woman who had it going on.

But I had butterflies in my stomach.

The memories were from a long time ago, but when my dad was *a dad*, he'd been a good one. He was about swinging you up on his shoulders and sneaking bowls of ice cream when Mom wasn't looking, and making different voices when he read to you at night.

Having opened the drawbridge to my Citadel, these memories were drifting through, and with them were remembrances of years of yearning to have that back. There was even recalling the anger I'd had toward Macy for taking it away, twisted tightly with shame for having that feeling when it was not at all her fault.

But I was a kid.

And I wanted my dad.

As I hit adulthood, and now facing a man who was clearly extending an olive branch, or whatever this was, what was also drifting along that lowered drawbridge was anger at Dad for taking so damn long to get his shit together.

Sure, one could argue I could have extended that olive branch.

But I'd learned a long time ago he was so lost to his pain, there was nothing getting through.

Not even me.

And it killed to keep trying something like that...and failing.

Hence, my move to Phoenix. But that didn't begin the estrangement between us, it just added distance to it. Distance that was a safety net, or in my case, a very wide moat around my mental health fortress.

And now the bridge over that moat had been lowered and my safety net was gone.

I heard the door open, then I heard Cap call, "Baby?"

I walked to the door to the hall.

Patches was lounged on the back of my armchair and Cap was scratching his head when his eyes went down the hall to me, and he stopped dead.

"Hey," I called. "Gonna grab my bag and be right there."

I went to the bed, nabbed the Cult Gaia pink clutch I'd already prepped and headed down the hall.

Cap, as I was coming to realize was Cap's way (and I liked this way), put his hands to my hips when I got to him.

"You look beautiful," he said.

So sweet.

He was in a navy blazer this time, light-blue shirt, another pair of dark wash jeans. He worked the semi-monochromatic big time, and it made the blue in his eyes stand out.

"You don't look so bad yourself," I replied.

His grip tightened. "No, Raye. You look *beautiful*."

I froze.

Cap didn't.

He asked, "You doing okay?"

I bested the herculean effort to recover from his words and how much they meant to me, and shared, "I'm remembering I'm pissed at my dad for not being my dad."

"Understandable."

"So I'm nervous."

"Again, understandable."

"I'm also really glad you and Luna are coming with me tonight."

"Wouldn't be anywhere else."

He was the greatest.

I leaned into him.

He kissed my nose, probably because he didn't want to ruin my pink lipstick or have it all over his beard.

"Ready?" he asked.

I nodded and turned to Patches. "No scratching the furniture."

He flicked his tail, which said, *You're not the boss of me.*

I gave his booty a scratch.

He squinted his eyes to say I was forgiven for trying to order him around.

Cap interrupted this exchange by taking my hand and pulling me out the door.

Alexis and Jacob were in the pool, wrapped around each other, floating in the deep end, making out so hard, I wondered how they didn't sink. Bill and Zach were sitting outside Linda's apartment in her woven bucket chairs with what looked like a pitcher of margaritas. Sally, a chick who lived opposite me, was out watering the plethora of pots that adorned her front door.

"Hey, all," I cried.

Sally whirled, "Hey, Raye! You look pretty!"

"Thanks!"

I got waves from Linda, Bill and Zach, so I waved back.

Jacob and Alexis ignored me.

"Man's making up for lost time," Cap said as he guided me down the stairs.

"He carried her to his Jeep on his hip this morning. I think she was going to rehearsal and he was driving her there. She has her own car. So that's a big, fat *yeah*."

Cap caught my gaze, his beard lifted up at the sides of his mouth and his eyes crinkled.

Our new security gate was a pale blue that worked really well with the new ocean of the walls. It was also a foot taller than the old one so, unless you were Cap's height or taller, you couldn't see inside. Last, it was pretty and decorative, but it had wicked spikes at the top so you'd think twice in trying to climb it.

"Landlord's not fucking around either," Cap noted.

All the painting and fence/gate switch outs were done by the time I got home.

"Nope. Not at all."

He put me in his Porsche (yes, he scored a visitor spot again, it had to be a kind of magic), and we headed to Luna's.

Cap had barely stopped at the curb before she was out the door, wearing a black halter maxi dress with a high, side slit and a print of large cream flowers and green leaves.

My best bitch had hella style. She looked great.

I felt my stomach dip when Cap got out to open the door for her.

Yeesh, he was something.

She folded in behind me, and I turned to look at her over the seat as he closed her door.

"I know I should be liberated, but he's pure class," she said.

"I know," I replied.

Cap angled in beside me as she inquired, "You doing okay?"

"I'm good."

"She's nervous," Cap put in as he glided from the curb.

I shot his profile a look.

"You're nervous?" she asked me.

"I'll be fine," I assured her.

"And she's pissed," Cap added.

"Cap!" I snapped.

Dude spilling all my secrets.

"What?" he asked. "Luna and I are a team tonight. You don't let your team member go in unprepared."

"Damn straight," Luna agreed.

I righted myself in my seat, seeing the error of my ways of fostering a kinship between these two.

"And just to say, I'd be nervous too, but more pissed," Luna said.

Hmm.

We weren't best friends for nothing.

Cap drove, and the nervous took over the pissed, so I was checking my lipstick in the mirror on the sun visor when Cap pulled around the fountain in the circular front drive of the Hermosa Inn where Lon's restaurant was located.

Thus, at first, I didn't know why Cap murmured a low, angry, "Goddamn it," and Luna emitted a surprised, "Holy shit."

I flipped the visor up and stared at the area in front of the adobe building with its double wooden doors, wooden benches, saguaro, paloverde and exceptional lighting.

Mingling there were Scott and Louise, Shirleen, and Tex and Nancy, Tex wearing what I assumed was fancy for him, jeans and a jean shirt.

Scott noticed our approach first and got to my door before the valet could, Louise and Shirleen close to his back. Once the doors were unlocked, Cap wasted no time knifing out.

Scott opened my door and helped me out, immediately explaining, "We couldn't let you do this alone."

"I called ahead, changed the reservation, got us a bigger table,"

Shirleen told Cap over the hood of the car while he handed off the key fob to the valet.

Scott moved to help Luna out.

"They got steaks here? Because I don't eat fancy shit."

Tex was there.

My head was spinning.

"Shirleen, a word," Cap bit off after he prowled around the Porsche.

"Ain't no word we gonna have will change our minds, boy," she replied. "Met up with them at the hostess stand, so been talkin' to Raye's real parents. They had the same idea as me. We warned the hostess. They're settin' us up with an even bigger table. It's all good."

"I want a word anyway," Cap demanded.

She heaved a beleaguered sigh, dramatically rolled her eyes then looked to me. "You look real pretty, child."

"Thanks, Shirleen."

"You too," she said to Luna.

"Thanks," she replied.

The valet drove off in Cap's car.

I stared after it longingly, wondering if I could run fast enough in my bubblegum-pink pumps to latch onto the bumper.

Cap took his mother's hand, tucked it to his chest and dragged her in her fabulous orange dress with the gold band belt behind a paloverde.

Scott sidled close to me and said low, "Please don't be angry, sweetheart. Louise has been a mess since Luna told us you were going to dinner with him tonight. If you want, we can ask for a different table. We'll take Shirleen, Tex and Nancy with us. We just need to be close."

Damn it, I was going to start crying.

I hadn't fought off this many tears since...since...

I didn't go there.

"My man," Tex said, "we don't do it that way. You make a decision to get up in someone's business, you stay the course. You back down, trust me, I been through this ten fuckin' times, these women will drag you through the gauntlet, and if you survive, drag you right back. Now, I'm not sayin' it ain't all kinds of fun, sometimes, if bullets aren't flyin', but you gotta get in on the beginnin' so you not only don't get left out of the action, but you can keep it under control."

"We *are* being very intrusive," Nancy who was now close said. "But Tex is right."

"What do you mean, you've been through this ten times?" Louise asked.

"We got ten girls," Tex told her. "They aren't ours through blood, though one a' them is Nancy's, but they're ours all the same." He turned back to Scott. "Listen to me, buster, when the cars start explodin' and the egg drop soup starts flyin', you'll wish you took a firmer hand."

Scott stared at him in horror mixed with confusion. Louise had the same expression.

I had a feeling I wore an expression not far from that, and I'd already heard some of the stories.

Cap and Shirleen reappeared with Cap looking like he was contemplating homicide, and Shirleen smiling a big smile, so I knew how their convo went.

"Let's get inside," Shirleen announced when she made it to us. "Shirleen needs an appletini."

Shirleen claimed Luna and drew her down the brick walkway that led to Lon's.

Tex claimed Nancy and guided her behind them.

Scott claimed Louise, and with a worried glance back at me, he walked Louise after them.

That was when Cap claimed me and started us moving, but a lot slower.

"I'm pissed as fuck, but you okay?" he asked.

"Yes," I said uncertainly.

"She knows what you mean to me, so she's being protective of you, but this shit still isn't right," he muttered angrily.

"I think it will be fine," I told him.

He stopped us and turned to me. "Cards on the table, she just told me she and the Rock Chicks got nosy, they looked you up, so she knows about Macy and your mom. Which is part of the reason why she's being so fuckin' out of line right now."

I nodded slowly.

In a strange and what I was learning Rock Chick way, that was sweet.

"So I'm pissed as fuck about that too," he continued.

I kept nodding.

"Her heart's in the right place. I'm still angry."

I put my hand to his neck. "This is what love is, I guess. Seems, even though we've had it for a while, we're both not used to it."

He jerked his head up to communicate he got me and then started us toward Lon's again.

Of course, I saw Tex seating Nancy at a long table because I could spot Tex in a crowded football stadium, but it was at the back of the patio, by the fireplace, and there were a lot of people milling around, and trees with fairy lights in the way, so I didn't see much more.

My chest tightened when I spied my dad, appearing confused and shaking Scott's hand.

We got ever closer when Louise and Shirleen cleared away, and I saw her at my father's side.

I halted in my tracks.

Cap halted with me.

"What?" he asked.

It had been years. I hadn't seen her since...since...

I wasn't sure, but I thought it was since the last time I was over at her house playing with Macy and her best friend, when I was eight.

She'd aged, but it was her.

It was the woman who'd been in her house across the street when someone took my sister.

And my dad had his arm around her.

He'd said "we" in his text.

Good God, until that moment, I'd totally forgotten the "we."

"Baby,"—Cap was curling my resisting body into his—"*what?*"

"That's...it's...with Dad, that's Deb. Debbie. Deborah." I swallowed and looked up at him. "That's Miss Deb, the lady who lived across the street from the playground Macy was taken from."

Cap's head whipped to the side, and I was in a daze, but even so, I felt his inner *Raye My Woman!* caveman take control with such savagery, it was like the ground shook under my feet.

Shirleen knew her son, she felt the vibe, and she was clicking over in her beautiful gold slingbacks double time.

She entered his line of sight and Cap shifted both of us so he didn't lose his lock on my father.

"Look at me, Julien," she demanded sharply.

He didn't look at her.

She dipped into his vision again. "Look at me, son."

His beard flexing, he looked to her.

"What are we dealing with here?" she asked. "I need to smooth things over while you take Raye away?"

"No," I said in a small voice. "I'm okay."

My small voice was a mistake.

A *big* mistake.

Cap's head snapped to me, his eyes narrowed on my face, and without a beat passing, he took my hand, placed it in Shirleen's, and there's no other way to put it, he bore down on my dad.

"Oh shit," both Shirleen and I said at the same time, and we clickety-clacked on our pumps, triple time, to Cap.

We got to him when Cap was finishing growling, "...a word."

Having no clue why they were doing it, but also feeling the vibe, Tex and Scott had taken his back. My dad, not missing the threat, had a pale face, and Deb, at his side holding his arm with both hands, had one too.

"Hi, Dad," I said.

He turned to me where I was standing at his side.

He got no chance to say anything, because Cap was speaking again.

Now, to me.

"Sit down, order a drink, baby. I'm gonna have a chat with your father."

"I think we should all sit down, honey. But first let me introduce you to—"

"Rachel," he clipped.

I closed my mouth.

Okay.

This was my guy.

And this was his job.

And honestly?

I didn't have it in me to find the words I needed to share with my dad in that moment.

I was relieved Cap was going to do it.

I didn't know what words he was going to say, exactly.

I was still glad he was going to say them.

I turned to my dad and said, "I'm sorry, Dad. This is Julien Jackson. He's my boyfriend. And he's very protective of me." My eyes swept through Deb, but I still saw her wince when I finished, "Especially around the issue of Macy."

"I told you, you should have warned her, Charlie," Deb whispered.

"I don't think that now's the—" my father began.

"Dad, you really need to go," I said softly. "Or I won't be here for another ten seconds. Cap will take me away."

Stiffly, now pissed too, a reaction that made my insides hollow out, I was so familiar with it, Dad lifted his chin, and with movements that were also rigid, walked away.

Cap followed him.

"Maybe I should go to our room," Deb murmured.

Our room.

"Are you two together?" I asked her.

"Honey, I think your father—" she started.

"You were going to ambush me," I cut her off. "I'm sorry, Debbie, but you don't get to make the decisions when the tables are turned."

"I told Charlie he should have this first dinner with you alone," she remarked.

"Well, that didn't happen. You're standing right here," I pointed out.

"Right. Then, okay." A big breath then, "We...we reconnected a... a little while ago," she told me.

"How long ago?" I asked.

She swallowed.

"How long?" I pushed.

"We were married three years ago."

I felt like she'd punched me in the stomach.

Married?

"Three years ago," I whispered.

"Yes," she admitted, practically squirming under my stare.

I didn't care.

Three years ago, my father remarried.

And he didn't *tell me.*

"Do you have a phone?" I asked sharply.

"Rachel," she whispered.

"Tell me!" I shouted. "Do you have a phone?"

"Yes, of course," she said quietly.

I pointed in her face. "So *you* could have called me. Or *you* as his *wife* could have made *him* call me."

She lifted her chin. "You have a phone too, Rachel."

"And I use it. How am I supposed to know my father is seeing a woman, and marrying her, unless someone fucking *shares that with me!*"

I felt Cap's hand on my back.

I looked up at him. "We're going."

"Rachel." Dad was in my space, speaking urgently.

"Back off," Cap snarled.

Dad was blurry with the tears in my eyes. "I'd want you to be happy. Don't you think I'd want that for you?"

"Deb and I didn't—" he began.

I could take no more.

"*What?*" I shouted in his face. "What didn't you? I didn't blame her. *You* did. But it was *nineteen years ago!*"

"Tex, get my car," Cap growled.

But I was all about my dad.

"Not cool, treating your wife like your dirty little secret," I sniped. "Springing her on me like a nasty little surprise."

"It wasn't me who brought seven people to a dinner without telling me," Dad shot back.

I got up on my toes to get in his face. "I didn't ask them. They showed. Think about that, Dad. Think about *why* the people who love me are so worried about me having a dinner with my father, they turn up to support me. My father who has not *once* bothered to come out and visit me, see the life I've built, the family I've made, the beauty I have. Think about *that.*"

"You didn't come home either," he retorted.

I threw out my arms. "To what? *Home,*" I scoffed. "Home to me is your anger and shame and guilt, and you forgetting every...*fucking*... day you may have lost one daughter, but you had the other one, and you didn't give that first *shit.*"

His head jerked like I'd slapped him.

"Look after your woman, Julien," Shirleen ordered.

She was a woman too, so she also knew me.

And I was about to lose it.

That was all she had to say.

It was me who had my hand tucked to Cap's chest, we walked through the beautiful, fairy light-strewn courtyard of Lon's down the brick walkway and to Cap's waiting car.

Cap opened my door.

Tex opened Luna's.

We got in. And Cap took me away.

"SHIRLEEN COULD GET USED TO THIS."

We were sitting in the courtyard of the Oasis.

Yes, all of us.

Since Luna had ordered in a bunch of pizzas, and Scott had gone out and got a bunch of craft beer, Linda, Martha, Jacob, Alexis and Sally had also joined us.

Luna ordered more pizza and added some boneless wings.

Shirleen was kicked back in a patio chair, her gold slingbacks on one of the tables, ankles crossed, sipping from a beer.

They'd all followed us to my place, and I'd begged Cap not to send them away, so he didn't. He definitely didn't take Luna to drop her off at her place first. He wanted my bestie close to me.

God, yes.

I was totally falling for this guy.

Jacob and Alexis were the only ones in the courtyard when we hit it. They were still frolicking in the pool.

Jacob took one look at me, though, and he hauled them both out, they dried off, got dressed and by the time Cap had opened the gate to the rest of our party, Linda and Martha had joined us, Linda with searching, gentle eyes on me, Martha waiting for someone to tell her who to eviscerate.

Sally just wandered down.

Luna and Alexis were in my space, Jacob standing sentry, like he needed to beat back a horde, and I'd pulled up the drawbridge on my Citadel of Denial and was drowning my sorrows in artisanal hops.

Tex had his jeans rolled up to his knees and his feet in the pool.

I heard Nancy ask him, "You like it here, don't you?"

"We got loads of grandbabies," he replied.

"They're pretty grown, sweetheart, and they'd like spring break by a pool," she said. "And I'd like a break from snow."

Though what she didn't say was that he wasn't getting any

younger, and maybe it was time to set aside the portafilter, load up the cats and kick back for a while.

Scott was crowding Cap, trying to distract him with every conversational gambit in his arsenal. He didn't have a son. He didn't know how to do this. But he was a man, and he knew where Cap's head was at with me, and no one needed Cap driving back to the Hermosa Inn.

Cap was at an overpopulated table with Louise, Shirleen, Martha and Linda, conversing with Scott, but his eyes often strayed to me where I was stretched out on a lounger, sandwiched between the two Luna and Alexis had pulled up tight to mine.

I watched Jacob wander over to Cap, but I didn't hear what he said, his back was to me. Though, I did see Cap get up and walk away with him, where they formed a huddle.

Maybe Jacob was asking what was going on, why we were all gussied up and gone for less than an hour, and I'd returned looking like I'd been hit by a truck.

Maybe he was sharing the best dispensaries to buy weed.

I was in my Citadel, so I wasn't thinking too much on it.

I was taking a sip of beer when I heard Ryan call from the gate, "Hey, Raye. You know this guy? He says he's your dad."

The pool area went wired.

My dad walked into the courtyard.

I tried to scramble out of my lounger, but had no egress with Luna and Alexis butted up against me.

Luna got out of her chair, took my beer and pulled her lounger away so I could get up.

I felt Cap at my back, and a lot of other people, both physically and emotionally, when my father made it to me.

"Can I have a word in private with you?" he asked me tautly.

"You can say no, Raye," Luna, at my side, reminded me.

"What's going on?" I heard Ryan ask somebody.

"Quiet," Martha, who was unsurprisingly close, shushed him.

I thought about Luke's lesson to Cap and I suggested, "Maybe we need some space to cool down. We can have dinner on Saturday before you leave."

Luna's body jerked.

Whoops.

That was her birthday party.

"Friday, sorry," I corrected. "I have important plans I can't miss on Saturday."

"We're in Phoenix to see you, Rachel," Dad pointed out.

"The fact that's a *we*, and it wasn't shared you've had a wife for three years and longer is the issue, Dad," I reminded him.

Dad shook his head and pulled his hand through his graying blond hair.

It was then I saw how thick it was. What a nice haircut he had. That it looked like he'd lost weight, firmed up. He was in a spot, but he was still standing taller. And when his eyes fell on mine, the same color of my own, they were bright and clear and...

Engaged.

I took a small step back and hit Cap's body.

He put a hand to my hip.

Right.

Better.

Dad watched this.

"I'm gla—" He cleared his throat. "I'm glad you have so many good people in your life, Rachel."

"So am I."

"You need to know, Deb told me, a long time ago, when we met again, when things sparked between us, that I should tell you. She said it often, and she was upset about the fact I didn't. She was upset you weren't at our wedding."

"She was right about that, and she was right to feel that way."

"I thought..." he shook his head and looked away.

I said nothing.

He came back to me. "I thought, with the way we lost your mom, your sister, that..." He shook his head again. "Dammit, Rachel, I thought you blamed me. Blamed me for not protecting Macy from being snatched from our lives. Blamed me for not looking after your mother so her grief drained the life from her so there was none to take when she hung herself."

I heard gasps, Linda and Alexis, and a sharp hiss, my guess, Martha.

I ignored those.

So now they knew.

They belonged in my Citadel with me.

Not the denial.

The fortification of my well-being.

"I didn't blame you, Dad. You blamed yourself."

"You escaped me the minute you could," he accused.

"I escaped the loneliness. *You left me alone.*" I swung my arm wide to my side, nearly hitting Luna, and Cap wrapped his around my belly. "You left me alone in dealing with all the shit around Macy. All the fear and hope and devastation and worry. You left me alone when Mom had already drifted away from me. And then when she finalized that. I was sick of being alone. Look at me. I'm not alone."

"I lost my baby." His voice cracked. "I lost my wife."

"I lost my sister. I lost my mother. I lost my *father.*"

"I'm right here," he said in a pleading voice.

"You've been married for three years and I didn't even know you were seeing somebody," I snapped.

Another couple gasps and hisses.

"Rachel—"

Martha stepped between us. "Enough."

"Martha, now is not—" I began.

She looked over her shoulder at me.

"Quiet, my lovely," she said softly.

I shut my mouth because she'd never called me an endearment (or anyone, even her grandchildren, not that I'd heard), and I'd never heard her talk quietly.

Ever.

She turned back to my father.

"I don't know what's going on, but the little I've heard, it's not good. It seems you got some shit to deal with, sir. So I encourage you to give your daughter some space and deal with it. But before you go, know this about the girl you left behind. This place,"—she indicated the Oasis with a flap of both arms—"it's a community. And Raye is the heart of it. I'm sure we'd all get along all right, but she doesn't walk out of her unit without calling, 'hey.' She looks after our pets. She's the ringleader of our shindigs. She organized us all to make sure Linda got fed and her sheets changed when she was down with Covid. I got a million different examples for you of how she unites us, and in my case, 'cause I'm ornery, puts up with us. But that's her too, she's a leader, so people look to her, and they follow that lead."

She took a sharp breath...

And kept going.

"But I'm not gonna get into all that, because I'm so damned mad to learn that she does all of it because she was hungry for a family. But I guess I got you to thank for what she gives us. Though, I'm not feelin' real thankful at the mo'. So you go away and you think on that, and you sit down to dinner with your daughter on Friday and figure out a way to fix this. Because let me assure you, you are *missing out*. We got her, so we're good. And it sounds like you lost a lot, but you had a diamond in your hands and you threw it away. It's up to you to figure out how to get it back. But now, she wants you to go, so you're leaving."

Jacob moved forward.

Sally did too.

Dad had tears in his eyes, and he looked at me.

"Darlin', I've always loved you."

"You can't just say it, sir," Alexis said quietly. "You have to show it."

Jacob got closer to my dad.

Dad stared at me.

"Jacob," Martha issued her order tersely.

Dad moved.

His arms shooting out, he caught me, pulled me into his body, wrapped me tight, pushed his face in my neck, and sobbed, "I've missed you, Raye, so damned much, honey."

Tentatively, I put my hands on his back.

He lifted up, cupped my face to his hands, ran his thumbs across my cheeks, and whispered, "You look just like your mom."

My body bucked.

Cap's hand wrapped around the back of my neck.

"I wanted you to go," Dad said.

"What?" I whispered.

Cap's hand squeezed.

"I couldn't protect you," he pushed out. "Christ, every day I woke up, terrified of what might happen to you."

And it happened again.

My insides hollowed out.

"Oh, Dad," I said softly.

"She was on a fucking playground. How can a kid not be safe on a fucking playground?"

Oh God.

I pushed into him, and this time held on tight.

"It wasn't your fault," I said, cheek to his chest.

"It was, honey."

"It wasn't."

"You'll have kids one day and you'll get it. It *was*." He pulled me away with my face in his hands again, and he said, "But I wanna work on it because it's torture, you being far from me. I thought I deserved it. I thought it was my penance. I thought you'd be safer, far away from me. But I couldn't hack it. Then, when it got too much, and I'd break down and think to come to you, I'd think again I was being weak. You went away, and I thought you did it to protect yourself from me. I thought you needed the distance. So I stayed away. But it's not that. It's not weak. I miss my little girl. So I'm gonna work on it because I need you in my life."

I put my hand over one of his at my face. "Does Deb make you happy?"

"Yes, but it's incomplete because you aren't a part of it. I hate that I do that to her too. I just can't seem to stop...fucking up."

"He left us with this, Dad. This is all on him. But he took Macy. We can't keep giving him pieces of us."

He nodded. "You're right."

I put my other hand to his and curled both around, taking his from my face, but I held them between us.

"You need to go back to Deb," I said.

"She lives with the guilt too."

I figured that was part of the draw.

Though, Deb was very pretty, and if memory served, really sweet.

"You're right. You have work to do. Both of you. But it isn't your fault. I don't blame you. Mom didn't."

"She did."

Hang on.

"What?"

"She blamed me, and she blamed Deb. I protected you from it when she'd lose it. The words she'd hurl at me. She hated me before she stopped feeling anything. I didn't want you to know. After we lost her. Your memories of her were already jaded. I wanted you to be able to keep hold of what little you had. I didn't want to tell you how much hate she had for me, how deeply she blamed me."

"How could she blame you? You had nothing to do with it."

"She sent Macy to Deb's so she could get her hair done. The truth of it is, darlin', she couldn't stand the guilt she felt herself, so she transferred it to me."

God, this was so *fucked up*.

He looked over my shoulder, so I looked over my shoulder to see everyone else had drifted away.

Everyone but Cap, Luna, Scott, Louise and Shirleen.

"I'm glad she has you," Dad said to Cap.

Cap, his hand still on my neck, gave it a squeeze, then he wrapped his arm around my belly again and gently pulled me away.

That was the only response he gave my dad.

"Right." Dad sniffed. "Friday. You bring whoever you need to bring, darlin'. We'll figure it out."

"Okay," I agreed.

His eyes moved over my face like he was drinking it in, memorizing it.

My eyes, I knew, were doing the same.

Then he nodded decisively and turned to walk away.

He got only a few steps in before I called, "Dad."

He turned back.

"I missed you too."

He gave me a small, sad smile, a low wave, then he was gone.

When I lost sight of him, I wilted in Cap's arm.

But he wasn't the one who caught me.

When the first sob came, it sounded against Linda's neck.

The next one, Martha's arms were also around me.

The next one, Alexis had burrowed in.

The next, Jacob had surrounded all of us in his embrace.

It was then, I realized I no longer lived in my Citadel, and I hadn't for a long time.

I'd moved to an Oasis.

EIGHTEEN

DAD INTERRUPTED

F leetwood Mac's "Dreams" sounded, waking me up.

I was spooning with Cap.

I turned around and saw his blue-gray eyes were open and on me.

So I said, "I'm glad you topped us both up with orgasms yesterday morning, considering I was such a wreck last night."

His beard twitched, and he murmured, "Baby."

I pressed closer and his arm tightened around me.

I was feeling a little hazy, which was how I felt the morning after I'd taken a pot gummie, something Luna urged me to do last night so I'd sleep, and Cap was right there with her.

"What did you and Jacob talk about last night?" I asked.

"First, how you doin'?"

I should have known he wouldn't let me dodge it.

"I'll live."

"Raye," he warned.

I sighed.

"That was a lot," I admitted.

"I take it you sought therapy, but your parents didn't get it for you."

"Oh, we talked to somebody. Family counseling. Mom was so vague, if I was old enough to consider it, I would think she was drugged. Her not engaging just made Dad madder. So, obviously, it didn't work real great."

"It fucks me to say this."

It might fuck him, but he didn't say it.

So I asked, "What?"

"He loves you, Raye. He loves you a lot."

I shoved my face in his throat, because last night Dad had made that obvious. "Yeah."

I just wasn't sure what to do with it.

"I got no advice," Cap started. "Got no idea what you should do. Only thing I know is, he really fucked it up, but he was giving it a shot. He wants to reconnect. And it's obvious he's wanted that a long time."

I tipped my head back, and he dipped his chin down to look at me.

"Yeah." I slid my hand up his chest and asked, "Do you think, this late in the game, I can get my dad back?"

"All I can say is, fifteen years ago, I had the clothes on my back, a dead best friend, an alive one who was as lost as me, both of us headed down the worst path in life there could be, and that was it. Overnight, and that's no exaggeration, overnight all of that changed. And now I got a beautiful woman and a huge family. So I think anything can happen."

I nodded and shoved my face in his throat again.

"As for Jacob," he said over the top of my head, "he wanted to tell me he met up with you at a sleazy motel to give you a universal key to uncuff a woman he was pretty sure was a sex worker, and warn me to keep an eye on that shit."

"Jacob's a good guy."

"Jacob's a good guy," Cap agreed. "You made yourself a huge family too, you know."

Oh, I knew.

I sighed again, contentedly that time.

Cap pulled me closer.

Safe in his arms, "Dreams" drifting through the room, I contemplated last night.

And then I noted, "He didn't give me much advanced warning he was coming because he was scared, if he did, I'd have time to find an excuse not to see him."

"Yes," Cap agreed in a way I knew he'd already figured this out.

"And he looks better than I remember seeing him since Macy. Healthier. More alert. Deb gives him something. He isn't healed, you can never heal from that, but having her has brought him back to life. He needs her. She's his touchstone. That's why he wanted her at dinner with us, because he was worried about seeing me again, he loves her, and he needed her at his side."

"Yes," Cap agreed again.

He'd figured that out too.

"He really wants this," I whispered.

Cap gathered me even closer, and whispered back, "Yeah."

All right.

Here we go.

"I built a Citadel of Denial," I told him.

"What?" he asked.

I tipped my head back to look at him again. "To deal. I built a Citadel of Denial. It has towers and a moat and drawbridge, and it's heavily fortified. I hid there and shut it all out."

He slid his hand up my spine so he could stroke the back of my neck before he said, "I can see that."

"She used to shriek at him. Mom did."

He put his forehead to mine and murmured, "Baby."

"It was scary. Terrifying, actually. It was so not her. She was the tough nut, Dad was the pushover. But she was also lovey and cuddly, and when she had to be bossy, it wasn't about yelling, instead, quiet disappointment. So that shift in her, especially coupled with my confusion that Macy was gone, was really scary. That was one of the things I buried so deep in my dungeon at the Citadel, I didn't remember it, until he mentioned it last night."

I gave it thought.

And then I shared, "I think he had a network. His best bud and his wife, definitely. Also, my friend's parents. Mom would get like that, he'd make a call, they'd whoosh in, and I was spending the night with somebody."

I closed my eyes tight as I allowed the next part to emerge, opened them and gave him it all.

"When he'd come get me, every time, he'd pull me in his arms and hold me so tight, sometimes, I couldn't breathe. I didn't get it then and never processed it enough to put it together until now. It was torture for him to send me away. He couldn't keep an eye on me if I was somewhere else. But he was torn between protecting me from what was happening with Mom, and just overall protecting me. He couldn't win, and one of his daughters was gone. He was in hell, Cap."

"He was, baby, but don't take on the guilt of not putting yourself in his shoes. You were a little kid. I'm not saying don't have the grace to put yourself there now and explore how you two can get your family back. I'm just saying that you both had your own hells to navigate, don't take his on too."

Good advice.

I wondered if I could take it.

I nodded regardless so he knew I heard him.

"Last night was a lot," I said, "but when I saw how healthy he looked, when I glimpsed the dad I used to have..."

Could I say it?

I could.

"It gave me hope."

"Scary, hunh?"

"How'd you know?"

"In the beginning, with Shirleen, always wondered when it'd end. When me or Roam would do something to make her put us out, or something would turn and it'd all go to shit." He moved his hand to the side of my neck so he could rub his thumb along my jaw. "It takes time, but you settle in. I know it didn't feel like it, but you two having those big blowups last night is good. He knows what you were feeling, you know where he was at. You built the springboard on top of the shit, so now you can jump off."

"You and me are a pair, aren't we?" I grumbled. "Connected by trauma."

He cupped my jaw, the haze of the gummies retreated and my focus pinpointed on him.

"That isn't our connection, Raye. Our connection is that we're survivors, with a healthy dose of you being gorgeous, funny, strong, dressing great, and in the end, giving phenomenal blowjobs."

I burst out laughing.

Cap was smiling at me when I finished.

"You wanna take the day off work and just chill?" he asked.

I shook my head on the pillow. "No. It's work, but The Surf Club is also a sanctuary."

"Then let's hit it, baby. We got a cat to feed."

It didn't take two to feed Patches, but I nodded again.

He touched his mouth to mine.

Then he pulled me out of bed.

I WAS TYING on my hot-pink server apron, which was the perfect pop of color to go with my army-green, linen crop pants and white racerback tank when I heard it.

"Keep your pants on! You'll get it when you get it, honky!"

Tex.

What was he doing there?

Shouting.

And...

Honky?

I raced through the kitchen, dimly noting Lucia had lifted her head from slicing red chilies to listen, and kept right on going until I'd rounded the bar and hit the front area and the coffee cubby.

I skidded to a halt when I saw Otis and Tex squeezed into the small area behind the counter.

Tex was at the espresso machine.

Otis was pulling a cherry muffin out of the display case.

He was also grinning like a loon.

He spied me and said, "I love this guy."

I turned my attention to Tex.

"Tex, what are you doing?"

He tugged at a portafilter in a way the entire heavy machine shifted an inch to the side.

"Makin' coffee. What's it look like I'm doing?"

"But...you don't work here," I pointed out.

"Nance is havin' a spa day with Shirleen. What else am I gonna do?" he asked.

"I don't know, sit by the pool, order in room service breakfast, read a book, do other vacation-type things."

"Why would I do that?"

"Because you're on vacation."

"Puh," he replied.

"Please don't make him leave," Otis begged. "He treats the customers like shit, but it gets hectic up here in the mornings. I've been meaning to ask Tito for help for months."

Tex indicated Otis with a stainless steel, steaming pitcher, and a slosh of milk escaped the side. "See?"

"I don't care he's loud and rude," a customer piped up. He was loitering in the corner cradling a paper cup in both of his hands like it was something precious. "Hire him. I've never tasted anything like this coffee. I actually think I'm dead, and I don't care, because this is heaven."

Luna came up to my side. "What's going on? Oh...hey, Tex."

"Yo, woman," Tex replied, then blasted steam into the pitcher.

She looked to me, apparently unsurprised Tex was spending his vacation working at the coffee cubby at The Surf Club. "You okay after last night?"

"What happened last night?" Otis asked.

"Reunion with my estranged father," I told him.

"Damn, you okay?" Otis inquired.

"Doesn't she look okay?" Tex demanded. "She's an Avenging Angel. It'll take a lot more than shouting at someone in a fancy-ass restaurant to bring her down."

Boy, the RCHB really did share the goss.

"Tex, loose lips," Luna warned.

Otis looked confused.

"Right," Tex mumbled (but it was still loud). What was definitely loud was when he handed off a paper cup to a waiting customer without sparing them a glance and boomed, "Next!"

Luna tugged me back to the main area.

When we got there, she repeated, "You okay?"

I nodded. "Processing through some stuff. But yeah. I'm okay."

"We can get into it before we go to The Slide tonight," she replied.

Oh yeah.

Right.

We were going to The Slide that night.

"Listen, sister," she began. "After you kicked ass and took names with that Jinx biz, I think you got this shit down, and we should ask Jessie and Harlow to come with us."

I considered this.

While I was doing it, she said, "It's better cover. The two of us might look like we're casing the place. The four of us makes it a party."

She was right.

Still.

"They work until seven, and we need time to give them the lowdown then figure out some way to perform a blood pact so they don't blab to anybody upon threat of voodoo magic claiming their firstborn."

"Yeah. We'll think on it."

"Agreed."

Byron, standing at the bar, asked, "Is anyone gonna serve me?"

Luna and I looked to him.

Then we got to work.

It was after the morning crush, but before the lunch crush, when Dream wandered in, laden with children.

I was clearing a table, Luna was behind the bar, and Dream made a beeline to Luna, so I did too.

I dumped the plates and cutlery in the busser tub, and Dream looked to me.

"I was too upset to say I was sorry to hear about your history, Raye."

"Thanks, Dream," I replied cautiously.

She turned to her sister.

I edged closer to Luna.

Dream launched in, her words saying good things, but they were still issued like a challenge.

"I asked Mom and Dad for my college/wedding fund. Since I didn't go to college, and marriage is an anchor for women that weighs them down, so I'm never gonna do that, I'm gonna use that money to get my child care certification and take in a couple kids at my place."

I hated to admit this, but this idea was genius, and if she could rearrange her tarot reading sessions, she'd be great at it.

Though, only my opinion, if she didn't do the things her parents saved the money for, it didn't mean it was her money. They'd saved it for her to do those things, and when she didn't, again my opinion, it should revert back to them.

I didn't share this opinion, however.

My phone vibrated in my apron.

Dream kept talking.

"And Dusk's daddy is thrilled he's got a son, and he wants him every other week, so I'm gonna lose my son half the time, so thank you for that."

She said thank you, but she was not grateful.

And not-so-side note: that wasn't at all Luna's fault.

"The man's his father, and it's good he wants to be in his life, but I'm not sure why you're up in my face about it," Luna said.

"They didn't dip into your college/wedding fund to look after me and the kids, so I don't know what your beef is," Dream retorted.

I edged even closer.

"You know what, I'm not gonna do this here," Luna replied. "I work here, Dream. I can't deal with your shit when I'm here. And it isn't cool you show whenever you want to do whatever you have a mind to do. I have a phone. Call me. I work Monday through Friday, seven to four. In those times, I'm off limits. And I'm a busy girl, but we can set a time to sit down and chat."

My phone buzzed again in my apron, reminding me of the text.

"Like you're gonna spend time with me," Dream returned.

"You're my sister," Luna pointed out. "If you have something to talk about, I'll listen to you."

"You think I'm a flake."

"You *are* a flake," Luna declared. "And whatever. Work it. I just don't need you flaking all over me. I have my own life to handle. It's called boundaries, Dream. My bad for letting you push through them. The thing you have to get is, I'm not going to let you do that anymore. That doesn't make you any less my sister, and I care about you. But I can't have you shitting all over my boundaries."

They stared at each other.

I didn't move.

They kept staring at each other.

I stayed put.

They continued staring at each other.

I loved Luna, but I wanted to know who'd texted me.

And anyway, someone had to help her defend her boundaries, and as her best bitch, that was my job.

"Right, Dream, Luna said what Luna had to say, and part of that was she can't do this here. So if you have more to say, text her and set up a time to say it."

Dream looked at me, muttered, "Whatever," and wandered out.

As she went, Dusk waved at us from his place at her back before he did that cute kid thing of smooching his splayed hand and flinging it out to throw kisses.

Luna and I watched her leave, and although neither of us was in the mood after that confrontation, since that wasn't Dusk's fault, we both threw kisses back.

When Dream and her brood were out of sight, Luna turned to me. "Whoa. That was easy."

"I think the intervention worked, kinda sorta," I remarked. "I still don't get why she blames you for everything."

"I don't know, and I've been putting up with it all my life. Though, it's gotten worse lately."

We both stood and contemplated this until we heard Tex shout, "What do you mean you don't have cinnamon syrup? What kind of operation is this?"

We then smiled at each other, because he was loud, but he was hilarious, and it was fun having him around.

After we stopped smiling, I dug out my phone.

My heart started beating faster when I saw who the text was from.

"Dad," I said to Luna.

She crowded close, and we read it.

Happy to give you time, darlin'. But Deb and me were shopping at this outdoor mall close to our hotel and I saw an ice cream joint. Thought I could buy my girl an ice cream. Just you and me, unless you want someone with you.

Which meant, he wasn't going to bring Deb.

I felt bad for pointing in her face and getting in her shit last night.

But I had my own shit to deal with first.

My dad...

And ice cream.

I texted back, *I think that's Frost. 4:30?*

And Luna asked, "Are you sure?"

I looked at her, "I'm nineteen-years-and-counting-for-us-to-be-beyond-this sure."

She nodded understandingly.

I hit send.

Dad texted back, *It's a date!*

The exclamation mark was cute and sweet, and full of hope.

My heart beat faster as I dropped a heart on his reply.

I texted Cap to tell him what was happening and got back to work.

Within two minutes, though, Cap texted back, *I'm glad you're doing that. Available if you need me.* He ended that with a red heart.

The red heart was just cute and sweet.

I glanced at Tito, who had sunglasses aimed at the coffee cubby even though now it was quiet.

He didn't seem to mind he had a guest barista.

And if he didn't mind, why should I?

I knew the answer to that.

So I headed to Byron to see if he needed his mid-morning dirty chai refill.

I DROVE to the Biltmore mall spotting the tail.

It was hard to miss, seeing as it was a bronze El Camino, and behind the wheel was Tex, and, get this...

Sitting next to him was Tito.

I had no clue how that unholy alliance sprung up, since I'd been in their presence all day, and I hadn't seen them in the same space once.

But in that current moment, the meetup with Dad looming, I didn't have it in me to figure it out.

Though, I did give some time to wondering how that old El Camino made it all the way down from Denver, and if the grenades were still in the back.

I parked.

They parked, not close, not far.

I got out and walked to Frost.

They got out and ambled to a bench outside True Food Kitchen, which was situated next to Frost. And it should be noted they were about as incognito as Tom Cruise would be strolling the mall in his *Top Gun* flight suit and mirrored aviators.

Dad was hanging outside Frost.

I hated that it was awkward, but no way around it. The hug we exchanged when I made it to him was awkward.

We walked in, and I knew why he picked this place. The sight of vats of creamy deliciousness and the smell of sugar and waffle cones took me back to a place I missed so bad, it was like intense chronic pain you get used to and just lived your life dealing with.

Dad, Macy and I didn't just sneak bowls of ice cream when Mom wasn't looking.

Dad took us, including Mom, to the local ice cream parlor as a treat, and he did this a lot.

"Wild guess," Dad murmured, looking down at the gelato on display. "Bubble gum."

Okay.

Right.

So he didn't forget I existed.

He knew his little girl.

"Double scoop?" he asked me.

Totally knew me.

I nodded.

We ordered, got our gelato, and he firmly shoved in to pay.

We then walked outside and sat at a table.

Tex and Tito still sat on their bench.

Dad glanced at them.

"I didn't ask them to come," I informed him. "They followed me."

"Who's the demented Santa Claus-looking guy?" Dad asked.

I grinned at him. "That's my boss, Tito. And that's not his name. No one knows his name. We just call him that because he likes Tito's vodka. He's weird and quiet, and has a very interesting sense of style, but he's a really good guy."

He dipped into his pistachio (and yeah, I could have picked his too). "You got an all-around interesting posse, darlin'."

He could say that again.

He took a bite and watched the people walking by.

I took a bite and did the same.

He took another one.

So did I.

I knew what this was.

We both had the same dilemma. When the wall between us was so high, and neither of us had a rope or a ladder, how did we even begin to climb it to meet at the top?

Dad, who had been a Dad Interrupted, was still a dad.

So he found a finger hold first and grabbed on.

"I'm more sorry than I can express that I didn't tell you I started seeing Deb. I hope it goes without saying that it gutted me you weren't at our wedding. It put a pall on the day, so it was a double gut, because Deb felt it, and I hate I left her with that being part of the memory of our special day."

"You look good. Fit." I smiled at him. "Handsome. Had to clean up your act to turn the eye of a pretty lady, hunh?"

He smiled back, not hiding his relief I lightened the mood. "Deb goes to the gym four times a week. Couldn't have the guys hitting on her while she's there, so I had to go with."

I loved knowing this about his life.

I loved it with everything I was in that moment.

"She talked me into selling the house and moving into a condo about six months ago," he shared. "I fought her on it. Thought I'd miss the yardwork. No clue why. Haven't missed it once."

This explained his text of six months ago, sharing his new address.

I downed a spoonful of bubble gum gelato and said, "I've never done yardwork. But I get that. Yardwork sucks."

He chuckled.

This sound ended abruptly before he said cautiously, "Remember Brittany?"

Yes.

I remembered Brittany.

She was Deb's daughter.

Macy's friend.

"I remember Brittany," I said quietly.

"She got engaged last month. She's too young, and the guy's a clown." A pause and then, "Deb and I are both hoping she'll wake up before Rich and Deb have to put any deposits down."

Rich was Deb's ex.

If memory served, he was kind of an ass.

I was glad she shook him loose.

"We ran into each other at a grocery store," he went on, moving us into the meatier stuff. "I hadn't seen her in years. I didn't want to see her then, because of the memories. But she told me she'd been worried about me...about *us*, all this time, and she asked if I wanted to have a cup of coffee and catch up. To this day, I don't know why I said yes. But I'm glad I did."

"The way you are, I'm glad you did too," I replied.

He shot me a look that was now dripping with relief, then shared sheepishly, "She told me she had a crush on me, back in the day before Macy."

I nodded.

I could see that. My dad was good-looking.

"She thought it was just a thing, not important," he continued. "You don't stop being a woman, or a man, even if you're married. Though, she realized it was more later, because in some part of her, she knew Rich and her weren't going to make it. He could be a serious ass."

See?

"I kinda remember that about him."

This time, he nodded before he continued sharing. "She didn't ask me to have coffee because of that. Fifteen years had gone by. She thought she was over it." His eyes twinkled. "And I wasn't the hot number in the neighborhood anymore."

He had definitely been that, tall, blond, blue-eyed, funny and loving.

He still had that now, I saw.

Deb had brought it back to him.

"I don't know." He shook his head, then shrugged. "Somehow, being with her, I tapped into a part of me I forgot was there. A spark ignited and...here we are."

"I'm so happy you two are there," I said it and meant it.

"I am too," he replied. "And that you're happy about it as well."

He went back to his pistachio gelato.

"I remember Mom yelling at you," I whispered.

Dad looked at me.

Then he put his cup of gelato down, turned to me and admitted, "After we lost your mom, I should have found someone for us to talk to. On our own and together. So we could figure out how to go forward with our family cut in half."

"By then, she'd convinced you it was all your fault."

He shook his head. "Don't make excuses for me, Raye."

I put my cup down and turned to him. "I really want to say let's bury all of that and move on from here."

Before I could finish my thought, he said firmly, "We can't do that, sweetheart. And we shouldn't. I need to make amends. And your sister and mom are a part of us, they always will be."

"I wasn't finished," I said gently.

He lifted his chin for me to go on.

"I'm not a mom, so I don't know how hard it was on her to not know where Macy was, to have her gone and then not have her come back."

I took a sec to see how he responded to me bringing up what happened to Macy, but his expression didn't change from intent on what I was saying, so I kept going.

"But if I'm honest and let myself feel it, I know it's rage I feel that she didn't think about me before she took herself away from me."

"She thought about you," he said quickly.

"Dad, I remember how we were before Macy was taken. Maybe it's idyllic now because of what happened, but we were happy. She was a good mom. And you loved her...a lot."

"I thought she was the love of my life," he whispered.

"Until Deb?" I asked.

He lifted a shoulder. "You can have two loves of your life, Raye. It doesn't make the feelings you had for one or the other any less. I didn't leave your mom, even as bad as it got. She didn't really leave me either. She was just in so much pain, she couldn't handle it anymore. She died. And it took too long, but I moved on. That doesn't have any bearing on how much I loved her."

"I don't want to hurt you, but she didn't just die, Dad," I replied.

"I understand you see it that way, I do, darlin'. If I was in your shoes, I would too. But we both lost our daughter, so I get it. And she sent her to Deb's, so I get that too. She might have blamed me through words, but she never stopped blaming herself. She didn't kill herself because she missed Macy and forgot she had another daughter who she loved, Rachel...*very much*," he stressed that last to drive it home. "She killed herself because she shouldered the blame Macy was gone, and she couldn't live with it."

He studied me after he said that, and kept on.

"If you need to hold on to your anger, that's your prerogative. I won't judge. I had a lot of anger at her too, before I decided her doing that was all my fault. But I hope you find it in you to forgive her. I still love her, and I want that for her."

I might get there.

I might not.

But right then, I was having ice cream with my father.

"I think that might be part of why the spark was ignited for Deb," he admitted. "Because I've been lucky enough to have two loves of my life. And yes, that's what I had with your mom, and it had a very unhappy ending, but I still feel lucky I had her, and not just because she gave me you and your sister. We had a lot of good years before we lost Macy, and she made me very happy. But I'm the only one Deb has had. And honestly, sweetheart, being that for her feels really freaking great."

That almost made me cry, I was so thrilled she gave him that.

"Does the, uh...Macy thing...?" I couldn't finish.

He got me.

"At first, yes. And I don't know if it's right or wrong, and where my life is at right now, I can't find it in me to spend too much time thinking on it, but it melted away. Not that I forget what I lost in Macy, or how, or what came after, just that, Deb played absolutely no part in it. Your mom and I would let you two girls go to that playground without thinking a second about it, and we couldn't even see it from our windows. It's something Deb and I share, but it isn't part of who we are. Does that make sense?"

I nodded.

Then I got into more of the meat of it.

"I hate it that you spent your whole life worrying about me, Dad."

"Raye-Raye," he whispered, calling me something he hadn't called me in a long time, making something that was out of whack inside me shift back in place. As if to solidify that feeling, he cupped my shoulder in his hand and gave it a squeeze before taking his hand away. "I'm sorry I blew it so bad with trying to get us back together."

I picked up my ice cream. "You didn't blow it. You unintentionally set up a scenario where we could say things we've been needing to say for a long time, doing it in the most dramatic way possible, so we could see where the other one was at and start dealing."

He chuckled again, and this time, it lasted a lot longer.

That made me happy too.

"Yeah, I'll look at it that way," he said. "Instead of how it was. I screwed up royally."

He wasn't the only one.

"I pointed in Deb's face and got up in her shit, and I wish I hadn't. This isn't on her."

"Sweetheart," he said, still smiling. "She wasn't mad at *you* about that. She was pissed as all hell at me. Why'd you think I came to your place last night? I was being a coward and saying you needed time. But she kicked me out of our casita and told me, if I didn't go see if you were okay, and at least make some attempt to start a conversation, she was starting divorce proceedings."

Just then, I remembered how much I liked Deb.

She was sweet, but she also had spirit.

I spooned up gelato. "Did she mean it?"

"I don't honestly know. She doesn't need me around to do the yardwork anymore."

That was when I started laughing.

"The man is intense," Dad noted. "But I like your boyfriend."

Yes. Yes, definitely.

It was time to move on to better things.

I grinned at him. "I do too."

"One thing I can say about that guy, he's no clown."

"He totally is not."

"Why do you call him Cap?"

"I didn't make it up, but it's his nickname. Everyone calls him that because he looks like Captain America."

Dad burst out laughing, and through it said, "Shit. He does." He spooned up some pistachio. "Who was that girl with you?"

I told him about Luna. And then about Scott and Louise, which led me to Dream. Also Tex, Nancy and Shirleen. And Jessie and

Harlow. I told him about The Surf Club. I told him about Oasis Square and everyone there.

While I was telling him all of this, Dad ate up more than just gelato.

And in the midst of it, Tex and Tito got up and went to the El Camino.

I had to stop talking when I was drowned out by "Smoke on the Water" blasting out of the El Camino's windows.

But after it faded away, I kept talking.

And my dad kept listening.

NINETEEN

WONDERS OF THE SISTERHOOD

I flew through the door of my apartment and saw Cap in the kitchen, his head coming up, eyes on me.

I skipped through the room, tossing the heavy bags I was carrying on the armchair, which made Patches go flying with an angry, "*Meow!*"

"Sorry, Patches," I sing-songed as I took a page out of Alexis's book, skipped to the kitchen and took a flying leap on Cap.

But I went for front to front, not the side, so he caught me with both hands on my ass.

My way was better.

"So after gelato, Dad took me shopping," I announced.

Cap shifted, set my ass on the counter, but didn't move away, so I kept my arms and legs curled around him.

"Yeah?" he asked, his lips tipped up.

"Yeah. We went to Sephora, and he bought me *loads* of new makeup and hair stuff and perfume. Then we went to Anthropologie, and he bought me new candles and two new dresses and a top. And *then* we went to Saks, and *there* he bought me my very first, not-secondhand, *or* on sale, designer handbag. A Fendi First in patent pink!"

"So my girl's totally taking advantage of the guilt trip," he teased.

"Totally." I smiled, knowing he knew that wasn't what it was, but still, I explained, "When we were leaving Frost, I mentioned that I needed to pop by Sephora to grab some mascara, and he instigated it by asking if he could come with. I knew he was trying to prolong our time, not only asking to come along, but encouraging me to stock up on things I might need and spoil myself a little. And he made excuses that Deb would never forgive him if he didn't pay for everything. Though, Saks was his idea. He saw the bag earlier with Deb, and she remembered my clutch from last night. She told him she thought that I'd like it. So I think the whole thing was an excuse to get me to the Fendi boutique at Saks so he could buy it for me."

"Awesome," he murmured. "So I take it this means your chat went well?"

I pressed my forehead tight to his, fighting tears.

Happy ones this time.

Cap helped by deducing, "It went well."

I nodded, my forehead rolling against his.

He shifted his chin so he could touch his mouth to mine.

When he moved away, I shared, "He wants to know if we want to try Lon's again tomorrow or go somewhere else." I belatedly sniffed the air. "What do I smell?"

"The bourbon molasses marinade the salmon fillets are in."

I mean...

Seriously.

Where did this guy come from?

"How about I cook for us here?" he suggested.

"I only have two barstools."

"We can take the food down to one of the patio tables in the courtyard."

"I'm not sure Dad would be feeling being on display to the Oasis, honey. His first time spent here wasn't the greatest."

"Right, then we eat on our laps up here," he kept at me. "I don't think your dad will give two shits he's balancing a plate on his knees. He'll want to see where you live."

He was right.

"I'll text him and see what he says."

"He's gonna say yes," Cap muttered.

"Cap?"

"Right here."

I said nothing, but I knew he saw the happy tears shimmering in my eyes, because he kissed me hard and closed-mouthed.

When he was done, he asked, "You call Luna and tell her how that went down?"

"I talked to her on the way home."

"Okay, baby, gonna say something now you won't hear often, but unwrap yourself from around me. I gotta put the fillets in."

I unwrapped myself.

Cap moved to the opposite counter.

I hopped off the one I was on, went to my purse, got my phone and texted Dad about Cap's idea.

It went off with a *swoosh*, the oven door closed with a *thunk*, and I took my phone with me when I hiked my ass on a barstool.

"So," I said in order to begin the rundown of my day. "Went into work to discover Tex making coffee in the coffee cubby at SC. Otis, our cubby guy, was thrilled. He's been needing help for a while. Tito obviously didn't care, because he and Tex hooked up to follow me to Frost to be close when I sat down with Dad. And Dream showed to give us an update on her sitch, at the same time be a bitch to Luna for no reason. She's going to do at-home daycare. And Dusk's dad is gonna be a part of his life."

Cap looked at me while bringing over the prep for a salad he was making so he could do it at the counter where I was.

Then he said, "It'll be nice you have a quiet night tonight. Your life is crazier than Jules's was when she was out trying to clean up the streets."

Uh-oh.

I hadn't told him my plans for that night weren't going to be quiet.

Cap kept talking.

"Speaking of Jules, Mace wants to know if you can come over on Sunday, sometime after your dad leaves. She's heading back to Denver on Monday, and she wants to meet you before she goes. She knows your dad is in town, and Luna's birthday party is Saturday so that's out. But she and Vance have three boys. They're hanging at the castle with Daisy and Marcus while they're gone, and she wants to get back to them and has to get back to work at the shelter."

"Castle?"

"Daisy and Marcus live in a castle."

"A castle in Denver?" I pushed.

"Precisely, it's in Englewood, a suburb of Denver. But yes, it is one hundred percent a castle."

That was just as weird and awesome as everything else I'd learned about the RCHB.

I moved on from that.

"Okay, first, I reserve the time to have my delayed freakout you're taking me to Stella Gunn's house for a get together, and I'm meeting Jules, and you're just going to have to put up with the intensity of that freakout when it happens. Because I have to have it before I meet them, so I won't act like a dork *when* I meet them."

We might be new, but Cap was getting to know me really well.

I knew this when he asked suspiciously, "What's second?"

"Luna and I need to go out and case a gentlemen's club tonight. But we decided to see if we can recruit a couple more Angels, so Jessie and Harlow are going to be here at eight thirty so we can see if they're in. If they are, we'll perform some kind of sacred rite to establish their allegiance, which will probably just be shots of Fireball and a pinkie promise. Then we all need to sit down with my wall before we head out."

Yes, we'd made that decision. Mostly because, if we didn't let

Jessie and Harlow in at the semi-beginning and recruited them later, and they discovered we'd been doing this for a while, they'd never forgive us.

Harlow would get over it.

But Jess could hold a grudge.

Cap said nothing and didn't move.

I sensed a struggle with his Inner *Raye My Woman!* caveman.

This time, with an operation imminent, the struggle took so long, I considered putting my shopping away while he was doing it, when he snapped out of it and said, "I'll ask Liam and Knox if they wanna meet for a beer after we eat dinner."

First things first.

"After we eat dinner and have a quick roll in the hay," I corrected.

His mouth quirked and he confirmed, "Yeah. After both of those."

Right.

Onward.

"Who's Knox?"

"He's a buddy of mine from the Army. He got out about a year earlier than me, and I talked to Lee and Mace about taking him on. He's been working with the team up in Denver and came down with Lee and Vance, since we're gearing up to be fully functional soon. Our new Phoenix team has been training back and forth between Denver, LA and here for a while now, with Mace, Liam and me doing setup down here the last six months, after Stella and Mace moved into their new house. But everyone is going to be heading this way to settle in within the next month."

"Okay, I haven't had enough time to evaluate how the scale is going to be set up, so you can't give me accurate readings at this time, but preliminarily, with you at a ten, and Liam at a nine, mostly because I'm not sleeping with him, where's this Knox guy at?"

"You mean in looks?"

"Yeah."

He chuckled. "Babe, I can't tell you that."

I gave him the side eye. "*Please.* I can tell you Beyoncé is gorgeous and Selena Gomez is cute without taking a hit to my womanhood."

"We'll just say he doesn't have a problem getting himself some."

Which meant this Knox guy was probably a nine too, at least on the Cap Scale. Which meant twenty-seven on the regular one.

I needed to ask Luna if she'd lift the ban off new acquaintances for her birthday party so we could feel these guys out (particularly her, I was digging coming home to my hot guy and bourbon molasses salmon, and I felt the need to spread that joy).

Then again, if this guy was our age, she didn't need to get in a cat fight with Jessie and Harlow over him. Someone might knock over the bowl of her famous pimento cheese spread.

My phone binged.

I read the text from Dad then told Cap, "Dad and Deb are in for dinner here Friday."

"Great."

"Anything I can do to help?"

"No, baby."

"You down with me putting my new stuff away?"

"Absolutely."

I hopped off the barstool to do that.

But I went to him first for a kiss.

This time I got tongue, so things escalated, and I was hot, wet and panting, and the salad wasn't finished, nor was my stuff put away, and we were about five minutes away from kitchen-floor sex, when the timer went off to tell us the salmon fillets were done.

"Can I borrow this?" Harlow, lounging across my bed, holding up my new Fendi, asked.

"I haven't even used it yet," I told her from where I was, standing by my wall, waiting to continue our briefing.

"After you use it," she amended.

"Girl, she got that shopping with her dad for the first time in eight years. Not even," Jessie replied instead of me. Then she, sitting cross-legged on the edge of my bed with Patches purring in the nest of her lap, announced to the room at large, "I need a cat."

"You barely remember to feed yourself, how are you going to remember to feed a cat?" Harlow returned.

"I remember to feed myself," Jess shot back.

As far as I could tell, Jessie existed on coffee and whatever struck her fancy at QuikTrip, and that was more about their massive beverage station, snacks were an afterthought.

This was why Jessie was slim and had a B-cup (maybe).

Whatever she ate, it gave her thick, glorious chestnut hair a healthy gleam. With her blue eyes and the olive tone to her skin, she'd be a way better Kelly Garrett than me.

Harlow, on the other hand, had light-brown hair (with high-lighted hues of honey) and dark-brown eyes, a wholesome Jennifer Garner thing going on, and she had a bombshell figure (like Luna and me, but whereas Jess was Luna's height, Harlow was an inch shorter than me).

Jessie had the personality of a goth on a good day, and the wardrobe to match. She didn't go the thick-eyeliner and pale skin route (the latter part of that was due to genes, the former part due to good fashion sense), but most everything she wore was black, with some white, red or neutrals thrown in so it wouldn't get boring.

Harlow had the personality of a cheerleader, also with the wardrobe to match. She was all about babydoll dresses, bows, ruffles and perfecting the art of wearing a ton of makeup and looking like she wasn't wearing a stroke.

I had no idea how they were besties, I just knew it worked.

We'd already ascertained they were in to be Angels. Considering their level of crazy matched, and sometimes surmounted Luna's and mine, I shouldn't have been surprised what an easy sell it was. They didn't so much as blink when we told them what we'd been up to, nor when we gave them the lowdown on "We" and asked them to become Angels.

We didn't even need Fireball and pinkie swears (but we did it anyway, with Jessie rolling her eyes and looking about ready to hurl, and Harlow giggling).

So we had shit to do.

I had a hot guy to come home to, and before he took off for beers with the boys, I discovered Cap had a particular talent with quickies. Even so, it wasn't going to keep my status where I wanted it to be on my newly invented Cap-Induced-Orgasms-o-Meter, so I didn't want to be at this all night.

But, as had happened often since Jessie and Harlow showed, we were way off topic.

Taking us back to that, kind of, having put my new patent pink baby aside, her eyes now to her phone, obviously having googled the sitch, Harlow announced, "I get to be Kris Munroe."

She was so totally not Kris.

"We can't have two Munroes," Jessie returned.

"Then can we move to the movies so I can be Dylan Sanders?" Harlow pressed.

"Bitches, will you two shut up?" Luna demanded. "Raye is briefing us on our current situation. Eyes to the prize."

"Okay, but I just wanna say, I call Dylan Sanders," Harlow muttered.

"I want to be whoever Lucy Liu played. I'm not Asian, but she's the shit," Jessie said.

"I can see that," Harlow replied, looked up from her phone and added, "We're gonna need to buy black leather pants."

"I already have some," Jessie said.

I exchanged a glance with Luna, and we both silently wondered if we'd made that right choice with our two friends.

However, the fact they didn't freak out, thought it was "rad" (Harlow's word) and were all in, taking it in stride and acting like they normally did said something good.

Didn't it?

Welp.

No going back now.

"Right!" I stated loudly. "This is what we've got."

I tapped the vertical line of pictures on the wall of the women who had gone missing with the baby crown end of my pink pen (mental note: requisition a laser pointer for briefing sessions, it could do double-duty when I was cat sitting).

"These are our victims, our first 'whos.'" I tapped the Post-its under them. "These are the 'whens.' We don't have the 'hows' and 'whys,' but we kinda have the 'wheres.'"

I followed the strings attached from various tacks to tacks on the big map of Phoenix, which were the two strip clubs that three of the women worked at. I then followed the strings attached from the victims' pictures who were sex workers to the patches they worked (a new addition to the wall, something Luna was clever enough to request from Clarice (or "We"), and got). I then followed the strings to the pictures I'd just put up, which Clarice gave us, of the possible other "whos" and kept speaking.

"These might be the perpetrators who, in my surveillance, I noticed were a cut above your normal skeevy. Men who hang outside those strip clubs a lot, which is not normally where guys hang out in those places."

I tapped repeatedly on Cyrus Gibbons' picture and continued my briefing.

"This is our number one suspect, considering he's done time, twice, for crimes against women." I tapped him again. "That means, this is our number one target tonight. Is he at the club? What's he do there, outside the obvious? Who does he associate with?" I tapped down the line of the other possible perp photos. "I've seen him with some of these guys, but not all. Do we notice him with any of the others, or any of the others at The Slide who I've so far only seen at The Pink Slip? Let's see if we can draw any connections outside of the ones I've already done with the blue yarn." I turned and jabbed the crown in the direction of my girls. "All that said, do not approach. This guy is not a good guy. This is a reconnaissance mission only."

"They definitely have a turf, Roosevelt to Van Buren, Sixteenth through Twenty-fourth Streets," Jessie noted.

"Yeah, it all points there," Harlow replied.

Luna brandished the notepad Cap wrote the outline of an investigation on. "Which might mean crime of opportunity. They're there because they hang there or they get their jollies with sex workers from there, and shit goes south."

"Exactly. These pins," I began, tapping all the black pins, "are where the suspects live. Which is also close to all of this." I circled ground zero. "However our girls,"—I indicated the scattered pink pins, which were the homes of the missing women—"live all over the place."

"This is a visual representation of not shitting where you live," Jessie noted.

This was true.

We all went silent and stared at the mess on my wall.

Harlow broke the silence by saying, "Your landlord is gonna freak at all those pin holes."

I turned to her. "This is why I'm a dab hand at spackle." Then to them all, I asked, "We ready to roll out?"

"I vote we take the Mercedes," Jessie said.

"We are absolutely taking the Mercedes," Luna declared.

Yes, we absolutely were.

It was time to launch the Merc on her maiden voyage.

Luna looked at me and grinned.

I grinned back.

Then I moved to take our possible perp pictures off the wall so I could tuck them away because people kept breaking into my pad, and so far, they'd all been the good guys.

But I was learning...shit happened.

And you couldn't be too careful.

"OKAY, I'm quitting SC and getting a job stripping," Jessie remarked. "Do you see how much money those women are making? Even here, and this place is all kinds of skanky."

We'd picked a table back from the stage, better vantage point for the whole space.

And I'd overestimated the night.

I thought it might give us more to go on, but also be some fun.

It had given us zero to go on.

And this wasn't fun.

This made cruising the streets looking for prostitutes feel like a road trip, complete with a cooler of root beer and a huge bag of Corn Nuts.

The strippers were working it, and some had moves, but I was going to have to take an hour-long shower after we left here, not only considering the company we were keeping as audience members, but that this place was rundown, dated and rank.

Worse, although one of the men I had on my wall was there—a Sergio Duzek, nicked for some petty crimes, including possession of a controlled substance and driving under the influence (twice)—none of the others were, including Cyrus Gibbons.

We'd been there for two drinks and two and a half hours. We went to the bathroom in pairs three times to further check out the joint (and the ladies left a lot to be desired). So, unless they thought we all had overactive bladders, we couldn't run that ruse again. Not to mention, outside of wondering which of the women on the stage might be next, perhaps the most unfun pastime I'd ever engaged in, this garnered nothing.

Jessie was on the same wavelength as me, I knew, when she called over the music, "Regardless of the mediocre talent of their bartenders, one more drink and go?"

I wasn't sure about the "one more drink" part of that.

I didn't get a chance to say that. My attention was taken by Luna, who had her face illuminated by the screen of her burner phone.

I grew alert.

She looked at me across our tiny table, then leaned toward me and said, "Jinx. She wants us back at Sun Valley. Now."

"Is she okay?" I asked, thinking Jinx might be a very appropriate name for her if she wasn't.

And this wasn't good news.

Cap was probably home after his impromptu boys' night out.

And I just wasn't in the mood to extort another Rolex.

But Luna shook her head. "She says she's got something we want."

We both stared in each other's eyes and then said at the same time, "Divinity."

We popped up out of our seats.

"We going now?" Harlow asked, looking between us.

"Yeah. Now," I answered.

Since we paid for our drinks on the go (we tipped our servers well, and considering our occupations, we always did), we headed out, Luna in the lead, Harlow, Jessie and me taking the rear.

I did not get a good feeling when, on our way out, my eyes fell on Sergio Duzek, his locked with mine, he shot me a smarmy smirk and lifted his fingers above his right brow and out in a mock salute.

Nope.

Not a good feeling at all.

In fact, my skin was crawling.

We got outside and I rushed up to Luna, handing her the key fob.

I'd driven there.

But now, I was shaken.

"You drive," I said.

"It's your night."

"I think Duzek saw me sitting outside in Tweety."

She stopped dead. So did Jessie and Harlow.

"How do you know that?" she demanded.

"I'll tell you in the car. Let's get out of here."

We hightailed it to the Merc while trying to look like we weren't hightailing it, and with Jess and Harlow in the back, me in the passenger seat, Luna reversed out of our spot and took off.

"Talk," she ordered.

"He gave me a salute when we were walking out," I shared. "Looked right at me and gave me a salute, like he knew me."

We'd been pretty thorough in our brief with Jessie and Harlow (though we left out my unhinged shenanigans with the wife beater, and my lunatic tomfooleries with the rapist, not to mention my deranged mischiefs with Paul Nicholson).

So Harlow asked, "You think he saw you when you were watching from Tweety?"

"Yeah. If not live and in person, they have cameras on the parking lot. I tried to park out of range, but I can't be sure I succeeded."

"So, say he didn't see you live and in person, which you would notice since you were there watching," Jessie said. "That means he saw you on one of the cameras. And as far as your intel goes, he doesn't work there, so how can he see security footage?"

"Maybe it's like Bibbidi-Bobbidi Boo from the Sopranos," Harlow suggested.

"What?" Luna asked.

"Bibbidi-Bobbidi Boo, Tony Sopranos' strip club where he and his boys hang out."

"You mean Bada Bing," Jessie corrected.

"Yeah, that," Harlow said. "In other words, a front."

I glanced at Luna to see she was glancing at me, and our glances weren't about how oh-so-very Harlow it was she thought a strip club would be called, Bibbidi-Bobbidi Boo.

Luna looked back at the road.

"Let's explore possible whys," Jessie said. "One, we have a serial killer, and I would hope like fuck the cops would cotton on to that."

I would hope so too.

However, I had considered this option, and I just couldn't imagine, if there was some connection that would say we had a Ted Bundy on the loose in Phoenix, they wouldn't be all over it.

"Two," she carried on. "Why would you nab sex workers and strippers?"

"Because less people might notice them gone, or less questions would be asked when they are gone," Harlow replied.

"That, for sure, but *why?*" Jessie pushed.

I should have added to my Angel posse a long time ago.

I knew this for certain when we all answered at the same time, "Human trafficking."

I couldn't say I hadn't considered this too. They were buzzwords because it was a problem.

I just never allowed myself to go there, not to the "why," because if I did, it'd hark way too close to what might have become of Macy.

But I couldn't turn away from the "why" anymore.

I had to face it.

And that was really our number one possibility.

Okay, it might be time to hand this over to Clarice.

Or Cap.

I wasn't sure where Nightingale Investigations and Security stood on pro bono criminal investigations. Considering how swank their office was, and the cost of what had to be a custom sculpture of a phoenix, my guess was, they weren't big fans.

So it would be Clarice.

"Where are we going now?" Harlow asked.

"To go see Jinx, our girl on the street," Luna told her.

"Right on," Harlow muttered, like this wasn't her first rodeo, when it was.

Luna took us to Sun Valley Motor Lodge and we parked.

I gave a crisp salute, and Luna gave a finger wave, to the dread night manager, Mr. Bad Mood, who was wearing his normal scowl with his eyes aimed our way, doing this as we headed to room number eight.

Luna knocked and called, "Jinx. It's us."

"Get in here, bitches," she called.

We went in.

And we nearly ran into each other as Luna, in the lead, stopped dead.

I knew why.

Divinity wasn't there.

But five other women, plus Jinx, were.

"You bitches are multiplying," Jinx remarked, eyeing Harlow and Jessie.

"You're one to talk," I replied.

"Close the damned door," one of the women said.

We shuffled fully in, and Jessie closed the door.

It wasn't a big room, and since our hosts had taken all the places to sit, we lined up just inside the door.

"Dylan, Natalie," I indicated each in turn, giving them their code names on the fly (I'd done my Angel research too), and seeing as they were semi-kinda second generation, I went with the movie, "this is Jinx and her friends. Jinx and her friends, this is Dylan, Natalie, Jill, and I'm Kelly."

"Charlie's Angels. Huh," one of the women, a light-skinned Black lady in a pink wig who was sitting at the head of the bed, mumbled, putting it together surprisingly quickly.

Outed.

Whatever.

"Persia, Genesis, Cameo, Skyla and Lotus," Jinx gestured to each woman, giving us their street names.

Pink wig lady was Persia.

At their monikers, which kicked ass, I wondered if we should have gone the stripper name route rather than the Angels, because, as just had very recently been proved, the Angels were obvious.

"You really walk up to that asshole's house and demand his Rolex?" Lotus, a white woman with fake breasts and a belly-button piercing, who was lounged back in one of the chairs by the window, inquired.

I was seeing why we suddenly had assistance from these ladies.

"Extortion isn't that easy," I educated. "His wife was home, and I laid on the doorbell about thirty seconds too long. His wife was worried about who was at the door. If she wasn't there, we'd be fucked."

"Dope," Lotus replied.

"Why are we here?" Luna asked Jinx.

"Divinity's missing," Jinx answered.

Oh snap.

I hadn't had time to peruse the *Republic* the last few days.

Did I miss the report?

My girls looked at each other.

Jinx's girls looked at us.

"Are there more women missing than are reported?" I asked.

"How would we know?" Skyla answered. "If I disappeared, no one would report me."

"I would," Cameo said softly.

Skyla gave her a surprised look, then her face gentled.

Aw.

"You need to find Jumper," Persia told us, taking us out of the moment.

We turned to her.

"Jumper?" Luna asked.

"Jumper. Think his real first name is Guy. Don't know his last," Persia said. "He was banging Bambi."

"You mean her boyfriend? Jazz?" I asked.

Persia busted out laughing, turning to her girls.

"Jazz," she said, his name shaking with her hilarity.

"More like Jizz," Genesis said.

"More like Numnuts," Cameo put in.

"Jackass." That was Skyla.

"Meathead." Persia.

"Mutt." Lotus.

"*Cabrón.*" Jinx.

This was familiar, and Luna and I exchanged a smile at the wonders of the sisterhood.

"Right. Jazz. Jumper. Numskull. Whatever," Jessie put in. "Is this guy Bambi's boyfriend?"

"Num*nuts*," Cameo corrected.

"Yeah, whatever," Jessie returned. "What's with this guy?"

"Probably a coupla reasons you don't give your real name to some stupid bitch you're porking," Jinx said. "Even your street name."

In other words, so the cops don't know who they're looking for, and therefore can't find him, when that "bitch he's porking" turns up missing.

A shiver slithered up my spine, because that smacked of premeditation, not crime of opportunity.

"Know where to find this guy?" Luna asked.

"Thought that was your job," Persia noted.

"Without a last name, it'd be nice to have a lead," I pointed out.

"He glides through here and there. Hits the streets. Hits the clubs," Skyla said. "He's not regular, but he's around."

"He been around recently?" Harlow asked.

Six heads shaking.

Shit.

"Jumper with any of the other women who disappeared?" Luna asked.

"Try...all of them?" Cameo said.

My skin started tingling.

My crew exchanged glances.

"Really? *All* of them?" Luna pressed.

"Don't know who all you're searchin' for," Cameo replied. "But Jumper is the grim reaper. For sure, Bambi. He also spent time with Divinity. And two others I know who weren't around for very long, and before they were gone, he was sniffing around them."

"Share our number," I ordered Jinx, then to all of them, I said, "You see this asshole, you call us."

"Dude's bad news," Persia remarked.

"No kidding?" I asked.

"Chill, mama, just sayin', with this guy, or all this shit, watch your ass."

"I'm more worried about yours," I replied. "Be safe. And thanks for the chat."

I lifted my chin to Jinx because Cap did that and looked badass.

She burst out laughing.

Whatever.

We left and headed to the Merc.

"What's his problem?" Harlow asked, her eyes aimed to reception.

I looked, and Mr. Bad Mood was making a lewd gesture with his fingers curled around and pumping toward his groin.

"He doesn't like us much," Luna answered.

"Why?" Jessie asked as we folded into the car.

"Because he's got a shit job and probably a shit life, and instead of finding a way to better it, he's sitting behind the desk at reception in a crappy motel in a crappy part of town, getting his jollies pretending to jack off in front of a bunch of women," I said.

"I guess that explains that," Harlow muttered.

Luna pulled out of the spot, and we motored.

WE SWITCHED OUT CARS, and since Jessie took us to the Mercedes in her Prius, she took us back to the Oasis.

We all saw the paint job on the east side of the building that faced Seventh, and it had a new addition that day.

It wasn't done, but it looked like it was going to be some kind of mural, which made me all kinds of happy. Phoenix was a city that had some crazy-cool murals.

"I hope I get off the waiting list soon," Jessie said.

"Me too," Harlow added.

Luna was grinning to herself.

She dropped them when she'd pulled just inside the entrance because they'd had to park on the street, and we idled until they got in their cars, their headlights came on, and they pulled away.

Then she inched up to the security gate and stopped again.

Cap's Porsche was in one of the visitor spots.

"I'll do the emailing again," Luna said. "Cops need to know they're looking for this Jumper character, first name Guy. Not Jazz, who they probably have no idea who that dude is." She paused a second, then said, "If this is what we think it is, we gotta think about getting out."

"We gotta think about getting out," I agreed, wondering how I'd feel about dismantling my wall, something I'd been nurturing and staring at for a year. And thinking I wouldn't mind doing it, but I wouldn't actually do it until they'd found those women.

"They did good," she noted, referring to Jessie and Harlow.

"They did," I agreed.

"Even Harlow," she remarked.

Yeah, this was a surprise.

A cheerleader doing amateur sleuth work in the underbelly of Phoenix didn't seem like it'd be a thing.

But...surprise!

She didn't even try to befriend any of the sex workers or ask them wig stabilization strategies.

"What do you think about Sergio?" she queried.

"Since we're never revisiting The Slide, I hope to never see Sergio again," I told her.

"Copy that. Are you gonna get another wild hair?" she asked.

She liked doing this.

"I don't know, are you?" I asked back.

"I don't know." We stared at each other until she said, "Go to your hot guy."

That sounded like a plan.

"Later, bitch," I bid.

"Later."

I got out, and she idled where she was until she saw me climbing the stairs, then she took off.

I let myself in my apartment.

The light over the stove was on, and since it was near midnight, that was it.

There was no Cap, so I headed to the bedroom to find him in bed doing something on his phone, chest bare, sheets and comforter up to his waist, Patches sleeping at his feet.

Ah.

It was good to be home.

"Successful night?" he asked me.

I slunk carefully onto the bed so as not to disturb Patches.

I settled on my belly beside him, up on my forearms.

"We think we got a lock on their recruiter, or whatever they call him. We're gonna feed that to the powers that be so the cops can pursue it." I paused and then shared, "And then I think we're out."

For the second time that day, relief washed through the face of a man in my life I cared about.

With Dad, I was glad.

With Cap, he had to suck it up.

If I got another wild hair, or Luna did, Jessie, Harlow, and we went after it, he'd have to deal.

It wasn't like his job was behind a desk.

Of course, he got paid to do what he was doing and had been training to do it since he was fifteen.

But...whatever.

"How'd you find that?" he asked.

"Shaking an asshole down for his Rolex and giving it to a woman who works the streets, we learned tonight, buys you some shit."

His beard twitched around his lips. "Yeah, that's pretty much how it works with all informants. You do something for them, they do something for you. And it usually goes just like that, what you do for them is a fuckuva lot bigger than what they give to you."

Handing over a Rolex sure was big.

Even so...

"Well, if it leads to those women being found,"—I jerked my head to the wall—"it was worth it."

His eyes drifted to the wall and back to me.

I knew what the expression on his face said before he started, "Babe—"

"I know, honey. They might be dead or taken somewhere we'll never find them. Still, there are people out there who love them, so if I can find answers..."

His face got soft before he set his phone on the nightstand.

He came back and started to reach for me.

"No," I said. "We'll disturb Patches. He's asleep."

"Patches is cute, but he eats off the floor and buries his own shit. I don't think he'll mind finding somewhere else to sleep."

"You're not a very good cat sitter," I informed him.

He grabbed hold, hauled me to him, then rolled us both.

Patches took off.

Chest to chest, Cap looked down at me.

"I don't care," he replied.

Then he kissed me.

And I didn't care either.

TWENTY

COMPOST

I woke with a jerk.

Cap was sleeping on his stomach.

I was tucked up to his side with an arm along the small of his back and a leg thrown over his thigh.

Yeesh, we were serious cuddlers.

This was why he felt me wake up.

He shifted and I rolled to my back. He slid his arm along my belly and semi-tucked me under his long body.

"Nightmare?" he murmured, sounding sexy-sleepy.

Sergio sitting beside me in Tweety, segueing to all the strippers at The Slide having Cyrus Gibbons' face, segueing to Christina Markovic swinging on the swings at the playground where Macy was taken from.

I'd say I'd had a nightmare.

"Yeah," I replied.

"Wanna talk about it?"

I could tell he was trying to shake the sleep so he could be there for me.

But hot guys needed their rest too.

And dreams were just your brain's way of processing your life.

No big whoop.

(I hoped.)

"I'm okay. Go back to sleep."

"Sure?"

"Yeah."

He tucked me further underneath him.

Okay.

That's what I needed.

I felt his body settle into mine as he reentered dreamland.

It would take me a little longer.

But with Cap right there, his smell and strength all around, it didn't take that long.

I was sucking Cap off, and really into it, when he put his hands under my arms and pulled me up.

I had a mind to protest, except as he pulled me up so I was on all fours above him, and he slid a bit down, when he was done moving us, his face was in line with my breasts.

Oh boy.

And...

Goodie!

He lifted up his head as his hand slid down my stomach and curled between my legs, and he hit the spot as he sucked hard on my nipple.

Goodie wasn't the half of it.

Yum.

I reached for his dick.

He released my nipple and said, "No, baby. This morning you take what I give you."

I shivered at this new brand of bossy, something I instantly liked.

A lot.

He alternated between my nipples while playing with my clit and sometimes finger-fucking me until I was trembling and moaning, I couldn't hold my head up anymore, and I knew I was *this close* to a climax that was gonna *rock my world.*

That was when he slid all the way down through my legs. Then Cap was on his knees behind me, and I should have heeded the earlier warnings so I'd be prepared, but I didn't, so I was caught completely unawares when he wrapped my hair in his fist and tugged my head back, at the same time he stroked into me.

Oh. My. *God.*

That was so magnificent, along with being way primed, I came immediately, the first time ever without any clit action, and I did it hard.

I also threw a hand out to the headboard to remain stationary as he pounded in me, holding my head back by my hair, the pads of the fingers of his other hand digging into my hip, the sound of our flesh slapping together our personal, hot, dirty symphony that accompanied my soul-shattering orgasm.

Cap let my hair go and slid his hand around my hip and in.

"*Cap,*" I breathed as my way to tell him it was too much.

I was wrong, I knew when his finger swirled my clit, and I went off again.

I was down on my forearms, forehead on the backs of my hands, panting and enjoying still taking him while coming down, when he buried himself and gave my ass a sharp slap that was so nasty-amazing, it made the walls of my sex contract.

He then grunted before he groaned through his finishing strokes, "*Fuck, Raye.*"

He took his time coming down before pulling out, rolling me to my back, then settling on top.

"For future reference, you can be bossy like that anytime you want," I told him.

With both hands, Cap smoothed the hair away from my face, and to share he accepted my offer, he kissed me.

I WAS FRANTICALLY MULTI-TASKING, eating Cap's eggs, bacon and toast (he even made scrambled eggs seem gourmet), putting on makeup and sorting through the police notices on the *Republic's* website, at the same time thinking we needed to change the alarm from 5:00 to 4:30 (no, 4:00) to accommodate our morning frolics, when Cap took the opportunity afforded him of me filling in my brows to turn my laptop his way.

"I thought you were letting this go," he said.

"I said I *think* we're letting it go."

He had no reply, so I looked from my brows in the mirror to him. "We found out another woman is missing last night, Cap."

"Chief of Police of Phoenix used to be uniform in Denver. Jorge Alvarez," he announced.

"Okay," I said, not sure why he was telling me this.

"He's the guy that came in while we were being interviewed about Elsie Faye," he explained.

"Right."

"He's a good man, Raye."

Oh.

Now I knew why he was telling me this.

I went back to my brows. "I didn't say he wasn't."

"Don't get pissed at me," he warned.

Oh shit.

I abandoned my brows and looked at him again.

"Mace and I went in, talked to him, ran those names on your wall by him. Every single one of those women has a history, Raye. Drugs. Solicitation. Petty theft. Stints in juvie. Domestic altercations, with her being the assaulter. Rough upbringings."

I didn't like where this was going.

What I knew was, it wasn't usually the girl with the upper-middle class upbringing, whose parents groomed her to look forward only to that day where she'd wear a beautiful dress and cut a cake then make babies, parents who had the money to pay for her college so she could be somewhere to find the right man to give her that life, who hit the streets.

And he knew this too.

So I didn't know why he was saying this stuff to me.

"So?" I asked sharply.

"They're known not to be real stable, and it's not their profession saying that," he said the last firmly, because I'd opened my mouth to retort. "I know sex workers and strippers and a lot of women in similar positions who are completely solid. Pay their mortgages or rent, pay their bills, look after their kids, got a good thing going with their men or women. Jorge says some of them burned so many bridges and pissed off so many people, or owed so much to their dealers, it's highly likely they left town."

I was still dubious.

And I was so because, to me, this made all of them even better marks to disappear for nefarious reasons.

Cap should know that too.

"Eight of them?" I said to relay these thoughts.

"Phoenix is the tenth largest city in America," he replied. "And it's growing exponentially with everyone moving in from California. Not to mention, Tucson, Vegas, San Diego, LA and Albuquerque are less than a day's car ride away. Easy to find new turf and the things they need. So yeah, honey. Eight of them."

"Clarice told us to find this Divinity, and not a week went by, and she's vanished."

"How deep have you looked into the first 'who?'"

Shit!

I was so focused on the second one, the only digging we did was into Christina.

And even with her, we didn't dig too far.

Even so, I told him about that. "On the face of it, Christina Markovic doesn't get along with her mom. But they're tight. They're just their personal brand of messed-up tight."

"You do what you gotta do, babe. I'm just telling you, this might end up as nothing. I've worked enough cases where a wife is certain her husband is cheating on her, and he isn't. Or an employer thinks an employee is stealing from a company, when they aren't, that not everything is as it seems. Some things have an explanation."

"In short, you think, with what happened to Macy, that I'm imagining bogeymen around every corner."

"I didn't say that," he replied gently. "What I will say is, you cannot do this kinda shit unless you understand yourself and your own motivations. If you don't, they can cloud your reasoning and judgement. So you should consider it."

He was making sense, therefore I went back to my brows and said, "I'll consider it."

"Raye—"

I looked to him and brandished my eyebrow pencil. "Dude, do you not know how delicate this operation is?"

His eyes crinkled and his beard quirked.

"You're heard, honey, so can I finish my eggs and makeup?" I requested.

"You got it, babe," he relented and moved away.

I looked at the clock on the microwave and let out little squeal.

At this rate, I was going to be at least fifteen minutes late to work, if not twenty.

I had to get my ass in gear.

Pronto.

I'D JUST LEFT my apartment and was walking down the walkway, when my next-door neighbor, Rhea, opened her door and poked her head out.

Her hair was a mess, her eyes still drowsy, and I was surprised she was awake considering she did the evening shift at Chopper

John's biker bar, this fact meaning she didn't often come to our shindigs, unless they were in the afternoon, because she was working.

"Dig it you're getting it regular, sister, but lay off the headboard at five in the morning."

"Oh God, can you hear us?" I asked.

"No, not until this morning." Her grin was as drowsy as her eyes. "Sounded good though."

I returned her grin. "It totally was. But we'll have a mind."

"All I ask."

Her door closed.

Fifteen minutes later, I was sitting in the suicide lane, staring at the front of The Surf Club.

Primarily the front window, which had been defaced with white shoe polish and said in big, oddly threatening letters, Today's Tex Special, Blood Orange Mocha.

And then there was a drawing of what looked like a blob with dots, but I sensed it was supposed to be an orange.

I guessed Tex hadn't yet caught the vacation vibe.

Someone honked their horn at me.

I looked in my rearview mirror and saw it was Byron.

I lifted a hand and waved, then I made a left when it was safe and slid into the parking lot of SC.

Sadly, I did it seventeen minutes late for my shift.

Per usual, no one noticed or said a word.

I waited until after the lunch crush to approach Tito's table.

He looked up from playing Stardew Valley when I stopped at his side.

"Thanks for the plant, Rachel," he said.

My gaze went to the succulent that was still pride of place, then back to him.

"Glad you like it," I replied. "Listen, are you cool with Tex being here?" I asked to confirm.

"Three customers came to me yesterday and personally thanked me for hiring him. And one did that at the same time telling me he called him 'turkey.' In other words, yes, Rachel, I'm okay with it."

I sensed this, but I had to check.

"How did you two hook up to, uh...you know, follow me when I went to see my dad?" I inquired.

"You went to your locker to take off your apron, and Tex came to me and said, 'Get up, we're goin' to take her back while she raps with her pops.' So I got up and went with him to make sure you were okay while you spoke to your father."

Right then.

That explained that.

I was a little surprised at how simple the explanation was, but there you go.

"You don't have to worry about me," he said.

"I wasn't—"

"You never have to worry about me, Rachel."

"Okay," I said softly.

"Though, I worried about you. But I feel a lot better after yesterday."

Tito was *such* a nice guy.

"I do too."

"Good."

He went back to Stardew Valley.

"Tito?"

He looked up and his bushy, white brows rose above the tops of his neon green sunglass frames.

"You know you're the awesomest boss ever, right?"

He smiled. "I try."

I wanted to hug him or something.

But he was back in Stardew Valley.

So instead, I returned to work.

Dad and I were sitting on stools watching Deb and Cap at the stove.

In a skillet, Cap was spooning some kind of buttery or olive-oily stuff that was sprinkled with some rosemary twigs on top of pork chops while Deb looked over his shoulder, oooing and aahing.

I'd changed from work clothes and donned the red dress with the pink flowers, flutter sleeves, tiered skirt, smocked waist with a cutaway at the small of my back that Dad bought me yesterday.

Cap was in jeans and a short sleeve, dark wash chambray-colored linen shirt.

I knew how nervous Deb was about this whole thing when she turned up in a sleeveless, blousy number and high heels that went better at Lon's than in my living room.

Dad knew where we were at in our reconciliation, that being in a good place, but he still knew how important this was, so he was in chinos and a navy button down.

Patches was in his normal outfit, curled into the corner of the couch with his back to us, sharing he was not a huge fan of too much company.

"That smells so good," Deb enthused. "We had lunch at a great Mexican place at that pretty, swanky mall, and I ate so much, I worried I wouldn't be hungry for dinner. But I can't wait to eat."

"Honey, quit hovering over Cap's shoulder and give the man some room to move," Dad said to his wife.

She jumped and put her hand to her chest before she made to skedaddle, saying, "I'm sorry, Cap."

"You're fine." Cap looked over his shoulder at Dad. "She's fine, Charlie. Thanks, though."

Deb left him alone and walked the half step (okay, it was more) to the counter opposite me and Dad.

"I like your apartment, Rachel," she said.

Update.

I'd had a slight drama when I got home and realized I wanted to give the full tour, and couldn't do that with my bedroom wall the way it was.

When Cap got home, I shared this dilemma.

So, while I was changing clothes, he tacked up the bright, flowery tapestry I sometimes threw over my rattan, Target, patio chairs outside my front door when I was feeling in a funky mood. This instantly solved my dilemma because it looked out of place on my wall, but not *that* out of place.

And thus, I could conduct the full tour.

"Can you get any better?" I asked when he was finished.

His eyes traveled the length of me in my dress, and he asked back, "That's my question."

Obviously, this comment was the answer to mine.

(It seemed impossible, but he kept demonstrating he could.)

And the way those pork chops were looking only served up more evidence to prove it.

"But...I don't mean to be funny," Deb went on. "Where are we going to eat?"

I could understand her concerns, considering she didn't want to be sawing into a pork chop with a plate balanced on her knees and maybe spill some pork juice on the silky material of her dress.

"I thought you and Dad could eat at the bar, and Cap and I will, erm...improvise," I said.

"Why don't we eat at one of the tables by the pool?" Dad suggested. "That courtyard is fantastic."

Cap looked over his shoulder again, this time at me.

"The complex is kinda busy, Dad," I said.

"Darlin', I hope you know, this isn't going to be our only visit," Dad informed me, and my heart swelled, because I'd hoped so, but his confirmation was awesome. "These people are part of your life. We had a rocky introduction, but we need to move on from that."

"Are you sure?" I asked.

"Sure I'm sure," he said.

"Okay!" I cried happily, because our courtyard *was* fantastic, and because I loved this indication that Dad was all in to stop hiding behind history, old and new, deal with shit and come out into the open.

I leaned in to kiss his cheek, ignoring the startled, happy look on his face when I pulled away.

I hopped off my chair and dashed to grab my eat-in-the-courtyard bucket from the shelf over the washer and dryer in the hall.

Stopping only to open a drawer and snatch my cloth napkins, which I dumped into the bucket, then opening another to nab the cutlery, I dashed out of the apartment, calling, "Be right back."

I ran down. Spritzed a table with all-purpose cleaner, wiped it down, shifted the chairs and laid out my placemats that I had rolled up and stored in the bucket. I set out the napkins and cutlery and raced back.

No one had moved from where they were.

I headed to the hall to put away the bucket.

"I could have helped you with that," Deb noted when I squeezed into the kitchen to get out my fancy plastic wineglasses and start the switch from what we were using.

"That's okay. You're on a mini-vacay. Sit down with Dad and relax." I said, getting sidetracked putting my marble wine holder in the freezer. From how those chops were looking, we didn't have a lot of time for it to chill, but every little helped.

"You've built a sweet life for yourself, Rachel," Deb noted, and I stopped pouring my wine into a plastic glass and looked at her.

"It got sweeter recently," I replied.

Pink hit her cheeks.

Dad ducked his head.

"Baby, help me with the finishing touches. We'll load up our plates here and head down," Cap said.

I did that. *We* did that. And it was Cap who did the extra trip up to go get another bottle of wine from the fridge and the holder from the freezer.

We were diving in when Patsy, standing at the railing on the upper walkway outside her unit, shouted down at us, "Hey, Raye! Hey, Raye's family!"

Cap, Dad and Deb looked up at her.

She didn't wait for their greetings.

She asked me, "Did you see the new compost bins?"

"Um...no," I replied.

"The landlord said I can maintain them and use the compost for my planters!" she cried excitedly.

Only Patsy would be excited at maintaining, essentially, garbage.

"That's great!" I yelled.

"You need to be sure to read my email about the rules of what goes in," she warned.

"I'll do that," I promised.

"'Kay. Sorry to disturb. Enjoy your evening!"

Then she was gone.

"She's the chick who looks after all the planters around the complex," I explained to Dad and Deb.

They looked around the space before Deb said, "She's good at it."

"They're great," Dad added. "But compost will make them awesome."

I wasn't sure how much more awesome they could get, and I envisioned a courtyard that was a riot of flowers, like Scott and Louise's yard was a riot of green, and I didn't think this would suck.

"Sorry to interrupt!" we heard from the other side.

I looked to see Jacob with a hand on the edge of his door, his head and shoulders sticking out, looking at us.

"Hey, Jacob!" I called.

"What time is Luna's gig again?" he asked.

"Starts at seven thirty," I answered.

"Right. Later," he replied, but Alexis ducked under his arm and shouted, "Hey, Raye. Hey, Cap. Hey, Raye's Dad and Missus."

"That's Jacob and Alexis," I murmured to the table.

Deb was game, she was so relieved no one had run them out on a rail—in fact, the opposite—she cried, "Hey there!"

Jacob was pulling her away when Alexis shouted, "Enjoy your dinner!"

The door closed on them.

"Just to say, this might happen all night," I warned them.

"That's okay," Deb bopped in her chair, settling in. "It makes it festive."

I loved she looked at it that way.

"So, I have to make my sangria for Luna's birthday party," I began. I also had to figure out a present for her, which was the reason for the trip to Anthropologie yesterday, from which I personally came out a winner, but my present-buying mission was a bust. "But other than that, we have all day tomorrow. Though, I have to carve some time out to figure out what to buy Luna. So what do you want to do? We can do brunch at Snooze, and then maybe go to the Botanical Gardens for a couple of hours. Or, if it's nice, we can take a walk down the canal and maybe hit up a restaurant in Scottsdale. Or—"

"I'm gonna sit by the pool," Dad declared. "And you can sit with me, though I think you should take Deb shopping. She can help you buy your friend a present. She's great at that type of thing."

Deb's eyes on me were bright.

"I'm a terrible gift-giver," I warned her.

She waved her hand in front of her face. "Oh, poo. I'm sure that's not true."

"She's my bestest bestie in all the world, and I gave her a gift card to Nordstrom Rack last year," I admitted.

Deb's expression of horror had me cracking up.

There it was.

Proof!

That gift stunk.

"Exactly," I said.

Deb immediately started quizzing me. "What's she like to do?"

We got into that, with only Ryan coming home and calling hey then leaving again disturbing us.

We were kicked back, the second bottle of wine open and

poured, and after Dad and Deb shared their gratitude and compliments for Cap's cooking, when Dad prompted Deb, "Ask her."

Deb turned her head to Dad. "I think you should ask her."

"It was your idea," Dad pointed out.

"It should come from you."

"Raye's a pretty laidback woman," Cap broke in, sweeping a hand out to indicate the table. "And if you haven't gotten it, she's all the way down with mending this rift. So it really doesn't matter who asks her whatever it is you're talking about."

Dad lounged deeper into his chair and sipped his wine.

I fought a smile, forgetting how stubborn he could be, and loving the experience of remembering it.

"Oh, all right," Deb said. She fiddled with the stem of her wineglass and couldn't quite meet my eyes when she said, "I suggested it, and your dad thinks it's a good idea, that maybe...and we'll pay for you to fly back, of course. Airline travel is so expensive these days, unless you want some cheapie flight where you're practically sitting on the lap of the person beside you—"

"Deb," Dad said low to get her back on target.

She twitched her head a little and reined it in. "I was thinking we could have a little, you know, not a big thing, just a nice dinner and a big cake and an excuse to buy pretty dresses."

She stopped talking, which was bad, because I didn't know exactly what she was talking about.

"You want me to come home for...a nice dinner?" I asked, trying to get the full lowdown.

"It hasn't been long, I mean, since the first, but, what I mean is a renewal of our vows," Deb said really fast.

I stared at her.

"Just a little party. Close family. And a photographer," she kept talking fast. "So you can be in the pictures."

Dad was watching me.

Cap put his hand on mine where it was resting on the arm of my chair.

I was silent.

"I know, it's a stupid idea," Deb mumbled, looking away.

"No, I think it's great," I told her. "I'm just trying really hard not to burst out crying."

Deb brightened up so vividly, I fought squinting.

Dad cleared his throat and became enthralled with one of Patsy's planters.

"Really?" she asked. "I mean, not you crying. That you think it's a good idea."

"I'd love that so much," I said, my voice husky.

"Oh, Raye," Deb said, her voice now also husky.

"Honey," Dad murmured, and I didn't know if it was to Deb or me.

But Cap muttering, "Baby," I knew was for me, and I knew that even without the hand squeeze he gave me.

"Can you get time off?" Dad asked, and that was to me.

I drew in a deep breath to control my emotion, turned my hand so Cap could link his fingers in mine (that did it), and answered Dad, "Definitely. When were you thinking?"

"Christmas," Dad and Deb said simultaneously.

Cap chuckled at their deviousness.

I burst out laughing.

Martha dragged a chair to our table, a bottle of beer in her hand, and with no greeting or request to join us, she sat down and declared, "Waited what seemed like a year for you to finish your chow. You all are the slowest eaters on the planet."

Deb was staring at her in shock.

Cap was looking at his lap, but his shoulders were shaking.

Dad, understandably, considering his last run-in with Martha, didn't seem surprised.

"Did you hear we're going to be cultivating garbage?" she asked me.

"It's called composting, Martha," I informed her.

"I know what it's called, Raye. It's still gonna smell up the joint," she shot back.

"Where are the bins?" I queried curiously.

"In the trash chute rooms," Martha said. "I guess we're all gonna get a little bucket, and the new garbage people are going to dump what we dump in the big containers they installed on the northeast corner of the parking lot. And Patsy's gonna go in and turn the piles with a shovel or something. It's positively barbaric."

"It's natural. It's been happening since the big bang," I returned.

She sat back and glugged some beer before she said, "Well, I'm not gonna save my egg shells and tea bags in a separate bucket."

"Don't tell me, tell Patsy. She'd *love* to hear all about you denying her your egg shells and tea bags," I retorted.

Cap scooted closer to me, because Linda was pulling up a chair.

Much like Martha, that was to say, without an invitation, she sat and asked, "Is Martha on about the compost?"

All of this was not rude, normally.

It was the unwritten rule of the courtyard: if you were in it, you were fair game.

Actually, I was surprised they waited for us to finish dinner.

Though, I worried about what Dad and Deb would think of it.

However, at a glance, I saw Deb appeared fascinated.

And Dad?

Well, Dad looked completely content.

I couldn't let myself linger too much on that look. My father being happy I'd found a safe place to land with good people around me, coming at me right on the heels of them inviting me to the renewal of their vows was too much.

So I set it aside in a cozy, warm place in my internal Oasis, shifted my attention to Linda, and answered, "Yes."

Linda looked to Martha. "You're going to compost like all the rest of us."

"Not gonna," Martha mumbled obstinately.

Zach strolled up, *sans* Bill (for once, those two really needed to get engaged, I didn't know what the holdup was, but I figured I might need to have a Jacob-style come to Jesus with them soon). "Are you guys talking about the mural?"

"No. Martha's complaining about the compost again," Linda told him.

Zach rolled his eyes before he aimed them to Martha. "My God, Martha, it isn't that big of a deal."

"Tell me that in a month when your little bucket gets slimy and smells up your kitchen," Martha shot back.

"You line it with a liner made of compostable plastic so it won't get slimy," Zach retorted.

"I'm not adding that to my budget," Martha returned.

"They cost maybe ten bucks for fifty of them. That'll last you a year," Zach stated.

"Can I just interrupt to introduce you all to my dad and step-mom, Charlie and Deb," I said.

"Heya," Zach replied.

"Nice to formally meet you." Linda smiled.

"Do you compost?" Martha asked.

"We live in a condominium, and no, they don't offer composting, unfortunately," Deb said.

"We should talk to the board about adding that amenity," Dad noted.

"We should," Deb agreed.

"I'm surrounded by weirdos," Martha groused.

"What about the mural?" I asked Zach.

He turned excited eyes to me. "The artist has the outline done, and it looks like it's going to be absolutely *insane*, with palm fronds and hibiscus flowers coming from the long, flowing skirt of a woman walking toward the southeast corner. We're going to have the coolest complex in Phoenix," Zach told me.

"We already got that, boy," Martha declared.

I heard a splash and turned my head to see Alexis had slipped into the pool and Jacob was diving over her head into the water.

When he came up for air, and after he did that man shake of his head to get the water out of his hair, Martha shouted, "If you two fornicate in the pool, I'm not speaking to you for a year."

Deb gasped.

Cap sounded like he was choking, but since it was on his laughter, that was okay.

Alexis's cheeks got red.

Zach muttered, "Oh my God."

Linda snapped, "Martha!"

"Hadn't planned on it before," Jacob called, snaking an arm out to claim Alexis. "Guaranteed we're gonna do it now."

"Behave yourselves," Martha yelled. "Raye's family is here."

Like *she* was behaving herself.

"Family is family," Jacob fired back. "So we'll do whatever we want."

My eyes hit my dad's on the "family is family" comment.

That was when my other hand was taken in a warm, firm grip by a man in my life I cared about.

"Well, at least they moved the copulation station from right next door to Jacob's unit, so I don't have to listen to it anymore," Martha declared. She looked between Dad and Deb. "Kids these days. Gluh."

Deb, who had scooted a little closer to Dad so Zach could stand with us, put her head on Dad's shoulder.

And I took a sip of my wine, wondering where I should go shopping for the dress I was going to wear to the renewal of their vows.

ON MY BACK, Cap on top, his cock moving inside me, his fingers threaded in mine on the pillow by my head, I breathed his breath, stared into his eyes and memorized how beautiful all I was seeing and feeling was.

"Best night ever," I whispered.

"Tonight was a good night," he murmured.

"No. I mean, the night I met you."

That did it.

He'd been taking it slow, lazy, touching and tasting and exploring and feeding the fire.

But right then, his pupils dilated, a fierce look moved into his face, and lazy went out the window.

I ended the festivities crying out into Cap's mouth, and not long after, he groaned into mine.

We were back to lazy and slow, touching and exploring silently as we came down.

Then Cap rolled off, and I got out of bed to go clean up and put on my nightie.

When I made it back to the room, Cap had turned out the light on my side of the bed.

I located my panties, slid them up and joined Cap in bed.

He turned out the light on his side and pulled me into his arms.

"I can't express how happy I am that this visit with Dad has been all it's been, but even so. I'll be glad when things calm down so maybe my boyfriend can show me where he lives," I hinted broadly.

Cap laughed softly and shared, "I'm renting a townhouse off Sixteenth around Bethany Home that's mostly full of boxes. Though, I got sheets on my bed and the cable hooked up."

I had no doubt.

It was my experience men and cable were a thing.

"I don't want to rent, I want to own," Cap went on. "But I didn't know, after we set up operations here, if I was going to stay in Phoenix, since Shirleen and Roam are in Denver."

My insides suddenly got super chilly.

"I thought they were thinking of moving down here," I remarked.

"They are. It's all up in the air."

"Oh," I mumbled to his chest in the dark.

"Sorry," he said. "That's past tense. It *was* up in the air." He started to draw randomly on the small of my back. "Recently, I decided I'm staying in Phoenix."

"Oh!" I chirped.

He laughed softly again before he shared, "Shirleen really likes it down here. It's not decided, but I see that happening, where I didn't really before. Not only because of Moses, and Roam, and Moses's daughters, but because of the Rock Chicks. But now she knows how easy it is to get here, less than a two-hour flight. So I can see that happening."

"I'd love that for you. I was in the midst of a drama at the time, but she's sweet with you. In a way I think only Shirleen can be sweet."

"Yeah," he muttered.

"Even if it's just boxes, can I still see your pad?" I asked, because I was curious about the place he'd chosen to spend his time not working, regardless that it was temporary.

"Sure, baby, but you missed a part."

"What?"

"I want to own."

Oh man.

I knew what he was saying.

I pressed my lips together.

"It's not gonna happen tomorrow," he said. "But I need to put it in your head. Because this place is not big enough for the two of us."

"They have two-bedroom units at the Oasis," I told him.

Another quiet laugh, then he found my lips in the dark and whispered, "We'll see. Now, go to sleep, Rachel."

"Okay, but just so you know, in the morning, we can't have headboard-banging sex. Rhea next door heard us this morning, and she works late at a biker bar."

"Got it."

"And also, I have a very small account that's going to be my down payment in about fifty years when I buy a house. In other words, eventually, I want to own too."

I felt his body relax against mine on his, "Right."

"Okay, 'night, honey."

His goodnight was to touch his mouth to mine again.

I'd take it.

And I did.

Carrying it right to dreamland.

TWENTY-ONE

PHONE TREE

T he bed moved when Cap got out of it.

Since he took my pillow with him—namely, his chest—I grabbed his and wrapped my arms around it to take his place until he got back.

I suspected he was going to the bathroom.

I was back to sleep when my hip was gently shaken, waking me again.

I rolled and saw Cap sitting beside me in bed.

It was dark, but since he slept either naked or in his underwear, and I figured I could spy his bare chest after having fallen while spelunking, and my flashlight battery gave out, and he was in my vicinity, I could see right then his shadow looked to be fully-clothed.

Therefore, my drowsiness partially cleared in surprise.

"Got a callout," he explained his state of attire. "Shouldn't be long. Just wanted you to know. You can go back to sleep."

I pushed up to sitting, resting back on a hand. "Callout?"

"Mace and Knox are into something, and they need an extra man."

I turned to look at my Alexa.

It was after one in the morning.

I went back to him.

"At this hour?" I asked.

"Babe, this is my job, and they're holding on me, so I have to go. I'm down to talk with you about it, but it can't be now."

"Okay," I said quickly.

He moved in to brush his lips against mine. "Be back, soon as I can."

"Okay," I repeated.

He got up, and I watched his shadow move to the door and disappear.

I laid back in bed, still mostly dozy from sleep, but also thinking that Cap had a job that could call him out after one in the morning.

Sure, philanderers philandered at times like these (and that was what I thought most private investigation was, catching cheaters cheating).

But that wouldn't need an extra man.

I turned my head toward the door where I saw Cap's shadow vanish, and I thought about the gun in the waistband in the back of his pants that first night when he broke in. I thought about how he'd been hired to find Elsie Fay.

And I thought that with all that had been going on, I hadn't had enough time to think about Cap's job.

Honestly?

Mace, Lee, Vance, Eric, Liam and Cap all looked like they could liberate a small country with only the members of that team.

And men like that didn't make enough bank to commission a bronze phoenix for their office if they were only catching cheaters cheat (and the like).

So, uh...*yeah*.

We needed a convo.

I wasn't going to pitch a fit. He'd been super cool with me, and what I was doing wasn't even my job.

But I had to know.

My eyes fell on my tapestry-covered wall. What was behind it, I'd looked at so much, it was burned in my brain.

So right then, without me calling it up, it hit my brain.

And then something else hit me.

All of a sudden, I sat up in bed.

I turned on the light, winced against the bright, but still threw my legs over the side and went to the wall.

I pulled the tapestry aside and stared at it.

"I'm such a dufus," I whispered, rushing to my phone.

I grabbed it off the charger and made the call as I hurried to my closet.

It took several rings, but Luna finally answered.

"Wha?" she asked, sounding half-asleep.

"Luna," I said, squeezing the phone between ear and shoulder while shoving my foot into the leg of a pair of jeans. "Who sees all and is in the middle of everything?"

Her "What?" was more alert this time.

"Who sees all and is just blocks away from The Slide *and* The Pink Slip *and* right in the middle of where the girls work?"

"Oh my God," she whispered. "Mr. Shithead."

Her name for him was better than mine so I immediately adopted it.

I struggled into my bra as I said, "We've half-assed this. Conducting an investigation, you follow the outline Cap gave me. I've been stuck on the beginning and end, mostly the end. He and I even had a conversation about it this morning and it didn't penetrate. But we need to go back to the beginning. We need to talk to people who might know the victims. And he's in the position to know, or at least have seen all the victims. Which means we need to go talk to him."

"He's not going to tell us anything."

"Nobody ever tells the cops anything, but they still find a way to get answers. We have to try."

"I thought we were passing this off to 'We.'"

"We are, but that doesn't mean we can't give them more if we find it." I sensed her hesitation, so I said, "I get it if you're done and don't want to come."

"You're not going alone," she replied firmly. "I'll activate the Angels Phone Tree."

I paused in trying to figure out how to pull on my shirt and still talk to her. "We have a phone tree?"

"Yeah, you call me, I call Jessie and tell her to call Harlow. Phone tree. You're up and sound like you're getting dressed. Which means you get to do the round of pickups. See you when you get here."

She disconnected.

I finished dressing, went to the wall, pulled back the tapestry, ripped all the women's pictures down, left my phone, turned out the light (climate change!), grabbed my burner and shot out of there.

We drove the Accord, me behind the wheel, and I was so fired up to do this, I was annoyed at the added delay in doing the switch out.

"First, we don't need to be driving practically to the airport to pick up our wheels. We need a centralized location for the vehicles," I declared. "So, I'm gonna ask for that and complete dossiers on all the missing women. We're going to pore through them. We're also gonna go talk to who reported them missing and any family they have in town. I missed it, even though Cap told me it was the first thing we needed to do. I'm not even sure who we're looking for, even though I know who we're looking for, but still, I don't know a thing about them. And that's the most important part!"

I was so worked up, I ended that shouting.

"Should Harlow and me meet this Clarice chick?" Jessie asked. "Because your dad's here, Luna's getting ready for her party tomorrow, and if she knew about us, Harlow and I could communicate with her."

"I'll email 'We' in the morning, share what we want and tell them you're on the team, so eventually, they'll hear from you. And I'll tell them you need to be kitted out," I said. "Also, I'll ask for a laser pointer."

"Rad," Harlow said.

"Did this 'We' entity give you anything on that Jumper character?" Jessie asked Luna.

"Nada, which is a little surprising," Luna answered. "Clarice told us we'd have something to go on within twenty-four hours, but they've been all kinds of thorough so far in what we've asked for. On him, nothing. Maybe this guy *is* a ghost."

"You mean, like, a *real* one?" That came from Harlow, and she sounded not happy about this. Then again, she'd shared that as a child on a visit to Disneyland with her family, taking the Haunted Mansion ride had messed her up for life, so she wouldn't be.

Another reason why it was a shocker that (so far) she was down to do all of this.

"No, I mean, like, he's doing some sick shit, and he knows how to cover his ass," Luna replied.

No one had anything to say to that, and not long after, I swung into Sun Valley Motor Lodge.

By the time we were out and headed to reception, Mr. Shithead was leaned all way back in his desk chair, eyes to the ceiling, clearly asking for deliverance.

Well, he wasn't going to get it.

I pushed in with my posse and rethought black leather pants.

We'd look kickass in black leather pants.

"Can I *pay* you not to show up here?" he asked when he stopped looking at the ceiling.

I slapped the pictures I brought down on the counter in front of him, spread them out and asked, "Have you seen these women?"

When he looked down at them, he lost some color in his face.

Holy shit!

It was just a hunch.

But not anymore.

"You have," I snapped. "Which ones?"

His gaze came to me, and I saw he'd gotten himself together really quickly.

This was why his reply was, "Fuck off and die."

"Do you know what happened to them?" I pressed.

He shoved at the photos so a couple fell off the counter.

Harlow moved to pick them up.

"You can talk to me or you can talk to the cops," I warned.

"Cops already came by, and if it'll get your asses out of my reception, I'll tell you what I told them. Yeah, I seen 'em. We rent rooms by the hour. I see 'em all. No, I don't know 'em, don't know who took 'em, don't know where they are, and I also don't care."

"Is it that they're dead that you don't care?" Jess asked. "Or you don't care because they're prostitutes who sold their bodies, and they're now forced into sexual slavery, and that's no big thing in your estimation?"

"Fuck off, I don't know dick," he returned.

But after Jessie's question, there was something different about him.

He was always such a jerk, and he seemed pretty down with being only that.

Now he seemed uncomfortable.

I knew Luna sensed it too when I felt her hand touch my back, encouraging me to keep at him.

"Bambi's mother is worried sick about her," I shared.

"Like I care," he said, no longer quite meeting my eyes.

"All these women have people in their lives who are worried about them," I pushed.

"Yeah? If they were, they'd keep their asses off the streets."

"Is this your dream job?" I asked. "What happened in your life to land you here?"

"I got it good, bitch," he snarled. "Sit and drink coffee and rent rooms and read my porno mags, then go home, jack off and go to sleep. Got no hassle in my life, 'cept you bitches recently. As long as I show up at work, it's all good."

"So that's what you wanted to be all your life, working reception at a crappy motel," I remarked.

"Fuck off," he bit, getting seriously angry now. "I don't give two shits what you think about me."

Luna touched my back again, this time to tell me I was following the wrong trail.

Mentioning Bambi got to him.

I needed to go back to that.

"Christina Markovic, you might know her as Bambi, would go to her mom's house every Sunday and do her laundry."

"This isn't gettin' through to you, *I don't care,*" he returned.

"Her mom still talks about her daughter in present tense. She still has hope she's going to come home. She was out asking around. Have you talked to Betsy?" I kept at him.

"If you're not gonna rent a room, you can get the fuck out of here, or it's gonna be me calling the cops."

"She just wants to know where her daughter is."

Both Luna and Harlow put their hands to my back at that, and they left them there, not communicating about my interrogation, communicating something else.

Me not knowing where Macy was.

I had to force myself to finish.

"Even if she's dead."

His eyes flicked to the windows and his demeanor changed again, and this time, it was a whole lot easier to read.

I couldn't look over my shoulder to the windows because, abruptly, he lost it.

We all took a step back when he pushed the pictures off the counter and shouted, "Get the fuck out of here, bitches, and don't fuckin' come back!"

Harlow bent down to pick up the pictures again, but Luna, Jess and me looked out the window.

Cold crawled over my skin.

Sergio Duzek was out there, leaning against the trunk of his BMW, arms crossed on his chest, eyes on us.

It was too bad he was kinda hot, with dark, curly hair he wore a bit long in the back so it brushed his collar, swarthy skin and good bone structure. He wasn't all that tall, but he had a decent body.

Considering he was clearly an asswipe, though, he sat at a point two on the normal scale, and about negative two hundred on the Cap Scale.

"You know what's good for you," Mr. Shithead said so quietly, it was barely discernible. "You'll leave this alone."

We turned back to him to see him pound on the desk angrily.

And he was shouting again when he said, "Get the fuck outta here! I mean it!"

One thing I knew about this, Sergio Duzek was in on the missing women.

The other thing I knew about it, Mr. Shithead was terrified of him.

The last thing I knew about it, I was terrified of him too.

With nothing for it, I had to channel my inner Rolex-extorting badass.

This was what I did.

I circled my finger in the air and said, "Let's roll."

We walked out to the car, and as we did, I caught Duzek's eyes and called, "Hey."

I was trying to play it cool.

Duzek wasn't in the mood to play it cool.

Instead of saying hey back, he asked, "How's it feel to be watched?"

Yikes!

They'd noticed me in Tweety.

Totally.

I gave him my best confused look. He openly didn't buy it. I looked away and stopped trying to sell it. And we all got in the car.

I pulled on to Roosevelt, and no one said a word.

We were nearing The Parking Spot when Luna noted, "I know you're fired up, Raye. But that was not good. I think we need to give 'We' Duzek and not be seen anywhere near Roosevelt and Van Buren between Sixteenth and Twenty-fourth until, maybe, my fortieth birthday."

"Those women are somewhere, Luna, maybe somewhere close," Jess said.

"Yeah, and my birthday is tomorrow, and I'd like to see my next one, not to mention all of yours, so my vote is, we feed this to 'We,' encouraging them to push the powers that be to look hard at Duzek and talk to that night clerk, then go back to our normal crazy."

No one said anything.

So Luna pressed, "Anyone else gonna vote?"

"It's hard to leave them hanging high and dry when we now have a prime suspect," Jess replied. "Some of them have been gone for years."

"I don't want to leave them high and dry either," Luna returned. "I hate the idea. It's fucked up. But we, in fact, are *not* Charlie's Angels, so until you can go hand-to-hand with four assailants without messing up your hair, maybe we should dial it back."

"It's my fuckup," I put in. "It got us something, but it was smack in ground zero. I was cocky. Now, I'll email 'We,' give them what we got and tell them we feel the danger level has elevated significantly, so we're dialing it back."

"Raye—" Jessie began.

"Jess, love you, babe, but I think you missed it. That was a direct threat from that guy. He sees me, or any of us again, he's not going to stay leaning against his car. And I already lost two people I love in my life due to shit like this. I'm not going to lose anymore."

That ended the discussion.

So we drove back to The Parking Spot in silence, and we did it feeling shit.

I was used to feeling shit like this.

And now I wished I hadn't dragged my girls to that place with me.

I was in a bad mood for obvious reasons when I let myself into my apartment after dropping off the girls.

The only good thing was that I saw Cap's Porsche in a visitor spot (I mean, *seriously*, how did he always score those?), which meant, when he told me what he was doing shouldn't take long, he wasn't blowing sunshine, and now, he was safe home.

At least that was something.

I walked into my place to see the light on over the stove, which wasn't a lot of illumination.

Even so, I saw Cap sitting on the couch.

Patches was curled up beside him, but they weren't cuddling and waiting for me.

No.

Cap had his long arms spread across the back of the couch, his legs open in a seriously aggressive manspread, and I could feel his eyes burning into me like lasers.

"Where have you been?" he asked in that ominous quiet voice of his.

Considering this seemed to be a dicey situation, and I tardily realized I should have left a note or shot him a text, I came in and put my burner, keys and the pictures of the women on the coffee table, before I shared, "After you left, I had an idea and rallied the girls to go look into it."

"And you didn't take your phone?"

"Clarice told us—"

"Fuck Clarice," he clipped. "Always take your fucking phone."

I stood in front of him like a naughty schoolgirl, and not the fun, role-playing kind.

And I didn't like it.

Right.

Considering what happened the last time we had words, I suggested, "I think we both need to breathe a little before any more is said."

"This is me, Rachel, *breathing*. If I wasn't *breathing*, I'd be in your space, shouting in your face."

"Cap—"

"I came home at two in the morning, and I didn't know where you fucking were."

Eek!

I copped to it immediately. "I should have left a note."

"You should have left a note *and* taken your phone."

"I don't think Clarice wants—"

"I don't give a fuck what Clarice wants, Raye." He dipped his head to the coffee table. "Do you have my number in that burner?"

"No."

"So you get in a situation, how are you gonna contact me?"

"I've memorized it." And I had, for just that occurrence (and, obviously, because he was my guy).

"So someone finds your dead body, mutilated beyond recognition, how are they gonna find who to give the death notice too?"

That was a little dramatic.

Sergio Duzek sprang to mind.

Okay, that was appropriately dramatic.

"We were just talking to a night clerk at a motel," I told him.

It ended up more than that, but I'd share that part later.

"I got home, you not here, knowing you're working some shady fuckin' business, which means rubbing up against shady fuckin' characters, no note, I call you, and your phone vibrates on the goddamned nightstand."

I knew how that felt, and I'd fucked up.

Royally.

I took a step around the coffee table to get closer to him, and said pacifyingly, "Okay, Cap. That wasn't cool. You woke me to tell me you were leaving, I should have shared why I'd gone and where so you'd know if you got home before me. Next time, I'll do that."

"You need to be really fuckin' smart doing this kind of shit on the streets, Rachel," he shared something I'd already learned that night. "And you not having the presence of mind to leave a note does not make me feel great about you being able to be as smart as you need to be."

I opened my mouth to retort, because I'd screwed up, but he was prodding something that was hella sensitive in that mo'. He lifted his hand to stop me from talking.

"I'm not saying you aren't smart. Don't read into that. But, Raye, I *lived* on the streets. You gotta know I know what I'm talking about."

He *so* did.

"Maybe we can chill this out or move it to the bedroom, or turn on a light and sit down and chat, because the way this is going down, I feel like a naughty child getting a talking to from her principal," I suggested.

"I've been sitting for the last hour, having no other choice but to sit and wait for you to come home, because the tracker we put on your car said it was parked and immobile at a lot near Sky Harbor. As far as I know, you had no reason to be there. And when our guy Brody hacked into their security cameras, you were nowhere to be seen. Fortunately, you and your girls showed about five minutes later. But do you feel me?"

I felt him.

And I was impressed they had a hacker who was that good.

Wow.

However...

"You put a tracker on my car?"

He shook his head. "Babe, seriously. Read the Rock Chick books."

"I'm not sure I'm down with you tracking me, Cap."

"We had a lead with that tracker on your car, Raye. Without that, you'd vanished without a trace."

My breath was escalating. "You should have told me."

"You're right, with how you and me are now, I should have. How we were when I did it, you'd think I was a creeper."

"When did you do it?" I asked curiously.

"The night I broke in."

Whoa!

If he wasn't him, total creeper.

I opened my mouth, but he got there before me.

"And I'll remind you, the first time you laid eyes on me, I'd just pulled a pedophile off you after he'd grabbed you and yanked you in his house. So be pissed and get over it. I knew you were the one, I also knew you were into some crazy shit, so I took precautions."

My breath regulated.

Because, okay.

Honestly?

I couldn't get ticked about that.

"Do you have a tracker on your car?" I queried.

"Yes, and my phone is tracked. Fuck, Lee would have chips embedded in our skin if he thought that extra measure of caution would save our asses if we had trouble."

The perfect segue.

"We need to talk more fully about what you do."

He shook his head and stood. "You're not gonna hijack our discussion with one about my job. You don't get to play the worry card right now."

"I actually wasn't worried." I thought about that and amended, "I was only slightly worried. You have it going on. I still want to understand what your job entails."

"Great, we'll talk about it after I fuck you in the morning, but now, Raye, I need assurances you get me. I don't wanna relive the last hour, dragging Brody in, putting Liam and Knox on call they might have to move out. Not ever again."

Shit, I'd blown it twice that night.

"I messed up," I admitted (or, repeated, though I wasn't going to point that out). "It won't happen again. You have my assurances. And anyway, we're definitely out now. We believe we've identified a major player. We'll feed it into the pipeline, then we're pulling back."

Cap made no reply.

"Do you need to call Liam and Knox and tell them they can stand down?"

"I did that when I saw your car was headed home."

"Are you still mad at me?"

"No."

Well.

Look at us.

It was iffy there for a bit, but we got through that without too much drama.

So I asked, "Can we go to bed now? I'm in a bad mood."

"You're in a bad mood?"

"Yeah. The Angels are out on this sitch, which means we have to wait and hope. And it's less of a crushing bummer to know those women are experiencing whatever they're experiencing and lost to the people who care about them when you're trying to do something about it. As you know I know all too well, waiting and hoping sucks."

"You're in a bad mood," he repeated, but it wasn't a question this time.

"Well...yeah. Because, again, waiting and hoping sucks. Though, since you're action man, and you probably don't experience it often, barring tonight, perhaps I should stress, waiting and hoping really, really, *really* sucks."

"You're in a bad mood," he said yet again, but this time explained why he was doing it. "And you didn't get up in my shit when I confronted you."

Ah.

At that, I moved all the way to him and put both hands on his chest.

"Although I commend you for the sinister waiting-in-the-dark move, I think you missed it, honey. I leveled up on maturity a few days ago. I'm all about communication and talking things out. Not acting like a brat."

"I know when you can act like a brat," he replied.

This was interesting.

"There's a time I can act like a brat?"

"Yeah."

"When?"

"Right now."

Then he did the shoulder-in-the-belly move, I was up in another fireman's hold, and not long after, I was bouncing on the bed.

I learned what acting like a brat meant through whispered encouragement from Cap.

And in the end, considering how hard we both came, we found, one try, and I had it down *pat*.

TWENTY-TWO

DRY ICE

I was on a stool at my bar with a mug o' joe.

Cap, his hair wet from his shower, having already donned his jeans and tee for the day (alas) was in the kitchen, pouring his second one.

While he was showering, I emailed "We" about the situation last night, shared about our recruitment of Jess and Harlow, and went on to explain we felt it prudent to bow out at this juncture.

It was harder to do than I thought, after having a night sleeping next to Cap, and the distance it gave from Sergio Duzek's threat, not to mention, I'd spent a year on this, it felt incomplete.

Obviously, I didn't like that feeling.

But Cap was right.

I needed to dive deep and understand my own motivations in doing this kind of thing.

And they all stemmed from Macy.

Last night, I gave my friends just a taste of the bitter pill that had been forced down my throat when my sister was taken, and I found doing it extremely upsetting.

In other words, as much as it blew, this was the right choice.

Cap moved to the bar opposite me and leaned into his forearms, cradling his mug between his hands.

He wasn't cooking breakfast because our plans for the day included brunch with Dad and Deb. After that, Deb and I were going to go shopping for Luna's gift, and Dad was headed to the pool at the Hermosa Inn. Cap was going to do Cap things and meet me back at my place at seven to help me with the sangria before we went to Luna's party.

The thing was, this brought to mind the fact that, since we met, we'd spent a lot of time together, and today, we were going to be separated for the first time for a reason that was not work.

Thus, I'd realized last night, he was learning a lot about me, my life, and the people in it, but I hadn't learned that much about him.

The afternoon soiree at Stella (oh my God!) and Mace's tomorrow would help with that.

But still.

"What are you gonna do after brunch today?" I asked.

"Go home, do some laundry, switch out my bag so I can bring new clothes over here, work out, then chill with some TV or something." He stopped talking and took a sip from his mug.

I stared at him.

I did this so long, he asked, "What?"

"That seems very normal."

His gray-blue eyes twinkled and crinkled, and he said, "That's because I'm a normal guy."

"I regret to inform you, you are not normal, Cap."

"What did you think I'd do today?"

"I don't know. Gather all your superhero friends to battle the evil alien being who wants to eradicate humanity, and in so doing, reduce half of Phoenix to rubble, then take a shower and come help me with the sangria. Just to say, if your plans change and that goes down, gratitude in advance for not taking down the Oasis in your rumble with the evil alien."

More twinkling and crinkling and then, "I like to run, if I have time, doing it hitting trails. It keeps me fit, but it also clears my head. I work out for my job. Working out is about goals and focus, and builds strength, and all of that is necessary for what I do. I'm not crazy into sports, but I follow baseball and basketball, and I won't say no to going to a bar and having a beer and watching any kind of game. I think you get I'm really into cooking, that's about focus too, and results, and it's a creative outlet. So I also like to go to restaurants to get ideas and dissect recipes. If I have a day or two, I go somewhere in the mountains, because it's quieter there than in the city and reminds me of home. I like going to movies. And if I need to chill, I do it reading or watching TV."

"That is, indeed, all surprisingly normal," I remarked.

"As I said," he replied, taking another sip from his coffee.

"Okay, now we need to get into your job," I noted carefully.

He cradled his mug again and replied, "Right. Let's get into that. We provide security for businesses in the form of keeping an eye on them, as well as for people who come to town who need it."

"You mean celebrities."

"I mean celebrities," he confirmed.

"What celebrities have you met?"

"A lot of them."

He then rattled off a dozen super famous people, from actors to sports stars to ridiculously rich folk.

"Wow," I said when he was done.

"For the most part, they're normal people too. They can be reserved, because so many people want a piece of them, they need to put up that wall. There have been some arrogant assholes, but Mace and Darius don't put up with that shit for very long. The money is good, but life is too short."

"Darius?"

"He's one of the partners. He's been with us since back in Denver, but he runs the LA crew now. He's also Liam's dad."

Definitely a family affair.

I nodded and refrained from asking who the arrogant asshole celebrities were, but jotted that down as a future follow-up question, and instead asked, "Who was your favorite celebrity?"

Without having to think, he answered, "Justice Lonesome is the shit. Totally down to earth. Even been to her place in the mountains of Colorado where she and her husband Deke and their kids live. Not for work, for a cookout. She's serious good people."

I had to take a moment to process the fact that Cap had hung out with another "Oh my God!" celebrity, the insanely talented singer-songwriter, who I was a massive fan of, Justice Lonesome.

"Are you breathing?" Cap teased.

I kinda wasn't.

I went about doing that.

Then I queried. "Okay. What else do you do?"

"We have private, corporate and government clients. And I'm sorry, Raye, the investigative work we do is all strictly confidential." He let go of his mug with one hand to reach out with his other and take mine. "I can't talk about it, ever. It's part of the gig."

"You told me Elsie Fay's grandparents hired you."

"I did that because I knew you were going to be there when we told the cops the same thing. Though, I also did it because it was pertinent to the situation, and I didn't have much choice. In the end, it was going to be necessary information for the police to know so they understood why we were there. And there might be other instances like that. Some of the shit we do gets in the papers."

Oh, I'd noticed that.

"But for the most part, we try to operate under radar and keep our work under wraps," he went on. "That said, you need to know it isn't a nine to five job, I get callouts like last night, though, those are infrequent. The team working a case tends to be the team that can deal with the case. But we absolutely take each other's backs. You need to know, that means I could be working late hours on my own cases."

"Okay," I replied.

He paused a second to ascertain I'd taken that in.

Then he kept going.

"And you know I started interning with NI when I was fifteen. They didn't involve us seriously when we were that young, but they knew we were interested in joining the team when we were old enough, so the longer we were around, the more they taught us. Then the Army taught me even more. The years of experience Lee, Mace, Luke, Vance and the rest have ratchets up into the hundreds. In other words, they know what they're doing, and along the way, they taught us that. They also are very thorough in how they curate their teams. We understand the job in an integral way, and we have each other's backs. This isn't about thrill-seeking and taking risks to get off. This is about getting the job done and getting home safe."

"So, it's not just catching cheaters cheating," I murmured.

He gave my hand a squeeze. "They got mortgages and mouths to feed, and the desire to live a good life and retire to better, so we take cases to pay the bills. So yes, we do that. But no, it's not just shit like that. And I'll admit, some of the shit we do can be dangerous, but that isn't our day to day. What I'm trying to impress on you is, when it happens, we have the skills to handle it."

"All right."

He studied me a beat before asking, "What are you thinking?"

"I believe you when you say it isn't about thrill-seeking and taking risks, but I'm sensing the risks are still there. It's not your average job. And after what you said to me yesterday, I'm wondering about your motivations for doing it. Because that kind of work draws a certain kind of person, and it has to be *a little* about thrill-seeking and taking risks."

He nodded. "I'll grant that. And yeah, that's a valid observation. What I mean is, we don't do stupid shit out in the field. But that's what I knew on the streets, Raye. Survival. Making it so I woke up the next day. It just wove into the fabric of who I was."

As much as I hated that he'd experienced that, he spoke sense, and there was probably no way around it happening for him.

He continued, "Then Roam and me saw the Nightingale men in action, and it was just done. I get that's because I wanted to learn how to be able to take care of myself as well as live a life where I commanded respect. A life where no one would shit on me or under-estimate me. I totally get that. But the bottom line, every day is differ-ent, and I always gotta stay primed to use my brain and my body. If I didn't do what I do, I'd be a cop or still in the Army." He smiled. "But this way, I make a fuck ton more money, and I get to work with men who, most of them, I've known half my life, and I consider them brothers."

"And once in a while, you get to do things like find Elsie Fay," I stated.

He nodded. "And once in a while, job satisfaction goes off the charts with shit like that," he affirmed.

"There are people who experienced what you experienced, who, if they had the chance, would be glad to put that behind them and be a banker, Cap. So maybe it also has to do with it being who you were meant to be."

His lips tipped up, he shook his head, and then he shared, "On the streets of Denver, I was known as Sniff."

I was confused. "Sniff?"

"I was a runt."

I hated he talked about himself like that, so I started, "Cap—"

"I'm not the first guy who had his growth spurt late and suffered from acne, Raye. It was what it was. And when Park met me, I was skinny and weak and my nose was always running, so he called me Sniff. He was a good-lookin' kid, all the girls liked him. Him and Roam. They were cool, they'd been on the streets longer than me, and I looked up to them. I was a goof. I ran my mouth a lot. Now I know I did this because I'd lived a life with a mother who didn't give a shit what I had to say. And when I was around people who did, it just all came out."

It was me squeezing his hand at that.

Cap carried on.

"Because of this, I get another part of my motivation is, I don't ever want to be that kid again. I don't know what would have happened to me if I hadn't met Park and Roam, but I'd seen enough boys like me who got used in ways they hated just so they could eat. Park and Roam, and then Jules, saved me from that. I owe that to them. But for me, it's a constant drive to put that kid behind me."

"You aren't that kid anymore, honey," I said gently.

"I know that, baby." He gave me gentle right back. "But we can't escape our pasts, so we have to find a way to use them to our advantage, and that means the good and the bad. I use what I was given to keep striving to be stronger and smarter. I use how I see the men with their women in what I give to you. The key is to make it all work for you."

He was being so out there, giving of himself, not making me work for it, it was a bit overwhelming, but in a very good way.

I gave his hand another squeeze. "I love how open you are with all of this. It means a lot to me, Cap."

"Now you know a little bit about how I've been feeling with you letting me be a part of all the shit that's gone down with you."

God.

This guy.

I tested the footrest on the stool again so I could make it to his mouth.

He pushed farther across the bar so it wasn't such a feat.

When we both moved back, he said, "You need to do the things you do that you don't need to do to be beautiful, babe. We got less than an hour before we're supposed to meet your folks at Snooze."

I looked at the microwave clock.

Then I cried, "Shit!"

I hopped off the stool and ran to the bathroom.

Then I ran back because I forgot my coffee.

I was sure to close the toilet seat because Patches liked to sit on it and watch me put my makeup on.

And I'd learned the last time I cat sat for him, he liked the feel of my blush brush on his face.

So, even if I was running late (no surprise), we did a little of that too.

I WASN'T GETTING good vibes when, after brunch, and after we dropped Dad, I climbed in Dad and Deb's rental car, and she drove us to Fashion Square, parked on the Nordstrom side and took me directly to the fine jewelry counter.

I mean, props to her that she'd scoped out all the local malls so thoroughly.

And sure, in a perfect world, I'd drop a load on my best bitch for her birthday, but I hadn't had the time to do much dog walking.

However, when we got to the jewelry case she was looking for, and Deb asked the associate if they had the delicate necklace with a tiny initial pendant fashioned from diamonds in the letter L, I knew it was the perfect gift for Luna.

I also knew that Deb didn't mess around and had done some research since they went home last night.

I further knew this meant a lot to me.

Bottom line, though, I didn't know the cost, but I knew I couldn't afford that necklace.

"I know what you're thinking," she said as the associate went off to see if they had an L. "And you're right. It *is* expensive. But I noticed your friend likes to layer her necklaces, and she's comfortable in herself and her style. I didn't spend much time with her, but it was obvious. I thought of trying to find someone who could make us a name necklace in a short period of time, but not only would that probably be impossible, it's too much *Carrie*." She shook her hands by her head on her last word. "So, if you'll allow us the honor, it can be from you and your dad and me. And since there are three of us, it'll be less than a hundred and forty dollars for you. Can you do that?"

I didn't answer her verbally.

I pulled her in my arms and hugged her.

She hugged me back.

We stayed that way while she whispered in my ear, "I love him very much."

She was talking about Dad.

"I can tell," I whispered back.

"It isn't about your sister."

"I know, Dad told me."

"But she's with us. Always."

My voice was croaky when I replied, "I know."

"Thank you for giving him a second chance."

"Thank you for your part in giving him back to me."

Her arms tightened.

We kept hugging.

Eventually, the sales associate cleared her throat.

We let each other go, and Deb adjusted the bracelets at her wrist. I twitched my head to get it together.

And with a sweet smile on her face, the sales lady said, "We have an L."

At the same time, Deb and I replied, "Perfect."

THE REASON why Luna wanted to be at Oasis Square so bad had a lot to do with the fact it was awesome.

It also had to do with the fact I was there.

And last, a lot to do with the fact her apartment was, no other way to put it...shit.

It was a one-bedroom, bigger than mine, but the carpet was stained (Oasis didn't have carpet, we had fake wood, but it was a whole lot better than this and easier to keep clean). Her balcony was tiny and had a view to a parking lot. And her kitchen was set up all wonky so it was hard to cook in it because she had zero counter space.

At least my old landlord had done a complex-wide upgrade of our kitchens and bathrooms about three years ago.

It was a massive undertaking, and a pain in the ass to live through, and it only happened because everyone was so sick of stuff breaking down or springing a leak (serious, I think it was all original from when the place was built) and then having to wait far too long to get it fixed.

Thus, Martha and I sent him a letter signed by everybody (but Mick). She wanted to threaten a rent strike. I toned it down to informing him, if things didn't change, we were complaining to housing code enforcement.

We were a little surprised he took it that far. I couldn't say my stove was a Wolf, but it also wasn't crap. Maybe even then he was considering selling, and a new landlord would know that would be an issue they'd have to tackle, so he got that investment back in the sale.

Though, that said, after he did all of it, he landed a rent increase on us.

I digress.

Regardless that Luna's place wasn't that great, she transformed it for her parties.

It took us years to figure out she had to do this on her own with no assistance from me, and then when they showed up in our lives, Jessie and Harlow.

This was because her "vision" was so locked in her head, she was always elbowing us out of the way to fix the things she thought we did wrong (we did not do them wrong, she was just a freak perfectionist about that kind of thing).

But she also loved doing it.

She could be a party planner for a living, if she was able to do it with no staff, considering she'd *so* be a micromanager.

For this event, she'd moved the furniture, and in a corner, created a midnight-blue, silver and white balloon festooned backdrop, with the words in script on it *Kiss the Moon!* as her selfie station.

The rest of the space was made magical with fairy lights, more balloons, including silver ones that spelled out TERRIBLE 29 hanging from the ceiling. And evening out what the balloon extravaganza would add to the landfill, she had fabulous paper plates, napkins and eco-friendly cutlery.

My sangria was Luna's favorite, but even so, Jessie had created a signature cocktail for the evening, something that included vodka, champagne, lemon juice, blue curaçao and a maraschino cherry, with a sparkly silver, sugar rim served in a stemless flute (and if you wanted to up the cool factor, Jess would drop a piece of dry ice in it to make it bubble and smoke).

With this, Luna had laid out her usual spread of finger foods, chips and dips, and her homemade pimento cheese spread.

The centerpiece of this was a tall cake on a cake stand with midnight blue frosting, and in it (actually *in the frosting*) were yellow streaks of shooting stars, white specks, purple and lighter blue gradation, with gold and silver macarons, candy stars and glitter stuck to the side, with a huge white moon on the top with a gold chocolate star that said HAPPY BIRTHDAY.

I'd be jealous of this cake, but I got the same from Willow, The Surf Club's baker. It was one of the presents I looked forward to every year, because it was always a spectacle, and it tasted divine.

Cap and I had taken our second selfie in front of the backdrop (and that one was *totally* going in a frame since we were kissing in it, though, the first one from the Botanical Gardens was too). Then he took a picture of me and Luna, I took a picture of him and Luna. After that, he took a picture of Luna, Jessie, Harlow and me.

There was music, laughter and loud conversation, and Cap was demonstrating his skill with small talk wasn't a one off at the Oasis shindig.

Now he was on the balcony talking with Jacob, which meant Alexis was with us, hanging by Jessie, who always manned the bar at

Luna's parties, not only as her way to give back, but also because mixology was not her vocation, it was her calling.

And that was when it happened.

Harlow saw them first, and therefore, her voice was breathy and wondrous when she asked, "What...is...*happening?*"

We all looked the direction she was looking, and we all froze.

Update: I'd asked and Luna had lifted the ban on newbies at her party.

In other words, she'd said Cap could invite his buds.

I knew Liam, and honestly, his tall, perfect skin, fabulous body, sweet smile, and gorgeous chocolate-eyed good looks were enough.

But with him was a man who was maybe two inches shorter than him. His close-cropped hair and neatly trimmed beard were black as soot but the hair had a healthy, midnight gleam. His eyes were a dreamy blue. His body was made up of bulky muscle. And his sex appeal was near on menacing. I was scared of him, and if I didn't have Cap, I knew I would have wanted to jump him, and these sensations hit me both at the same time.

If this wasn't enough, with him was a dude that had to be taller than Cap by two inches, and he was *built*. His dark-brown hair was cut close at the sides, but styled to messily flip back at the top (though, the top was still short, just short-*ish*). He had dark scruff, deep-set, hooded eyes, the color of which I couldn't decipher from my distance, but they looked hazel. There was a subtle cleft in his chin, and he had the most perfect jawline and nose I'd ever witnessed *in my life.*

This meant one of these guys was Knox, but I had no clue who the other one was.

Liam spied me, tagged the other two and headed our direction.

"Oh my God, they're coming over here," Harlow whispered, grabbing hold of my arm in a way I nearly spilled some of my cocktail.

Liam smiled at me.

When he did, one of my crew made a noise like she'd been socked in the stomach. Another one whimpered. A third one (Harlow) let out a nervous giggle.

The last one, Luna, whispered, "I'm actually having an orgasm *right now*."

"Hey, Raye," Liam said when he made it to us.

"Hey, Liam," I replied, and I didn't know him all that well, but I still went in to touch my cheek to his.

He put his hand on my waist lightly when I did it, which told me I did the right thing.

I moved back, and he looked to Luna.

"Hey, Luna. Happy birthday," he said, then offered her the bottle of Dom he was carrying.

"Class," Jessie mumbled.

Totes!

"Thanks, Liam," she said, taking it.

Harlow had let me go, but now she was tapping me incessantly on my arm.

She wanted an introduction.

I took in the other two guys and stated, "I know one of you is Knox, but the other..."

I let that trail.

The dark-haired guy—and yes, his eyes were hazel—jerked up his chin. "I'm guilty of being Knox."

"Hey," I said.

His lips spread in a smile so white against his dark scruff and tanned skin, I blinked and fought reaching out to grab hold of something, not only because I'd lose my cocktail, but also because I'd look like a dork.

"This is Gabe," Liam introduced the other guy.

He was looking at Luna. "I crashed the party, babe. Hope that's cool."

"Yeah, uh...yeah, well, sure...of course...plenty of food...and booze, you know, the more the merrier..."

I turned to stare at her while she babbled because that was so not Luna.

She kept doing it.

"My door is always open. I mean, it isn't *always* open...I just said that because this is a party. Normally, I'm very safe. You can't be too careful. It's just that—"

"You can stop talking now," I said under my breath.

She lifted her cocktail and said over-loudly, "Right! What I mean is, welcome. You boys want one of Jessie's cocktails or some of Raye's sangria?"

I waded back in. "And this is the rest of my posse, Harlow, Alexis and Jessie." I indicated each with their name.

Before they could say anything, we heard, "Hey."

I turned my head and Cap was there.

He slid an arm around me.

I settled into his side and smiled up at him.

After he smiled down at me, I noted Jacob claimed Alexis in much the same way.

Good for them.

They could now check off "Indisputable Gesture of Possession" on their to-do lists.

So noted, even if we invented the wheel and learned how to fly, you couldn't take the caveman out of the cave.

Not a complaint, just sayin'.

"Kickass selfie station," Knox commented, his head turned that way.

"Luna blew up all the balloons!" Harlow exclaimed over-excitedly.

All three of the men turned eyes to Luna at this.

Her face went up in flames.

I burst out laughing.

"Hey."

Cap's body went taut.

My laughter died an instant death and my body went taut.

56 KRISTEN ASHLEY

Luna's body jerked.

And this was because Dream was there, elbowing in rudely between Knox and Gabe.

They stepped aside, partly because I sensed they were gentlemen, partly because she gave them no choice.

Side to side, she looked them up and down, including Liam in this, not trying to hide her distaste of them, even if she had no clue who they were.

Her dis silently accomplished, she shoved a jar toward Luna that was filled with a candle and tied with a bow of rough twine with a hand-written label that said PATCHOULI on the side.

And she said tartly, "Happy birthday."

I felt my lips get tight.

First, because Luna and I could have been separated at birth. Sure, I rocked the glam-boho-sophisticated vibe, and her vibe was more boho-glam-sophisticated, but all in all, samesies.

In other words, a jar candle tied in twine was an even worse gift than a Nordstrom Rack gift card. But at least with a gift card, she could get what she wanted.

Second, Luna detested the scent of patchouli with such a red-hot hatred, it was a little unhinged.

I mean, that wasn't my favorite scent in the world, but I'd actually seen Luna gag when she'd smelled it.

Last, I didn't like Dream's tone.

Luna tried to rise above, taking the candle and saying, "Thanks, Dream. And this is Liam and Knox and—"

"I don't need to know them," Dream cut her off.

My body got tauter, so Cap dug his fingers warningly in my hip.

"And thanks so much for the invite," Dream went on, but she didn't mean this, she said it in a way that meant Luna didn't actually invite her.

Luna looked as confused as I was, since I knew she'd asked her sister to her party. "I invited you."

"By text," Dream shot back.

"That's how I got my invitation too," Jessie put in.

"Me too," Alexis added.

Dream barely glanced at them before she asked her sister snottily, "You gonna offer me a drink?"

Okay.

I was done.

I'd actually been done awhile.

But now, seeing as it was Luna's birthday, not to mention, she'd spent all day creating the extravaganza that surrounded us, and that was some serious hard work, therefore, this was even less okay than the other shit Dream pulled.

In other words, it was time to wade in.

"I'm gonna offer you the door if you don't park the attitude, Dream," I said.

She turned her attention to me.

"I'm talking to my sister," she replied.

"No, you have an audience, and you're at a party, and you interrupted a conversation, so you're actually not," I retorted. "You're trying to make a scene."

"I'm not about drama," she shot back.

I couldn't even think of what to say, that was such bullshit.

"Yeah, and I'm trying out for the Cardinals cheerleaders next year," Jessie muttered.

I figured out what to say. "Right, time to exit your the-world-revolves-around-me bubble and look around. Luna spent all day setting this up. If you're here to celebrate her and have a good time, great. If you're here to be a bitch, spare your sister that on her big day, at least."

Dream squared off on me, and how she did, I knew things were bad and about to get worse.

I was not wrong.

"That's the second time you've called me a bitch."

And then she made a grave mistake.

She finished it by leaning toward me and sniping, "*Bitch.*"

In the flash of an eye, I found myself staring at Cap's back, and Dream finding her space seriously invaded by my guy.

Oh shit.

"I get a woman like you doesn't like men like me because you can't shit all over us and lead us around by our dicks," he said in a low, dangerous voice. "But women like Raye who are strong enough to want a partner like me get some bonuses from that. One of them is that they don't stand by and let a woman who's regretting the choices she's made in life take her shit out on *his* woman. Hear me, Dream. You do not call my woman a bitch in front of my face or ever. And it's not my place to handle your shit, except when it's Luna's night and she's put a fuck ton of work into throwing a party so she can enjoy the people she cares about. Newsflash, she invited you, so she cares about you. Fuck off with this damage you bring into her house. If you can't be cool, get the fuck out."

"Stand back, man, you're leaking your toxicity all over me," Dream returned.

"You're mistaking who brought the toxicity to the party, Dream," Cap fired back.

Luna shifted between them, but not to ask Cap to stand down.

She said to her sister, "Go."

Dream's eyes rounded. "You're gonna just let him get in my face like that?"

"Dream," she said in a small voice that gave me the opposing reactions of needing to pull her in my arms and making my head want to explode, it doing this before I delivered a bitch slap. "It's my birthday."

Dream glared at her, then Cap, then me, then for some reason, Gabe, Liam and Knox, then she turned on her hippie sandal and stormed out.

I didn't even try to hold myself back.

I was done with this.

So I went after her.

"Raye!" Luna called.

I stopped, whirled and ordered, "Stay here."

Then I took off.

I felt Cap with me, but kept going and shouted Dream's name on the walkway.

She stopped and looked back at me. "I've had about enough of you tonight."

"Never again," I warned as I pulled up in front of her.

"What?" she asked.

"I waited eleven years to have a sister again, and believe me, Dream, I do not know what your problem is, but no way in fuck I'm gonna stand by and watch you treat her like shit."

"This isn't about you and your sister, Raye. You don't know what it's been like to play second fiddle to Luna the Magnificent all my life."

I knew for a fact she was now talking trash about Scott and Louise.

And that just pissed me off more.

"You're right about me and Macy. You're so very wrong about Luna. And you know it. You know it's about you being confused, and not sure what you wanted in life, like all of us are, Dream. Then you thought you figured it out, but you found it wasn't as easy as you expected it would be. And now you have to watch your sister throw parties and go to work at a cool place, and spend her money on things she chooses, her time doing whatever she wants, and you're jealous as all fuck. And being you, still confused, and not knowing what to do about it, and being hella prideful, instead of sorting yourself out, you're taking it out on Luna. And that's what's gonna stop, Dream."

She shook her curls back. "I love my kids."

"Maybe so, but you're thirty, nearly thirty-one, alone with two kids, and it's a lot. More than you bargained for. And now you got yourself pregnant again and that's too much for you, so you've snapped, and you're taking your shit out on your sister."

I was guessing, of course, but what she said next proved it was a damned good guess.

"I didn't mean to get pregnant," she bit back.

Whoa.

"I can't do it," she said. "I can't take care of another baby."

And there we were.

"I'm sorry you're facing that without it being in your plans, but it isn't Luna's fault," I said much more calmly.

"It isn't cool, inviting me to her big party knowing Mom and Dad are fed up with watching my kids, and knowing I don't have any money."

Somehow, she made it to the party anyway.

I didn't mention that.

I said, "First, Scott and Louise love those kids. They're fed up with *you* taking advantage of them, not their grandchildren. Second, you're in control of your own life, you can say no to a party if you can't come, and do something else for Luna to celebrate her. And last, she asked you not only because you're her sister and she wants you here, but because you've created a situation where she can't win. If she doesn't ask you because she's being sensitive to those issues, you'll get ugly with her. If she does,"—I indicated where we were—"you got ugly with her. *That* is what's uncool, Dream."

"Of course you'd take her side."

Oh my God.

"Right, I'm done and—" I started to finish it.

I didn't get to finish what I started.

"Raye!"

The way Jessie shouted my name, I whirled, Cap put his hand to my back, and when I saw the look on Jessie's face, my heart started hammering.

"Get in here!" Jessie ordered.

I didn't even look at Dream. I glanced at Cap, then ran as fast as my high-heeled sandals would take me back into the apartment.

But we didn't go to the party.

We went to Luna's bedroom.

And weirdly, not only was Harlow there, but Liam, Knox and Gabe were too.

The men shot Cap stony-faced looks.

I went right to Luna, who was holding her flipped open burner.

Oh no.

"What's going on?" I asked.

She looked from the phone to me and rocked the world under my feet.

"Jinx texted. Jumper is back. And he's taken Cameo."

TWENTY-THREE

YOU CAN SAY THAT AGAIN

Cap took one look at my reaction to that, then he took over, and I had zero problem he did.

He told Luna to text Jinx to get to a safe place, tell us where that was, and we'd meet her there.

He then tried to get Luna, Harlow, Jessie and me to stay at the party while he and his boys went to Jinx.

I had a problem with that.

"She's ours, Cap," I said.

"You're not doing this," he returned.

"I am, and you're coming with me, but Jinx trusts us. I need to be there at least to be the go-between."

"I'm coming too," Luna declared.

I turned to her. "You're having your birthday party."

"It's Jinx, Raye," she replied. "And they have Cameo."

It was, and God help her, they did.

I went back to Cap. "Luna and I are with you." I looked to Harlow and Jessie. "You guys make excuses for Luna."

"But—" Jessie started.

I cut her off. "Babe, we don't have a lot of time."

Jessie nodded.

I grabbed my bag off Luna's bed and said, "Let's roll."

Cap, Knox, Liam and Gabe were a lot more efficient with their vehicle switch outs, and part of that was that they didn't have to deal with an app to free their SUVs.

Another part was that their office was on the way to where we were going.

See?

Centralized location, so much better.

And yes, Knox, Liam and Gabe followed us to the underground parking at Cap's office, and then they rolled out in two extra vehicles, so we were a convoy of three when we hit a diner I'd never been to and never wanted to see again that was not in Ground Zero, but instead in a 'hood southwest of that, which was even worse.

Even though Jinx looked pissed as shit, as did Persia and Skyla, both of whom she had with her, all their faces went slack when they saw Luna and I strutting in with the Hottie Squad at our heels.

"You bitches don't play," Jinx said as we stopped outside the booth she and the girls were sitting in, and the men fanned out around us.

I decided to go with it for the sake of time.

"No, we don't. Talk to us."

Skyla launched right in.

"No fucking around, asshole rolls up, he's got a buddy with him. They stroll out, grab her, shove her in the back seat and ride off. Just like they had every right to do that. I got a scratch in on the friend, but he pushed me off, and it isn't like I got a good center of balance on these shoes. I went down. By the time I got up again, they were gone."

"Genesis followed them," Persia put in.

My blood ran cold.

"She followed them?" I asked.

"She's got a headache. Not feelin' it tonight," Persia said. "She was getting in her car to go home, saw the whole thing, took off after them."

"You know where she is?" Cap asked.

Persia closed up instantly. "Who am I talking to?"

I looked to Cap.

He nodded.

I turned back to Persia. "This is Cap, Liam, Gabe and Knox."

"We're with them," Cap added.

Aw!

My man was so sweet!

"She's sittin' outside some warehouse, close to The Pink Slip," Persia told us.

And it was all coming together.

But...

Why Cameo?

I had a sinking feeling I knew.

And Jinx knew what I was feeling.

"Don't take that on, *linda*," she said in a tone I didn't know she had in her arsenal. It was kind, even tender. "We know the way it's been going. We were out in pairs. We were checkin' in. We carry mace. Keepin' an eye on the new girls. Because we were watchin' our asses, the pickin's for them were slimming down. If they needed fresh blood, they had to snatch it. It wasn't about her talking to you."

I nodded, but that creeping feeling was still creeping.

I was so into this exchange, I hadn't realized Liam had peeled off, and now he was outside, talking on his phone.

"She got an address?" Cap asked.

"Sure," Persia said.

"Text it," Cap ordered. "And tell your girl who's sitting at that warehouse to get out of there."

"Copy that, Captain America," Persia mumbled while looking down at her phone.

That would have been funny in any other circumstances.

I'd laugh about it later.

"Can you stay here or get somewhere safe tonight?" Cap asked the girls.

Jinx's eyes skimmed through me before she said, "I got the resources to cover us for a few days off. We good, *guapo*."

Translation: she didn't waste time pawning the Rolex.

"Get safe," Cap ordered. "Someone will update you later."

We got three nods.

Then Cap took my arm, Knox took Luna's, and they escorted us out of there.

We were in our Denali and on the road before Cap said, "We gotta swing by your place. I want all the descriptions of the men you're looking at for this from your wall."

"I can do you one better. I got pictures and sheets on all of them, courtesy of Chuck," I told him.

"Chuck?" Cap asked.

"We usually refer to him as 'We,' the wizard behind the curtain," I explained. "But that's awkward. We can't call him Charlie, because that's my dad's name, and it's unoriginal. So I'm going with Chuck."

"I don't like Chuck," Luna chimed in from the back. "How about Charles?"

"Charles is also my dad's name," I pointed out.

"Then something else," she said.

"Dick?" I suggested.

"Good, but no." She snapped her fingers. "I got it. Arthur."

Arthur was perfect!

"Word on Arthur, sister," I agreed.

"Jesus," Cap muttered.

I decided it was time to get my head in the game and grew quiet.

Luna got quiet with me.

CAP HAD a mini-battle with his inner caveman when we were at my apartment, and I not only grabbed all the goods we had, I quickly changed out of the cute dress and heels I wore to Luna's party and put on jeans, a long-sleeved tee and my Nikes.

Luna was a size larger than me, so she confiscated some joggers, another long-sleeved tee, but fortunately we shared the same shoe size, so she put on my Adidas.

To help him get over it, I shared, "We're not going to go storm the warehouse. But in this sitch, we can't be in heels."

My assistance worked, Cap bested the beast, and we trooped out to the Denali he'd parked behind the visitor spots.

We then hit the road.

Cap played fast and loose with appropriate city driving on the way back to his offices, and this normally would both annoy me and frighten me, but the ease with which he did it was kinda surreal. So in the end, I was just glad he didn't mess around and got us there as fast as we could go.

We hit the reception of his offices, and the transformation was so complete, and it was such sheer class, even in the current sitch, my gait slowed so I could take it all in.

The reception desk had floor lighting built in its base to illuminate it, and above it was a kickass gold and glass light feature. The paintings were positioned to perfection, the modern furniture, sumptuous and expensive. All of this making the gleam coming from the rich wood paneling on the walls gleamier.

If reception at Nightingale Investigations and Security didn't say "We get the job done!" nothing did.

Cap took us right to a door that was almost invisible in the paneling, if it didn't have a gold door handle. He slid open an invisible panel and punched in a code in a keypad recessed to the side of the door that I'd not noticed before, and it wasn't functioning the last time I breached the inner sanctuary the night we rescued Elsie Fay, or it was set to open, because he and Mace didn't use it.

We were through, down the hall, two doors in to the right, and we went into Mace's office.

And again, it had been transformed. More kickass paintings and lighting and furniture.

But I couldn't take it all in.

That was because Knox, Liam and Gabe were there.

But also, Mace, Lee, Eric, Vance...and Tex.

I was more than a little surprised at the addition of Tex, but I didn't mention it, mostly because Mace pinned me with his jade eyes and demanded to know, "What we got?"

Me and my manila envelope went to his desk.

I pulled out what I had, first the pictures of the women I'd stashed in there that morning because I didn't have time to put them back up on my wall, and I didn't want them sitting out. Next came the pictures of the men.

"Sheets, photos," I said, dropping the first, then putting the second on top of them. I stopped at Sergio Duzek and tapped his pic. "We believe he's definitely involved. We found that out last night."

Cap immediately slid the sheet out from under Duzek's picture and started reading it.

I kept dropping, and when I finally got to the end, that being Cyrus Gibbons, I tapped him too.

"I was pretty sure he was the ringleader. Don't ask me why. But..."

I trailed off because I felt the vibe in the room shift definitively, and it was pressing in on me.

"Get them vests," Lee all but barked at Gabe.

Gabe took off.

I looked to Luna.

Her eyes were huge.

She felt it too.

"Lee," Cap said low.

"Not taking them in," Lee said the words like a prolonged grunt, his handsome face so intense, it was scary. "But they got this far.

They cracked it. We're taking them with us." His gaze cut to Tex. "Tex, you're on the women."

"Got it," Tex said.

"Get a vest," Lee ordered Tex.

"Don't need a vest," Tex returned.

"Get a vest, Tex," Lee said in a tone that brooked no argument.

Tex made a noise that the only way to describe it was a wordless grumble, and he lumbered off.

Lee looked to Mace. "You got Jorge?"

Mace, who was on his phone, jutted out his chin.

"What's going on?" I asked.

Lee looked at me, and if his intensity was a lot when he was ordering other people around, having it aimed at me was knee-weakening at the same time it was awe-inspiring.

He, too, tapped Cyrus Gibbons' picture, but he did it harder than me.

"Thirteen years ago, my sister, who's also a PI, and my team took this guy down. I warned him, when he got out of prison, to get out of my town. Apparently, he listened. Also apparently, his time in the joint didn't teach him any lessons. I told him he didn't want to see me again. He's gonna see me again. And this time when he goes down, he's not gonna get back up."

He meant this.

Maybe literally.

Ho...

Lee...

Shit.

They gave Luna and I bulletproof vests.

They didn't really fit great in the boob area, and I wasn't a fan of why I might have to wear one, but I'd never thought I'd try on a bulletproof vest. I was deciding to regard it as a wardrobe adventure, like when I'd tried skinny jeans. They weren't comfortable, and they looked shit on me, but at least I gave them a go.

There had been a lot of activity in the twenty minutes we were in Mace's office. Lots of phone calls. Eric sat down behind Mace's desk with a laptop. Vance, with Knox and Gabe, going back and forth to somewhere in the offices and returning with stuff like our vests, but also utility belts, guns, extra clips and little canisters with pins on top that were either smoke bombs, tear gas or grenades.

Luna and I exchanged glances at all this too, so much, it was a wonder we didn't get dizzy with it.

We stayed out of the way, though, and watched it all closely.

One thing you could say, this crew knew how to work as a team. After the preliminary commands Lee issued, they just got on with it, everyone understanding the role they played, and they played it.

And Cap was all kinds of *hawt* in work mode.

Not to mention in his vest and gun belt.

I didn't think I was that girl.

But Cap was that guy, and he was mine, so I was now that girl.

In other words, after they rescued the women (hopefully), I was fucking him so hard, he was going to think he was beamed to an alternate universe populated by sexbots that existed solely for a man's pleasure.

We rolled out in another convoy that had more vehicles, but our convoy didn't stay a convoy.

SUVs started peeling off.

I didn't know why and I didn't ask. Tex was driving and being quiet for once, so I decided he should set the mood.

We followed the two vehicles in front of us, one driven by Mace, Cap at his side, Knox in the back, one driven by Eric, Liam at his side.

Lee, Gabe and Vance were the ones who peeled off and went somewhere else.

We entered the alley I knew ran behind The Pink Slip, and they cut their headlights in a synchronization that was uncanny, Tex doing it at the same time, and he didn't even get a text or a command on the walkie-talkie they'd given him.

Tex slowed to a stop a building away from where the men went.

But we sat and watched as the vehicles in front of us also rolled to a stop, rather than actually stopping, in other words, no brake lights.

Then doors opened and men moved out, jogging back to the building that was situated between the one they'd stopped behind and ours.

It had a chain-link fence against the alley, and I held my breath in stunned surprise as they scaled it with the same ease as they'd walk through a gate.

Luna broke the silence to whisper, "Holy wow."

She could say that again.

But Cap just did that.

Cap went in there.

Cap was in there.

"Are the police coming?" I whispered to Tex.

"No, darlin'."

It was hard to keep my voice quiet when I asked a terrified, "Why?"

"Because they have no probable cause to enter that building," Tex explained.

"But Genesis saw them take Cameo there," I told him.

He turned his head from having his eyes locked on the warehouse and said, "Okay then. The truth. Because those men are going to deal with the jackasses in that building in a way the police can't. And your girl who gave you that information probably has to go back out on the streets. So she can't be known as a rat by reporting what she saw to the police. They'll get the job done, darlin'. The police can clean up."

"Oh," I said.

He nodded and looked back at the warehouse.

I looked at the warehouse.

Luna, I knew but didn't check, was looking at the warehouse.

All was quiet on the warehouse front. It didn't seem like

anything was happening in there. There weren't any lights coming from inside. There wasn't any motion. There were no men screaming in agony, at least not that we could hear from where we were.

But my heart was beating so fast, I could feel it pumping in my chest. And I was getting sweaty like the temperature in the cab of the Denali had ratcheted up thirty degrees.

We waited and nothing.

We waited more, and more nothing.

This was followed by even more waiting, and nothing.

"Maybe we should call the police," I suggested.

"Hold," Tex replied.

"Tex, this is taking a long time."

"Hold," Tex repeated.

"Tex—"

"There it is," he murmured, pushed open his door and got out.

Even in the shadows, I knew that body, I knew that gait.

And sauntering purposefully to the chain-link fence was Cap.

I got out.

Luna got out.

"Hold!" Tex called.

It took everything I had, but I held.

I'd know why in short order.

When he got to the fence, Cap didn't scale it again.

He took a weird step to the side, then the flash of his gun momentarily lit the dark, the blast of it silenced so it just sounded like a *zing*. He pulled a chain off the gate and opened it.

I sprinted to him.

He'd holstered his weapon, so when I got to him, he settled both hands firmly to my hips.

Okay, got it.

You didn't girlie throw yourself in your man's arms when he was in the middle of an operation.

So noted.

I didn't get a word in, like *You're the greatest* or *I love you* (too soon for that, still, I couldn't deny, I was feeling it).

He said, "You're needed inside, baby."

I looked to the warehouse and started that way.

He halted me by gripping my hips.

I shifted my attention back to him.

"What you're gonna see, Rachel, you can't unsee. No shame you get back in the Denali."

I stared into his shadowed face.

Then I nodded.

I squared my shoulders.

I looked back to Luna, who was standing close to us.

"You good?" I asked.

"I'm good," she said.

That was all I needed.

We walked through the gate toward the warehouse.

And then we walked in.

IT TOOK a while to find them, the place was that big, a labyrinth of rooms and cubbies, and the things I saw in them I immediately expelled from my Oasis because they didn't belong there.

But, we found them.

We found *her*.

Someone had located blankets, and all of the women—curled into themselves and each other, sitting on their asses and lining a wall—had them wrapped around them.

The second she saw us, Cameo came out of her curl and launched herself at us.

We hugged her.

She dissolved into sobs.

Luna took over.

Freed from Cameo, it was then I walked to her, crouched in front of her, caught her lowered gaze, and whispered, "Hey, Christina. I've been looking forward to meeting you. Your mom wants you to know she can't wait for you guys to fight over the phone again."

I barely finished speaking, in fact, it was on the words "your mom," when, clawing the blanket to her, she managed to roll to her knees and collapse into me.

By some miracle, I kept my crouch, wrapped my arms around her and held on.

It wasn't my love I was giving her in my hold, it was her mom's.

Even so, I knew she felt it.

Jorge Alvarez was a good-looking Latino man around the same age as Lee and Mace et al. (in other words, the first generation).

And from the beleaguered looks he gave me, even though our introduction was brief, he didn't like me much.

Oh well.

It took a whole heckuva lot longer to deal with this mess than it did the Elsie Fay thing (and, uh...I saw it, none of them were dead, even if they looked it, but you couldn't groan like that and be dead, but we could just say Cap and the guys didn't fuck around with the men in that warehouse).

Therefore, Luna and I were hanging out, texting Jinx and Jessie and Harlow with the updates when she came tearing in.

She was wild-eyed, wild-haired and out of control.

Some of the uniforms made a move to the waiting area, where we were hanging, and where she was racing, but she was on such a mission, they didn't get to us before she did.

Betsy Markovic pulled me out of my chair first with a yank so strong, I feared she dislocated my shoulder.

Luna came up next, and I heard her grunt of pain, so I knew she got the same treatment as me.

Then she hugged us both.

"She's sleeping at the hospital. Sleeping, breathing," she said in the cadence of an excited prattle. "They say there's nothing wrong with her, physically, I mean. A little dehydration. They're on that. She can come home tomorrow. Tomorrow. Tomorrow, she can come home."

She jumped away from us but cupped her hands on our cheeks with too much excitement, thus she nearly knocked our heads together.

"I had a feeling about you girls," she said. "I'd lost hope. Then you girls showed up. And I knew. I knew my Christina would come back."

"We had help," I told her.

She shook her head in a crazed way. "I don't care. I don't care how it happened. She's coming home tomorrow. That's all I care about."

She then moved her hands to the back of our heads, pulled Luna down to press a big smooch on her forehead, then me, and she let us go and raced out of there, just as wild and out of control as she'd arrived.

Luna and I watched her go.

Then we looked at each other.

After that we sat down.

"You good?" she asked.

"Yep," I answered.

"Raye, my sister," she said with a gravity that made my eyes go to her. "Are you good?"

I knew her question now.

Dad, Mom and I didn't get that relief. Macy wouldn't come home any of our tomorrows.

But Betsy had a lot of love for Christina, so no matter how messed up their relationship was, I had faith they'd be fighting again, if not soon, then someday.

And that really, really, *really* worked for me.

I bumped her with my shoulder and answered, "I'm great."

She examined my face before she looked away and complained, "This is taking forever."

"I know. I guess it's not kosher to storm a warehouse and beat the shit out of a bunch of bad dudes."

"Yeah, they got some 'splainin' to do," she mumbled.

She stretched her legs out in front of her.

I perused my phone to see what game I could play to pass the time.

A couple minutes later, we heard a bing.

We looked at each other again, then Luna fished her burner out of the pocket of my joggers and looked at it.

"Voicemail," she whispered.

Voicemail?

As in an actual *voice* sending us a message.

"Holy crap," I replied.

She flipped open the phone and I huddled closer as she put it to both of our ears.

We listened to a three-word message.

We sat immobile when it ended.

Slowly, Luna pulled the phone away from our ears, and equally slowly we turned our heads toward each other.

"Fucking hell," she said.

"You can say that again," I replied.

I watched the smile creep over her face at the same time that happened to mine.

"Awesome," I whispered.

"You can say that again," she replied, whispering like me.

Why were we acting so weird?

Because, not in John Forsythe's voice, but in a voice that sounded like Morgan Freeman, the voicemail said...

"Well done, Angels."

TWENTY-FOUR

BEER PONG

Cap was naked, sprawled on his stomach diagonally across the bed, the sheets covering his ass (which was a shame), when I walked in with two mugs of coffee the next morning.

Patches knew a good thing and was curled asleep by his hip.

I put the mugs down, bounced on the bed beside him and smacked his beautiful ass.

He groaned.

"Wake up, stud," I called.

"I think you broke me," he mumbled into the bed.

I started laughing, plastered my chest to his back and kissed his shoulder.

He dislodged me and sent Patches scurrying by rolling.

So I plastered my chest to his front and kissed his mouth.

When I lifted my head, he said, "If you want me to fuck you, I'm game. But you're gonna have to ride my dick, cowgirl. It shits me to say this, but I'm not up to doing the work."

I was unsurprised by this.

I was so jazzed and happy the women were safe (as I suspected, we missed some, all in all, there were fourteen, but all the ones I was looking for were there, including Divinity), and I learned a fun fact: after an operation, Cap got jazzed too.

So last night, we barely got through the door before we were fucking on the floor.

We'd made it halfway down the hall before I was on my back and Cap was going down on me.

We eventually tripped into the bedroom, where Cap bent me over the side of the bed and did me.

And it didn't end there.

So you get the picture.

Not to mention, it wasn't me who scaled a chain-link fence then beat the absolute crap out of seven guys.

So...

"I don't think, with how pretty your dick is, I'll ever be fucked out, just a nugget of wisdom about me you should know," I told him. "But you're off duty, and I brought coffee, because we need to rally. Dad and Deb are gonna be here in an hour to meet us to go out for breakfast. And we can't delay. Dad was making noise about coming back for Thanksgiving. Their flight leaves at two, so we don't have a ton of time with them."

He threw an arm over his eyes.

I kissed his chest.

He pulled his shit together, pushed himself to right in bed, shoved pillows behind him and lifted a hand, which I took to mean, "Coffee."

I grabbed our mugs, gave him his, then curled on a hip by his side, sipping.

He was sipping too, and when he was done, he asked, "You think dicks are pretty?"

"No," I answered. "I think *your* dick is pretty, because I get to play with it, and you use it to fuck me. Generally, dicks are gross. And dick pics are grosser." I took another sip and queried. "Why do guys do that?"

"The men who do that think with that part of their anatomy.

Their personalities are so tied up in it, they believe everyone will think it's as awesome as they do. That's another way to say, they don't have a lot to offer. If they have anything."

"I take it that means you never sent a dick pic."

"No, I have absolutely never sent a dick pic."

"Have you taken a pic?"

"Why would I do that?"

I shrugged.

He narrowed his eyes at me. "Have you taken pics?"

I shook my head. "No. Euw. If I wanted you to have it, you'd see it live and in person."

He smiled lazily, it was a sexy AF smile, because I wanted him to have it, so he saw it live and in person, and then he drank more coffee.

"I need you to put your thinking cap on," I told him.

His gaze slid sideways to mine. "Why?"

"Because I'm thinking candles and incense and maybe some chanting."

His "What?" shook with laughter.

"The ceremony we're gonna perform while we take down my wall."

He turned and wrapped his arm around my lap, performing a minor miracle by holding up his weight in his other elbow all the while keeping his coffee safe, before he said, "Babe, call Luna and the girls to do that with you. Proud of you. You got great instincts. You got the job done. Those women are safe. They got a bitch of a road to travel to work through what they were put through. But it's better than where they were. But I'm out on any of your ceremonies. Especially if they involve incense."

Since I liked to burn incense occasionally, this was concerning.

I didn't get into that.

"You're proud of me?"

"Well...yeah."

I could see it then, in his gorgeous face.

He was.

I curved my back to kiss him.

When I lifted up, I said softly, "That means a lot to me, Julien."

"I can tell, Rachel."

I used my free hand to smooth his hair back.

It fell over his forehead again.

I gave up and drank some more coffee.

After I swallowed, I noted, "I didn't see Sergio Duzek or Cyrus Gibbons at the warehouse last night."

"That's because that mess was their brainchild, and the big dicks have flunkies who do the dirty work. It keeps their hands clean."

The buzz went off my morning.

"So they got away."

He laid back, put his mug to his lips and said against it, "Didn't say that."

"Where are they?"

He took a sip and said, "Contained."

And that was all he said.

"You're not going to tell me?"

His gaze hit mine. "I'm going to tell you that you, and Jinx and her friends, and nobody, have to worry about them again. And that's all I'm gonna tell you, baby, so you gotta be good with it."

I wondered if I could be good with it.

I decided I could.

At least I knew what Lee, Vance and Gabe peeled off to do last night.

"Okeydokey."

That was when Cap grinned at me.

"Do you know which one of those guys went by the street name of Jumper?" I asked.

Another slide to the side of his eyes. "The one who got a ride in an ambulance and who's now cuffed to a hospital bed."

I was good with that too.

And that's all the thought I gave to an asshole called Jumper.

"I'm gonna hit the shower first so I can start getting ready," I announced.

"We're gonna shower together."

My nipples liked that, but my timeline was unforgiving.

"We have less than an hour now before Dad and Deb get here."

"We'll be quick."

"With the shower?"

"With fucking in the shower."

My nipples liked that so much better, they invited my clit to the party.

But I tipped my head to the side. "I thought I broke you."

He swung his mug my way. "I've rallied."

I looked at him.

He looked at me.

Then I turned and put my mug on the nightstand, jumped off the bed and dashed to the bathroom, losing my nightie on the way.

Cap followed a lot slower, but not that slow.

And Cap was quick with doing me in the shower.

I shouldn't have been worried.

Like I mentioned, he had a talent with that.

EVEN THOUGH WE had to wait as long for a table as we would at Hash Kitchen, I picked Prep and Pastry for brunch because it was awesome, but also because it was close to Deb's and my Motherland: Fashion Square Mall.

Anyway, the time flew as we waited outside and gabbed.

Of course, we didn't tell them about our activities of the night before, except Luna's party, her selfie spot (and I showed pictures, Deb was impressed, Dad seemed confused), her awesome cake (I showed a picture of that too, both Dad and Deb were impressed by that). And last, I filled them in on Dream.

Needless to say, both Dad and Deb were unimpressed by Dream.

After we were seated, I noted Cap's interest in the pastry counter and the way he perused the menu.

So I leaned into him in his seat at my side (Dad and Deb were in the booth seat opposite us), and told him, "If you decide to explore making pastries, I'm totes down with that, just sayin'."

He gave me a smile and a soft kiss then went back to his menu.

I went back to mine, trying not to feel the pain of knowing Dad and Deb were leaving soon, at the same time lamenting the fact I didn't ask Luna, Scott, Louise, as well as Shirleen to this brunch.

I wanted my family to get to know each other.

That said, we still had a lot of catching up to do, so maybe when they came back for Thanksgiving (I was going with "when" rather than "if" to help with the fact they were leaving that day, though I had no idea how we'd manage a Thanksgiving feast in the courtyard, but if they came, by God, I'd find a way).

In the midst of eating, Luna sent a text that was a selfie of her wearing the necklace we gave her and a big ol' smile with the message *I love it! Thank you!!!!!!* and she added about twenty double pink hearts after that.

I showed that photo to Deb too, and we shared a moment the likes of which I never thought I'd have again.

Mom and daughter who done good while shopping.

Sure, she was my stepmom, but it worked for me.

We were lingering over coffees, and I was trying to figure out what we should do next because we had some more time, but we should also give up our table so the crowd outside could be thinned out and the establishment could make more money.

I was leaning toward trying to talk Dad and Cap into hanging out in the shoe section of Nordstrom while Deb and I tried things on when Cap pulled out his phone.

He looked at it, his brows drew down, he murmured to the table, "Sorry, gotta take this. Work," then he kissed the side of my head, got up and strolled out of the restaurant.

"Uh..." Dad began, and I looked from watching Cap outside (okay, he had his back to us, so I was staring at his ass) to my dad. "What work does he do that he has to do it on a Sunday?"

"He's a private investigator," I informed them.

They both looked shocked.

"At his age?" Dad asked.

"He was in the Army, and he kinda sorta grew up with the team at the firm where he now works. His mom, the Black lady at Lon's?" I asked to confirm they remembered her.

They nodded.

Even in all that was going on, I figured Shirleen was hard to forget.

"She's the receptionist at the firm."

"Ah," Deb said.

"His mom is Black?" Dad queried.

I wasn't going to share Cap's story, not unless he gave me permission.

So I said, "He's adopted."

"Oh," Deb murmured, her gaze going soft and drifting to the windows to outside.

"I should have guessed he was in the service. He knows how to hold himself," Dad remarked.

Oh, he knew how to do that all right.

I felt it before I saw it, so I turned my attention to the front of the restaurant to see Cap, with a carefully blank look on his face I obviously couldn't read, I just knew I didn't like it, coming back in.

He went right to our server, pulled out his wallet and handed her a credit card.

"Well, that was sneaky," Deb said, sounding both annoyed and impressed.

Cap came to the table and sat down in a manner I knew he wanted to get back up.

Dad immediately shared something Cap had to know, since

they'd had this conversation the day before (with Dad winning), "Deb and I wanted to pay for brunch."

"I need to ask you to go somewhere with me," Cap stated instead of responding to what Dad said.

"Well, we have a few hours before we have to get to the airport," Dad replied cautiously. "So, sure."

"No, sir, you mistake me. I can't explain how right now, but I need you to trust me."

Deb and Dad looked at each other.

After I saw them do that, I pinned my eyes to Cap.

I still couldn't get a read on what was going on, and why he was being like this, and what he wanted with Dad and Deb.

The server brought the bill folder and Cap took it.

He stood after he was done signing and put his card back in his wallet.

Uncertainly, Dad, Deb and I stood too.

"If you'll follow us in your car," Cap requested with strange formality.

"Is everything okay?" Dad asked.

"Yes, everything is fine," Cap told him, though his tone didn't confirm that...*exactly.*

I just didn't know how I knew everything was not fine...*exactly.*

Cap took my hand and guided us all out of the restaurant.

I waited until we were in the car to ask, "What's going on?"

He reversed out of his spot, saying, "Need to ask you to trust me too, baby."

"Cap, you're kinda freaking me out."

We were out of our spot, he was idling with his eyes to his rearview, waiting for Dad and Deb to come up behind us, but he looked to me, lifted a hand to cup my jaw and whispered, "Please, Raye, just trust me."

I was still freaking out, but this was Cap, so I nodded.

Dad and Deb pulled up behind us, and Cap drove out.

There was zero conversation as Cap headed out of Scottsdale and into Paradise Valley. Cap's vibe was so off, my freakout was in overdrive by the time he hit his blinker to turn left into a neighborhood at the base of the mountains in Clearwater Hills.

A neighborhood that screamed *Money!*

And part of the reason why I knew this was, I spied a security gate that had two men staffing it.

"Text your dad and tell him, if they stop him, he needs to share his name and that he's a guest of Kai Mason."

Oh God.

We were going to meet Stella Gunn.

That was huge, but she was a member of his family, so this couldn't possibly be why Cap was acting so strange.

Again, I didn't ask.

Without a word, I texted Dad immediately.

Cap turned left, and I looked back and saw Dad and Deb do the same. Then Cap stopped at the guardhouse even if they'd already pulled up the heavy-duty (but still attractive) arm of the stanchion in front of us.

"Morning, Mr. Jackson," the guard said.

"The car behind me is with us."

"Yes, Mr. Mason told us to expect you."

Cap nodded and rolled through.

Dad and Deb rolled through with us.

The houses in this 'hood were few and huge. My guess, they were on three acre lots, at least.

Cap wound his way up to the top one, an enormous modern marvel of glass and adobe, including several outbuildings, as well as lots of patios and balconies with amazing views.

We pulled into a drive that had numerous cars in it.

Cap got out, I got out, and I didn't know if my feeling was better or worse when I saw Shirleen open the front door of the house and stand in it.

I went to Cap, Dad and Deb joined us, and Cap took my hand and led us to Shirleen.

When we got to her, I couldn't read the look on her face either, and not only because I didn't know her very well.

But she didn't hesitate to pull me in her arms and give me a big, tight hug, whispering, "Child," in my ear.

Okay, suddenly, even though her hug was awesome, I didn't like this at all.

I also didn't want to do this, and I still didn't know what "this" was.

She let me go and offered her hand to Dad. "Charlie." After he took it she moved to Deb. "Deb." They squeezed hands and she said, "Come in."

We walked in, and I couldn't dally to marvel at the bright, airy living room with white couches and rugs, accented in colors of sand and stone with touches of Hawaiian art carved in wood.

And I couldn't do this not only because I wasn't in the mood, but because Shirleen led us right through it, down a short hall that was lined in pictures of Mace, Stella with a little girl and a little boy, from the time they were babies to the girl being in her early tweens (the boy, it seemed from the photos, was still very young).

I knew this was bad when we hit what had to be the family room, which was sunken, much warmer, anchored by a very shaggy rug in a deep blue, the rest of it a wonder of the shades of the sea, the earth and the sky.

I took it in, and I didn't.

Because hanging there were Mace, Lee, Vance, and Tex, and they'd been joined by four other guys. One of them had to be Lee's brother. Two of the others also had to be related. The last one reminded me a little of Gabe.

Mace came forward immediately and touched his cheek to mine, murmuring, "Raye."

And yes, this too was sweet, but no, I didn't like it.

He then turned direct to Dad, held out his hand and said, "Mr.

Armstrong. I'm Kai Mason. Cap's a member of my team. And my family."

Wordlessly, also obviously feeling the vibe and not liking it, Dad took his hand and nodded.

"Mrs. Armstrong," Mace said to Deb with a dip of his chin.

"Deb," she squeaked.

She was feeling the vibe too.

Then again, you couldn't miss it.

"And I'm Charlie," Dad put in.

Mace gave him a tight smile then turned. "These are my partners, and brothers, Lee Nightingale, Vance Crowe, Hank Nightingale, Eddie Chavez, Luke Stark and Hector Chavez. I believe you've met Tex."

He indicated each in turn.

They all nodded.

And I vaguely noted I was right about the double set of brothers.

"Please come in and sit down," Mace invited.

Sneaking peeks at each other, we moved down into the room, Dad and Deb going to one couch, I started to the other one.

Cap stopped me and said, "Sit with your dad."

I went still before my head twisted to him and shivers slithered over my skin.

"Do it, please, baby," he urged.

Even if my muscles felt atrophied, I walked over stiltedly, and Dad and Deb made room for me on the couch, with Dad sitting in the middle.

It was Hank Nightingale who came and sat on the edge of the armchair that flanked the couch, his body angled our way. Eddie Chavez came down with him but sat on the arm of the couch opposite us.

Last, Lee came and sat on the couch beside Eddie, also on the edge with legs open, torso bent forward, elbows to his knees, eyes on Dad and me.

I was right.

Whatever this was, I didn't want to do it.

At all.

Hank's attention was directed to Dad when he stated, "Eddie and I are detectives with the Denver Police Department."

"All right," Dad replied.

Lee picked it up. "And Nightingale Investigations and Security has a computer guy on our team who's exceptionally talented. So much so, he's built some apps that have made so much money, he doesn't have to work for me, or anybody. He just likes what he does, and as I mentioned, he's very good at it."

Dad said nothing to that, he just nodded.

Back to Hank.

"So, Brody wrote an algorithm which swiftly and effectively searched all computerized police case files in this country with careful parameters around crimes against children with the MO of how your daughter was taken."

Dad's hand darted out and took mine. I saw out of the corner of my eye Deb's fingers curl around Dad's knee.

After that, we all sat immobile and stared at Hank.

But now it was Eddie's turn.

So we stared at him.

"Brody pinpointed a suspect who is now in prison in Wisconsin who we thought was good for what happened to Macy."

Wisconsin?

We lived outside Philly.

Eddie kept talking.

"Hank and I spoke with local law enforcement and flew out to have a conversation with him," Eddie went on. "The crimes he committed were against boys, but we were riding a hunch due to some of the things he said during interrogation. That hunch proved true, and we were able to elicit a confession of his abduction of five girls, along with the seven boys he'd been convicted of abducting and murdering. He gave us locations for where he buried the bodies. Luke and Hector attended the excavations."

Back to Hank, "And we're sorry to inform you that one of the bodies recovered was Macy."

I heard Deb's sob, but Dad made no noise or movement, neither did I, except his fingers tightened so tightly around mine, they caused pain.

I didn't care.

Hank kept at it.

"I understand this probably gives no measure of comfort, but this perpetrator had a daughter. He seemed relieved to be free of the burden of the secret of taking the girls. He also didn't abuse them. As he was molested by his uncles, he molested the boys, but he was adamant he did not do the same to the girls. He appeared openly repulsed by the idea. Why he took them and did what he did to them, we don't know. We can only deduce that he couldn't fight the urge to kidnap them, and he didn't want to get caught, so he had to...I'm sorry to frame it this way, but in his mind, he was burying the evidence. Though, after Macy was recovered, we further interrogated him, and he shared he had Macy for two days before he bludgeoned her, buried her and moved on. We've been assured by the coroner that she died very quickly, and she would have been rendered unconscious by the blow, so if it wasn't immediately, it would have still been without pain."

At that, Dad surged to his feet.

I came up with him, as did Deb.

She latched onto his arm with both hands.

I got in his space.

"Dad—"

"Two days," he spat.

"Dad—"

"*She was dead two days after he took her!*" Dad bellowed.

I crowded him as I sensed all the men retreating, which was a surprise, but I also sensed they did this because they would stand back and let him tear apart the room if that was what he needed.

And I knew why.

Because I saw the pictures of Mace and Stella and their kids as we walked to this room.

"Dad, look at me," I urged.

He looked at me. "All that hope and fear and all the *shit!*" he exploded on the last. "Years of it! And she was already dead."

"Okay, but—"

"I'd convinced myself," he spoke over me. "I'd convinced myself it was some guy who lost his daughter and Macy reminded him of her, and all this time, he loved her and took care of her. And she lived a good life and was in love with some clown he hoped she'd snap out of before he put any deposits down."

Oh *God*.

Knowing Dad thought that, I couldn't hack it.

I fell into him.

He wrapped his arms around me and shoved his face in my neck, so I did the same to his.

"Two days," he whispered.

My body bucked as the tears came, and his arms got tighter.

"Fuck, honey, she was only away from us and scared for two days." He took a ragged breath. "And then it was over for her."

I burrowed into him.

"Only two days," he said, his voice cracking.

I cried harder and held on stronger.

I felt him shaking with his tears before I felt them on my skin.

I had no idea how long we stood like that, crying and holding each other. But eventually, Dad lifted his head, but he didn't move away.

I tipped my head back to look at him.

With both hands to my cheeks, he swiped at my face with his thumbs.

Then he caught my eyes.

"Now we know," he whispered.

"Now we know," I whispered back.

I fell into him again and recommenced crying.

Dad gathered me close and cried with me.

ONE GOOD THING about finding out your sister was murdered by a notorious, murderous, serial pedophile was that I didn't act like a dork when I met Stella Gunn.

Not to mention, Cap's beloved Jules.

And I didn't have it in me to react too much, after meeting the famous Hot Bunch, when their counterpart Rock Chicks entered the scene.

Mace and Stella had been really cool, asking if we'd like to stay and offering a bedroom to Dad and Deb after Deb called the airlines and switched their flight to one that went out on Wednesday.

Though, they were clear that if we felt we needed to leave and give the final licks to a wound that had been festering for nineteen years, but now maybe we could allow it to close, they were down with that too (they didn't phrase it that way, but that was the gist).

Dad and I had already started working on healing that wound. It would leave a scar, but I figured Dad and I were okay with it. The scar would represent Macy, as well as Mom, like an emotional tattoo, and neither of us wanted rid of it.

I didn't know why Dad took Stella and Mace up on their offer to hang out (though, Deb also rebooked them into the Hermosa Inn, so they didn't accept their other kind offer).

Maybe he thought these were my people and I'd want to be around them. Though, he didn't know Cap and I had known each other less than two weeks (which meant they had solved a nearly-two-decades-long mystery in that time, which, even as emotionally lacerated as I was, I was together enough to think was super impressive).

Maybe he just realized what good people they were.

Once it was ascertained we were staying, Cap took over and got Luna, Scott and Louise there.

I really didn't know how they did it. And I often caught Luna looking at me like she was checking some gauge I had on my face, the same with Scott, however, his glances held sorrow and pain for me (he shot the same looks to Dad). Not to mention, Louise, Deb and Shirleen flitted around, not hiding they were taking our pulses.

Even with all of that, eventually, it started to feel like a party.

I knew why.

The Rock Chicks.

And it took one to know one, and they were keeping it under wraps considering the circumstances.

But I knew to my bones those bitches were the good kind of crazy.

Indy was Lee's. Jet was Eddie's. Roxie was Hank's.

As mentioned, I finally met the fabulous Jules, and she actually *was* movie-star gorgeous, but more importantly, really nice. And as previously noted, she was Vance's.

Then there was Ava, who was Luke's. And Sadie (who looked like a fairy princess, and that was not me, but I did recognize a look embedded deep in her eyes, so I got what Cap meant when he spoke about her), and she was Hector's.

As you could see, I now totally understood how two people belonged to each other, because Cap was mine, and that meant I was lucky enough to be Cap's.

Two other couples that weren't involved in the family room drama were Ally, Lee and Hank's sister, and her man, Ren, and Daisy and Marcus, Clarice's benefactors (and I knew why Clarice didn't put up a fight when Daisy threw a fit, she was diminutive, and honest to God, was the spitting image of a younger Dolly Parton, including her bedazzled, stone-washed denim sundress and massive bosom, but I sensed she wasn't a woman to cross, no way).

Last, we met Moses, Cap's stepdad. And he was so sweet, I loved he was in Shirleen's life...and Cap's.

Oh, and then there was Tallulah, Mace and Stella's spunky, hilarious daughter, and Walsh, their adorable three-year-old son.

And if this conflagration of people landing on Phoenix to take the back of Cap's woman, who most of them hadn't even met, didn't prove why he was so tight and so clearly loved his family, nothing would.

Who was not there was Roam, Cap's brother, which I found surprising, until Cap explained his absence.

"He wanted to give you privacy for this."

There was something so profoundly beautiful about Roam offering that to me, giving me the opportunity to meet Cap's brother, and the person he was closest to in this world, when I wasn't mired in this emotional morass, I almost started crying again.

Fortunately, I did not.

This was a lot, but it was also Cap's family, and they were so comfortable with him, and embracing of all of us, that "a lot" dwindled to nothing the minute Stella put out a bowl of cashews, heralding the feel of a party.

And I was kinda down with it being a party.

Because after years and years, now we knew.

We knew Macy hadn't been touched that way.

We knew she wasn't frightened and alone for very long.

And we were going to get her back, so we could put her to peace.

And that might be a whacked thing to want to celebrate.

But I wanted to celebrate it.

I'd stepped away from the rest to have some time to process and was out on the balcony, close to their kickass zero edge pool, staring at Stella and Mace's view, when Cap came to me.

He slid a hand along the small of my back, curled it in at my hip, kissed my temple then pressed his front to my side.

"You okay?" he asked.

"Give the rest to me," I demanded.

It took him only a second before he said, "It was the boys he took that put them off. When an offender has an MO like that, it doesn't tend to deviate. He made no mention of the girls. He also didn't bury the boys, he discarded them, which was why they were looking for him. This meant they didn't know there were girls."

I flinched at his word, "discarded," but said nothing.

Cap kept going.

"If a perpetrator has a certain predilection, it is very rare there's more to that story, so they didn't even consider that he was also taking girls. Also, he got the fuck out of Pennsylvania. Macy's body was found in a state park in Indiana."

I turned my head and looked up at him. "So how did this Brody guy know to pinpoint him?"

"Partly, it was how audacious he was with his snatch and grabs, and the fact he left no witnesses but other children. But they didn't pinpoint him. He was one of several people they looked into. Once Eddie and Hank and the guys got hold of the interrogation tapes and transcripts, it was noted he seemed to have an unhealthy protective streak for girls, which might have to do with him having a daughter. And also the fact he had a sister, who he reported he protected from the abuse he endured from his uncles. This is not shade, but all the kids taken were playing close to home without close adult supervision."

"Yeah, because kids should be able to play across the street from their best friend's house without someone snatching them," I returned.

"I said it was no shade," he noted softly.

"I'm not mad at you, Cap," I told him, then went back to the view.

"He also had two sons, he abused both of them," Cap shared.

"Great," I muttered sarcastically.

Cap gave me a squeeze with his fingers. "In the end, the cops missed it not only because they were looking for a man who hurt boys, but also because Macy was the only child taken in Pennsylvania. He lived in Wisconsin, was in Philadelphia on business. Why he was in your neighborhood is anyone's guess, because he refused to share that with Hank and Eddie. Though, he did cast a relatively wide net, taking only one kid from Wisconsin. His first. The rest were from Michigan, Illinois, Indiana and Ohio."

"You don't shit where you live."

"Maybe."

I said nothing.

I just knew you didn't shit where you lived, and this asshole didn't do it because he didn't want to get caught.

"Wisconsin has no death penalty," Cap informed me. "But he was serving seven consecutive life sentences, obviously with no chance for parole. He'll be resentenced for the girls. For Macy. Even so, he already was set to live his life in maximum security."

"Good. I don't want him to die. That's too easy."

Cap pulled me deeper into his body.

I looked up at him again. "So how long did your band of super-heroes work on this before they cracked it?"

"We're not superheroes, Raye."

"Yes, you are, Cap."

He bent to press his forehead to mine, raised away and said, "Mace was concerned about what you were doing with Elsie Fay, that we were entering a new era of Rock Chick shit, because he knew you were it for me. He looked into it, and the minute he discovered your history, he brought in the team."

"Did you know they were doing it?"

For the first time since I met him, he appeared uncomfortable.

"You knew," I said.

"I didn't think they'd find him, which was why I didn't tell you, because I didn't want to get your hopes up. I was also surprised by what happened today. But yes, I knew. And I knew they were onto something. I just didn't know they got the coroner's report confirming it was Macy, and then they all decided to show up here to do this as soon as they could before your Dad left so you two could hear it together."

"I'm not mad about that either, Cap. Now we can move on. I think Dad is experiencing that small measure of comfort Hank didn't think he had, knowing it didn't last long for Macy. And that it wasn't as bad as it could have been. And we're getting her back."

"Yeah, honey."

"We'll never be able to thank them."

"They don't need thanks, Raye. This is one of the reasons we do what we do. Hank and Eddie especially. They've dedicated their life to this."

"The really good cops you know," I deduced.

"Yeah."

I gave my attention back to the view, took in a deep breath and let it out.

The heat wasn't overbearing, autumn was definitely in the cards. The clouds were fluffy against the pale blue of the sky, and the view was ridiculously gorgeous. It would be downright insane at sunset.

And I wished with all my heart my sister was standing beside me so she could see it.

On that thought, entirely tuned to me, Cap spoke.

"Mace wanted me to tell you, or more to the point, offer his time if you want to talk about Macy. His little sister was also abducted and murdered..."

My head snapped his way.

"...she was older than Macy. It was a kidnap and ransom situation, and Mace was there, trying to do a hostage exchange, him for her, when they killed her. And yes, he witnessed it. So he doesn't get you, but he gets you."

"Oh my God," I whispered, thinking about that tall, strong, handsome man, who was such a brother to Cap, he pulled out all the stops to bring my sister back to me, and who was openly happy with his wife, daughter and son.

"It took him a while," Cap said softly. "But we all learn to put it behind us, move on and live as much life as we can in the time we have. Mace knows Caitlin would want that for him—"

"And Macy would want that for Dad and me," I finished for him.

"Yeah, honey," he repeated tenderly.

She'd never grown old enough to have adult thoughts like that.

Even so, she loved her daddy and her big sister, so I knew that to be true all the way to the deepest part of me.

I twisted my neck further to look through our shoulders, and I caught Dad and Shirleen, standing together at the window, quickly moving their heads to cover the fact they were watching us.

I turned my attention back to Cap. "You know this means we can never break up. Dad already thought a lot of you. Now he'll love you for all his days."

"I never intend to break up with you."

Wait.

What?

I blinked. "Never?"

"Did you miss the part I said just a second ago about you being it for me?"

"I know you're into me, Cap, you've told me and shown me. But we haven't even been seeing each other for two weeks."

He cracked a smile. "Really, straight up, babe, you gotta read those Rock Chick books."

Whoa.

That was huge.

And I loved it.

However, I decided in that moment I was never going to read those books, or at least, not for a good, long while.

And I decided it because I hated spoilers with an all-consuming passion.

So I was just gonna let it unfold, because, so far, it was working hella great for me.

A door opened and Luna shouted out, "Get in here, bitch. Ally's setting up a game of beer pong!"

Beer pong?

"Jesus," Cap muttered.

"Be right there," I shouted back. Then to Cap, "Beer pong? She's a mother in her forties."

"Welcome to the RCHB," he replied.

I was digging the RCHB.

Though, I had a feeling I was going to like the AAHS better.

Cap and I went in to play beer pong.

And...surprise!

(Not.)

Cap rocked at it.

TWENTY-FIVE

THE WONDERS OF THE
AVENGING ANGELS, UNITE

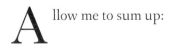llow me to sum up:

A WEEK LATER, The Surf Club was dark for three days.

This was because, sitting behind us as Dad and I occupied the front row, Deb by Dad's side, Brittany by Deb's, me on Dad's other side, Cap on mine, all of us staring at a pretty, shiny, tiny cream-colored casket covered in little pink sweetheart roses, we had a crowd of people.

From my family: Luna, Scott, Louise and even Dream, Feather and Dusk (Scott and Louise paid for their trip). Also, Jessie and Harlow.

From SC: Otis, Hunter, Lucia, her husband Mario, and of course, Tito.

And get this...

Byron.

From Oasis Square: Martha, Linda, Bill, Zach, Jacob, Alexis,

Patsy and Rhea. But the rest of the complex got together and paid for that beautiful spray of pink roses on Macy's casket.

Last, the entirety of the RCHB.

Roam, by the way, had it going on.

I knew this because he allowed me privacy for the drama, but he did not miss this.

He hugged me the instant he met me at Dad and Deb's condo and said when he did, "Shit reason to meet you, Raye, so fuckin' sorry."

I didn't have a reply, because I agreed with him.

I also hung onto him.

I didn't know why (and it wasn't because he was as gorgeous as Cap and all the rest).

I did get confirmation of what I already knew. He was a great guy, because he let me hang onto him. He allowed this for a long time. And it was only when Cap was done with it that Roam carefully unlatched me and guided me into Cap's arms when it stopped.

At Macy's funeral, where we laid her to rest next to Mom, although I heard the weeping from behind me of family and friends I hadn't seen in years, in the front row, we didn't cry.

Our tears had been spent.

Now, it wasn't about closure, nor was it about healing, because our hearts would never be closed to Macy, nor would they ever be healed at losing her.

It was about settling in the knowledge we knew where she was, and in a way, we had her back.

It seemed simple, and maybe even weird, but it had been a yearning we'd learned to live with that now was fulfilled, so in it, we found nothing but peace.

Though, I was overwhelmed by the show of love and support that was behind me.

And for that, later, when we were in bed together in Dad and Deb's guest room, safe in Cap's arms, I allowed myself to cry.

Two asides:

First, Tito cast aside the Hawaiian shirts and shorts and wore all black to the funeral. Black suit, shirt, tie, and opaque black sunglasses. Also, a black fedora with a grosgrain, black ribbon around the band.

He looked like a visiting mafioso.

And he sat directly behind my chair at the funeral.

He didn't touch me, and he may have only said two words to me (okay, four, "I'm so sorry, Rachel.").

But he was there, right there, for me.

In other words, I lost a mom and a sister.

In doing so, I got three dads (my own, Scott and Tito), two moms (Louise and Deb, perhaps three, including Shirleen) and three sisters (Luna, Jessie and Harlow).

I hated they made that sacrifice for me. I hated it with everything that was me.

But that didn't negate the fact that their loss gave me great bounty.

And I knew both of them would be very disappointed in me if I didn't treasure the gifts they'd given me.

So, I did.

And again, I did it with everything that was me.

Second, I met Brittany's fiancé.

And Dad was right.

I couldn't put my finger on it, and perhaps I was measuring him against Cap's stick, which no one could compare to.

Still, I hoped Brittany scraped him off because she was as sweet as I remembered.

And her dude was a total clown.

HAVING a Hottie Squad had its perks, and they weren't just the ones you normally got by having them around occasionally to look at.

They were the ones that made moving Luna into Oasis Square a breeze.

A new member of the team in from LA joined us.

He was a dude named Brady, who had dark hair with an auburn cast to it (definitely his thick, somewhat long beard was red). He was the same height as Cap, but he had the powerhouse build of Knox.

I called him Lumberjack Hottie, and oh yes, we made up names for them like they were the uber-gorgeous, testosterone-abundant Spice Girls—Cap was Captain Hottie (obvs), Gabe was Menacing Hottie, Liam was Sweetheart Hottie and Knox was Football Hottie (because I found out he was the quarterback of his football team in high school).

As such, with all this muscle, Luna was ensconced in the Oasis in no time.

Oh, and a bit of news.

Gabe looked like Luke Stark, one of the OGs, because he was Luke's cousin's son. Gabe's last name was also Stark.

So that explained that.

The unit Luna took was Mick's (I could have called that), so she was on the top floor, across the courtyard, a door to the south of me.

It was when, two days after Luna was in, that Jessie got a notification that a unit at the Oasis had opened up, and after signing the lease, she was free to move in November first, that I again grew suspicious.

"That can't be a coincidence," I said to Cap one evening after he got home from work at a decent hour, and I was at my normal spot on a stool, and he was in his normal place in the kitchen, cooking for me.

By the by, he showed me his place. It was a nondescript townhouse with more space than mine, with another bedroom and a dining area. He didn't have a lot of boxes, but as he'd said, most of his stuff was still packed. My kitchen was better than his, there was no personality to the place, and wouldn't be, even if he unpacked, and thus, we spent only a few nights there, and all the rest, Cap was at mine.

He even managed to squeeze some of his shirts, jeans, pants and cargoes into my closet, and I'd managed to free up space in a drawer (I was planning an epic trip to the Container Store to do some organizing and hack some space, and Harlow, who had a talent at this, had already been over to assess and "draft a sketch" (her words), so I was thinking good things).

By the by part two, as he said he would, Cap had looked into my new landlord and shared nothing was amiss. Indeed, Dreamweaver, Inc. owned a variety of rental properties in four states: Arizona, California, New Mexico and Colorado. And every time they bought one, they not only instigated updates and upgrades with a lean into eco-consciousness, they froze rent rates for one to two years.

"People leave," was Cap's reply to my assertion.

"Not the Oasis," I returned.

We would find it was Robyn going, and because I still thought this was suspicious, I nosed around (by that I meant I went to her door, knocked and asked), and she said, "I've been thinking of going for months, Raye. Jacob getting with Alexis cut it. They're always making out in the pool. Or on a lounger. It's gross. I don't need to come home to that. My lease is up, so I'm out."

Jacob and Alexis weren't gross, but whatever.

Different strokes.

And Jessie wouldn't care that Jacob and Alexis were open with how into each other they were, so Robyn out and Jess in worked for everybody.

Thus, on November first, the Hottie Squad was requisitioned again, and Jessie was in, just a few doors down from me.

Oh yeah.

That worked for everybody.

Make no mistake, when the news hit the media that the cretin who killed seven little boys also killed five little girls, for me, it was like a slap.

Enter stage left was a hassle I could do without, when a bunch of reporters called me, emailed me or hung out by the gate trying to get to me.

This didn't last very long, and it wasn't Cap who accomplished it, but our illustrious landlord who called the police, shared that gate was on private property, so they could fuck off (I doubt the cops used the F-word, but whatever, they fucked off).

It was reported to me they hung around at the two entrances for a few days, but since those days were the ones I spent the night at Cap's, after I hung up on them without fail without saying anything (and Dad and Deb did too), some other juicy story struck, and they disappeared.

This could also be because Martha made it her pastime to go out and harangue them as vultures who fed off misery, demanding to know how they could sleep at night when my family went through what we went through, and they were harassing me.

And as we all knew, when Martha had a bee in her bonnet, her words were not few and she dedicated her existence to whatever it took to complete her task.

Though, I'd never know which it was, because I wasn't going to ask.

Nevertheless, they had my name, and they printed it.

Therefore, I suspected this was why the reverend found time to sit down with Ben and Emily, Elsie Fay's parents.

So I guessed it was no surprise they showed at The Surf Club one day (though, I was curious to know how they knew where I worked, and suspected that had something to do with NI&S, where I apparently moonlighted when I wasn't serving according to Mace and Cap's statement to the police, however, when I asked, Cap told me no one there said anything, therefore, it was a longshot, but I thought it might be Arthur).

They sat at the bar.

Lucia made Elsie Fay a hot fudge sundae, something we didn't have on the menu.

We talked while I worked.

Gratitude and sadness shone in Emily's eyes when she looked at me, anger and protectiveness in Ben's, and I found it uncomfortable.

But soon, Tito came over and took a stool by them, starting a quiet conversation, which freed me to gab with Elsie Fay.

Her favorite color was purple, and her mom and dad got her a kitty she named Tuna, and she was going to take skiing lessons... *finally*...after she'd begged...*for years*...when they went to Flagstaff to spend Christmas with her grandparents.

In other words, bottom line, their visit worked for me.

I WOULD BE REMISS if I didn't share that this was the time I approached Mace.

I didn't pry, neither did he, but since his dad had been some huge-ass billionaire, and when his sister was killed, there was a lot of media attention, when the same happened to me, I just needed to be around someone who'd made it to the other side.

I told Cap this, and he wasted no time getting me back to Mace and Stella's.

I got it then, because Mace tried to make it so it was just him and me in their family room, rapping, but Stella found every excuse she could to check in on us, Cap wasn't far behind her, and Tally, her kiddo senses buzzing, did the same (Walsh was busy decimating the house by rolling a toy recycling truck through every inch of it).

So, after one of the times Stella left us alone once she'd dropped fresh Fat Tire beers on us (and we weren't finished with the ones we already had, not even halfway!), I said, "It's about her, isn't it?"

I meant Stella.

Mace knew what I meant, so he looked me dead in the eye and replied, "It's *all* about her."

"Tally and Walsh?" I asked.

He shook his head. "If Stella didn't ground me, Tally, Walsh and I would live in a cabin in the woods far away from anybody so no one could harm them."

Serious as shit.

I dug this guy.

I sensed movement, looked down the hall, and just caught Cap strolling by the mouth at the other end of the hall, his head turned to check us out.

My lips tipped up.

"It's all about him, yeah?" Mace asked me.

He, obviously, meant Cap.

That was when I looked him dead in the eye. "Oh yeah. Abso-freaking-lutely."

Mace chuckled, sat back and slugged some beer.

I did the same then queried, "How long should we torture them with our heart to heart?"

He tipped his handsome head to the side. "What are your thoughts on that?"

"Fifteen minutes," I told him. "They need to keep their senses sharp, but we shouldn't be cruel."

He pointed the neck of his beer bottle at me and winked.

Oh my.

And...

Mm-hmm.

Totally got that Hot Bunch thing.

Totally.

Oh!

Almost forgot.

Cap organized another night out for beer with the boys when Luna, Jess and Harlow came over to help me take down my wall.

I totally did incense and candles, but Jessie refused to chant (I was thinking "Oh, Arthur, our Arthur" or "The wonders of the Avenging Angels, unite!" but she rained on my parade).

Though she did create a cocktail for the evening. And I got seriously tipsy.

So later, Cap got an epic blowjob, after which he thanked me by eating me out so well, my orgasm was unusually noisy (I knew this when I saw Rhea the next day, and she smirked at me).

Thus, in the end, our ceremony worked out splendidly.

Dream got licensed to take in a couple of kids (which she did). Feather's dad got his head out of his ass and horned in to get his time with his daughter, and the bun in her oven's daddio lost his shit because he was not down to be a dad or pay child support.

And yeah, I was right, partially.

She told him she had it covered, but she didn't think she was lying. She didn't know she would be fertile so soon after delivering Feather.

I mean, only Dream could dream she could use no birth control, and the universe would protect her from getting knocked up. Even after two pregnancies. I mean, she had to have that OB/GYN shit down pat by now, but apparently, *no*.

Yeesh.

So, a lot going on for Dream.

The good news: she was making money (and she augmented this by crafting hippie bags and totes, because apparently, the one she carried she'd made herself, as she made the candle she gave to Luna for her birthday, all of this she sold on Etsy and at markets on the weekends).

The bad news: she lost her kids to their dads every other week, and this didn't make her happy.

Obviously, I filled Luna in on my conversation with Dream on the walkway at her party, and Luna gave it a go (more than once) to try to talk her sister into not unloading her shit on Luna, but these efforts failed.

This ended in a stalemate, which meant now, they were avoiding each other.

This didn't make Scott and Louise happy, but their hands were tied.

And it was going to make Thanksgiving interesting.

ALTHOUGH TEX AND NANCY, Shirleen and Moses all came to Macy's funeral, they went back to Denver after.

I sensed Cap's loss at this (yes, even Tex, and FYI, I felt a loss at this too, so did The Surf Club coffee cubby—Tex was a crazy man, and he left a big hole when he was gone).

Cap had been a kid without any family, and although Mace and Stella were close (and sometimes, we went over to dinner at their house—Stella Gunn cooking...*for me!*), and it was obvious he was tight with his buds (particularly Liam and Knox), I'd played beer pong with the Rock Chicks and the Hot Bunch had returned Macy to Dad and me, so I got how much he was missing.

Therefore, I was sure to give him quality Oasis courtyard time and encouraged him and his boys to come to The Surf Club for lunch so he could get his dose of crazy.

THE TRANSFORMATION OF THE OASIS, by the way, jetted forward swimmingly.

The mural was kickass. The window boxes were affixed and gave the flow of the woman in the mural's skirt more depth and personality. The solar panels were installed on the roof, and they gave hella relief on the electric bill. The cameras were mounted, aimed to the parking lot. And in November, when it was officially too cold to swim, the pool deck was torn up, the pool itself drained, and work began on new decking and resurfacing.

Not to mention, Luna and Jess living so close was *everything*.

So things were coming up roses all around.

And it just got better when Ryan told us he put money down on a house, and within a day, Harlow got word a unit had opened up for her at the Oasis.

But really, seriously, are you with me?

That was fishy!

JESSIE AND HARLOW were not invited to go in and meet Clarice.

However, we received an email from Arthur that we could collect the keys from the management office of a storage unit four blocks away.

We were given three keys, one each to units eleven, twelve and thirteen.

In eleven was the Accord. In twelve was the Merc. And in thirteen was a blue Kia Sportage.

The Kia had two more stun guns, Tasers and burner phones in it. All three cars had two sets of handcuffs, with keys, in the glove compartments. And on the hood of the Merc were four boxes of business cards, one that said Kelly Garrett, one that said Jill Munroe, then there was Dylan Sanders and Natalie Cook.

And on the driver's seat of the Merc was a laser pointer.

So yeah.

We were set.

Not to mention, on the back walls of all of the units, there were side-by-side bulletin boards and whiteboards (so my wall was free to be just a wall...if there was a next time).

We only rolled in these wheels to meet up with Jinx and some, or all of her girls at that crappy-ass diner.

Though, we found they had great burgers. Not as great as Lenny's, but they didn't suck.

Cameo was hanging in there, but she hadn't been taken for that long.

Though, weirdness of weird, someone told Betsy they'd paid for therapy sessions for Christina.

I thought at first that might be about Cap and his team, or Arthur.

It was Persia who gave it up that it was Jinx and the Rolex.

"Bitch better get her head on straight," Jinx said when Luna's, Jessie's, Harlow's and my eyes moved to her. "I'm not payin' for her to gab at a shrink for the next century."

I didn't know how the other girls who were found in that warehouse were faring.

But before Thanksgiving, Luna and I listened to three voicemails on the burner (she kept getting disconnected, but that didn't stop her from calling again to get it all out) from Betsy that could be described as nothing but a diatribe about how "my Christina is doing my head in!"

So at least we knew Christina was making progress.

But now was now.

And Cap and I were getting ready to head over to Scott and Louise's for Thanksgiving.

Dad and Deb were again at the Hermosa Inn, and they were meeting us at the house.

And by "getting ready," I meant Cap was crafting some kind of green bean casserole, which bore no resemblance to the one I made that had three ingredients (his had about eighty! (slight exaggeration)).

As mentioned, my pudding had to have time to cure, so I'd started that yesterday, and finished it half an hour ago.

And we were having an interesting conversation.

"ABOUT ALL THAT shit from The Container Store," he began.

I stopped blending my eye shadow where I sat at the bar doing my makeup, and looked to the plethora of Container Store bags that were piled up in a corner.

I thought he was on about Nala, the gray and white semi-kitten (she was only eight months old) who was batting at the bags while her sister, Godiva (not a sister by blood, Godiva was much older), a Siamese, sat on my couch and stared at her like she was an idiot.

These were Shanti's cats. Shanti lived under me and a couple over. Shanti had gone home for Thanksgiving. And Shanti gave gratitude in the form of Nordstrom gift cards.

I went back to blending, at the same time assuring, "There's nothing in there she can hurt."

"No, I'm talking about me installing all that shit in your bedroom closet, hall closet and laundry nook this weekend."

As mentioned, Harlow was a master at this kind of thing, and as far as I could tell, with the sketch she delivered, she was going to double the space, and I didn't even *need* the space doubled in the hall closet and laundry nook.

But I bet I'd use it.

I again stopped blending. "Yeah, I thought you and Knox were down to do that."

"We are. Just saying, when we're done, my pans are better than yours, so we can pack yours up and put them in storage if you want to keep them."

I could do nothing but stare.

Cap kept talking.

"I like your bed, and I have a king, so it'd be too big for your bedroom, so we can put that and my furniture in storage too," he went on.

Was he...?

Was he...?

"Are you...asking...to *move in with me?*"

He finished pouring something that smelled divine over green beans he'd roasted to perfection, put the pot down and looked at me.

"No reason for me to pay rent at a pad I'm never at. And I'm not a big fan of using your water and electricity without paying my share. You're not gonna leave the Oasis. We'll get on the waiting list in case a two bedroom opens up. But in the meantime, I don't need a lot of space, I like your space, you obviously like your space, you're not gonna leave the Oasis until we're ready to buy. So...yeah, I'm asking to move in with you."

I abandoned blending altogether, dropped the brush, hopped off my stool, and Godiva raced into the bedroom, but Nala lost interest in the Container Store bags and pranced after me as I rounded the column and jumped on Cap.

With my arms and legs around him, his hands on my ass, I kissed him all over his face.

He was laughing and saying, "I'll take this as a yes."

I stopped kissing. "Damn straight it's a yes."

"You might have to move some of your summer clothes to the storage unit I rent so I can put away my shit."

"We live in perpetual summer in Phoenix, Cap."

"Please don't try to convince me you don't have different clothes for the different seasons."

He was too shrewd.

Though, I wasn't exactly secretive about being a clotheshorse.

"Whatever, okay. I'll do a seasonal purge."

He grinned. "Awesome, baby."

He could say that again.

I kissed him again.

This time, I aimed at his mouth.

Cap didn't laugh at that.

Not even a little bit.

ONLY TWENTY MINUTES late after our moving-in-together festivities (yeah, we did it, though Cap took it to the bedroom so we didn't do it on the kitchen floor), we forged our way through the jungle and into Scott and Louise's house, with me shouting, "We're here!"

A black lab mixed with something (a pittie?) came and jumped on me.

Cap, balancing the tray of casserole in his other hand, pushed him off.

"We are too!" Louise called from the bowels of the house.

We hit the living room, were surrounded by other dogs, but that wasn't why we stopped dead.

Tex was on the couch, his arms along the back, and Scott and Louise's cats were crawling all over him, with one curled up, apparently asleep in his lap.

"Yo!" he boomed.

"Tex," I cried, tossing my purse off, but still keeping hold on the trifle bowl while dashing to him.

Cats scattered as I juggled the bowl and hugged him, even though he didn't move a muscle on the couch.

"Woman!" Another boom. "I don't hug!"

I popped back, still smiling at him.

"Fuck the turkey," he proclaimed. "I just want whatever's in that bowl."

My smile grew to a huge-ass grin.

Then, out of the corner of my eyes, I saw Shirleen come in, wearing one of Louise's aprons around her waist to protect her gorgeous burnt-sienna sweater dress.

"That better be your green bean casserole, son," she said to Cap.

I just caught the happy grin that spread on his face before I raced to her and gave her a hug.

She hugged me back, and when we broke, she looked me up and down. "My girl, Raye. Always turned out *good*."

"Same to you," I replied. "And what an amazing surprise! I'm so happy you're here!"

She smiled at me and moved to her son.

Nancy and Louise came in, both also wearing aprons, and Deb followed up the rear.

I was giving Nancy a hug while Deb took the casserole from Cap, and Louise nabbed the pudding from me while talking.

"I told Scott no football in this house, so he set up a man cave on the back patio. I suspect they'll file in to stuff their faces, then go right back out."

I turned to Tex. "Why aren't you out with the guys?"

He was pushing out of the couch. "Because I had a cat in my lap. There's rules, woman. Now it's gone, I'm gone."

And he pushed through the crowd to get through the kitchen to the back patio just as Luna and Dad showed.

"Hey, sister," Luna greeted.

But she didn't come in for a hug, because Dad was doing it.

"Heya, darlin'," he said in my ear.

"Hey, Dad."

He hugged me tight, like he hadn't seen me in months, even though we had dinner together in the courtyard after their flight landed yesterday.

I let him, and not only because I was hugging him the same way.

"Hey, man."

Dad and I broke at this new voice, and I turned to see Roam there, smiling at his brother.

Then I watched as they went in for a man hug, pounding on each other's backs in a way it didn't look like they felt it, but it hurt me.

They let each other go exchanging another smile before Roam came in for a hug from me.

"Oh my God," I said, still hugging him (his were nearly as good as his mother's). "I'm so glad you're here."

He moved away, saying, "I am too, if the smell in the kitchen is anything to go by."

Moses came in next, and I got another hug and a "Hey there, darlin'. Lookin' good."

"You too, Moses," I replied.

He let me go, and Dream strolled in.

Since she'd hogged Dusk and Feather without telling their fathers they existed, she'd had to give them up for this Thanksgiving to their dads, even if Feather hadn't had a Thanksgiving yet. They got testy, so to keep things copasetic, she'd given in.

"You left me out there," she accused Luna.

Luna made no reply to her sister, she turned to me.

"Brady and Knox also came," she explained (part of) Dream's bad mood.

Whoa.

Cap didn't give up too much, because it wasn't his to tell, but although Gabe was home in Grand Junction with his mom and dad, and Liam had gone to LA to spend Thanksgiving with his parents, Darius and Malia, and his little sister, Antonia, Knox and Brady had some family issues going on.

They'd been at loose ends for the holiday, and NI&S suspended operations for Thanksgiving (at least this branch did, they didn't have any cases that required them to work).

Apparently, Luna (or Louise, or both) had stepped in.

"We've had to put in all the leaves for the dining room table, and it's gonna be a tight squeeze, but we borrowed some chairs from the neighbors, so we'll all fit," Louise declared.

"Glad I doubled the green bean casserole," Cap muttered.

I was too.

Though, I'd learned my pudding fed an entire apartment complex, so we were all good there.

Cap was ushered out, and I was pressed into table-setting duties, doing this with Luna.

Then we were shooed out of the kitchen by the mothers, and Luna and I hit the back patio and scrunched in with the men (and Dream, who was sitting with her arms crossed on her chest, glaring at the TV, but...whatever).

"Cap and I are moving in together," I told Luna.

She frowned. "You're leaving the Oasis?"

"No, sister, he's gonna do the setup so I can organize the crap out of my closets. I'm going to cycle out spring/summer and fall/winter wardrobes, we're gonna switch out to his pots and pans, and we're gonna put our extra stuff in storage and stay put."

"Rad!" she cried.

Totally.

"That's news," Roam noted to his brother.

"You knew it was gonna happen," Cap replied.

"Yeah. Took your time. I lost a hundred bucks on you," Roam returned.

"What's this?" Luna asked.

"We had a pool. When they'd move in together," Roam explained.

"I lost a hundred bucks too," Brady said.

"I lost mine two months ago," Knox added.

"I think Mace had October fifteenth, so he wins," Brady put in.

October fifteenth?

That was around a month after we met.

"Oh my God! Why didn't anyone tell me?" Luna snapped.

"Next time, we'll do that," Knox said.

"You better," Luna warned.

Dream got up. "I'm gonna help the moms."

She swanned out.

Scott sighed.

No one else paid attention.

What I was paying attention to was Roam and Moses giving each other looks.

Eventually, Moses muttered, "Don't you dare."

"What?" Cap asked.

"I can tell my shit," Roam said.

"Your shit is tied to our shit," Moses retorted.

"Oh for fuck's sake," Tex boomed. "Roam is joining the Phoenix team, and Shirleen and Moses are moving down. So are Nance and me."

"*Oh my God!*" I screeched, jumping out of the loveseat Luna and I were wedged into with Scott.

I was so happy about this for Cap (and me), I was not embarrassed I did a girlie cheerleader jump (I would have done splits if I wasn't in a cute, faux leather mini-skirt, cowl neck sweater and booties—totally had a fall/winter wardrobe—also if I could do the splits, which I couldn't).

Cap was grinning at Roam.

That just made me happier.

I hugged Moses first, Roam next and Tex last.

Only for Tex to boom, "What'd I say about hugs?"

I jumped away from him and retorted, "Suck it up, big man. This is cause for celebration."

"Tell me you did not tell my son we're moving to Phoenix without me being there," Shirleen demanded from where she was standing in the door.

"We didn't, Tex did." Roam threw Tex under the bus.

Tex reached forward, grabbed some party mix, tossed it in his mouth, and with that only partially chewed, he said, "Don't know what the big secret is."

"I have no idea how one of us hasn't whacked you yet," Shirleen replied.

I ran to Shirleen and gave her a hug.

She lost her tiff and hugged me back.

When I moved away, she said, "You're gonna have to help us find a house."

"Scottsdale, you're totally Scottsdale," I decreed.

"Nope, Arcadia," Luna corrected.

I turned to her. "You think? That's populated with entitled moms wearing Lululemon all day."

"Oh, right, scratch Arcadia. Then totes Scottsdale. Though, maybe Paradise Valley. Or possibly Biltmore."

"We'll figure it out," Shirleen said, then wandered in the kitchen.

I twirled, lunged forward and did a devil's horns.

Luna had her phone out, mumbling, "I'm pulling up Zillow."

All the men smiled at me.

Including Cap, but he also ordered, "Get over here."

I went over there, and he pulled me in his lap and wrapped his arms around me.

Oh yeah.

Per usual.

This was *much better*.

It was after dinner.

The men were out with football and all the dogs, alternately going in to do dishes (apparently, a deal was struck before we got there, and since my part of it was setting the table, and clearing it, I was done, so it worked for me).

The women were sitting around Scott and Louise's patio table by the pool, drinking cocktails and gabbing.

Dream had left shortly after we ate (and as far as I could tell, did nothing to help, and again...*whatever*).

Luna had been in the room with me, draped over a chair with a cat lying on the back, until she made the herculean effort to get up because she had to go to the bathroom (the cat, as they were wont to do, went with her).

I was flat out on Scott and Louise's couch, covered in what seemed like all the rest of the cats, nursing my food coma and trying to rally because I wanted a cocktail, when Luna called, "Babe?"

I looked her way.

She held up the burner.

I looked from the phone to her.

Then I dislodged the felines as I rolled off the couch, and due to my body still coping with the food coma, nearly landed on my hands and knees (told you the effort was herculean). But I was able to right myself, and I walked her way.

"What?" I asked.

"I don't know. Missed call. But, Raye, I recognized the number. It was from Harlow."

My head jerked, and I asked, "On the burner?"

"Yeah."

"She leave a voicemail?"

"No."

"Is something up with her?"

"I don't know. I didn't think so."

I went to my purse to get my phone to call Harlow.

As I did, Luna's burner binged.

I stopped and looked back.

Luna was reading the text.

I returned to her. "What's it say?"

"It says..." Her eyes came to me, and they were sparkling. "'The wonders of the Avenging Angels, unite.'"

A thrill raced through me.

Another bing came from the phone.

Luna read it out, "'Tomorrow. Eight. My pad. Over and out.'"

"Over and out?" I asked on a giggle I couldn't stop from bubbling up and out of me.

"Time to fire up the Merc again, it seems."

We stared at each other, and I couldn't see me, but I still knew my eyes were sparkling too.

Then we did a high five, bumped hips, Luna shoved the phone in the pocket of her killer, high-waisted, paper bag trousers.

And we went to get cocktails.

The End

The Avenging Angels will return in...
Avenging Angels: Back in the Saddle

KristenAshley.net
NEW YORK TIMES BESTSELLING AUTHOR

The Avenging Angels series adventures
continue in Phoenix with

Avenging Angels: Back in the Saddle
The story of Jessie and Eric.

READ MORE OF KRISTEN ASHLEY'S AVENGING ANGELS SERIES

Avenging Angels: *Back in the Saddle*
Avenging Angels Book Two

Jessie Wylde is on a secret mission. She's trying to find her brother. She hasn't told her friends; this is about family.

She doesn't think it's dangerous.

Eric Turner disagrees.

Eric is a member of the Nightingale Investigations and Security team. Therefore, Eric knows what he's talking about.

Eric isn't only badass, he's also a seriously gorgeous guy, and Jessie has a huge crush on him. She doesn't think he knows she exists... until now.

Eric steps in, and so do Jessie's besties, the Avenging Angels. Soon, the Angels and the Hottie Squad are on the case to find Jessie's missing sibling.

There's more happening when it comes to Eric, though. Jessie's so worried about her brother, she's not paying attention. Eric sets about changing that, and just like all the Hot Bunch before him, when he finds his one, he doesn't mess around.

However, something is afoot in Phoenix. And as the Angels uncover the sinister workings behind people going missing, and Eric and Jessie unpack their emotional baggage, the Angels dive deeper into the dark underbelly of the city...

Finding heroes, more hot guys, lots of hijinks...and heart.

Continue reading for Chapter One.

AVENGING ANGELS: BACK IN THE SADDLE

AVENGING ANGELS BOOK TWO

Chapter One
Catch Me if You Can

It was dark as pitch in the area around the makeshift encampment that sat in the parking lot of an abandoned warehouse, in what had become a kind of no man's land just south of the heart of the city.

This darkness might have to do with the fact it was nearing one in the morning.

It wasn't a great time to do my search, but in the last six months, I'd been hitting up the encampment at random times, day and evening. I always came up empty handed. But due to safety issues, I'd never gone so late (or early, depending on how you looked at it).

This time, I was giving it a shot precisely because it was so late (also because I was getting desperate).

He had to sleep somewhere, and I was hoping it was here. At the same time, I died a little death thinking it might be.

It was the night before Thanksgiving.

I'd hoped he'd be somewhere with someone on Thanksgiving,

even if that someone wasn't me, and, well, that somewhere was here.

I'd learned, and I had the requisite materials with me.

Four bags full of bottles of water (sorry environment) and a backpack stuffed with packs of beef jerky, boxes of protein bars and hydration packets.

Oh yeah, and an empty used sharps container.

Homer shuffled out first, as Homer always did. I wasn't sure Homer slept. I was sure Homer was King of the Homeless Encampment.

I was sure of this because I'd learned something else. I had to make Homer trust me before anyone else did.

This took time.

And lots of bottles of water and packs of beef jerky.

He said nothing as he took two of the bags and the sharps container from me.

Then he mumbled, "Late night."

"Is he here?"

My eyes had adjusted to the dark. I'd hit the encampment, and in the dim light that came from the city and various camp lanterns dotting the space, I saw his eyes in his dangerously tanned, leathery, whiskered face catch mine.

And I saw my answer.

No.

My brother wasn't there.

"Seen him?" I asked as we began to move through the oddly organized labyrinth of tents, tarps that created crude shelters, loaded grocery carts and the scattering of debris.

"Did you bring clean syringes?"

This wasn't an answer to my question, and sadly, my answer to his was, "Not this time."

He nodded, reached into a bag, made a noise, and a hand came out of a tent.

He put a bottle of water in it as I shrugged off the backpack to pull out a bag of jerky.

Homer took that, tossed it into the tent, and we moved on.

We did this at two more tents before I said, "Homer."

That was all I said, but he got me, so he stopped and turned to me.

And he stated it plainly. "You find him, you quit coming."

Oh my God.

On the one hand, it felt good that he trusted me, and him saying that meant he and his brethren appreciated me. I didn't have the resources to give much, and I knew I didn't help their situation at all, but it was nice to understand the little I did meant something.

On the other hand, I needed to find my brother.

"Are you...keeping him from me?" I asked.

He shook his head.

But he said, "Others might."

That meant, since Homer knew everyone and everything, others *were*.

Damn.

I pointed out the obvious. "I've gotta know if he's all right."

Homer gazed around the dismal space that looked bad and smelled worse.

I took his point.

If Jeff was here, he wasn't all right.

Then again, I already knew he wasn't all right.

Just as I knew, the minute Mom kicked him out seven months ago, and he didn't do his usual—bunk with one of his buds, then figure his shit out and get back on his meds—I would be doing what I was doing right then.

And there I was, doing what I was doing right then.

We moved through the space, silently handing out waters and protein delivery systems, with me looking closely at faces and trying to peer into tents.

I came up empty.

As usual.

When we were back at Homer's tent, he took the spent plastic bags from me (something else I'd learned: Homer had a thing for plastic bags), but handed me the clattering sharps container.

"It'd be good you bring syringes next time," he said.

With that, he ducked into his tent and disappeared.

I stared at it, the feelings I was feeling balling up inside me, the weight so heavy, the urge was almost overwhelming to open my mouth and shriek my fear and frustration to the skies above Phoenix.

I didn't do that.

I carried that weight with the container and my empty backpack to my car.

Though, I didn't make it to my car.

I stopped dead twenty feet away when I saw Eric Turner, investigator at Nightingale Investigations & Security. The place of business of Eric, Cap (my friend Raye's boyfriend) and a number of other badasses who were all ridiculously attractive.

Yep.

Every.

Single.

One.

His ass was resting on the fender of my black convertible Mini, his long legs stretched out in front of him, ankles crossed, his arms also crossed on his chest.

He'd been there a while.

Waiting for me.

Okay, one could say, until I met Eric, I hadn't been into older guys.

And he wasn't older, *as such*.

It was just that he belonged to the first generation of the Hot Bunch guys of NI&S (Raye had dubbed the younger generation the Hottie Squad so we could tell them apart, something that was necessary due to their overall concentrated level of hotness, which was so high, it was immeasurable, so we had to pry them apart somehow).

The first generation were all married (except Eric) and had wives and children (except Eric).

But the minute I clapped eyes on him, I was into him.

That was because he was mega hot.

It was also about other things, which I wasn't in the place to contemplate fully at that moment, seeing as it was now closer to two in the morning, and he had no reason to be leaning against my car at that time—or ever.

Yet there he was.

I restarted walking toward him, and when I arrived, I quipped, "Of all the gin joints."

"I'm not finding anything funny, Jessie," he replied.

Hmm.

One could say we hadn't had very many deep conversations (as in...*none*).

But I'd been around him somewhat frequently, seeing as Raye, one of my three besties, was not only hooked up, but shacked up with Cap. This meant they often came to The Surf Club to have lunch or grab a cup of joe. And The Surf Club was where Raye, my other two besties, Harlow and Luna, and I worked.

Obviously, I'd heard his voice, which was normally deep and mellow, but it could get smooth, rich and warm as fudge when he said things like, "Thank you," after I put one of Lucia's (our chef) divine creations in front of him.

Now, it was still deep, though not at all mellow, or smooth. Instead, rough and edgy.

In other words...pissed.

"Eric—"

He cut me off. "Have you lost your fuckin' mind?"

"No, I—"

"Wrong," he bit off. "You have. You've lost your fuckin' mind."

Now, hang on a second.

Avenging Angels: Back in the Saddle
will be unleashed
December 3, 2024

CAST OF CHARACTERS

AVENGING ANGELS SERIES

Avenging Angels

- Rachel "Raye" Armstrong
- Luna Nelson
- Harlow O'Neill
- Jessica "Jessie" "Jess" Wilde
- Clarice Davis
- "Arthur"

Hottie Squad
Phoenix Branch: Nightingale Investigations & Security

- Knox Chambers
- Brady Houston
- Julien "Cap" Jackson
- Roman "Roam" Jackson
- Gabriel "Gabe" Stark
- Liam Clark Tucker
- Eric Turner

OG Rock Chicks
(In order of Rock Chick books)

- India "Indy" Savage Nightingale – owner, Fortnum's bookstore (Denver)
- Jet McAlister Chavez – barista, Fortnum's bookstore
- Roxanne "Roxie" Logan Nightingale – self-employed website designer
- Juliet "Jules" "Law" Lawler Crowe – social worker, King's Shelter (Denver)
- Ava Barlow Stark – self-employed graphics designer
- Stella Gunn – world-renowned rock star
- Sadie Townsend Chavez – owner, "Art," a gallery
- Alison "Ally" Nightingale Zano – Owner/Partner, Private Investigator - Rock Chick Investigations
- Daisy Sloan – Owner/Partner, Office Manager - Rock Chick Investigations
- Malia Clark Tucker – Paralegal
- Shirleen Richardson – Partner, Nightingale Investigations & Security, ex-Office Manager Denver Branch (by end of *Avenging Angel*)

OG Hot Bunch
(In order of Rock Chick books)

- Liam "Lee" Nightingale – Partner, Nightingale Investigations & Security, Managing Partner, Denver Branch
- Eddie Chavez – Denver Police Detective
- Hank Nightingale – Denver Police Detective
- Vance Crowe – Partner, Nightingale Investigations & Security
- Luke Stark – Partner, Nightingale Investigations & Security

- Kai "Mace" Mason – Partner, Nightingale Investigations & Security, Managing Partner, Phoenix Branch
- Hector Chavez – Partner, Nightingale Investigations & Security
- Lorenzo "Ren" Zano - Businessman
- Marcus Sloan – Businessman
- Moses Richardson – Corrections Officer, Juvenile Detention (Denver)
- Darius Tucker – Partner, Nightingale Investigations & Security, Managing Partner, Los Angeles Branch

Raye and Luna's Family

- Charles "Charlie" Armstrong
- Deborah "Deb" "Debbie" Armstrong
- Macy Armstrong
- Dream Nelson, Children, Dusk and Feather
- Louise Nelson
- Scott Nelson

Informants

- Betsy and Cristina "Bambi" Markovic
- Cameo
- Divinity
- Genesis
- Jinx
- Lotus
- Persia
- Mr. Shithead
- Skyla

Oasis Square Residents

- Alexis
- Bill and Zach
- Jacob Brewer
- John Campos (ex-landlord)
- Jenn
- Linda
- Martha
- Mick (former resident by end of *Avenging Angel*)
- Patsy
- Rhea
- Robyn (former resident by end of *Avenging Angel*)
- Ryan (former resident by end of *Avenging Angel*)
- Sally

Phoenix Police Chief

- Jorge Alvarez

The Surf Club

- Tito – Owner
- Byron – Regular
- Hunter – Staff/Barista
- Lucia – Head Chef - HUSBAND, MARIO
- Otis – Staff/Barista
- Tex MacMillan – Guest Barista - WIFE, NANCY

Villains

- Bobby (thanks for the Rolex!)
- Sergio Duzek

- Cryus Gibbons
- Jazz/Jumper "Guy"
- Paul Nicholson/Donald Walken

ACKNOWLEDGMENTS

First, to my readers, who have been asking for this series for a *really long time*. I love how much you all wanted to be back with this cast of characters, and to meet the next generation. I truly hope you found Raye and Cap's story as much of a thrill ride as I did. I cannot begin to tell you how delighted I was to be back in this world and bringing these characters' stories forward. It felt like coming home.

I hope you felt the same.

A shout out to my cheerleaders, Liz and Donna, for taking this journey with me as I wrote it and for spurring me on.

Also, I don't say it often enough, thank you to Emily Sylvan Kim, my agent since this whole dream began, whose support and guidance through the years has been such a tremendous blessing.

Last as ever, to my fabulous team, Donna Perry, Amanda Simpson, Kelly Brown and Stacey Tardif, thank you for keeping my shit sharp and making me look good. You're the best!

Rock On!

ABOUT THE AUTHOR

Kristen Ashley is the *New York Times* bestselling author of over eighty romance novels including the *Rock Chick, Colorado Mountain, Dream Man, Chaos, Unfinished Heroes, The 'Burg, Magdalene, Fantasyland, The Three, Ghost and Reincarnation, The Rising, Dream Team, Moonlight and Motor Oil, River Rain, Wild West MC, Misted Pines* and *Honey* series along with several standalone novels. She's a hybrid author, publishing titles both independently and traditionally, her books have been translated in fourteen languages and she's sold over five million books.

Kristen's novel, *Law Man*, won the *RT Book Reviews* Reviewer's Choice Award for best Romantic Suspense, her independently published title *Hold On* was nominated for *RT Book Reviews* best Independent Contemporary Romance and her traditionally published title *Breathe* was nominated for best Contemporary Romance. Kristen's titles *Motorcycle Man, The Will*, and *Ride Steady* (which won the Reader's Choice award from *Romance Reviews*) all made the final rounds for Goodreads Choice Awards in the Romance category.

Kristen, born in Gary and raised in Brownsburg, Indiana, is a fourth-generation graduate of Purdue University. Since, she's lived in Denver, the West Country of England, and she now resides in Phoenix. She worked as a charity executive for eighteen years prior to beginning her independent publishing career. She now writes full-time.

Although romance is her genre, the prevailing themes running through all of Kristen's novels are friendship, family and a strong sisterhood. To this end, and as a way to thank her readers for their support, Kristen has created the Rock Chick Nation, a series of programs that are designed to give back to her readers and promote a strong female community.

The mission of the Rock Chick Nation is to live your best life, be true to your true self, recognize your beauty, and take your sister's back whether they're at your side as friends and family or if they're thousands of miles away and you don't know who they are.

The programs of the RC Nation include Rock Chick Rendezvous, weekends Kristen organizes full of parties and get-togethers to bring the sisterhood together, Rock Chick Recharges, evenings Kristen arranges for women who have been nominated to receive a special night, and Rock Chick Rewards, an ongoing program that raises funds for nonprofit women's organizations Kristen's readers nominate. Kristen's Rock Chick Rewards have donated hundreds of thousands of dollars to charity and this number continues to rise.

You can read more about Kristen, her titles and the Rock Chick Nation at KristenAshley.net.

facebook.com/kristenashleybooks

instagram.com/kristenashleybooks

pinterest.com/KristenAshleyBooks

goodreads.com/kristenashleybooks

bookbub.com/authors/kristen-ashley

tiktok.com/@kristenashleybooks

ALSO BY KRISTEN ASHLEY

Rock Chick Series:

Rock Chick

Rock Chick Rescue

Rock Chick Redemption

Rock Chick Renegade

Rock Chick Revenge

Rock Chick Reckoning

Rock Chick Regret

Rock Chick Revolution

Rock Chick Reawakening

Rock Chick Reborn

Rock Chick Rematch

Avenging Angels Series

Avenging Angel

Avenging Angels: Back in the Saddle

The 'Burg Series:

For You

At Peace

Golden Trail

Games of the Heart

The Promise

Hold On

The Chaos Series:

Own the Wind

Fire Inside

Ride Steady

Walk Through Fire

A Christmas to Remember

Rough Ride

Wild Like the Wind

Free

Wild Fire

Wild Wind

The Colorado Mountain Series:

The Gamble

Sweet Dreams

Lady Luck

Breathe

Jagged

Kaleidoscope

Bounty

Dream Man Series:

Mystery Man

Wild Man

Law Man

Motorcycle Man

Quiet Man

Mathilda, SuperWitch:

Mathilda's Book of Shadows

Mathilda The Rise of the Dark Lord

Misted Pines Series

The Girl in the Mist

The Girl in the Woods

The Woman by the Lake

Moonlight and Motor Oil Series:

The Hookup

The Slow Burn

The Rising Series:

The Beginning of Everything

The Plan Commences

The Dawn of the End

The Rising

The River Rain Series:

After the Climb

After the Climb Special Edition

Chasing Serenity

Taking the Leap

Making the Match

Fighting the Pull

Sharing the Miracle

Embracing the Change

The Three Series:

Until the Sun Falls from the Sky

With Everything I Am

Wild and Free

The Unfinished Hero Series:

Knight

Creed

Raid

Deacon

Sebring

Wild West MC Series:

Still Standing

Smoke and Steel

Other Titles by Kristen Ashley:

Heaven and Hell

Play It Safe

Three Wishes

Complicated

Loose Ends

Fast Lane

Perfect Together

Too Good To Be True

Printed in the USA
CPSIA information can be obtained
at www.ICGtesting.com
LVHW091741011124
795358LV00001B/58